BIG AS LIFE

BIG AS LIFE

Stories
About Men

RAND RICHARDS COOPER

For Neil,
The consummate gentleman —
and killer competitor — on the
tennis court. I look forward
to our occasional matches.

Best wishes,

Rand

July 1995

THE DIAL PRESS

Published by
The Dial Press
Bantam Doubleday Dell Publishing Group, Inc.
1540 Broadway
New York, New York 10036

"Kerenyaga" was originally published in *Harper's,* "The Hoax" in
Confrontation, "Fireworks at Nine" and "Magendo Men" in
Northwest Review, "Exit 99" and "Big as Life" in *American Way,*
"Going the Distance" in *Amelia,* and "The Way Things Always
Happen" in *Story Magazine.*

Book design: Barbara Berger

Library of Congress Cataloging in Publication Data

Cooper, Rand Richards.
    Big as life : stories about men / by Rand Richards Cooper.
        p.   cm.
    ISBN 0-385-31422-1
    1. Men—Social life and customs—Fiction.   I. Title.
PS3553.O623B5   1995
813'.54—dc20   94-48922
                                                        CIP

Manufactured in the United States of America

Published simultaneously in Canada

June 1995

10   9   8   7   6   5   4   3   2   1

BVG

für Z

Wer nie sein Brot mit Tränen a,
Wer nie die kummervollen Nächte
Auf seinem Bette weinend sa,
Der kennt euch nicht, ihr himmlischen Mächte.

Ihr führt ins Leben uns hinein,
Ihr lat den Armen schuldig werden,
Dann über lat ihr ihn der Pein,
Denn alle Schuld rächt sich auf Erden.

—Goethe

Acknowledgments

Many thanks are due to my intrepid editor, Susan Kamil, and her assistant, Kathleen Jayes; to my daring duo of agents, Gloria Loomis and Nicole Aragi; and to a whole bunch of guys who've been mentors and friends over the years: Chick High; Fast Eddie and Cabey Baby; Paul Baumann; Meester Gotwals; VB; Jon Wool; the Feen Machine; the Beck, the Geek, the Mint, Jefferson, Andy, Kurt, and Geoff Moulton; John Elder; David Huddle; WHP; Bob Stone; Sanford and Jonathan; Joseph N. Gorra; the late Reggie Eccleston; the late Dennis Shortell; Mutiso Mwalili; Wolfgang Stein; LD; Lou B; Dave Jackson; Brian Berkey; Terminator, Lehrer Görtz, Pride of Prague, Erich, Carsten, Mister Meister and the rest of Mannschaft Vorwärts Orient; my grandfather, the late Clarence Cooper; my uncle, Dick Hook; and my father, Donald W. Cooper.

CONTENTS

BIG AS LIFE

Exit 99

The first time, you've been telling yourself, was an accident. By pure coincidence you were in the area; really nothing else to it.

It was last Friday. You'd gone after work to see a guy about a lawn mower up in the woods north of the highway, and when you got there nobody was home. Nearby, you remembered, was that new Indian casino, Three Lakes, your best buddy Jack has been trying to drag you to since the day it opened. You're a family man, you always tell him, not a gambling man. Still, there you were, with an hour to kill.

So you went and checked it out. A huge place, like a mall: waterfalls, T-shirt stores, a restaurant with a $9.95 all-you-can-eat buffet. Guys in Red

Sox shirts and old ladies with towering hairdos were playing roulette, craps, and cards. You found a $10 blackjack table and in a half hour managed to turn $30 into $60—not bad, you thought, for an amateur. You cashed in your chips and left.

Over the weekend, you kept meaning to tell your wife about your little excursion, but something always got in the way, the groceries needing to be picked up or the baby changed; then it was Monday again. And now all week you've been wandering back to how you doubled your money in that half hour and walked away, clean and green. Driving home from work you feel the thought tugging like a beggar at your sleeve, and it takes an effort not to turn off at exit 99 and head for the casino.

What's eating you? your wife asks.

Nothing, you say. *Why?*

You're not a gambler, you remind yourself. Never have been. In a football game it's the play on the field you care about, not the point spread. On the slopes at Killington you can bash the moguls with the best of them, but you're no risk freak, you don't have any interest in courting death. Life itself is risky enough, you believe. You like telling people your chief vices are Bud Lite and your two girls.

Once you picked up the phone and overheard a girlfriend of your wife's saying "What do *you* have to worry about, you have *Tom!*" You liked the sound of that. But sometimes you wonder. You're a foreman at the plant, pulling thirty-nine G's before taxes, and still it sometimes feels like you're barely making it. What with the monthly nut on the house and cars, the credit cards to pay off, the secondhand piano you bought to go with your daughter's lessons—with all that there's never anything left.

I can't catch my breath, you tell your wife. *I'm always two steps behind!* It burns you to think of all the guys out there who are always two steps ahead. You see them on the highway, zooming by in their $50,000 BMWs, wheeling and dealing on their car phones while you, meanwhile, are struggling to budget a family trip to Disney World two years from now.

Arriving home from work you sit in the driveway, thinking again about how the $30 became $60. Some of the people who go to a casino, for them it's an illness, an obsession. But you're not that kind of guy. For you it would be a limited, one-time thing, a way to make a quick hundred or two and spread a little happiness around the house.

You think about your wife and girls. Sure, they're doing all right. But they deserve better.

When you were a kid, for your eighth birthday, your father took you for a ride in a hot air balloon. You were scared of being scared, but when the thing lifted off, just you and your father and the pilot on board, it turned out your old man was the scared one, while all you felt was the thrill of it, the dizzy tingling rush as the ground pulled away and you went up and up.

It's Friday afternoon at Three Lakes, you've got the center seat at a $25 table, and you're winning. At the bank you hesitated before scribbling $300 on the "Less Cash Received" line of the deposit slip and handing it over with your paycheck to the teller; and half an hour later, when the dealer scooped up your six fifties and gave you twelve green chips, you felt a second twinge of nerves. But then you began to win. You're not flashy: no playing the sevens, no splitting or doubling unless it's perfect. But bit by bit you're eking it out. As you do, you sneak chips into your pocket for safekeeping. Your wife doesn't know you're here—you told her you're putting in overtime on a shipment—but if she did, she'd like this careful way of handling things.

The dealer is a woman named Cheri with a dynamite figure and a gold-capped front tooth. Cheri smiles when she deals you a winner, and she's dealing you a lot of them. Again and again you win, and it's like that memory of rising in the balloon, the tingling in your legs and stomach. By six o'clock you've got the original $300 safely pocketed and $425 more on the table in front of you. Just two or three more hands, you decide. Get to an even five hundred, then get out.

You lose the first, taking a hit on an eight-four and busting with a queen. So now you put out three chips, $75, your biggest bet of the night. Cheri lays down a six and a five, perfect for doubling—except she's showing a king. *Come on, Cheri,* you say, tossing out three more chips, *do it for me!* She deals you a ten—*yessss!*—but when she turns her card over, it's an ace. Blackjack. "Sorry," she says, taking the chips away. You shrug to let her know you're not taking it personally, and push your chair back.

On the way to the cashier, you count ten chips in your hand—$250. You're still way up, but it hurts to think of the $425 you had just minutes ago; it's a desolate feeling, like someone has died. You gravitate toward a roulette table where players are spreading chips around the grid like farmers planting seeds.

Two chips, you tell yourself. *One shot. Back up to $300 and out.* You step forward and put $50 down on red.

The avalanche that follows is so quick it's over before you know what's happening. It begins with the wheel spinning, the croupier calling out "Thirty-one black!" and a cute girl next to you calmly collecting $10 from black and leaving her original chip in place. Quickly you lean in and slap four chips down on red. The ball spins and tumbles.

Black again.

A dull pressure thrums in your temples, but there's no pulling out now. From your pocket you borrow four chips from the $300 to go with the four left in your hand—eight chips, exactly enough to get you out of here. The wheel spins, and then— *sonofabitch!*—there's the girl, taking her chip once more, and you're groping in your pocket, fingers filmy with sweat. A monster roars in the back of your mind, but you haul the door shut on it with the knowledge that this can't happen, not four times in a row, no way. The wheel spins.

"Twenty-two," says the croupier. "Black."

It's over; your pocket is empty.

The whole nightmare has taken all of ten minutes. Like a sleepwalker you wander across the room, picturing yourself driving away in the pickup, the radio playing some bullshit song.

There's no way you can go home like this, a voice says. *You have to undo the damage.*

At the cash machine out in the front hall, you find today's deposit hasn't been credited yet; there's only $229 in your checking account. You can punch in $200, but it's not going to clear you enough room to make things good. You flip through your wallet, the monster roaring louder now, and take out your credit card.

Back at the table she's still there, the cute girl, still playing her crazy $10 bet. You've got eight fifty-buck chips in your fist, black-and-white checkered ones, and when the croupier spins the wheel you push your way to the edge of the table and unload all of them on red.

People crowd like vultures; you feel the hot breath on your neck. The ball slides for an eternity along the rim, and as it does, the curtains in your mind part and you see with a sickening certainty exactly what is about to happen—how you've fooled yourself into believing the girl can't win five in a row against you when the cold truth is that every spin is a new beginning, it's fifty-fifty every time, and you've put everything, all four hundred bucks, on a single wild bet against a girl with luck running her way; and now you're going to walk out $700 down, a whole paycheck that's going to have to be made up somehow, and fast, either by borrowing or by selling something, or else it will open like a hole in the ground and your family will fall right smack down into it.

The ball drops from the rim and clatters across the grooves. You turn away, raising your eyes toward the ceiling.

Outside you're shocked to find it's still light; it seems like weeks have gone by. The Friday evening rush is on, Caddies and Jeeps pulling up to valets in the front circle. Back in the truck, engine idling, you separate out the original $300, then the $400 from the Visa card, and you're left with one crisp new hundred in your hand. You haven't felt this bushed since high school, when you wrestled in the 145-lb. class and would come home limp as a rag, your muscles trembling as you sat at dinner shoveling down your mother's good food.

You're glad you came, you think as you drive away. It was a little ragged at times; still, it was an experience. Your wife won't be too happy about it, but she'll come around. You'll have to work a little on a few of the details. Everything that happened after the blackjack—the cash machine part, the whole roulette part of it—is no good. The feeling of rising in the balloon; the thrill and terror as you heard the ball dancing across the numbers; the surge of relief when the croupier called out "Red!": you try to imagine explaining this to your wife. *You did WHAT?* you hear her saying, with that look that can crack ice cubes.

Off to your right the sun is setting, flooding pink through the trees. You find yourself thinking about the one and only time in nine years of marriage you cheated on your wife: a five-day fishing trip in Pennsylvania, a sweet young thing at the lodge who made her intentions very plain. You worried yourself raw for three days until finally you acted, and as soon as you did you knew you were in the clear, knew it would be once and once only and wouldn't touch anything at home. You could build a wall around it so nothing could get in or out, and that way it would stay separate and wouldn't matter.

It's five of eight when you pass a spanking new minimall a quarter mile before the highway. There are a dozen stores, including a florist; a girl is wheeling a display cart of flowers across the parking lot. You pull in and climb down from the truck.

A big bunch, you tell her. Load it up nice.

She picks from this and from that. Even in the dim light you can see it's going to be beautiful. You pay and drive off, the flowers propped on the seat beside you.

The dangerous thing about talking, you remind yourself, is that it punches a hole in the wall you've built, and pretty soon things start leaking out and you can't control them anymore. You picture the smile on your wife's face when you pull the flowers out from behind your back.

If you were the kind of guy who was going to do this all the time, who couldn't control it, that would be one thing, you tell yourself.

But you're not that kind of guy. Right?

FAITH IN THE SYSTEM

I. THAT GREENISH LOOK IN THE SKY

It is the summer of 1969, and Andy Hatter is in the back of his parents' station wagon, heading to camp. He's riding with an arm draped over his suitcase, thinking about what's packed inside. It pleases him to picture the red block letters of the name tags sewn on his clothes, ANDREW E. HATTER. He's ten years old; this is his first time away from home.

"Got your envelopes, honey?" asks his mother, who has prepared six for him, with addresses and stamps. "And your Dopp kit?"

"Hilda," his father sighs over the steering wheel.

"I know, I know," says Mrs. Hatter. She falls quiet. Leaving the highway, they drive through the woods of Connecticut—a name mysterious to Andy compared with his own state, Rhode Island. Mr. Hatter turns on the radio, and Andy is surprised to hear "Build Me Up, Buttercup," one of his favorite songs.

"Enjoy it while you can," his father says. "Tonight it's good-bye, civilization, hello bears."

Andy knows he's just kidding; still, when he thinks about the coming two weeks, a small knot of doubt forms inside him. First, he's not sure football will be played at camp. At home Andy has a pair of cleats painted white in the style of his hero, Joe Namath. After school he likes to act out spectacular passes from Namath to Don Maynard in the front yard—tossing the football high and diving to catch it, dancing deliriously in the end zone between the magnolias.

He's also worried about thunderstorms. It's wrong, he knows, for a boy entering sixth grade to be as afraid as he is of storms. But he can't help it. Whenever the afternoon sky gets that greenish-yellowish tint, the air staticky, Andy begins to keep a worried eye on the situation. He is so practiced an observer of the sky that he believes himself a better weather predictor than the meteorologist on Channel 6, John Ghiorse. Still, he's ashamed of this cowardice, and considers it a dark defect in his character which, like his humiliating tendency to cry, he must keep hidden.

Shortly after two, Mr. Hatter turns by a sign that says CAMP MOHEGAN in letters of painted logs. Andy sees cabins and a lake, a tremendous green lawn, a flagpole with a loudspeaker on top. Boys are everywhere, already finding things out, building a head start Andy feels will be hard to make up. He jiggles his foot on the floor.

At Cabin 7 they're greeted by a man with a mustache who shakes Andy's hand. "Andy, I'm Drew Hartusian, your counselor," the man says. He points him to a bunk in the musty cabin, and stays outside talking while Andy unpacks. Andy's mother slips in to help, arranging his socks and underwear on the wooden shelves, patting them like friendly pets.

"You be brave," she says to Andy.

His father ducks in and taps his watch; Andy is kissed and hugged; and then they are gone. Outside he hears the next arrival. "Richard, I'm Drew Hartusian, your counselor. . . ." Leaning over to unroll a T-shirt, he glances out the window and sees his parents walking across the green lawn. It's an exciting moment, one he's been waiting for; and so he's confused, as his parents reach the car and the door winks open, to find he has to fight back a sudden lump in his throat, and the astonishing urge to run after them.

II. BUGLES AND GIMP

At an all-camp meeting in the activities hall, he looks around at boys in dungarees and in shorts, in Yankees and Red Sox T-shirts. One red-haired kid is busily picking his nose and eating it, and as Andy watches he knows it will be impossible to erase such a first impression, and that, for him at least, the boy is already damned.

"And now," says the founder, Mr. Sperry, an old man with bags under his eyes, "I'd like you to meet our director, Mr. Jim Squires of Tennessee—better known around here as the Rebel."

The man who stands is tall and rugged, like the lieutenant on *Rat Patrol*. Even though it's night and indoors, he's wearing sunglasses. "Now, I bet you've all been hearing some wild stories about the Rebel," he says in a slow drawl, as if speaking about someone else. "For instance, that he once killed a wolf with his bare hands." Silence fills the room. "Truth is, I actually used a baseball bat."

Boys sit with their mouths wide open. Even the counselors look solemn, and with a tingle Andy realizes here is a kind of person he has never encountered back in Rhode Island. The Rebel informs them that the key to camp is being where you're supposed to be, when you're supposed to be. "And to help you *git* there," he says, "we've got us a little system." As if by magic, a horn sounds outside; Andy remembers the loudspeaker and the pole. "When y'all hear that little bugle, y'all just think of it as the Rebel whispering in your ear, all right?" The Rebel smiles.

The next day, whenever Andy hears the bugle, he thinks of that sinister smile, and hurries along. In the morning he has Archery, Riflery, and Rocketry; in the afternoon, Swimming and Leatherworking. In between there's lunch and a rest period in the cabins, when mail and candy are brought by a girl, Suzy, who is fourteen and Mr. Sperry's granddaughter. Andy has an account at the camp store with twenty dollars in it, and he's eager to use up all the money, since if there's any left over he isn't sure his parents will let him keep it. Apart from candy, or necessities like toothpaste, the only thing you can buy at Camp Mohegan turns out to be something called gimp—long flat strings of colored plastic you weave together to make bracelets or belts. At first Andy is suspicious: making bracelets sounds dangerously like a hobby of his older sister's, a person whose entire value system he considers frivolous in the extreme. Looking closer, however, he sees that some of the coolest kids at Mohegan are involved in gimp. And so on the third day he goes to the store and picks out some strings: nothing fancy, just some green and white to make a rope for a coach's whistle. It will allow him to assume the role of Weeb Eubank, the Jets' coach—much more in keeping with the Rebel's toughness, he reasons, than any bracelet could be.

That night he wakes in pitch blackness to find himself falling out of his bunk—his whole sleeping bag sliding away, legs first. His elbow smacks the floor, sending a jolt up his arm; still half-asleep, he calls out, *"Ma!!!"* The word is out before he can grab it back; all he can do is scramble up onto the bunk and lie there dead still. Drew Hartusian's voice rises from his cot in the center of the cabin: "Everyone okay, guys?" Andy affects a light snore. The next morning, when someone asks who was crying for his mommy last night, he shakes his head in disgust; and by noon he has half convinced himself that what he really called out was not "Ma!" but "Aaa!"—not much of anything, considering his bone-crushing, death-defying, Rebel-style plunge from *six feet up!* in the air.

III. COOL

He learns who's who in Cabin 7. There's Sammy Ecker, from Florida, and a tall boy, Trip Taylor. Leo DiMarco has a ragged purple scar from a heart operation. Beneath him is a loudmouth named Phil Lubberfield with gleaming braces who's always boasting about his father's cabin cruiser; and in the far corner Ed Brickman and Mikey Dempsey, the quiet ones.

Andy's bunkmate is the only black person at Mohegan, and the coolest kid in camp. What's cool about Richard Wills begins with the fact that he is called "Richard" instead of Rich, Dickie, or any of the usual nicknames. Richard is skinny, with dark hairs

on his lip that look almost like a real mustache. His walk has a
funny hitch in it, as if he's riding a slow wave; and when he
laughs he cocks his neck back and goes *chee chee chee, yuk yuk yuk*
in a high rolling chuckle. Richard knows how to joke his way
out of trouble. During rest period one day he strolls in twenty
minutes late, and instead of apologizing to Drew Hartusian he
calls out, "Hiya folks, y'all miss me?" Then he goes straight over
to Ed Brickman, tousles his hair, and says, "Been behaving yourself, Junior?"; and the whole cabin, including Drew Hartusian,
cracks up. Richard is the best slapfighter Andy has ever seen,
dancing around the cabin, feinting and jabbing and talking in a
stream like the boxer Muhammad Ali. But the most remarkable
thing about him is his hat—a soft, shapeless thing of red felt, with
wavy edges that drop low over his ears and forehead; a present
from his older brother that Richard wears everywhere, even to
dinner.

Richard has a kind of cool that can't be imitated. One day by
the store, Andy's stitching gimp with him and some others when
Phil Lubberfield comes up, calling out, "Hey *Richard,* man, it's
me, *Philip!*" Lubberfield tries to laugh like Richard, but all that
happens is a weird honking in his throat. Richard turns to Andy.
"Some people," he says, and shakes his head.

As the days pass, Richard seems to be choosing him as his best
friend. Honored, Andy makes the friendship a centerpiece of his
first letter home. He writes,

> *Dear Mom and Dad,*
>   *I'm having a great time here. In Swimming I will
> make Flying Fish if I can pass the test. The water is pretty
> warm.*

> *My best friend is Richard Wills, a Negro boy from*
> *Haddonfield, New Jersey. His father is a lawyer. He*
> *wears a funny red hat. XXXOOO,*
>
> *Andrew E. Hatter*

It's Andy's first letter ever, and he's pleased by how different his writing is from his sister's, with her looping curves and *i*'s dotted with flowers and hearts. Thinking of his sister makes him frown. He knows his mother will be angry with him for leaving her out of the letter; and finally he pulls it out of the still-unsealed envelope and scribbles *(& Tracey)* after *Dear Mom and Dad*. He takes consolation in knowing his sister will see he has added her in at the last minute, and then only because he had to.

IV. The Corner of Bedford and Orange

He wonders where Richard Wills would live if he lived in Rhode Island. In Andy's town the kids whose fathers are lawyers live in one neighborhood, the same one the Hatters live in; and everyone there is white.

There are two black kids on Andy's Little League team, Jimmy Hollister and Darryl Bennett. Sometimes after practice Andy walks with them to the Cumberland Farms on Bedford Avenue, where the three sit drinking sodas and watching cars go by. Jimmy and Andy do most of the talking, Darryl sitting there thumping his fist in his mitt and saying "Sheeeit!" or "That's the *damn* truth!" every now and then. When it's time to go, Andy heads down Bedford toward the beach, Jimmy and Darryl along Orange Street toward Scott. Scott Street is a neighborhood of two-family houses with tiny yards and sagging porches. The sidewalks are cracked and broken, and in summer crowded with people sitting on folding chairs. Andy knows these people are poor, and he's supposed to feel sorry for them; but sometimes as he watches Jimmy and Darryl head off to Scott Street, he feels a curiosity that borders on envy. They're curious about his neighborhood too. One day when the three have finished their Cokes and are standing on the corner of Bedford and Orange, Jimmy Hollister asks him about the Hatters' house.

"You got your own room?" he asks. "All by yourself and nobody else?"

"Sheeeit," says Darryl Bennett.

"Hey Andy," says Jimmy. "How big is your bed?"

A bed is a bed, Andy thinks. But then he realizes what Jimmy expects, and while he knows boasting is wrong and lying worse, he doesn't want to disappoint him; and so he says his bed is extra big—eight feet across and ten feet long. Both his teammates explode with laughter.

"That ain't no bed," says Jimmy. "That's a boat! You better watch out, one day you gonna float straight out to sea!"

A month before Andy left for camp, Darryl Bennett started missing practice. He skipped three times, then showed up for a game; then disappeared for two whole weeks. At the next game Coach Sal called the team to the dugout.

"Now, you guys know Darryl's been cutting practice," he said.

The dugout went silent. Coach Sal kept his arms folded, and looked down at the ground to where he was digging up dirt with the toe of his cleat. "Now, maybe you got family problems, okay—hey, we all got problems! But if you wanna be on a team, you still gotta work for it."

The final decision, he said, was up to the team. By the time

Andy realized they were actually going to *vote* on Darryl, kids were already putting their heads down, and Coach Sal was saying, "All those for Darryl?" As if it had a hesitant life all its own, his hand went up.

"All against?"

His eyes closed, Andy heard a distinct "Aw, *man*!" from the end of the bench, where Jimmy Hollister was sitting.

"Okay," Coach Sal said. They opened their eyes. "Fair is fair."

When Andy told his parents about it that night, his mother, busy clearing the dishes, tossed a spatula into the sink with a loud clank.

"That little runt!" she said. To his shock, Andy saw she meant not Darryl but Coach Sal himself. She turned to him. "And how did you vote?"

He was about to answer when his father broke in. "That's your business," he said.

His mother frowned and went back to the pot she was washing. "You be extra nice to Darryl," she said to Andy. He told her he would, and started toward the door, then stopped. "Hey Mom," he said. "Can I sleep over his house tomorrow?"

"Whose house, honey?"

"Darryl's. Darryl Bennett's. He invited me."

The words had popped out by themselves—a lie, and for no reason. Andy didn't even know where Darryl's house was, exactly.

"He invited you?" His mother was studying him. "For when?"

For Friday night, he said, looking away. His mother was quiet, and he looked up at her. "You just told me to be extra nice to him, didn't you?"

"I did, but . . ." She glanced over at Andy's father, who raised an eyebrow. "Well," she said to Andy. "Couldn't you be nice to him *here*?"

V. INTERNAL COMBUSTION

At nine it's lights out in the cabin, and they lie in their bunks listening to the bugle play taps. If Andy turns he can look out and see the moon on the lake, its light shattered into a million gleaming bits. Drew Hartusian stays for ten minutes, then quietly leaves.

The first few nights everyone goes right to sleep. But soon they begin to wait for Hartusian to go so they can talk. Each night they laugh a little harder, get a little noisier. One night the counselor's hardly out the door when someone unleashes a loud fart.

"Aw, who ripped?" "Who cut the cheese?" "Aw Leo, gross me out!"

Sammy Ecker announces he's going to barf—a word Andy has never heard before. "One time my sister played a piano concert," Sammy says, "and right in the middle she *barfed* all over the piano!"

"What's really gross," Leo DiMarco says, "is when you barf and there's *corn* in it!" The cabin rocks with laughter. Andy considers what to contribute, but nothing he can think of is guaranteed to be funny.

"Hey, you guys," says Phil Lubberfield. "You ever light a fart?"

Light a fart? they ask.

"Yeah. It's gas. You can light it with a match. Like a blow-torch."

Challenged to show them, Lubberfield falls silent. Andy sees his chance. "What're you gonna do," he says, "order one? 'Hi, this is Philip Lubberfield in Cabin 7, and I'd like one large fart.' "

"Very funny, Hatter," he hears—but the others are laughing. "I'd like that fart with peppers and onions, please," says Leo DiMarco, and when someone else adds, "And extra *cheese*!" laughter erupts again.

"Okay, you douchebags," says Lubberfield. "Okay."

The talk shifts to school and teachers. Trip Taylor tells them about sex education classes at his school, taught by a lady named Mrs. Shanahan, who's divorced and wears a tight purple sweater.

"Hey Trip," Andy says. "Do you stay after and get help with your homework?" Everyone laughs again, and he's pleased to hear Richard Wills chuckling beneath him—until now he wasn't sure Richard was even awake.

"And those boobs . . ." says Trip Taylor. His voice fades away.

Suddenly, a match flares in the dark. Lubberfield is on his back in his bunk, legs drawn up. All he's wearing is underwear, and he brings the lighted match close, closer, until you can see golden hairs on his legs.

"Okay," he says. "Now everybody watch!" Andy hears a *fffft!* and the fire at the end of the match leaps up.

"Wow!" says Leo. "Boss!"

"I told you guys." Lubberfield sits up. "Just like a blowtorch."

It's another chance for Andy. "You know, with gas like that," he starts to say, "you should work for the gas com—"

The door bangs open, the light snaps on. "All right!" booms Drew Hartusian's voice.

They all turn to the wall, eyes clenched shut, as the counselor patrols the room. He's been outside listening, he says, and he's ashamed of them. "What would your parents say if they heard? Huh? Phil? Leo? Andy?" Hartusian sighs. "Just today I was giving the Rebel a positive report about you guys, but now . . . ? I tell you, he's gonna be *extremely* disappointed."

Finally the light blinks off, the screen door closes, and the counselor's step fades away on the path. As silence descends, Andy feels despair at having been lumped by Drew Hartusian with Leo and Phil, whose sins he believes more serious, and of a more disgusting nature, than his own.

In the darkness, a *chee chee yuk yuk yuk*. "You all got some strange hobbies," says Richard Wills. "Talking about your teacher's boobies! Shoving lit matches up your butt!"

"Yeah," says Lubberfield, "well, at least we didn't pretend to be asleep the whole time like a little pussy-shit."

"You already fried your butt, boy," Richard says. "Now you wanna get it whupped too?"

There's a rustle, and Lubberfield is standing there in the dark. In whispers they shout at him—*go to sleep, you big jerk!*—until he goes back to bed. Briefly Andy tries to envision what would have happened if Lubberfield had been stupid enough to fight Richard Wills. But even this thought can't distract him from his own troubles. He falls asleep replaying the sound of Hartusian's disappointed *Andy?* and lamenting the stupidity of trading his good name for a few lousy laughs.

VI. What Makes the World Go Round

Richard Wills is knowledgeable about sex.

On the raft one hot afternoon, they discuss girls and what one does with them. It's a subject Andy has gone into only with his friend Tommy Sebastian, in the dim back of the Sebastians' garage where Tommy's father keeps stacks of *Playboy* magazines; to be talking about it in the middle of the wide open day, out on a lake, makes him nervous. Richard's telling about his brother Lawrence, who is nineteen and a student at New York University. At New York University, says Richard, boys and girls live together in the same dormitory. Sometimes they even take showers together. Lawrence's girlfriend frequently spends the whole night in his room. "He's a sex hound," says Richard— Andy glancing to see if a counselor might be floating by. "He even does it when she's on the *rag*!"

Andy is disturbed to realize he isn't exactly sure what this means. For the millionth time he finds himself longing for an older brother; it seems an overwhelming advantage for getting ahead in the world.

"Your brother," he says. "Doesn't he want to marry her first?" Richard stares, and he has to fumble for a way out. "I mean, like my parents tell my sister—you know, a girl should save herself and everything."

"You think your folks didn't do it first?" says Richard.

Andy feels pretty sure his father didn't, and absolutely sure his mother didn't. But Richard scoffs at the idea. No one is a virgin anymore, he informs Andy. "Walt Frazier. He's not married; you think he's a virgin? Joe Namath, you think *he* is?"

Andy shrugs helplessly; he has spent hundreds of hours thinking about Joe Namath without ever remotely considering this question.

"You know what makes the world go round, Andy man?" Richard Wills leans close. "Pussy," he says. "Pussy makes the world go round."

Nodding, Andy tries to imagine what to do with this information, how to use it to begin to bring himself up to Richard's level of knowledge. He thinks about Suzy Sperry, Mr. Sperry's granddaughter. When she passes by in the cabin, delivering candy, he has a good view down the front of her shirt, and several times he's caught a glimpse of her bra.

Richard Wills interrupts this thought with a cackling laugh. "Hey, Andy man—didn't your mama ever show you a Q-tip?"

"Huh?" Andy says, confused.

Richard leans close, peering at the side of his head. "You got all that waxy shit in your ears. You gotta scoop that shit out, man!"

And with that, Richard picks himself up and dives off the raft.

VII. An Incident by the Piano

The least popular kid at Mohegan is a skinny boy named Neil from New York City. Neil has a silly way of pursing his lips together, rolling his eyes, and throwing up his hands when someone asks him a question. At foursquare he looks happy to be knocked right away to the end of the line; and when some mean boys play keepaway with one of his shoes, Neil seems actually to *like* it, running from one tormentor to the next with a shrieking, girlish laughter.

There's one thing Neil is good at. In the rec room, over by the pool tables, stands a beat-up piano. Neil is always playing it. Not the usual things, like chopsticks or "Heart and Soul," but real piano music. There's one song Neil plays over and over—a clear, light melody that for some reason makes Andy think of a stream in sunlight. Sometimes when he listens to it he's afraid he's going to cry, and has to think hard about something else until the stinging around his eyes goes away.

One morning in Riflery he cuts a finger on a nail and has to go to the Nurse for a Band-Aid. Passing the activities hall on his way back he hears the song, and goes inside. The rec room is empty except for Neil.

"Hey," Andy says, "how come you're here?"

Neil just shrugs. "How come not?"

"I mean," says Andy, "don't you have to be in activities?"

"Nope," Neil says. "They don't make me."

"Why not?"

"Cripesy, don't ask *me*!" He rolls his eyes and looks at the ceiling.

Andy realizes his question sounded meaner than he meant it to. "Go ahead and play some more," he says. Leaning on the pool table, he studies the Band-Aid the Nurse put on his finger as Neil resumes. Out of the corner of his eye he sees the boy's slender hands fluttering like birds over the keys. He feels the stinging sensation and squeezes it away.

"Hey," he says, "that's kinda neat, that song. What is it?"

"It's nothing," Neil answers. "It's just some silly nonsense."

To prove his point, he bangs the keys with a loud, clanging sound. It's as if he has crumpled up the melody and thrown it away.

"What did you do that for?" Andy asks.

"Oh, because," Neil says. Then he pushes the stool back and walks out of the room, leaving Andy standing there alone.

A few days later, Neil is gone. Andy looks around for him in the rec room, in the mess hall, but he's not there anymore. Trying to sound casual, he asks Drew Hartusian if he's seen the kid who plays the piano.

The counselor looks at him. "Are you a friend of Neil's, Andy?"

"Well, not really, he just . . ." He feels his face turning red. "I lent him fifty cents, and I was kinda wondering . . ."

"Oh, I see. Well, Andy—I'm afraid Neil had to go home."

"Was he . . . was he sick or something?"

"Something like that." From his pocket Hartusian pulls a handful of change and picks out two quarters. "That was nice of you to lend him money," he says. "I wish a few other people were half as considerate."

Andy wonders what was wrong with Neil; but more than that, what strikes him in the next days is how little difference Neil's not being there anymore makes to anyone. He wonders if it would be different if *he* left, and decides it would. He himself does not exactly miss Neil; though when he looks over in the rec room and sees the piano in the corner, he feels guilty about the fifty cents.

He also can't get the pretty song out of his mind. All over camp—in the morning, splashing cold water on his face at the outdoor sinks; at night in his bunk—he finds himself humming it, and picturing the boy's white, birdlike hands.

"What *is* that jive tune, anyway?" Richard Wills asks as they cross the lawn one night, heading for dinner. "I know I heard that somewhere."

"Huh?" says Andy. "What tune?" And after that he's careful not to hum it out loud anymore.

VIII. THE SACHEM BOYS

Up in the woods somewhere is a mysterious place called Sachem Village, where the oldest boys stay—legendary figures who move from place to place at whim, painting their faces and wearing loincloths, sleeping in caves with bears. One evening Andy and Leo DiMarco set out to find Sachem, but it isn't long before the quiet and the tall trees press in on them, and they flee back down to camp, where they report being chased by a shadowy figure carrying a hatchet.

In his heart Andy knows that most of what is said about the Sachem Boys cannot be true, that finally they are just ordinary boys who were brought here, as he was, by parents. But as he lies in his bunk at night he also knows it takes a different kind of person than he is to sleep out in the dark woods, and that while bears and loincloths may be imaginary, they express something which itself is real. Possessing that something, he understands, is the job of heroes; and so he adds the Sachem Boys to the list of Joe Namath and Carl Yastrzemski, Tom Sawyer and Chip Hilton.

Some friends of his consider their fathers heroes; but for Andy this is impossible. The father of his best friend, Tim Harnisch, is a brain surgeon, and of his next-best friend, Tommy Sebastian, a state trooper. Andy's father is an accountant; and no matter how Andy looks at it, adding numbers can't compare with drilling open someone's skull or chasing crooks on I-95. Mr. Hatter is old—forty-four—and bald, so on Parents Day at school it looks to Andy like a grandfather has slipped into the group. He watches no TV, and spends long hours in his study, paying bills and reading. Reading the newspaper, he holds it up high, and the smoke from his pipe drifts over the top; sometimes Andy imagines him on fire behind it.

Sometimes, guiltily, he wishes he had a different father—like Mr. Sebastian, for instance, who in April scored thirty points at the school's father-son basketball game. At home Andy mentioned the game to his mother. Why hadn't he said anything about it to his father? she asked.

"To Dad? Why?"

His mother frowned at a fingernail.

Two days later he was out in the yard with his football after dinner when the door opened and his father came out, in sneakers.

"Hey superstar," he said. "Toss the pigskin with the old man?"

"Well," Andy said, "I'm kinda expecting Tommy to come over."

He hoped his father would go back inside; but instead he stepped out onto the lawn. "I'll warm you up till Tommy gets here." He rubbed his hands together and held them out. "Come on. Let 'er rip."

"Well, okay." Andy hefted the ball. Feeling queasily that his father would get hurt, and that it would be his fault, he stepped forward and tossed a floater which, to his relief, his father managed to catch.

"Not bad—for Joe Namath. Now lets see how Johnny U does it." His father licked his fingertips, cocked his arm—and suddenly Andy found the football bearing down on him, hard, in a perfect spiral.

"Hey!" he said. "How'd you do that?"

"It's all in the laces," said his father.

That night his mother came to his room with a box full of old pictures. In one, an arrow pointed to a boy dribbling a basketball past a defender, his mouth open, hair flying. Taped to the back was a yellowed clipping: *High man for St. John's was Ernest Hatter with 19 points.*

Andy stared at the photo, wondering what had happened to change that boy into his father—whether he had simply forgotten what it meant to drive past a defender toward the hoop, or whether he had discovered something better in life as a grownup. In the days afterward, Andy studied his father's life, trying to see what that something might be. There was golf, which was boring, and on Wednesday nights bridge—more boring. On Sunday came church, which Andy was convinced his father secretly hated as much as he himself did and went merely because Andy's mother made him. There was paying bills, and shaving in the morning, and driving, and the great unknown of the office and work; and there were parties. One night his parents gave a party, and Andy lay awake in bed, listening to the murmur of conversation below. It astounded him, the way grown-ups could stand around for hours on end doing nothing but talking. His father, he concluded, had made a bad trade, and he determined not to make the same one himself.

IX. FROG MAN

Trip Taylor, the tallest boy in camp, has webbed toes.

Andy discovers this intriguing fact as the two are scouting for a launching place in Rocketry, and he happens to see Taylor's sandaled foot. "Hey!" he says.

"What?"

"Your toes! They . . . there's skin between them!"

Oh, yeah, says Taylor matter-of-factly. Those are his webbed toes.

Andy asks for a closer look, and the tall boy slips off his sandal. Sure enough, instead of space between the second and third toe, there's a panel of soft, earlobelike skin. It's no big deal, Trip insists. A cousin of his had a whole extra *finger* on his hand, he tells Andy. "Just like a little sausage. They had to snip it off."

Andy asks if the toes hurt when you run on them.

"No, why should they?" Taylor puts his sandal back on. "They're normal toes. They're just not separated."

Andy nods. He's a little envious, because having feet like that would be a distinction. At the same time there's something freakish about them, like the pictures of people in Tim Harnisch's father's medical books; and though the thought makes him more than a little disgusted, he secretly likes to imagine trying to pull the toes apart or separate them with a knife.

At lunch one day there's a discussion of the upcoming camp swim meet. The favorite is a boy from Cabin 12, Derek Slater, who practices with a high school team during the winter. Andy announces that Slater doesn't have a chance against their cabin's entry, Trip Taylor.

"Trip's got a secret weapon," he says. "He's got built-in flippers."

"Built-in what?" says Leo.

"Flippers. Go ahead, Trip—show 'em!"

They gather round. Taylor takes off his sneaker with a sigh, and it occurs to Andy that maybe it's not so much fun to have to keep showing your webbed toes around. He leans in and says,

"You're gonna win all the way, man!" But Taylor ignores him, and he realizes he has gone too far.

After that, Trip Taylor is polite, but a curtain has come down between them. The thought agonizes Andy. He likes Taylor and feels guilty for hurting his feelings; but more than that, there's something grown-up about the tall boy, something calm and mature, and to have earned the dislike of such a person seems a bad sign for the future. With jokes and friendly looks he does what he can to change the situation, but to no avail.

In the swim meet, to everyone's surprise, Trip Taylor edges out Derek Slater with a burst of power on the last length. Later in the rec room Andy overhears him talking about the race. How did he pour it on like that at the end? one kid asks. Taylor smiles and slips off a sneaker.

"My secret weapon," he says. "Built-in flippers."

Hearing this, Andy feels something like joy. A wave of relief carries him, smiling, to Trip Taylor's side.

"Heya Tripper," he says, and slaps his shoulder. "How's it going?"

"Oh," says Taylor. "Hi."

The curtain is still there.

X. OUT OF THE BLUE

A sunny morning, and he has dashed to the cabin between activities to get a letter he has written to his grandparents. He's surprised to find Phil Lubberfield there, lying in his bunk in the corner.

"What's wrong with you?" Andy says.

"Headache." Lubberfield watches him root around in his drawer. "So where's your friend the cool guy?"

"Who? You mean Richard?"

"Yeah, Mister Cool. Mister Always Showing Off."

Even if there is a speck of truth to this, coming from Lubberfield it doesn't matter. "I'd like to hear you say that to him," he says.

"My dad, he says they're all like that."

Andy glances out the window to see none other than Richard Wills himself, way on the other side of the lawn. "Hey!" he calls out. "Hey Richard!"

"What're you doing?" says Lubberfield.

Andy goes to the door. With so much bright blue sky he has to squint to locate Richard's red hat, about to disappear into the activities hall.

"Richard!" he yells through cupped hands. He hears a noise behind him, and before he knows what's happening, Lubberfield is standing at his shoulder, screaming past his ear: *"You lazy nigger!"*

Turning, Andy pushes the other boy back into the cabin. "What'd you go and say that for, huh?" He races out the door into the bright sunlight. The red hat is gone, the big lawn empty. Standing there, he considers whether to go find Richard and explain what just happened. But he can't get around the word Lubberfield yelled—a word so poisonous, he can't imagine repeating it to Richard's face—and so all he can do is silently pray that his friend didn't hear. "You're lucky, you big jerk," he calls back to Lubberfield, and hustles off to mail his letter.

But someone, it turns out, *did* hear: the next morning at breakfast he gets the terrifying message that the Rebel wants to talk to him and Lubberfield. In silence they walk to the white cottage at the edge of the woods where the Rebel lives. There's a screened-in porch, and as they approach they can see him sitting there. A nightmare vision of being kicked out of camp flickers in Andy's mind, and he vows to tell on Lubberfield, if necessary, to prevent this. They knock on the door.

"Come on in!" the deep voice drawls.

The Rebel is sitting in a wicker chair, writing on a clipboard.

"Ah," he says. "I guess you two know why you're here, right?"

"Yes, sir." Andy squeezes the words out over a thick urge to cry.

"Now, maybe you think that because I'm from Tennessee I don't care about this kind of garbage." He stares at them. "Is that what you think?"

In a menacing voice, the Rebel tells them they need to think long and hard about how to treat other people. In order to help them think about it, he says, they're going to spend the morning scrubbing the bathhouse.

"Now *git*!" he says, turning back to his clipboard.

They stop at the maintenance shed to pick up buckets, sponges, and soap. At the bathhouse they squirt cleaner into their buckets and fill them from the showers. Praying Richard Wills won't come along and ask why they're being punished, Andy dips his sponge into the hot foamy water, determined to scrub until everything is sparkling clean.

"Hey," says Phil Lubberfield. "Thanks for not snitching, buddy."

"I'm not your buddy, so shut up, you fat blubberface!"

Lubberfield stares, then snorts and turns away. Andy knows he's being given one insult free; a second and he'll have to fight. He thinks about it, but rejects the idea as too little, too late, and grimly sets to work, flinging water on the wall and watching it sluice down in filthy streams.

XI. MISSION HQ

They mount a spy mission to the counselors' wood-shingled house by the lake. At ten sharp on the chosen night, Andy, Leo, Richard, and Trip Taylor, watches synchronized, slip from their bunks and gather outside.

"Your mission, should you decide to accept it," whispers Leo, "is to infiltrate HQ and observe the organization's activities."

Richard Wills clicks his tongue in scorn. "That's baby stuff," he says. "Me, I'm just going strolling."

"Me too," says Andy. Since the near-disaster with Lubberfield, he's been looking for any sign that Richard knows, and he's beginning to feel safe again. He follows along down the path.

It's a five-minute walk to the beach, then a dash across to the porch of the counselors' HQ. Crouching behind a wicker couch, they can spy through a window screen to the room within.

The place is not as nice as Andy has expected—mismatched chairs and couches, a dangling bulb overhead. Half a dozen counselors occupy the room: Andy's archery teacher, Barry LaGrange, sorting albums by the record player; his swim teacher, Roger, writing at a beat-up desk. Drew Hartusian's there, too, playing cards with three others, leaning back in his chair.

"Well," says one of the other players. "What's it gonna be, Tuse?"

Hartusian tips forward. "Son of a bitch," he says, tossing his cards on the table. Taking a cigarette from his shirt pocket, he lights it and squints through the smoke as the others play on. A counselor named Jerry arrives with beer—Andy recognizes the red, white and blue of Budweiser, which Tommy Sebastian's father drinks.

"Jesus," whispers Trip. "They're getting *bombed*!"

"Well, what did you *expect*?" hisses Richard. "Milk and cookies?"

"Hey, look!" It's Leo, tugging at Andy's sleeve.

Along the cinder path, headed straight for HQ, strides the Rebel.

Andy watches with a thrilled and queasy feeling, wondering whether the counselors will be fired right now, on the spot, or tomorrow after breakfast. The door opens; the Rebel stands in the room.

"So folks," he says. "How're the kiddies tonight?"

"Babes in the woods," says Barry LaGrange.

The counselors smile. The Rebel pulls up a chair at the card table. "Hope you boys have deep pockets tonight," he says, grinning.

"Tell us about it, Jimmy," says Drew Hartusian. "Just like last night and the night before, right buddy?"

The Rebel smiles and pops open a beer. "Hey, what can I tell ya, Tuse?" he says. "You can't make chicken salad out of chicken shit."

The group roars with laughter.

Lying in his bunk an hour later, Andy tries to reflect on all he has seen and heard. Beneath him Richard chuckles, repeating the Rebel's joke about the chicken salad. But Andy is troubled. He pictures Hartusian sending a spout of smoke toward the ceiling. He's never seen the counselor smoke, and it makes him wonder who he really is—or the Rebel, who apparently is also called

Jimmy, who drinks and swears and plays cards, and whose Southern accent disappears when he's not talking to campers.

To Andy, the truly disturbing thing about all of it is not how wicked it is, or even how unexpected, but how little any of it has to do with *him*. Apparently there are lives in which he exists, but barely, and far, far from the center of things: like a picture on the wall, perhaps, or a leaf blowing down the street.

XII. GIANT STEPS AND SMALL

A special bugle sounds one night, and they proceed, two hundred strong, to the mess hall, where a TV has been brought in for the landing on the moon. Mr. Sperry informs them that if they live to be ninety, they'll never forget this night, July 20, 1969. But Andy finds the landing disappointing. The fuzzy picture keeps skipping a frame, and he's too far back in the crowd to decipher the squawking voices of the astronauts. On the screen, a blocky, statuelike figure glows bright white against the grayness. The figure stumbles forward; everyone cheers.

Soon they're trooping back to their cabins. Andy hopes his lack of excitement isn't unpatriotic. But he doesn't see why the moon should be singled out for a mission when other, more exotic planets are available, like Saturn with its mysterious rings. In general, such things as space travel and science fiction don't interest him much. What people do in galaxies that don't exist, or in equally unimaginable future eons, is far less compelling to him than what real boys do on real islands, or in haunted houses, or on football fields.

The next morning, however, he wakes at dawn with a troubling question: If there's no gravity in space, how do you know up from down? And if you don't know up from down, how do you know that the northern hemisphere, where he lives, really *is* the top of the world, and the southern hemisphere the bottom? He tries to figure it out. He knows that the Hatters' street in Rhode Island, Locust Lane, runs north–south. But what does this mean, really? What if it turns out to mean nothing? The questions open up an empty area inside him that fills with something like panic. For a moment he feels the way he did back in first grade, when he'd wake from a nightmare, sweating and confused, unsure of where he was, unsure even of the simple words like *bed, door, window* that described where he was.

Outside his cabin window, meanwhile, morning is coming. Thunder mutters in the distance; but the soft, steady pace of the rain tells him the storm has already passed and he is safe. Though he knows the planet is actually hurtling through space, he decides to believe for the time being in the stability of the trees and ground taking shape in the gray light. The panic subsides. He lies listening to the familiar sound of rain in the leaves, and waits for day to happen.

XIII. DOWN BUT NOT OUT

Suddenly it's Friday, the last full day. His green-and-white gimp rope is done, his six letters mailed. Tomorrow the lawn will fill with cars and parents. To Andy it seems impossible that camp and home belong to the same world; he imagines his parents setting out and never showing up, never finding the camp because, after all, it's in another dimension.

He hopes that if they do show up, his sister isn't with them.

In the afternoon there's a scavenger hunt, and after dinner, a campfire sing-along and the annual Mohegan Boxout. The boxout is a challenge tournament. One round of four minutes, with the loser sitting down and the winner fighting on; win five in a row and you "retire" as undefeated champ.

Andy and Richard arrive in the rec room to a big crowd. Boxers circle and jab on the blue mat as Barry LaGrange keeps time with a stopwatch. Andy analyzes the different styles. Some boys throw wild flurries. Some stick both gloves out and hold their heads back in terror. He and Richard cheer for Sammy Ecker, who fights hard but loses to a bigger boy named George from Cabin 4. As Barry raises George's arm, Andy calls out, "All right, Sammy!"

And then Ecker turns and tosses him the gloves.

If there's one thing Andy knows about himself, a fact as familiar as his shoe size, it's that he's not tough. He knows plenty of tough kids back home, kids like Spiros Lalakos and Jimmy Donnelly, and the encounters he's had with them—like when Donnelly chester-backstered him all the way home from school—have always been filled with misery and hot shame. Over the years he's learned to recognize these situations before they develop, and get out fast. It's a coward's skill, he knows, but one he depends on.

Once he's caught the gloves from Ecker, however, there's no way out. There's a roar from the crowd around him, and all too soon Andy finds himself standing on the mat, his legs rubbery as he faces the maroon circles of the other boy's gloves. George pushes in cautiously, and dishes out a light left jab. Andy covers up. He feels sick to his stomach, certain it's all going to come spilling out now, all the fear and weakness he has succeeded in keeping hidden these two weeks at camp. What he wants above anything else in the world is to run—to dash through the crowd and out into the night, throwing the gloves behind him.

Confident now, George has him backed to the far edge of the mat. There's nowhere else to go, Andy realizes; no escape. And so, fists clenched inside his gloves, he lowers his head and charges, swinging out as hard as he can in all directions.

And as he does, a strange thing happens: his panic evaporates. He's aware of George hitting him, but to his amazement the blows are soft, almost pillowy, and he can ignore them. Meanwhile his own hands flail away. A punch connects, another. George falls back, and Andy watches his own foot step forward. It's as if some other person has taken control of his body while his mind floats high above, free and easy. Nothing hurts. Nothing is going to hurt. He sees how ridiculous it is, the way he's spent his life afraid of getting hit. Up to now he always believed that boys like Lalakos and Donnelly were physically different from him, that they didn't feel pain. Now he sees the truth, and it makes him want to shout with joy.

The round flies by. Everything blurs together, the flashing gloves, the shouts of the boys watching; and then the whistle shrills, and Barry LaGrange grabs his arm and raises it.

With the next boy it's no different. Andy takes the first few blows, then his nervousness lifts and he bulls in, and the other boy moves back. He's not only winning, he realizes, he's winning big; he's unstoppable. The crowd knows it too. He can feel his reputation building. His third fight, against a big fat kid named Eric Abel, ends almost before it starts. When Barry gives the cue to box, Abel stands in his corner, raising his hands in front of his face and peeking out with a look of blank terror. Andy crosses and punches him once in the stomach, and Abel goes down as if a chair has been jerked out from beneath him. "My rib," he gasps, struggling to one knee. "I think I got a bruised rib." This time when Andy's arm goes up, he raises both hands and dances in his corner, throwing jabs toward the crowd.

From behind him he hears a familiar chuckle. "Yup," he hears, "I guess I'm gonna have to give him the best friendly whuppin' he's ever had!"

He turns to see Barry lacing up the gloves on Richard Wills.

Shirtless, still wearing his red hat, Richard throws a blindingly fast combination in the air while doing his famous Muhammad Ali shuffle step. Boys ooh and aah. A speck of dread lands in Andy's stomach. He tries to catch Richard's eye, but Richard is busy talking to the crowd.

"Gentlemen," says Barry. "Box!"

The room shakes with excitement, and Andy senses he has gone from favorite to underdog. Wary, not exactly afraid, he waits as Richard comes dancing across the mat. The maroon gloves flash, and a patter of jabs, too many to count, lands on Andy's arms and sides. Richard hisses with each punch, making a crunching noise through his teeth, like breaking bones.

Andy covers up, creating a shell with his arms and gloves, and the crowd howls, sensing a knockout. Inside the shell, however, he assesses a surprising fact: Richard's punches, despite all the scary bone-crunching noises, don't really hurt. It's not all that different from the other boys Andy has already beaten. He prepares a mental image of himself breaking out of the shell, fists flying.

The first punch catches Richard on the shoulder; the red hat flies off. Andy sees surprise and anger on his friend's face. Charging in, he delivers two more solid hits, the second one landing smack in the center of Richard's chest, staggering him. Then the chase is on: Richard backing and dancing, Andy boring in. At the end Richard stops running; for the last thirty seconds they stand at the center of the mat, trading furious punches. But when the whistle blows it's Andy's hand that goes up.

"That's bullshit, man!" Hurling the gloves down, Richard picks up his hat and pushes into the crowd.

Andy would like to mull over what has happened, but there's no time for that. The boxout continues. "One last shot!" Barry LaGrange calls, and a boy steps forward—a quiet, sturdy boy from Cabin 10 with the funny name of Danny Doctor.

"Go Andy!" someone screams as Danny Doctor laces up. "Eat him up, champ!" Andy taps his gloves and smiles toward the crowd.

But this time it's different. This time, though the punches don't exactly hurt, he finds he can no longer move forward after absorbing one; sometimes he's even knocked back a step. Looking across at Danny Doctor's face he finds no fear there, just a calm, waiting look. He lunges with his right—and the next thing he knows, he's sitting on the blue mat. The shriek on all sides and a ringing in his ears tell him he's been knocked down. Wobbling to his feet, he tastes something salty on his lip.

He looks over to see Richard Wills clapping.

When it's over, and he has lost, he sticks around to watch Danny Doctor win his next match, then leaves. The crowd parts, hands reaching to pat him on the back.

Outside he crosses the lawn, sampling the swelling of his lip and the rusty taste of blood, the noise of the boxout shrinking away behind him. He hears guitars playing at the sing-along, *The cat came back, the very next day, the cat came back, you know they thought he was a goner* . . .

On a rock near the cabin he sits looking out over the lake. The moon is bright and almost full; he wonders if the astronauts are still up there, and whether they can see its face from so close up.

After some time, a noise approaches on the path and turns into Richard Wills.

"Hi," Andy says.

Richard jams his hands in his pockets. "How's your lip?"

Andy says his lip is okay. He asks what happened in the box-out, and learns that Danny Doctor retired as undefeated champ. He nods. "Why'd you root for him, anyway?" he asks Richard.

"Me? I didn't root for anyone. I'm objective."

In his mind Andy checks the image of Richard cheering his knockdown. He has no wish to argue. "Where's your hat?" he asks.

Richard pulls a wad of red felt out of his back pocket. "It got dirty when it—when you knocked it off my head, sucker!" He chuckles. "Shit, Andy man, next year I'm gonna have to take you *serious*!"

They laugh and then fall silent.

When Richard goes to the cabin, Andy stays behind, tossing pebbles in the dark and listening to them *plish* into the water. His body aches pleasurably. He feels cut loose from the world of two weeks ago; he has learned things, has changed, and wonders how he can communicate these changes at home and thus prevent them from withering away. He wishes that instead of being picked up in the morning, he could set out on his own, hitching rides, tramping through woods and across highways before emerging, dirty and lean, in his parents' backyard—his mother throwing her hands to her face at the ragged sight.

He surveys the stretch of life just ahead of him. Sixth grade, the kings of the school; Mr. Haberman for homeroom, said to crack you over the head with a wooden pointer if he doesn't like you. After that, seventh grade and the huge world beyond, in a new and impossible-sounding decade, the Seventies. By the time that's over he'll be twenty-one, as old as Drew Hartusian is now. Though he finds that hard to believe, he sees how it will go: the circle of things he understands getting bigger year by year, and the circle of things he doesn't getting smaller, until at some distant point in the future, it will disappear altogether, like the last pinprick dot when you turn the TV off; and then he will be a grown-up.

He considers how to handle things tomorrow with his parents. The key will be to take charge and make them listen. They'll have to realize that what he has lived the past two weeks is not something cute or childish or temporary—but, on the contrary, something that's going to come back with him and form the core of his life from now on. His parents will benefit from it, particularly his mother, because he's going to be so much more responsible with his chores. On the other hand, he's going to need his parents less, and tell them less as well. All this must be made clear from the start.

He sees how he'll do it, too. When he greets his father he'll shake hands instead of hugging; his father will raise an eyebrow and smile out of the corner of his mouth. His sister, if she's there, will be greeted not with the old antagonism, but with cool politeness. And when his mother leans forward to kiss him, he won't pull away—that would be mean—but he won't hug back either. Instead he'll just stand still, arms at his sides, and calmly offer his cheek. It's a small thing, he knows; but that's how bigger things are built, one step at a time: the only way, if you want to cross even a very big room, you can get from here to there.

LAUGHING IN
THE DARK

ALL LAST SPRING I was depressed. Even when I felt okay, the okayness was like a papery membrane, and feeling bad was beating hard underneath. My life was a disaster. There was the F in precalculus, the college applications I never sent, the question of would I even graduate. But most of the time I obsessed about bizarre little things, like the faces people wear. My father's You-Are-Disappointing-Me stare, or my advisor Mr. Latimer's Passion-for-History look, or my mother and her Pretending-I'm-Not-Worried-About-You glances. I wondered: What if you just locked the personality closet one morning and didn't let people put their faces on?

As Ms. Angela T. says, they'd have to *be real*.

I knew something was wrong with me, but I

didn't know what. Sometime during the winter, just when everyone else had shifted up a gear, I'd gone into neutral. At school I'd get a pass to the library and sit with the college essays I was supposed to be doing. *Describe two people who have influenced you. Tell about an event that had an important effect on you.* I'd sit there just staring. And it wasn't only this. It was other things, like how when Mr. Latimer was telling me *I'm not going to let you fall through the cracks, Danny,* he glanced toward the Faculty Room and I knew he was picturing his next cigarette.

It was a lot of stupid little nothings that somehow added up to everything.

May eleventh was part of it too—my sister Janice's birthday. Janice ran away from home after a fight with my father when she was fifteen and I was four, and I never saw her again. It's not a topic anyone talks much about, but I think about it all the time. Last spring I guess you could say I was obsessing about it.

On May eleventh I was at my father's, hanging out in the garage while he worked on his toy planes. I was telling him about my Senior Project, a portfolio of photos showing people whose relationships other people in test groups had to guess at. (This was supposed to be my original idea, but basically I'd stolen it from an article called "Social Intelligence—Do *You* Have It?" in an old *Psychology Today*.) My father designs ventilator systems for nuclear submarines at the Boat Works. He wanted to know how it was going in my "real courses."

"Fine," I said, lying a little.

"You're lying," he said. "I don't need any social intelligence to see that." He took the Stuka he was working on out into the driveway. "You, Danny. You stick to your bread and butter subjects, okay?"

I followed him. "Hey Dad," I asked. "Do you know what today is?"

When Janice ran away, my parents hired a detective, but after two years my father decided enough was enough. He told my mother to clear out Janice's room. She took down the horse drawings and Woodstock posters, rolled them up and tied them with red ribbons. I was thinking about those ribbons now as I watched my father's face, looking for a blink, a twitch, anything.

"Friday," he said. "It's Friday, Danny."

I turned and went for my bike.

When I got home, my mother was in the front room at her easel. I don't see how she paints nature pictures inside while smoking Tareytons, but she does. It's something she started sometime between when Janice ran away and when my parents got divorced seven years later. Her paintings are scenes of boats and beaches, mountains and waterfalls. The details are terrific— little butterflies in the background, or the petals of a daisy lying in a pile. She uses a magnifying glass.

"Hi honeybunch," she called to me.

"Hi," I said, but I didn't go in. That beating-against-the-membrane feeling was hitting me again. I didn't know what to do. I considered going up to my room and standing in front of the mirror and pulling my eyebags off my eye, like they do to Malcolm MacDowell in *A Clockwork Orange,* and watching my eye become completely round like a Ping-Pong ball. But then I imagined Angela Tourtelotte's nosy little voice going, "Oh gross, that's like, so *twisted*!"

So instead I went over to the phone.

★ ★ ★

The thing with Ms. Angela T. began a month before that, in April, when Mr. Latimer decided I needed an "assistant" for my Senior Project and gave my name to a kid who was writing a Most Compatible Person program for his project. I lied blatantly on the questionnaire. Yes, I loved junk food and football, and yes, men *should* open doors for women "out of respect." When the list came back, the girl for me was a tenth grader named Angela Tourtelotte.

I went down to introduce myself. Angela Tourtelotte must have done some serious lying on the questionnaire, too, because she definitely did not look like someone who wanted doors opened for her out of respect. She was into some retro punk act —hair shaved on one side, six earrings, plastic handcuff belt, and bowling shoes, the green-and-red ones with the size in big numbers on the back. I asked her: "You really think people trust someone in bowling shoes?"

She made a honking noise like post-nasal drip. Was that really her laugh? I wanted to know.

"God, let's *be* boring!" She banged her locker shut and took off down the hall.

For some reason we started hanging out anyway. First we went around taking photos for my project. Her strategy was to hover like a vulture, then swoop up to someone and say, "Hi, we'd like to take your picture!" When people asked what she wanted them to do, she said: "Just walk like you were walking. Just be you." They loved it. I circled around, snapping and clicking.

You'll be a famous photographer, Angela Tourtelotte told me. *You'll go across America and write a book about people who look like their gerbils! You'll be on* Oprah*!*

I liked going over to her house. It was always loud, with the twins, Rickey and Mickey, cruising around yelling, "Do the Giants *rule,* or *what*?!" and the dog, Ralphie, barking, and the TV on, and Mrs. Tourtelotte shouting for a little *help* here, please! in the kitchen. Mr. T was always slapping me on the back. *This is the first normal person you've brought around here in years, Angie,* he'd say. *Stick around, lemme enjoy it a little!*

For someone supposedly so punk, Angela Tourtelotte had some pretty homey ideas. Like humming the theme song from *Leave It to Beaver,* and calling people "Wally" and "Beave." Or riding go-carts at Kart-O-Rama, or hanging out at the bowling alley, or keeping a lock of her mother's hair in a little silver box. I asked her, did Mommy serve her cookies and milk after school?

"Don't be a Wally," she said.

Sometimes Mrs. Tourtelotte let us use her car. It was bizarre to find myself driving the Estate Wagon through town on a Saturday night with Angela Tourtelotte sitting on the passenger side, putting purple lipstick on in the visor mirror. Her idea of a terrific time was to cruise back and forth past her friends' houses, blasting music on the tape deck—horrible bands like King Missile. She begged me to let her drive. She'd have her license in six months, so what was the big deal? I told her I didn't think she'd get her license.

"Oh yeah? Well, I'll be sixteen, and that's the law, Wally."

"Not in your case. In your case they'll make an exception."

"Why in my case?"

"Because," I said, "you're dangerous. You're a public menace."

She liked that. She slid over and whispered, "I'm public enemy number one!" and kind of nuzzled into my shoulder.

"Hey," I said. "I'm driving." And she went back over to her side.

I was only seventeen, so there was no law against doing with Angela Tourtelotte all the things everyone always talks about doing. But I never knew whether they really did those things. Sometimes I wasn't even sure what those things *were*. I didn't have an older brother to tell me about it. I'd hear the way people talked at school, the way guys talked, about who was scamming who, who hooked up with who over the weekend. It all seemed like a foreign language to me. It just froze me up.

Whenever I thought about two people doing it, I always used to get this image of fish flopping—how they curl back and forth on the dock, sucking air and slowly dying. I also used to think a lot about my grandparents' golden wedding anniversary down in Virginia, when I was ten. My parents were separated by then, but they were pretending not to be, and my father wasn't too happy about it. "This charade, Martha," I overheard him saying. "It nauseates me." That night in my room I woke up and I could hear them through the wall. First I thought they were fighting. When I realized they weren't, I wrapped my pillow around my head and squeezed. The next morning at breakfast they were back to hating each other, as if nothing had happened.

One Saturday after the driving incident, Angela Tourtelotte dragged me to Kart-O-Rama, where we raced around the track like maniacs with a bunch of ten-year-olds. In the middle of it she pulled her cart over and waved me alongside, like she wanted to tell me something. Then, instead, she stuck her tongue in my ear.

I knew I was supposed to be experiencing maximum passion, but all I could think was, Who *is* this person with her tongue in my ear?

My father called and asked me to lunch. We met at the Fast Attack Deli, over by the Boat Works.

"So," he said when our grinders came. "Tell me, Danny— what exactly are your plans these days?"

I babbled about the pictures Angela T. and I had been doing for my project; I tried to emphasize how *professional* the whole thing was.

"That's a hobby, Danny," he broke in. "You can do that in your *spare* time." In exactly three weeks, he reminded me, I was graduating. He was wondering what I was planning to *do*.

"Maybe I'll travel," I said. "Go across America and take pictures."

"Pictures?"

"Yeah, you know. Photographs. I'll make a book out of it. A travelogue or something."

When he's stressed out, my father runs his hand over his head in an Ancient Hair Reflex. "Do I sense your mother behind this?" he asked.

"It's my life, you know."

"Yes, son. Yes, it is." He heaved a sigh that made it sound truly sad, even to me, that it *was* my life. Then he went on, talking about some medical-technician training program a friend of his had told him about. I started thinking about Janice. All spring I'd been wondering what was going through her mind the day she ran away. I believed she must have had a good reason for going.

"You're not listening, Danny," my father said.

"Dad," I said. "Where do you think she is right now?" I wanted him to say her name, just once. I wanted to see his lips make the motion.

"I'm sitting here trying to help, and you're not even—"

I aimed it right at him, point-blank: "You can't even say her name, can you?"

"Son, I don't think—"

"You can't! She ran away because of *you,* and you can't even say her name! Janice! *Janice!*"

I was shouting, and people were looking. My father turned away, then changed his mind and came back hard with a finger in my face. "Now you listen to me, son. Your sister made her decision. She abandoned her family and threw herself on the mercy of strangers—"

I tried to break in—I hate it when he starts calling me "son," like I'm the Universal Son and he's the Universal Father—but he held up his hand. "A damned foolish thing to do, but if you want to worship it, go right ahead, that's your business. In the meantime, I suggest you do some hard thinking about your own situation."

He took a ten-dollar bill from his wallet and tossed it on the table, then walked away.

After he left, I sat there for a while, looking out the window across Sub Way to the Boat Works. It's like a city over there. There are brick buildings and glass buildings and a massive green building where the subs are built. There's a huge sign shaped like a sub that says SUBMARINE CAPITAL OF THE WORLD in pink neon letters.

I tried to imagine where Janice could be. I always pictured her in some green and breezy place, with horses. In my mind it was always Montana, but not really Montana—not Montana itself. I'd see her standing in the sunlight, swinging her leg up over a big reddish-brown horse. She'd start to ride off, toward a mountain. I'd go closer and try to get a look at her face, but the sunlight coming over the mountain was too bright.

The bill was $9.15, so I added another dollar to my father's ten, then put on my jacket and left. Out on Sub Way I took a last look at the shipyard. I thought about the weeks and months and years my father had spent there.

Maybe he was right about Janice, I thought. But he still hadn't said her name.

The night it all finally caved in, we were at Angela Tourtelotte's, babysitting. Her parents were out to dinner and the twins up in bed. Around eleven we were watching *Magnificent Obsession,* the old version with Robert Taylor, where he becomes a brain surgeon just to save the life of this girl he loves. Angela was sitting next to me on the couch.

"You know what?" she said. "You should do something wild and totally weird your father out."

"Like what? Become a brain surgeon and give him a brain transplant?"

"No!" She gave me her Sweeping Scorn look. "I mean something *dangerous*. Like, I don't know—like going and becoming a male stripper and dancing in some bar for sexually frustrated women, or something."

"Gee," I said. "Great idea!"

"God, I was just *kidding*." She took the remote control and fast-forwarded, making everything ridiculous. I stared at her. "Hi there,'' she said, batting her eyelashes. Her face came toward mine. We kissed, sort of.

She pulled back and licked her lips like she was trying to figure out what I tasted like. ''Do you always get so nervous?'' she asked.

''I'm not nervous,'' I said.

She looked at me. ''Aha!'' she said. ''A virgin!'' Then she burrowed her face into my neck and started yelling *the Virgin Danny!* over and over.

''Hey, come on.'' But she kept doing it, and I pushed her away. ''Cut it out.''

When Angela Tourtelotte gets mad, it happens fast, the switch just gets flipped. ''You know,'' she said, ''you're always rejecting me. I mean, like, totally.''

''No,'' I said. ''Look, it's just . . .''

''You think I'm like, hideous or something, right? You think all this stuff is totally bogus!'' She was pulling off her plastic bracelets. ''Well, it's not like I was born with all this crap on, you know!'' She started in on her earrings, and I was afraid she was going to tear right through her ear.

''Look,'' I said. ''I'm not rejecting you.''

''No? Then what *are* you doing?''

I just didn't want to wake up the twins, I said. Plus who knew when her parents might show up? And weren't we supposed to be watching a movie, anyway?

Angela sighed and rolled her eyes. ''You know, sometimes you're like an old man or something,'' she said.

''Old man? What do you mean, old man?''

''Like, look at you right now. I mean, don't you ever get happy?''

Sure I did, I said. Everyone got happy sometimes, didn't they?

"No, not like *that*. I mean HAPPY! I mean screaming and yelling happy! Obnoxious happy! Freak-people-on-the-street-out happy!" She stared at me.

"Think about it," she said.

I did think about it. We sat there watching the movie and I thought about it and thought about it and thought about it until the membrane started pounding and I felt bad again.

At some point the door opened, and Angela's parents barged in.

"Hiya gang!" said Mr. T. "Everything okay here at the ranch?"

Instantly Angela Tourtelotte had her earrings and bracelets gathered up in an inconspicuous pile. "Yeah," she said. "But poophead here wouldn't let me drive the car, even though I *told* him you'd let me."

"My ass I would," Mr. T said.

"Jack!" Mrs. Tourtelotte pretended to be shocked.

"Okay then," he said, "*your* ass I would!" He pinched her, and she slapped his hand away.

"I gotta go," I said, and stood up.

Mr. Tourtelotte took me home. He was one of those drivers who steer with their wrists resting on the crossbars of the steering wheel. Even at the sharp corners he never actually grabbed the wheel with his hand.

We drove along. Every time a band of light from the streetlights went by, I saw him smiling, as if he were remembering a great joke. "So," he said eventually. "Angie behaving herself these days?" I didn't know what to say, and he kept talking. "Christ, she puts any more metal in that ear of hers, she's gonna start picking up radio signals!'' He laughed, a soft *hunh hunh hunh*.

The house was dark when we pulled in.

''Thanks a lot for the ride,'' I said.

Mr. Tourtelotte leaned close. ''Dan,'' he said. ''I'm gonna let you in on a little secret.'' I could smell whatever he'd been drinking, rum or something. ''It's hard to be bad,'' he whispered.

''Excuse me?''

''I said, it's hard to be bad.'' He put his hand on my shoulder. People thought it was hard to be good, he explained, but they were wrong, dead wrong. ''Oh, you can be bad all right, Dan— for a while. But you can't keep it up! It's just too damn hard! You always end up being good again!''

He squeezed my arm and chuckled as I got out. Backing out of the drive, he gave a little toot. Then he was gone.

I turned to the house. I could see now that my mother's light was on, and I pictured her lying in bed reading and smoking. And suddenly, right then and there, I felt the membrane tearing away, all the way off, and I was falling through to the other side. I thought about Angela Tourtelotte's question. No, I would *never* be happy, I decided, never in my life. For me, being unhappy was a life calling, it was like the priesthood, or like the bad breath some people have, you can cover it up but you can't get rid of it. I remembered how my mother used to take me down to the beach to watch the submarines when I was a kid, and one day we saw a sub going out with all the men on deck—and suddenly I was terrified my father was there, and he was going to sink into the water, and I cried and cried until my mother shook me and said *Hey! Dad is sitting at his desk, right now, on dry land, honey!* But that was how it went with me: every single happy thing had some twist in it, some moment where it started to go bad.

I went inside, locked up, and went to bed.

The last two weeks of school, everyone else was going wild, but all I wanted to do was sleep. In the middle of the night I'd come downstairs and eat. Then in the morning my mother would bang on the door. "Is the Snooze King gracing the court with his presence today?" she'd say.

At school I avoided Angela Tourtelotte. She followed me around, sulking. *Why are you harshing on me?* she kept saying. *What did I do?*

"Nothing," I told her. "I'm just hibernating, okay?"

She had a friend, Teddy, who kept giving me sinister little messages in the hall, like "You know, if you don't treat her right you could *lose* her!" Finally the whole thing blew up. I was heading toward the caf and they were following me. It was like in a detective movie—I'd stop, they'd stop. At the water fountain I went to take a drink, and when I bent over there they were, huddling together.

"This is ridiculous," I said, standing up.

Teddy came over. "Angela isn't talking to you," she said.

"What are you," I said, "her bodyguard?"

"She's like, totally disappointed in you, you know."

Teddy's one of those people who wear pointy black glasses with fake diamonds in them and think it's cool. "If you'll excuse me," I said, "I was going to get a drink of water."

"Okay," Angela Tourtelotte called. "Let's *be* boring!"

I turned and faced her. "Do you realize you say the same things over and over again?" I said. "You have these three expressions. 'Let's *be* boring!' 'Go-carts *rule!*' 'Stop *harshing* on me, Wally!' That's it—that's your whole vocabulary!'' Then I walked past her down the hall.

"You are like, so lame, it's *pathetic!*" she shouted after me. "Go *be* alone, see what I care, you big . . . LUMP!"

I kept on walking.

After school that day I rode my bike down by the beaches. The streets were so familiar it felt almost sore riding down them, that comfortable soreness like around the edges of a scab when you pick at it. I parked my bike and sat on the hurricane wall. An old man was flying a kite with a little kid, but there wasn't enough wind. He'd run a few steps and the kite would bob up, then sink down again. I thought about Montana. States out there were huge, their lines perfectly straight. The towns had names like Pierre and Helena. When it snowed, they got four feet, and the snow never got dirty; it just stayed there, shining white.

On Thursday before graduation we had rehearsal in the gym after school. First we got plastic packets with our gowns inside. Then the vice principal, Mr. Pellard, explained how to get your diploma: "Take with your left! Shake with your right! And whatever you do, please *keep moving!*"

Afterward I sat until everyone was gone and the janitor, Fred, started folding up the bleachers. I liked how they folded and unfolded, creating hundreds of seats out of nothing, then taking them back again.

Someone coughed behind me. It was Angela Tourtelotte, standing by the door. Since our fight we hadn't talked. I went over.

"What, no bodyguard?" I asked her.

"Ha, ha." She was holding something wrapped in newspaper. "Here. It's not like you deserve it or anything, but . . ."

I unwrapped the paper. It was a pair of bowling shoes. And a can of the disinfectant they spray on them when you turn them in.

"Thanks," I said. "It's, uh, it's terrific." The truth was, I'd missed Angela Tourtelotte, but I didn't know how to say it. So I just stood there.

"Hey," she said. "Wanna go get scenic? I happen to know a *looovely* spot."

She held out her arm and I took it.

We walked over to Beaufort College, this junior college near school, and sat out in front of the Student Center. People were already gone for the summer, the campus was practically deserted. Every now and then someone would come out of the building and head across toward the library, carrying books or a briefcase.

"I wonder what I'm going to do," I said.

Angela looked at me. "You're going to go inside and get me a Coke."

I looked across the lawns. There was a little breeze, and the trees overhead rustled. Angela rolled the sleeves of her shirt up to the shoulders. Everything stood still.

"The leaves," I said.

"Huh?"

"You asked when was I ever happy. At your house that night. Remember?" She nodded. "Well, I was happy when my sister used to throw me in the leaves in the fall. Out in the backyard. We used to rake leaves—"

"Rewind, rewind!" Angela Tourtelotte held her hands up. *"Sister?"*

And so I told her everything I hadn't told her, or anyone else for that matter—about Janice, my mother and the red ribbons, the detective, Montana and the mountain in the sunshine; it all came flying out. I hadn't remembered those leaves until just then. We'd rake them up in the back, a giant mountain of leaves, and Janice would swing me back and forth and then let me go and I'd float into the crackly pile.

When I was done, Angela picked a blade of grass and twirled it around. She shook her head. "Life is so weird. It's so, like, secret, you know?"

I waited. I guess I was expecting her to make some comment about Janice. But instead she proceeded to tell some story about how her father had blatantly cheated on her mother three years before, how he'd bought his girlfriend a Mustang convertible and how then, after he got guilty and bagged her, the girlfriend traded the car in for lottery tickets and won two hundred thousand dollars.

I stared at her.

"It's true! Right now she's on this island in Indonesia somewhere with a personal slave giving her total body massages."

Whatever the point was supposed to be, I didn't feel like getting it. We sat there. Angela Tourtelotte started doing the blade-of-grass routine again.

"You like it this way, don't you," she finally said.

"What way? What do I like?"

"You know, the whole lost-sister situation. The whole Montana thing. You're into it."

I just looked at her.

"That's right, you're into it. You're into it because it's, like, so impossible and perfect and everything. It's so, you know . . . so *done*. That's what you want to be. Totally *done*."

"Done?" I said. "Done? What am I, a steak?"

She flicked the piece of grass away.

"Your sister could be anywhere, you know." She pointed to a girl in a jeans jacket sitting on a bench reading. "She could be her. Or she could be, like, a taxi driver somewhere. Or she could be one of them." The door to the Student Center had just opened and two women in cafeteria outfits were standing outside talking.

"Yup," Angela Tourtelotte said. "I think that one's definitely her. The tall one. That's Janice."

"You are very strange," I said.

"Just check it out," she insisted. "Just try to imagine it."

I watched as the woman reached into her purse and took out a cigarette. She had purplish-brownish curled hair. She was at least fifty. Angela went on. "Maybe Janice has kids. Maybe she has twins, like Rickey and Mickey. Maybe triplets—you know, three pink little screamers. What do you think about that?"

"Who knows?" I said.

She reached over and grabbed my arm.

"Hey, I love you," she said. "What do you think about *that*?"

She let go of my arm and looked at me. I couldn't look back at her—I wasn't upset, I just couldn't look at her—so I closed my eyes and pretended to be enjoying the sun on my face. After a minute I really did start enjoying it. When I thought about it, it *was* funny to imagine Janice underneath the same sun some-where, a waitress smoking a cigarette and boasting about her kids, bitching about taxes, telling someone how to make a killer avocado dip.

I opened my eyes; Angela was standing up.

"Come on," she said. "Time to get scenic."

What she wanted to show me was the college greenhouse, way across campus. It was locked when we got there, so we walked around the outside, looking in. Angela started naming all the plants: snapdragons and coleus, dusty miller, sago palm. She and her mother, it turned out, did garden club together.

"Do a lot with sago palms in garden club?" I asked her.

"Oh, you're so *funny,* it's hysterical!" She did an exaggerated nasal-drip laugh. Then she looked around and grabbed my hand. There was a little tool shed right by the greenhouse, and the door stood partway open.

Inside was dark and cool, with one tiny streaky window. My eyes adjusted and I saw shovels against the wall, trowels like claws, big bags of wood chips. I took an old chair and wedged it under the doorknob.

"My hero," Angela Tourtelotte said.

She was standing right in front of me, so close I could feel her breath on my chin. Her lips looked purple and shiny in the dim light—they *were* purple and shiny, I remembered.

"Hey," she said, "do you think I'm a sexy mama?" Someone in the library had written *Angela Is a Sexy Mama* in the last carrel, she explained. She was hoping maybe it was me.

Me, a vandal—? I started to say, and then she kissed me. We rolled over on the bags of wood chips. She was on top of me, then I was on top of her, and then she was on top of me again, and we were doing a kind of full-body rub.

After a while I had to stop. "What's wrong?" she asked.

"I don't know how to say this, but . . ." I put on my AM-radio voice. "I think I'm in the grip of the sexual urge."

"Ooh, dangerous!"

"No, seriously. Listen, uh, I've never actually, you know—"

"God, you make it sound like we're *doing* it or something. I mean, this is just, like, cuddling." She kissed me.

"Hey. If we keep cuddling like this, I think I'm gonna explode."

"Don't worry, silly," she said. "I'll put you back together again."

We rolled over, and then a lot of things happened at once: Angela slid her tongue into my ear, and I shivered and heard my own voice moaning; a shadow crossed outside the window and then the door was rattling and Angela was whispering *shhh!* to me but still rubbing as someone outside croakily said, "What's going on in there? You okay in there?"

Through the window I could see a campus security uniform. The door rattled again. I leaned over to Angela and whispered, "I think I exploded."

"We're just fine!" she called out. And the two of us held on tight and did the nasal drip together, looking out at the greenhouse and the sago palm, laughing like idiots in the dark.

THE PRICK
OF THE SEASON

I WAS SEVENTEEN and strictly mediocre. An anonymous B− in school, I didn't play guitar, didn't own wheels, was headed for the state university in the fall and not some hot-shit college, and my father, of all things in the world, was a teacher. I had one secret hope—a smile I'd discovered was catchy, like a yawn in public places. *Don't expect to get by on your looks,* my father told me. But we lived in a beach town, and it was summer, and all around me people were doing just that.

Though I loved my father, the dingy life of a teacher repelled me, with its cigarettes and clouds of chalk dust, its cheap shirts and beat-up briefcases. I knew I'd been made for more than that. Sometimes I felt I was living in a movie—*Downhill Racer,* say, with Robert Redford. Passing a woman walking her dog or a couple sharing a sundae at the Kool Kreem, I'd experience a giddy charge, as if only my presence gave these bit players and routines their existence. Exactly where I was headed in life wasn't clear, but I was sure that when I got there, the tired old adult world would welcome me with gratitude, like an infusion of rich red blood.

My two best friends, Eddie Boyce and Tom Krajewski, were definitely *not* cut out for the movies. Eddie was short and funny-looking, but made up for it with cool. When you were still listening to Jethro Tull, he was into country rock; by the time you'd bought all the new Pure Prairie League and Marshall Tucker, he was off into Bob Marley; you could never catch up. Tom Krajewski, the K-Man, wore his hair back in a bandanna and had the terrible kind of acne that makes you wince to look at. His chief love was his van, a beat-up, sludge-colored Plymouth fitted out in back with curtains, carpet, and speakers the size of small clothes hampers. Tom was the only one of us not going to college in September, and it wasn't clear what he was going to do with himself, other than smoke dope and fight with his parents. He talked about heading to California and opening a surf and cycle shop. Because he was the K-Man and the K-Man was king, Eddie and I believed Tom could do whatever he wanted; but in the back of my mind I wondered. Eddie was smart, I reasoned, and would get by on his wits; I was charmed and had luck; but Tom was one of those people who was just . . . there. Sometimes I could imagine him getting himself in trouble. He had a temper. When he got mad he'd go into a zone where no one could reach him, brooding, then bursting out in wild rages he always regretted later.

The three of us spent our weekends cruising in the van—aimless rides late into the night, past the stone walls and tilting farmhouses of rural Connecticut. Pulling over, we'd light up a joint and listen to the Grateful Dead do "Truckin'" for the millionth time. Eddie did his impersonations of teachers, reducing them to dust. Someone would open the door and we'd tumble out in a rush of smoke, laughing. Usually we ended up driving out to the marshes at Mallard Point to listen to the ducks gabble away like munchkins. It was a small town, and we wanted to escape.

After the endless senior spring, June had finally come around, summer shifting into gear. Eddie was helping out at his father's furniture store, Tom filling in with a construction crew and waiting for something to happen. As for me, I'd gotten a job as a lifeguard at Sandy Neck Beach.

I loved the beach. In school I'd been on the football team, and sometimes on a warm September Saturday when a whisper of ocean air would pass over the field, I'd turn seaward, away from the game, and experience a small rush of bliss. Spending my last summer before college getting paid to gaze out over the Sound was perfect for me. The continent at my back, crammed to bursting with real people and their messy, familiar fates—for me that world was hopelessly flawed. The ocean, on the other hand, presented a vast blank, and I could write on it whatever I wanted.

What I wanted most immediately was to get a car and lose my virginity. Sandy Neck looked especially promising on the second front. The beach was loaded with females. In fact, for me every day at work involved a conflict, for I was in love with two women there—or rather, I was in lust with a woman and in love with a girl.

Lifeguards at Sandy Neck had to take turns doing "porter duty"—waiting by the gate to fetch people's chairs and umbrellas from big storage boxes along the sea wall. My very first day "toting for tips," as the guards called it, I'd looked up to see a woman in a leopard-spotted bikini coming down the steps. This was mid-June, but Lola Kellerman had an August tan. Her body, as Eddie Boyce liked to say, was a true work of God. She stood smoking a cigarette and squinting across the beach with a challenging smile. I rose to get her chair.

"Don't worry about it," she said, tossing her cigarette into the sand and starting toward the storage boxes. I followed, trying not to stare, and caught up to her at the second box.

"*I* don't know where he put the damn thing!" she said to me, leaning over the side and looking in. I couldn't tell if she meant her husband or some chair porter from last summer. The sand up by the wall was hot, and as we stood there I did a little dance from foot to foot. She smiled the tiniest smile, then pulled a chair out of the box and started across the beach. "I can set it up myself," she said over her shoulder. "Maybe you'd better go cool those toes."

Lola Kellerman was thirty-two years old and outrageously sexy. She carried herself with a reckless, swinging stride, and her upper lip curled in a sly-cat way that reminded me of the actress Lee Remick. Her cigarettes of choice were Lucky Strikes, which she dragged on intensely, blowing the smoke hard out of the side of her mouth—a gesture that called to me from a world of illicit pleasures. I soon became aware Lola considered me "cute." Wherever I lifeguarded, she'd stroll over to the foot of my chair to smoke a Lucky and shoot the breeze. *You got a sweet smile, kiddo, you know that?* she said one day; and after that I smiled even more sweetly.

The other half of my Sandy Neck dilemma was a chaste, noontime love anyone's parents would have approved of. Janet Alford later became a star swimmer at the University of Florida and just missed making the U.S. Olympic team; but in the summer of 1975 she was a tall sixteen-year-old with silky brown hair and a forehead round and white like the moon. The local paper was already following her career—her specialty was the butterfly —and a few times that winter I'd wandered over to the school pool to watch her practice. Each time, I'd found my throat constricting in a helpless feeling, the stroke was so beautiful: her graceful body rippling along, as if in passing through the water she became water herself.

Hearing that Janet Alford had also been hired to lifeguard at Sandy Neck, I'd made a plan. Everyone knew Janet was going places in life, and this, my reasoning went, had caused a space to gather around her, a moat of advance celebrity inside which she sat trapped. I liked the thought of throwing a bridge across that moat and waltzing on in. On Memorial Day, when we lifeguards were summoned to listen as the beach manager, Mr. McGuirk, explained how unheroic the job really was, I edged over to Janet and said hi.

"Tony, right?" she said. Our school was small, you knew who people were.

"Call me . . . Antoine," I answered. "My stage name. And I'll call you . . . Jeannette."

A quizzical little smile played across her mouth.

The season under way, I traded shifts so that whenever Janet Alford had porter duty, *presto!* Antoine had it with her. There we sat, in low-slung beach chairs near the gate, listening to the radio while waiting for our customers. The AM stations spun tunes like "Tighter and Tighter," or Janet's all-time favorite, "The Night the Lights Went Out in Georgia," but I flipped around until I found a college program playing reggae. I asked Janet whether she didn't think the Wailers were extremely excellent.

"I don't know," she said. "It sounds kind of . . . slow-motion-like."

She looked skeptical, and I ransacked my brain for things Eddie Boyce had told me about Rastafarians. Getting high was their religion, I explained, their First Commandment. I leaned toward her, glancing around. "Jeannette," I growled. "Antoine says, a toke a day keeps the devil away!"

The goal was to keep her always slightly off balance. Racy jokes made her blush bright red; compliments made her look away, blinking. I told her tall women were descended from the noble concubines of pharaohs; I told her I wished she were a milkshake and I could drink her.

"You're weird," she said, laughing.

So the summer developed along schizophrenic lines, running me from one side of the beach to the other, from Janet Alford to Lola Kellerman. It was the traditional good girl/bad girl arrangement, even I could see that. But years were to pass before I'd see that dividing womanhood into the sainted and the fallen only mirrored deep divisions in myself, and that conducting one's identity as a greenhouse where separate selves were nurtured, each to its own audience—now Antoine the Savvy, now Tony the Innocent—made for a tricky business indeed. And so my deepest feelings remained strange and disturbing to me. Some mornings I'd gobble down the breakfast my mother gave me and rush to the beach early to spy on Janet swimming in a roped-off area of the Sound, sending small ripples out to sea as her coach stood by with a stopwatch. Looking on, I'd find myself beset by a hollowing-out sensation that started in my chest and gouged its way outward until I felt empty to my very fingertips. When Janet emerged and stood listening to her coach, a shudder passed through me, and I winced to think of Antoine—his accomplishments seemed so puny, his ploys so trivial and insincere. Thus, adrift in a Bermuda triangle of worship, envy, and self-loathing, did I manage to delude myself into mistaking for love a vehement desire, less to have Janet Alford than to *be* her; less to sleep with her than to swallow her whole.

I was requested to stop by at Lola Kellerman's to fix a lamp.

A sizzling afternoon in July, and I'd toted Lola's chair to her spot by the dunes. "Oh, Tony," she said when I turned to go. "Last night I knocked over this *stupid* lamp. . . ." Could I stop by that evening and help her out?

"Yeah, sure," I said. But first I needed some clarification. I'd done some nosing around, and from what I'd been told, it seemed there was one thing Lola was leaving out. "Do you, uh, live alone or something?" I asked.

She sighed. No, she didn't; but her husband, unfortunately, was away.

Lola's house stood on a newish street on the west side of town —a big split-level place with a tremendous living room picture window and one of those gravity-defying mailboxes perched on a serpentine length of welded chain. I stashed my bike behind the garage, and when I came back, Lola was standing at the door, wearing pressed jeans and a printed blouse. She looked older in clothes, and even more sexy. "Come on in," she said.

Having tantalized myself with visions of her leading me into the bedroom and quietly closing the door, I was perplexed to find that there was, in fact, a broken lamp. The bulb had shattered on impact, and in attempting to remove it, Lola had loosened the whole socket casing.

"See," she sighed over my shoulder. "You turn and turn and the stupid thing doesn't come unscrewed."

"No problem," I said, tightening the casing. But when Lola got a new bulb and I twisted it in, nothing happened.

"This stupid little shit–ass lamp!" she burst out. Eyes closed, she raised two fingers to massage her temples. "Know what I'd like? Some grass. God, I'd kill for some grass."

For a moment I thought crazily of the green lawn outside. Then it clicked. Lola Kellerman wanted *reefer*. She wanted to get high! I didn't by any chance have any, did I? she inquired.

"Not on me," I said. "But I can get some."

And so I found myself cruising across town behind the wheel of a glistening black 1974 Ford Thunderbird, V-8 engine, white leather, power everything, the ashtray full of butts and the glove compartment of tapes I hated, like the Beach Boys and the Eagles. I drove swiftly, admiring how the merest touch of the brakes gripped the car to a total stop.

Fortunately, Tom Krajewski was at home. I found him in the garage working on his motorcycle, an old, wrecked BMW with a sidecar he was forever trying to get going. He sat on the floor, parts strewn around him.

"K-Man," I said. "I need some weed."

"Oh yeah? Where's the party?"

The party was private, I told him. One on one.

"Aha! But the K-Man's gotta do the atmosphere, huh?"

Look, I said, it was cool, I'd owe him one.

He laughed. "You *already* owe me one, dip-shit." In fact, I already owed him about ten. "Who's the babe, anyway?"

"K-Man, come on," I pleaded, looking at my watch.

"Christ, all right already." He tossed aside a wrench and stood, wiping his hands on his pants. "Let's go see what's in stock."

We went into the house, saying hi to Mrs. Krajewski in the kitchen, and up two flights to the attic. Tom's room always depressed me a little—tiny and dark, a single window, a shelf of dusty old motorcycle models he'd made in grade school. When you slept over, somehow there was always sand in the bed, it drove you crazy. His stash sat in the top drawer of his bureau, among dubious-looking underwear. He pulled out a small plastic bag and separated half of what was in it into another, empty one.

"Want me to roll it, Junior, or can you handle that yourself?"

"Hey, you're saving my life, K-Man," I said, reaching out for the bag. Too late: he'd just looked out the window and seen the Thunderbird.

"Whoa!" He snatched the dope back. "Who is this babe—Liz Taylor?"

I explained that it was someone from the beach.

"The beach." He nodded. "Why doesn't anyone give *me* a fucking job like that, huh?"

I was silent, focusing on the weed like a dog. Finally he tossed it to me.

"Okay," he said. "But I want the *details*. In three fucking D."

"You got it, K-Man," I promised, and pounded down the stairs.

Back at her house, Lola was sitting on the living room couch. A Heineken, beaded with sweat, waited on the coffee table. I eased down in front of it, taking out the bag and setting to work, licking along the edge of the rolling paper in a way I hoped was highly erotic.

It was interesting to discover that Lola smoked dope like a novice, raising her eyebrows and sucking in too much air. "God, it's good to relax," she observed, tipping her head back and sighing. "I've been a wreck lately. A total wreck."

"Yeah?" I said. "You don't look it."

She laughed. That was just her facade, she said. People saw her as bold and sexy, but she considered herself timid and ugly.

"Ugly? That's crazy! How can you even *say* that?"

Her husband Barry was to blame, she told me. Barry had destroyed her confidence. A real estate developer, he'd gotten her to drop her modeling career in New York, marry him, and move up to Connecticut. He'd told her she never would have made it as a model; she was too big, all models were slim. She'd started taking diet pills, then making herself throw up, so that she'd finally had to go to a psychiatrist. Barry was a true bastard, she said. He was violent, he drank too much, and he cheated on her —had already been cheating on her during their honeymoon. She hated him. Once she'd thought about killing herself just to get back at him.

The things Lola was telling me had no place in how I'd imagined the evening would go; they were things which at seventeen I had no idea whatsoever how to respond to. I was setting myself to try anyway when I noticed she was peering at me with a cool, sly grin.

"You don't have these problems, do you, dream boy?" she said. "You don't have any problems at all."

"Sure I do," I said.

"Oh no you don't. Not you." She smiled, beckoning with a finger. "C'mere. Come on over here to bad old me."

With girls my own age, fooling around had always been a muffled thing, a kind of petty shoplifting, full of trickery and stolen pleasures. No one had ever looked me in the eye like this, and surely no one had ever done what Lola did now—peeling her jeans off, then her shirt and underwear, until she was calmly and completely naked. I managed to do likewise. Lola ran her fingernails up and down my body.

"God," she breathed, "you're so *smoooooth*."

I was a virgin, but as it turned out, not a particularly nervous one. My ideas about sex resembled those letters in *Penthouse*—actually, they came from those letters in *Penthouse*—where tireless men perform like heroes all night long. I was sure I knew exactly how moments like this one were supposed to go. Lola started kissing me, and I kissed her back. There was a touch of competition to what came next—a grit-your-teeth, grappling quality. I wanted to *win*. We stared at each other, our bodies thrashing away beneath us, until finally she couldn't hold out any longer, she had to close her eyes; and that was my victory and the signal that I, too, could release myself, which, in a rush of groaning sound, I did.

"Oh God," Lola said, and gulped.

A few minutes later she was glancing at her watch.

★ ★ ★

One might have expected Tony the Innocent, having lived out his own version of the *Summer of '42,* to be in seventh heaven. In fact, losing my virginity to Lola Kellerman plunged me into a moral crisis so grave that one week later, as I sat perched on my lifeguard's tower at Sandy Neck, I reached a momentous decision: I would forswear a repeat performance with Lola, and would instead devote my life to Janet Alford.

One step toward this pledge was Lola's decision, two days after our encounter, to show up at the beach with her husband. Barry the Bastard turned out to be a burly, friendly guy who tipped me a buck for setting up his umbrella, in the process moving up in my world from the status of an abstraction to that of an all-too-real person, one moreover whose wife I had lusted after, pursued, and enjoyed—right in the middle of his living room, no less.

I was also about to turn eighteen; and the more I'd thought about it, the clearer it seemed that the type of man who sneaked around messing with other men's wives was not the type I wanted to be. If I was doing this at eighteen, what would I be doing at thirty? No, only if my aspirations were higher would my fulfillments be higher too.

On the morning of my birthday, my father came to my room to wish me the best. I accepted with the friendly detachment that was standard policy in dealing with my folks. But this time my father wasn't having it. He studied me, nodding as if he'd just put some new thought together for himself. "You've got all the answers, don't you Tony?" he said. "You're in the driver's seat, and everyone else is just along for the ride."

I fumed at the monstrous injustice of my father's remark. In some dark corner of my heart I believed he hated me for having gotten his share of life's luck along with my own. What I ex-

pected from him was the same sweet deal sons have always expected—that he continue not just to love me but to *like* me, even
as I held a hundred petty things against him, from the embarrassment of his hobby, gardening, to the dandruff on his shoulders or
the loathsome state of his toes. These resentments made me feel
guilty, and guilt in turn fed my resentment: it was that old dismal
cycle of childhood, where you believe yourself first the best person in the whole world, then the worst.

But if someone like Janet Alford liked me, I reasoned—and all
signs were she might—then I couldn't be all that bad, could I?
For wasn't Janet better than good? In fact, wasn't she excellent?
Wasn't she *superior*? All summer I'd observed how nice she was to
the old ladies who made you carry four lounge chairs across the
beach and then tipped a dime, or to McGuirk, one of history's
most boring persons, a man who could lecture for an hour on
how to grow tomatoes. I'd noted the way, when you talked with
Janet, she really *listened,* not trying to shove herself into what you
were saying but rather effacing herself, disappearing into pure
listening the same way she disappeared into swimming. To disappear into things like that: that, it occurred to me, was holy.

All day long in my lifeguard's chair at Sandy Neck I sharpened
my new resolve, turning now and then—for reinforcement—to
wave at Janet on the next tower. One by one I ticked off my
transgressions. I would not be lazy. I would do something in
school for once in my life. I would treat my mother with respect.

And I would not commit adultery again.

That night I went out with Tom and Eddie. For my birthday
K-Man had given me the rest of the ounce of Colombian, and
the three of us drove to Mallard Point to go to work on it.
K-Man was talking nonstop about my night with Lola. "Come

over and fix a *lamp*," he was saying. "Come over and screw in my bulb, Sir Tony!" He shook his head. "I kick in the reefer and he gets the babe. Life's a pisser."

Eddie handed me the joint. "Ah, eighteen! He votes, he drinks, he gets nooky. And it's all legal!"

Yeah, yeah, I said, but I was hardly listening. Inwardly I was reflecting on having reached a turn in life that forked off from where Tom and Eddie were headed. It was an important moment, I thought.

I passed the joint on without taking a hit. K-Man took it, stuck it between his lips—then leaned over and punched me on the arm, hard.

"Fucking Sir Tony!" he said, and dragged on the weed till it glowed and popped in the dark.

I started calling on Janet Alford. I took her to the movies, to the Kool Kreem; we "dated," as my mother liked to say. At swim meets I watched Janet demolish her opponents and then, peeling off her cap in the lane, smile up at me. We walked through the town park, holding hands. I'd noticed she had a funny habit of swishing her tongue around inside her mouth, and when I asked about it, she turned her trademark red, then told me: she'd had braces and still wore a retainer at night; one of her front teeth was a little loose, and she could move it slightly with her tongue, making it click. I leaned close to listen. *That's Morse code for "I want your body," right Jeannette?* I was about to say. But Antoine's days, I'd decided, were numbered. Already I was at work in the greenhouse, busy preparing a new self for Janet, someone dedicated and serious—an Anthony, perhaps.

My new righteousness put a strain on life with Tom and Eddie. They showed up at the beach one day, lumbering across the sand to where I sat with Janet on porter duty, both of them in filthy jeans, Tom in black motorcycle boots, beer bottles dangling from between his fingers.

"Hey, fuck face," he said, sprawling down. "How's your love life?" He held out a Miller to Janet, who politely declined.

An awkward silence followed. Eddie took out his harmonica and wah-wahed some Dylan. K-Man pointed with his beer toward the lighthouse out in the Sound. "Whaddya think?" he asked me. "Those guys blowing some serious weed out there, or what?"

"Could be," I said.

"Whaddya mean, 'could be'?" said Eddie. "Those guys are outta their freaking minds out there! The only way they keep from going freaking *nuts* is to hit the holy bong! We're talking sunrise to sunset!"

A sidelong glance at Janet Alford. "Yeah, well," I offered. "They've got a job to do too, you know. I mean, the boats have to come in."

Eddie put down his harmonica. "The boats have to come in," he repeated. "The boats . . . have . . . to . . . come . . . in!" He turned to Tom with a show of astonishment. "I think we got a philosopher here. I think we just heard . . . brace yourself now . . . a *metaphor*!"

They howled. Eddie whistled the theme from the Old Spice commercial and started calling out *Top of the mornin' to ye, Cap'n!* in my direction. Tom adjusted his red bandanna, raised his arms to the sun, and belched—a long, two-toned honking, like a fog-horn.

It seemed to take forever, but finally they left, clumping their way across the beach, K-Man chucking a bottle into one of the garbage cans where it exploded with a loud pop.

"So those guys are your friends, huh?" Janet Alford asked as the van squealed off, horn blaring, on the road above the sea wall.

"Ah, they're jerks." I shook my head sadly. "They're not . . . I mean, they're not what you'd call *good people* or anything."

Janet giggled. "I think they're funny."

I think they're funny. Boom, there it was again, that goodness of hers, catching me when I least expected it, eluding me when I tried to join up with it; and again that thickness in the back of my throat. In such moments I'd think about Ingrid Bergman in *Casablanca,* who turned men into saints just by staring at them. Could there be a purer emotion than the love I felt for Janet Alford? It was cleansing me, I believed; it was bringing me back from the edge, the way Ingrid brought Humphrey Bogart back.

And yet, while Janet was bringing me back from the edge, Lola Kellerman continued to prowl my dreams, whispering from around every corner. Night after night in my bed I conjured up images of her legs parting, her face clenched in ecstasy, and stroked my lust to perfection. If anyone had pointed out the contradiction between who I was by day and who I was by night, I would have been baffled. I thought of those nighttime sessions as something merely physical, with no more meaning than a sneeze. And so my virtue was a house of cards, set to topple.

The phone rang on a Sunday night. I answered it myself.

"Long time no see, dream boy," Lola's voice said. "Save any lives lately?"

"Nah," I said, scooting out of the kitchen, where my mother was doing the dishes. "You know how it is."

"And how're things with your little angel?"

"Little angel?"

"Hey, it's okay, I think she's cute. You make a nice little pair, the two of you." Music wavered in the background. Lola sounded strange. "By the way, I'm alone here, you know. Barry went to Florida for three weeks." She yawned. "He's developing some properties."

I heard the mucky sound of myself swallowing.

Lola had something for me, she said; a belated birthday present. She'd considered bringing it to the beach, but on second thought had decided it might be better if I . . . unwrapped it at her place.

"Then again, if you don't want it . . ." Her voice trailed off.

I stared close-range at the wallpaper, a pattern of jumbled paisley that repeated itself over and over in crazy curlicues.

Oh no, I told her; I wanted it.

When I was a kid, my favorite TV shows had featured someone under cover or on the run, the Secret Agent, the Fugitive—a hero slipping from alley to alley, caught in a life of aliases and narrow escapes. I needed this training now, for suddenly my summer, which had had a secret in it, *became* a secret, and I lived with the jumpy sensation of someone looking over my shoulder. Barry Kellerman was off in Florida, developing his properties, and I was at his house, making love to his wife. I was also chastely courting Janet Alford. More than once, in fact, I was doing both on the same evening—leaving Janet on the front porch at her parents' and riding off on my bike toward Lola's street, where I'd circle until no cars were coming, then shoot up the drive and around the side of the garage. I used the back entrance now, where no one could see. *Just this once more,* I'd tell myself as I came through the door. *Just tonight and that's it!*

My dream boy, Lola would say, unzipping my pants.

During sex, she'd watch me closely, as if taking the measure of my need. This made me work extra hard to get to that point where she'd lose her cool control, where she'd turn her head and bite the side of her finger, eyes squeezed closed, so that now I'd be the one watching and measuring. We didn't do a lot of talking. One time when we were done, Lola put on her robe and sat on the edge of the bed with her back turned toward me, and smoked a cigarette. *You might be surprised to know,* she said in a low voice, *that I've never cheated on Barry before.* I said nothing, and she asked: *Does that surprise you?*

I shrugged. I was sitting half-propped up on pillows, regarding the long stretch of my legs down the bed. After a moment she turned away and went back to her cigarette. *You're dangerous,* she said. *You don't even realize how beautiful it is.*

Two days before Barry Kellerman was due to return, a balmy evening in early August, I was invited to the Alfords' for dinner. Janet's father was a doctor, a dry person who wore a tie to dinner and gave the impression of saving his personality for people not present. Her mother, however, had Janet's own girlish twinkle, tipping out over half-rim glasses. I soon saw I wasn't making much of a dent in Dr. A., but Mrs. A. seemed to like me. After dinner I scored points by juggling oranges for Janet's two younger brothers, and in the middle of it I glanced over and saw a smile pass from Janet to her mother and back, and my heart went *lurp* with joy.

Janet had a meet the next day and had to be in bed by ten. At nine we adjourned to the porch. There was a wicker swing, and we nestled back in it so that the tips of our feet just touched the ground.

"My parents really like you," Janet said.

"Your father?" It seemed optimistic.

"No no, that's just how he is. He . . . he expects a lot." She thought it over. "I guess he's strict."

I nodded. I loved this moment, the quiet of it, moon generously shining, crickets blurting, a car hovering indecisively two streets over. Using my toe, I rocked the swing a little.

"Janet," I said. "Listen, I think I'm in lo—"

Shhhhh, she cut me off; and then tilted her face up to be kissed.

We sat murmuring to each other until her mother came to the door and politely coughed. It was past ten; I'd managed to steal a quarter of an hour from Janet's swim schedule—no mean feat, I knew. Minutes later I was riding home, elated, bursting with the urge to shout through the sleeping neighborhoods, *Hey you stiffs out there, I'm in l-o-v-e LOVE!!*

My perfect joy was marred by one small blemish, however. And I knew what I had to do about it too. I had to do what any hero in a movie would do, even a jaded hero like Robert Redford in *Downhill Racer.* Leaning low over the handlebars, I veered west off Atlantic Avenue.

I only hoped Lola wouldn't cry. It would be hard on her, I warned myself, because she clearly had fallen in love with me; but I would be firm. And if she wanted to go to bed one last time, I would resist kindly but categorically, even if she wailed, even if she pleaded and begged.

As it turned out, Lola didn't plead or beg, but listened calmly while the western she'd been watching galloped onward in front of us. She nodded when I told her how important it was to be honest about the situation, how summer was one thing but life another. "You've got big plans to think about," she said. "Absolutely."

She was taking it very well, I thought.

At the end I assured her there was no need to feel guilty about Barry—after all, he hadn't exactly been Mr. Faithful himself, right?—and then, on an impulse of goodwill, I stuck out my hand. Lola stared at it for a long second before taking it.

"Adios, dream boy," she said.

Summer's end found me concentrating everything on Janet Alford and our glorious future together. The UConn campus was only an hour away, and I'd already decided that if the Alfords wouldn't let Janet visit me there, I'd drive back to see her in the blue 1969 Firebird convertible I'd spotted at a used-car lot downtown. That car cost $1900, and I figured that with my earnings from the rest of August, plus tips over Labor Day, I'd have just enough to ensure many afternoons spent squiring Janet, top down, through the splendor of Indian summer. For the more distant future, I'd checked into the swim program at UConn, and while it wasn't exactly famous, I concluded that Janet could do nicely there, a pool being much the same everywhere you went.

With all these shiny new plans in place, Lola Kellerman soon seemed like part of my distant past—so distant that I felt something like nostalgia when, one week after our final meeting, she showed up at the beach. Her husband was with her; the two passed ten feet behind where I sat up on Tower 3, and proceeded down to the dunes. A couple of times I swung my binoculars over to spy on them, both reading magazines, Kellerman sipping beer from a can, a breach of beach rules I was not inclined to pursue. My attention drifted back north to Tower 1, where Janet Alford was stationed, twirling her whistle and thinking, I was sure, of me.

Sometime after three I became aware of a commotion to my right. The breeze carried tufts of sound, a woman's shrill voice, a man's blunt and meaty one. Down the south shore two figures stood face-to-face at the high-water mark.

Lola and her husband were having a fight.

With mounting dread I watched through my binoculars as over and over Kellerman jabbed a finger in Lola's face. She let him rage away, then raised a cool eyebrow and said something that froze him dead still.

Kellerman turned, looked, and started striding up the beach.

Only the certainty that he would come after me, bellowing my sins for all to hear, kept me from leaping to the sand and fleeing as he marched to the foot of my chair. He took his sunglasses off and slipped them into his pocket, though the sun was behind me and forced him to squint.

"Get your ass down here," he said.

I couldn't seem to budge, and in one fluid motion Kellerman came up the ladder, wrested me from my chair, and threw me off. He jumped down to go after me and jerked me up by my T-shirt.

"Okay, punk," he said, spitting out the word. "I'm gonna make this simple." One hand twisted my T-shirt hard while the other pointed in my face. "If I ever, *ever* catch you sniffing around my wife, if I ever catch you so much as *looking* at her, if I catch you within two *miles* of her—!"

As he enumerated the ways he would hurt me, I glanced to see whether Janet was watching. If only he would let go of my shirt! I thought. When he finally did, I reached up a hand to smooth down the bunched material.

"Now," he said, "do we understand each other?"

By this time McGuirk had arrived on the scene. "What's the trouble here?" he inquired, drawing his stomach in and trying to look official.

"No trouble," Kellerman said.

Behind McGuirk, other guards were approaching, including, a dozen paces back, Janet Alford. Kellerman was about to walk back down the beach, I could see that. All I had to do was let him go.

For years afterward I'd replay the moment that followed, trying to pin down my motives. Was it that I was angry at Lola's betrayal? That I wanted to snatch back some of the honor lost in the humiliating dive from the chair? Or that my impulses had been trained by a hundred movies in which a hundred heroes always got the last, zinging word?

Whatever the case, I didn't let Kellerman go. "You know, maybe if you just *treated* her a little better," I heard myself saying, "then maybe she wouldn't have to—"

He snapped around.

"You little zero," he snarled. "You think this is about you, don't you!" He stared as if at a cockroach. "You wanna know what this has to do with you? You're diddly! You don't even *register!*" Now he was shouting. "Six months from now you think she's even gonna know your *name,* you little prick? You're just this summer's fuck, that's all you are!''

Then he had me by the shirt again, and McGuirk and the others were trying to pull him back. But Kellerman was strong; he was shaking me like a doll. Finally he flung me against the tower stanchion and turned away, the crowd parting to let him through.

I pushed myself up. The onlookers buzzed, and McGuirk was gaping like an idiot, but the only person who mattered in the whole wide world was standing in the circle to my left.

"Listen, Janet," I said, moving toward her.

For a frowning moment she studied me closely, then walked away without a word.

I turned to start the long climb back up my tower. Behind me someone coughed, *Ahem!* McGuirk was looking at me.

"Uh-uh," he said, shaking his head.

Life's full of lumps, better learn to take 'em. This was a favorite saying of my parents, for whom the idea that adversity molds character was an article of faith. In truth, what adversity does to most people isn't pretty. It pins them to their misfortunes, making them bitter and cowardly. It primes them for revenges that end up being taken against the wrong people.

The day after the disaster at Sandy Neck, I called Janet Alford with a well-rehearsed recital of half-truths, apologies, and pledges of devotion. She listened, then chose her words with chilling care. "Tony, if there's nothing else you can tell me"—she meant, of course, about the *facts*—"then I think it's better if we don't hear from each other."

Somehow I didn't quite believe it. In a week, I told myself, maybe two, she'd come back, and my plans would snap back into place. In the meantime, I had Eddie and Tom to fall back on. K-Man in particular was sympathetic. My losing everything, job, girl, car, seemed to revive our bond, wiping away the whole Sir Tony business and cementing us in a brotherhood of the have-nots. He raged against Lola Kellerman, that traitor, that bitch, and I played to it, the two of us ratcheting each other upward in a kind of tandem resentment machine. Retelling the drama of the beach, I stressed how Kellerman had called me a punk, how in his eyes I was just another no-consequence townie: a zero, he'd called me. It made Tom seethe. "I'll show him who's a fucking zero!" he said, pounding his fist into his hand.

I believe it was K-Man's idea to drive past Lola Kellerman's house that Friday night before Labor Day. The three of us were out cruising in the van, and around 1 A.M. I recall Tom saying, *Come on, let's go check out where the bitch lives!* When we reached Lola's street he turned down the music, and dead quiet reigned in the van. The house was dark as we glided by.

"Check out that bullshit mailbox," said Tom. "What does the sonofabitch do, anyway?"

"Develops properties," I said.

"Oh, a sleazebag rip-off artist." Tom knew sleazebags like that, he told us. They hired third-rate builders who cheated the subcontractors and built pieces of shit that fell apart in five years.

At the end of the street we turned around. "Okay," Eddie said. "You guys got your kicks now? Can we maybe get outta here?"

Tom slowed the van to a crawl.

"Come on, let's book before they call the cops, huh?" Eddie turned to me. "Tony, man, this thing's *over,* okay?"

K-Man banged the dashboard. "That sonofabitch sleazebag and his bitch wife!" He was getting heated up. Eddie looked over and raised an eyebrow.

But I was far away. Eddie's last words—*This thing's over, okay?*—had hit me hard. It was true, I saw: I would not get Janet Alford back. In all likelihood I would never even get to talk to her again. Over. It was over.

Down I spun, free-falling toward the black pit of an awareness that my life was not at all what I'd thought it had been. There *was* no movie, no script; anything I might want to become in the future would have to be built from scratch. And my tools for doing that were few and crude. Kellerman had called me a zero, but in fact, given all that had happened this summer, I was less than that; I was a negative. Not an arch-villain, not the world's worst sinner, not the world's best or worst anything. Just a very slight negative, something marginally less than zero. For the first time in my life I felt anger—not the pretend anger I'd known before, but real rage, the kind that sweats helplessness and fear.

The van had stopped, we were idling at the curb directly in front of Lola's house. Tom hunched glowering at the wheel.

"Do we trash something here, or what?" he hissed.

Whatever I said now would have to be just right. I wasn't exactly sure what Tom would do. There were the cars in the garage, the welded-chain mailbox, the plate glass living room window. . . . Then in a flash I saw it: I saw him tearing the mailbox loose, humping up to the side of the house and hurling it through to a splash of breaking glass—then lights coming on, sirens, Eddie yelling *Oh fuck! Fuck!,* and Tom himself coming back across the lawn with his wild look already giving way to sheepishness, fear, and guilt at having involved us in his misdeed, when actually I'd dragged him into mine, a cover I'd maintain later, *Officer, he's my buddy, how can I say anything against him?* And if Eddie Boyce was smart enough to figure things out, well, he'd convince himself otherwise, and in a few years' time we'd all have gone different directions and wouldn't be friends anymore anyway.

How much of this I actually thought out in advance and how much I merely saw later on, after everything that happened happened, I really don't know. I do know that words have effects, quite apart from what we later decide about our motives in saying them. I know that finding the right words as I sat there in the van meant that for me a difficult episode would come to a close, while for Tom Krajewski a much more difficult one would be just beginning. And I know that of the two things I'd learned to do that summer, the more useful one was to deceive. In the dimness of the van I turned a little toward Tom and shrugged. "I dunno, K-Man," I said. "This guy's no pussy, he's got a baseball bat under his bed."

"Oh yeah?" Krajewski turned to me, eyes blazing. "Well, let's just *see* about that!" And he opened the door and stepped out into the street.

KERENYAGA

THE STREETLIGHT DRIPPING through the trees splashes monsters that swarm about his feet. He has one hand in his pocket, the other knocking at the door. "Mrs. Jackson? Mrs. Jackson, are you there?"

Again he pulls the money out and counts it. "Mrs. Jackson, it is just me, Zeke. Can you open please?"

A spot of blood lands on the top note. He smears it away, then presses his sleeve to his face. A dog in the next yard growls.

Somehow they always know.

Money. The whole life was a struggle for money. It was on every face—the smile that said, I will get something from you, the frown that said, Will you ask something from me? *You wake on a Sunday, and you know that if you don't get that cash by evening, you are out on the street. It is like waking to find someone is holding a gun at your head.*

Sunday morning at the park near Mrs. Jackson's. *I was looking for a guy from the Equator who had promised me some little cash.* Half a dozen cars are parked by the basketball court. Men sit lacing their shoes. No one notices him until it's time to divide teams and there are only nine.

"Yo, man! You wanna run?"

He shrugs and joins one team, rolling up his shirtsleeves.

It doesn't take long for the others to see. "Yo, that nigger's got some freakish tendencies!" "Where you from, brother—Mars?"

"I am from Africa," he says.

"Brothers don't play no ball in Africa?"

He gets the ball and shoots wildly, far over the basket. Hey, they say, calm down, baby, calm down! After that they keep it away from him; he runs up and down, trying to follow the movements, never touching the ball.

They sit on the grass when the game is over. "You from Africa?" they ask him. "You living with tigers and all that wild shit, man?"

"There are some wild creatures here and there. But we have also got cities. We have got theaters and taxicabs and skyscrapers."

"I hear you all got some system over there where you can have three, four wives?"

He starts to explain, but they break in—"James, you can't hold on to one wife, what you gonna do with four?!"—and then the talk flows on around him. He leans back on his elbows and looks at the cars. A church bell clangs. *Ten o'clock and still my pockets were empty.*

At the start, a year before, things had been better. There was the room in his cousin's apartment in Alexandria, the job running errands at the embassy where his cousin worked. For a while there were classes at the community college. He would stroll across the big lawn, notebooks under his arm. Girls sitting on the library steps smiled.

I am Ezekiel Kimanja wa Mwangi, he would say, drawing the syllables out.

On weekends there were parties. He liked to stand by the speakers and let the sound roll through his bones. People brought cocaine in small plastic packets. *This one friend of mine, Chris, he was extremely generous. He was earning the degree Master of Parties with distinction!* Often they went into the District to the Equator Club, where palm trees swayed over bamboo tables and a volcano puffed real smoke. The bartenders smiled and called out, Zeke, Zeke my man! when he came through the door.

His cousin began to lecture him. Kimanja, he said, I don't like this crowd you are running around with.

Since when has my cousin become my judge? he answered. Kinuthia, we are not back in Kamiri village digging yams. So please do not try to tell me how to do my work and run my life!

Work? His cousin laughed. What work? As far as I can see, work has become an alien concept! Is this why I've paid your flight—for this fast living?

On Saturday nights he drove with Chris to a housing project near the Beltway. People came and went in the darkness, murmuring. One of the big cocaine sellers had a moon-white Rolls-

Royce parked in the street. They would buy the stuff and then, when his cousin was out, head back to Alexandria and sit in the apartment.

"Tell me about Africa, Zeke," Chris would say, laying out thin lines on a mirror. "Tell me about a place so radical I can't even imagine it."

The results from the first term of classes were posted, and he had failed. Two days later his cousin put his things in the hall, handed him a fifty-dollar bill, and shut the door in his face.

"You are crazy, Kinuthia!" he shouted at the door. "If I go back to our home and say how you have treated me, you will be humiliated!" *But the guy remained silent. He was fast becoming an infamous villain in my mind.*

He got a job at a Roy Rogers and a tiny apartment with no furniture save a mattress and an old black-and-white TV. The rent was $400, his wage $5.05 an hour. Finding himself short, he would go to Alexandria to ask his cousin for money. *The guy was feeling guilty, and he would just shoot me some few dollars to sweeten his sour conscience.* But it was never enough, and one day he gave in and sold a half gram of cocaine to one of the cleanup boys at Roy Rogers. Soon he began making more trips to the housing project where the Rolls-Royce was. He stood in the dark imagining himself riding in the fancy car like a head of state, flags whipping on the hood.

One afternoon the manager at Roy Rogers took him aside. "Now, it just so happens I like you, Zeke," he said. "And that's why, instead of calling the cops, I'm just gonna have you take off your apron, haul your ass through that door, and never come back here again."

He started to speak, but the man held up a hand. "Not . . . one . . . word."

In Alexandria he found a strange woman in the apartment. "He went back," she said when he asked about his cousin.

"Back? Back to where?"

The woman shrugged. "Wherever it is you all come from," she said.

Out on the sidewalk again, he felt dizzy. He was breathing hard but couldn't get enough air. *I never believed he could do that to a cousin. Just to run away and leave somebody totally stranded.* He sat down on the curb until his breathing slowed, then stood and stuck his thumb out.

In Bethesda the houses towered like fortresses; his feet crashing through dead leaves made the only sound on the street. When he knocked at Chris's house, a dog began bellowing on the other side, smearing its fangs and snout across a panel of glass next to the door. A woman appeared and opened up a few inches. In her hand she held the choke collar on the dog, which lunged forward, hoarsely raging.

"Don't think I don't know who you are," she said, staring at him.

"Excuse me, madam . . ." he began.

"You're the one who got our son involved in this . . . this—"

"Now, wait one second, if you please—"

"I'm calling the police!" the woman yelled. Her face bulged red. "I'm calling the police and having you arrested right now!"

A minute later he was crossing the front lawn, half running. He heard a siren far off.

It was the beginning of a bad time.

★   ★   ★

The phone rings and clicks, and again he gets the recording.

"Muita," he says. "This is Kimanja, still trying to break in on your Sunday afternoon." He pauses. "The situation is getting rather urgent."

From the phone booth he watches a construction crew digging a deep foundation. The hacked-off remnant of a neighboring building shows zigzagging black-and-white up a wall where a stairway once ran. A huge crane is devouring the earth. He puts another quarter in, dials, and hangs up as soon as Muita's machine clicks on; but the quarter doesn't come back.

"You bloody thing," he says, and walks out into the street.

For almost a year he's been working on and off for Muita. The car wash on Fourteenth Street is only one of Muita's businesses. There is a restaurant-cleaning business, a moving van, and for a while there was a business in which Muita bought used washing machines cheap, cleaned them up, and sold them back, much dearer, to other landlords. *He was like certain people in desert places who can spot an underground root, dig it up, and squeeze out a drink. Muita, he knew the secret of squeezing cash from the world.*

At Union Station he takes out his last quarters and hesitates before paying the fare. The woman Muita has married, a black American woman, has a way of looking at him that makes him feel like an insect on the wall. It makes him want to turn back. But then he thinks of his room at Mrs. Jackson's; he sees her sitting at the kitchen table shaking her head, saying Ezekiel, what am I gonna do with you? He buys the ticket and merges with the stream of people flowing toward the platform.

On the train he thinks about the time he has put in for Muita. At the beginning Muita worked right alongside. The two of them might drive up to Baltimore or Pennsylvania to steam-clean a kitchen. Coming back very late, he would sing and joke to keep Muita awake at the wheel. *But all that while, the woman was working against me. She hated me. She hated that we were speaking a language she could not understand. She wanted her husband to be a big boss and not to associate with peasants.*

At Muita's town house in Silver Spring he taps until the door opens, and he recognizes Byron, the fat fifteen-year-old boy of Muita's wife. The boy scowls and retreats into the living room, to a couch in front of a TV.

"I am Zeke Kimanja." He steps inside. "I work with your father."

"My father doesn't know you. My father's in the army in Germany. You mean Eddie."

"Yes." He waits, but the boy does not turn the television off. He clears his throat. "Can you tell me where Muita . . . where Eddie is?"

"I don't know. They went to some picnic thing in Virginia."

"I see. And can you tell me when I can expect them to return?"

"What am I, the man's secretary?" Byron shrugs. "Late, probably."

"I see."

He stands there while the boy eats corn chips and watches TV. On the tables and on the floor are magazines, magazines everywhere, more than any person could read in a year. *This woman, she was costing Muita a whole hell of a lot of money: hiring someone to cook, someone to clean, and so forth. I wanted to tell him Look here, this woman of yours is totally useless—in fact, she should take a thrashing or two and quietly learn from it.*

On a table near the door sits an ashtray piled high with spare change. He looks at the quarters and dimes, as Byron flicks through the TV channels with a remote control. He thinks about Muita and his wife playing with their two daughters in Virginia somewhere—the two little girls in pink dresses and white socks, speaking English and only English, ignorant of their father's tongue.

The light on the telephone machine is blinking.

"I see you have got some messages here," he says. The boy pays no heed. "In fact, those are my messages."

"I know," Byron says. "I was here."

He stares at the flashing light—one, two, three, four—and crosses to the boy. "Why did you just sit listening while I was pumping my money into that phone?"

Byron shrugs and sticks out his lower lip. "It wasn't for me."

"You are rude!" he shouts down at the fat boy. "You are rude and totally spoiled! I won't waste my time with a totally spoiled boy whose hands have never known work!" He charges across the room and out, slamming the door behind him.

Outside in the parking lot, he leans against Muita's pickup truck and smokes his next-to-last cigarette. He sees himself as he was a few months back, sitting in the driver's seat of the truck. It was three in the morning, coming back from a restaurant job in Philadelphia; Muita had turned into a rest area and told him to take the wheel. Pulling back onto the highway, he felt how the engine responded to the slightest increase of pressure on the pedal. It was as if power surged forth from his foot itself, from his arms and his hands on the steering wheel.

I have been wanting to ask you, he said to Muita. To ask you about how one squeezes some success out of this crazy country.

Muita was drowsy; his eyes were closed and he spoke in a muted voice with long spaces between his words. Success? he said. You work and you worry. Work and worry all the time. Even when you enjoy, you keep one part worrying. It is like a bicycle. Stop moving and you will fall.

I see. But you know, I myself am also working and worrying.

Muita sighed. Kimanja, your worries are too small. Look at me. One week I am very very rich, the next week I am—temporarily—very very poor. The important thing is that I am steadily *big*. The gains are big, the losses are big. One way or the other, but always I stay big.

I see, he said, yes, yes, I see.

A businessman, murmured Muita, he has got to be big.

He nodded. And perhaps you could give me a clue to the first step, he said. I mean, how does one *get* big? What is the direction?

He looked over to see Muita asleep, his lips soundlessly moving. Turning on the radio, he found some low music and gave his attention to the roadway. He accelerated, switching lanes. The white stripes on the surface shot forth and disappeared beneath the hood; he had the feeling of consuming them, one by one, in a never-ending meal.

At the beginning of time there was a first man. The first man was called up to the mountain. At the top he looked down and saw the hills and streams and fig trees. He heard the voice of Ngai saying, Descend and live well, the country now belongs to you. This is the story we were told.

From our place you could see the peaks of Kerenyaga. They were jagged and covered with whiteness. Sometimes clouds would come for two days or three, and when they left, the whiteness was greater and brighter than before.

As a boy I was always fearing. My brothers were putting the old ideas into my head. They said the thunder and lightning was Ngai stepping from place to place, stretching himself and cracking his great joints, preparing to smash his enemies. Who could be such a fool to look up and risk being smashed as well? If I lay on my back in bed during a storm, my brother was pushing me over on my side and ridiculing me for boldness.

The Europeans who came to climb the mountain were bringing heavy clothes and special claws for the hands and feet. Their vehicles passed on the road, rumbling up a lot of dust. My brothers told me they would never return. But they returned. They said the place up there was very cold and it was hard to breathe. We said Ngai was invisibly squeezing the lungs.

One year the short rains and the long rains failed, and then the short rains again in the next season. We were eating dust and drinking it too. There was one old man in our place, a man who knew about the traditional things. This was a filthy, wild old man, with hair that was tangled and only a stinking animal skin to cover himself. His feet were tough and rounded, like stones. He had a deformity of the neck and back.

One day he called certain children out of school. We were called to a field. The old man had a container with sour beer. He was drinking and then spitting on the ground, left and right, north and south, drinking and then spitting. A goat was held down by some other men. The old man looked up to the mountain and screamed, Ngai, Ngai who dwells in the brightness, whose anger destroys homesteads, who makes mountains tremble and rivers flood . . . ! Then he jumped down and began to strangle the creature.

A week later we were still lacking rain. The old man decided to go to the extreme of climbing the mountain. I could just imagine his bare feet striking that hard, cold brightness.

This is the end for him, my brother said. He is already dead.

Eventually we got rain. But the old man never came back. Sometimes I would stand outside my mother's door and look up at Kerenyaga and imagine how the brightness had covered him and melted him away.

During the bad time, things had happened one after another, with no space in between for rest. He went from apartment to apartment. He would pay the rent for a few weeks, then fall behind. He did gardening work for two old ladies in Arlington, sisters who never came out of the house without plastic bags on their hands—they were afraid of dirt. When the job was done, they paid him exactly half what they had promised.

You didn't understand us, they said. Poor boy, it's not even his language.

Excuse me, I told them, but I am a Form Four finisher in English!

Everyone cheated, he learned. If they could get away with it, they did it. He rented a tiny room in Northeast from a West African named Pierre who spent his evenings buried in big text-books. One night when Pierre went out, he and the other tenant, a Nigerian named Henry who drove a taxi, searched Pierre's desk and found the lease. The rent was $550. The two of them were paying $250 each.

He confronted Pierre. "How is it that you exploit a fellow African in this way?"

Pierre squinted through narrow lizard eyes. "I advertised. You took."

It was an outrage. He screamed at him—"You say you study economics? I say you study exploitation!"—and stormed out.

That evening he spent the few dollars in his pocket on cans of beer and settled down in a small park to drink them. It was September and still warm. Music drifted from cars passing in the street behind. He sat beneath a statue of a man on horseback. Finally sleep overtook him; when he woke he saw the hoof of the horse outlined against a milky dawn sky. He had slept and risen, and it had not cost a dime.

Why not? he said to himself. Why not cheat the game a little? *Better to be sleeping in the free and open than to be robbed every night for the privilege of lying down under the same roof with the robber.*

So he began staying outside. At night he covered himself with a sleeping bag bought for four dollars at a secondhand store. He avoided alleys and underpasses; they stank of urine and were frequented by dangerous and demented people. He was not like them, he told himself. He kept his clothes and body clean. On Friday nights he showed up at the Equator Club in freshly laundered jeans, a few dollars in his pocket for beer, and no one knew. If he got work for a few days and had money, he took a cab to the housing project where the Rolls-Royce stood in the moonlight. He was generous with the cab drivers, tipping what he could.

In late October he realized the season had turned. It was not yet cold, but there was a different sound in the trees at night. Lying outside, he felt something pressing down on him from far, far above. He slept poorly. Nightmares flooded his dreams and seeped out into the day.

It got colder. He worked five days for a Lebanese who hired illegal laborers. At the end of the week he looked for a room but found nothing; instead, he bought a coat and went for a night on the town. *I decided to seek the shelter of a woman over the shelter of a roof.* Cleaning himself in the shower at a YMCA, he realized how dirty he had become, and scrubbed his skin until it stung.

There were women everywhere at the Equator. Most were with boyfriends, but others sat in twos or threes, drinking colorful drinks with palm-tree stirring sticks and moving their bodies to the music.

One sat alone, in a purple dress that glittered in the light. He approached and bowed. "May I take the liberty of joining you?" he asked.

"You some kind of Jamaican?" she said, looking at him suspiciously.

"No, I am no kind of Jamaican. No kind at all."

"Well, I don't mess with no Jamaicans, so don't even try."

"But I am not a Jamaican." He held up his hands. "I am an African."

She nodded. "I thought you talked funny."

"That is the Queen's English. Here it is not recognized."

They danced and drank. He bought her drinks, keeping up a steady talk. *Some women, they want to be entertained. You must chat them up and never let the game slide.* When she wasn't looking he stole glimpses of her body. *Her breasts were full and rounded. In fact, I was aching just to reach over and caress them. Her name was Angeline, a beautiful name.*

"I believe you must be descended from the Tutsi people," he told her.

"The whoosi people?"

"The Tutsi. From the region of eastern Africa. They are

known as the most beautiful women in the world. Very tall and slender. And very proud.''

She chuckled. "If you got so many beautiful women over there, what're you doing over here?"

"I was a rebel," he answered. "I was not seeing eye to eye with the expectations of my parents. So I just skipped the place altogether."

At the bar, buying another round of drinks, he imagined the moment when he arrived with Angeline in her room and she lifted the purple dress over her head. She would fling the dress into a corner, eager to begin. But he would pick it up and fold it, teasing her, making her wait, making her crazy. That was how American women were—crazy to play the game.

Twisting his way back through the crowd, he found his place taken by someone in a white suit who sat talking to Angeline.

"Excuse me," he said. "But you are sitting in my seat."

The man in the white suit looked at him as if at an annoying mosquito. "Now who," he said, "might you be?"

He put the drinks on the table. "I am Ezekiel Kimanja wa Mwangi."

The man's finger stroked a scar on his neck. "You best be real watchful now, Mr. Banjo Wango, or that's the last introduction you'll make in a long time."

"Angeline. How long has this fellow been disturbing you?" He turned to her, but she looked away.

"I don't think you hearing me right," the man said. "This here's *my* lady. *You* the disturbance."

"Look here. The entire evening I have treated this woman—"

The man stood. He shook his head; he couldn't believe a

mosquito was talking back to him. "I *still* don't think you hearing me right, sucker—"

Then I got steamed. Look here, I said, I won't have some grandson of a slave abusing me! Some scavenger, picking where another has done the work! If you want to find out who I am, then you will find out!

He didn't see the blow—just a flash of white, then a crushing pressure in his chest. He fell back, knocking into a neighboring table and sending drinks tumbling.

"You one lucky motherfucker," the man in the suit snarled. "I'll *kill* you, you hear?" Angeline stared straight ahead. In the center of the room the volcano puffed with a soft whoosh. He watched the smoke rise toward the ceiling to pool among the blues and reds of the disco lights.

The taxi driver outside agreed to take him to Alexandria but wanted the money up front. He handed over the rest of the bills in his pocket and sat back. "That fucking grandson of a bastard slave," he said aloud. "Next time I will have a brick or a gun, and he will know who I am."

They motored through the city. The cab had its heater on, and the window was cold to the touch. Miniature cyclones of garbage and dust whirled in the gutters. Three whores stood on a corner outside a wrecked apartment building, clapping their hands and jumping up on their toes to keep warm. As the cab veered by, he saw how ugly they were, their faces old and battered under the makeup. When he went past they shrieked at the cab, showing their teeth like hyenas.

"They call this the Capital City," he said. "The capital of sin."

He thought of all the people he had seen on the streets in the past weeks: drunken people, stinking people, a woman with a bandage covering a stump of a leg that dripped brown juice; fat people, people with potato faces and yam faces and calabash faces. People with teeth like rotten fruit, people talking with demons and laughing at nothing; people hurling curses and bottles from their autos; people who would beat and beat and beat you just for existing.

I began to see the policy. Let only the smart and wealthy Americans go abroad. Keep the rotten ones here. It was a public relations trick.

When they reached Alexandria, he gave instructions at random. After a while the driver turned to him. "You ain't goin' nowhere, am I right?" he said. "You just jerkin' me around."

"Not at all." He looked out onto a street of brick houses and fenced yards. "In fact, we have arrived."

The man pulled to the curb without a word.

When the cab drove off it took all warmth away with it. He turned to the houses. *If I could just set myself down close to the light, I thought, I would be somehow warmer—like the hungry man who sits outside the rich man's kitchen and eats his bread together with the aroma of cooking meat.* He saw a place out of the wind, a corner between a house and a garage, with a bed of leaves and a canvas sheet covering a motorcycle.

He was lifting the sheet off the motorcycle when a dog heard him and began calling out a rubbery rage that bounced through the neighborhood, *No! No! No! No! No!* Lights went on. He fled, taking the sheet with him.

Wind numbed his ears. He thought of the dogs in every place, lying warm on their cushions—dogs with human names, living in houses like people, eating food from bowls, drinking milk with a ferocious, greedy sound. They lay with eyes open, their hairy warm sides heaving in and out.

By an apartment building sat a huge trash bin. He climbed in, lay down, and wrapped himself in the cloth. The smell of oil from the fabric chased the other odors from his nostrils. He shivered himself into sleep.

When he woke it was neither day nor night. Something was crawling across his face. He swatted at it. Tiny sounds crept on all sides. He looked up and saw what he thought were insects hovering in the steam of his own breath. They were landing on his face and urinating.

He stood up. His legs were stiff and he groaned; the voice that came out of him was exactly his father's voice, cracked and ancient. Over the top of the bin he looked out at a world covered in ash. Ash clung to the sides of buildings, it bearded the trees and glowed on the ground.

"Snow," he said aloud.

An auto crept by, making no sound. The snow brought with it a silence that spilled to the center of his bones. *And even though I was no longer believing, still I heard inside myself the voice of my brother saying, So Kimanja, Kimanja, now you are already dead.*

He has almost given up when he sees her coming along the sidewalk, waving. *Bonjour,* she says. "I am late—it is insupportable—my apologies!" She is wearing her waitress costume. The restaurant has called her for an extra shift, she explains. "The bastards, they think they own me." *Zey tink zey hown me.*

He looks down from the Capitol building toward the Mall, crowded with tourists and joggers. "They are all bastards," he says. "It is a dog-eat-dog kind of society. I am sure it is better in France."

"France?" She laughs, shaking her head. "In France it is worse. In France they are still living in the eighteenth century."

When she smiles, she has a way of tossing her head back to inhale deeply through her nostrils. He recalls meeting her three nights ago in the bar in Georgetown where she served him beer after beer and he joked and grew bold with her, forgetting for the moment Mrs. Jackson and the rent. At the end of the night she let him hang on to her shoulder but would not leave with him. I never go with a drunken man, she laughed. I am not a nurse!

All right, he said. Then meet me Sunday afternoon in town. By that time I will be sober, and you can be a woman, not a nurse.

"So Ezekiel," she says now. "What have you done this Sunday? Were you to the church to forgive your sins?"

"Today I have played basketball, I have been out to confer with a business partner in Silver Spring. The day has been quite full, but with no church anywhere in it. So I guess my sins are still my sins."

"Myself," she says, "I stayed in bed all the morning, and then in the bath. I was very naughty."

They walk west down the Mall. She sings a song in French. Men in business suits let their glances climb up and down as they pass.

"What is it, Ezekiel?" she asks. "You are sad today? You think to your home and family?"

"No, I am not sad." *In fact I was recalling a guy who used to loiter around Kamiri town, begging. His name was Jengo, and he had a foul smell.* "I was just listening to your song, trying in vain to pick out some few words I might recognize."

She sings some more. "Ah, I love music! Painting also. Unfortunately I have no ability for art myself." She sighs. "It was a great sadness, but then I surrendered. I decided merely to live."

At the Monument in the center of the Mall they stand outside the circle of flags and watch tourists looking up and up. *I was still thinking of that Jengo. In town he would approach you with a pitiful expression and repeat the only words of English he had ever learned— "A friend in need is a friend indeed!" Everyone hated him.*

"This thing," he says, looking up at the Monument. "It reminds me of a spear. A spear with a sharp, sharp point."

Helene laughs. "It is a penis," she says. "How does one say this in your language?"

He looks around. *Mboo,* he says in a low voice.

"It is a national *mboo.* The great American erection."

"You are very funny," he tells her.

"But it's true! For the Americans, to be the biggest does not suffice. They must show it—and see it! The president, he needs to see it. The senators, they need to see it. That is why they put it here, in the center." She leans close. "It's a malady, when you want to show everyone how big is your *mboo.* A psychological malady."

They walk toward the avenue. "You know," he tells her, "one reason I left my country is there were too many people wanting to be big."

"They were showing their *mboos*?" She laughs, then sees he is serious.

He lights his last cigarette; the flame trembles on the match and then leaps into the tobacco. "There was one guy named Chulu in that place. He had a camera and left for the city to work as a photographer. If you traveled there, you could get your picture struck while standing next to the New Africa Towers.

There was a way of doing that picture and making the people seem as tall as the skyscraper. Chulu showed me how it was done." He draws the cigarette smoke in and releases it with a sigh. "It was just another trick."

"Please, Ezekiel." Her hand touches his shoulder. "I must go now. Tonight you come late to the bar and I give you free drinks. You can use that, free drinks? You can feel better?"

"Hey," he says, "I am okay." He pushes a smile out. "Who knows—maybe I am even coming round to buy you a few drinks when you are through."

"Comme tu veux." She raises her arm, and as if by magic a taxi appears. *"A bientôt,* Ezekiel!" She kisses him on the cheek and gets in.

He is alone again; it is a sickening feeling. *My pocket was empty. My stomach was empty. I had just smoked my last fag.* The voice of Mrs. Jackson speaks in his ear: I'm soft on you, Ezekiel; you remind me of my boy. But I can't afford a son; I need a boarder. And that means paying.

That means paying by the weekend or I'm gonna hafta get somebody new.

He walks along Constitution Avenue. The brightness of the buildings aches in his head—buildings scrubbed clean for visitors. He wants to shout: It's a lie, a bloody fucking lie! He passes a T-shirt vendor and, without breaking stride, snatches a pair of sunglasses. No one sees.

Tourists are queuing at a memorial, a black wall carved with names. People take pictures and babble in many tongues. He goes through the line. A family of Japanese stand before him, a man and a woman and two boys eating ice cream off sticks. They are like all the rest, the British and the Germans and the French.

Today they are here, tomorrow in California, the next day Europe or Japan or Africa. They go where they please; moving from place to place at will, charging everything on their cards.

The Japanese man takes pictures, talking as he does. There is enough wealth in his camera to pay rent for weeks and weeks. The boys speak, the mother speaks; it is hard to believe they understand such sounds.

He follows at a distance. The family stroll about and enter a path through trees. He slows for a moment to let them get into the shadows, then steps quickly forward.

"Mrs. Jackson? Mrs. Jackson, can you open please?"

It is late. He tastes the salt of his own blood and tilts his head back. Again the creature next door erupts into howling. Perhaps they smell that he is wounded.

"Mrs. Jackson? I have not got my key. Hallo?" He looks down the street. No lights. He pictures people peering out at him.

The thing did not happen as he had imagined it would. Grabbing the camera strap, he was terrified to find that it did not break or slip off, but instead jerked the man around like a puppet. The woman jabbered in short scared barks. The man stared in amazement and then started pulling back with a silent fury. Finally the strap broke.

At the pawn shop, a place he had often passed but never entered, he carried the camera in a bag. I am needing four hundred dollars for this, he said.

The man laughed. You'll get ninety. Take it or leave it.

He went with the money into a bar nearby. A row of white faces turned, frowning. The bartender looked at him, then moved away to the far end of the bar and lit a cigarette. He pounded on the bar. "Service! Service here! I won't be insulted by racialist bastards, damn it to stinking hell!"

The door opens. Mrs. Jackson is standing there. "Now will you tell me just exactly what— Oh Lord, look at his face!"

He stands in the kitchen, under the light. She has put her glasses on. They are attached to a cord studded with jewels that wink in the light. She dabs his nose with a towel and turns his face side to side.

"Oh, Ezekiel, what have they done to you?"

"I was visiting at the so-called Sportsman's Bar," he tells her.

"The what? You foolish child. Ain't you got enough trouble?"

Taking out the bills, he lays them on the counter. "Rent," he says.

Mrs. Jackson pulls back and squints at him. "I'm not even gonna ask," she whispers. "Not even gonna ask."

He sits at the table, closes his eyes, and lays his head down on crossed arms.

At night my father was crying and moaning. He had a problem in his leg—someone was trying to do evil to him, he said. But I could see he was simply like everyone else in the place: too old. In town the old men were sitting on the steps, day in and day out, with their stiff legs stuck out like sticks. There was one ancient woman, Wanjiru, who roamed about at night, laughing and speaking nonsense. We children were believing that when she encountered a cat or a dog she would devour it whole.

The choice along the street was mud or dust, depending on the season. The dust choked you, the mud joined your toes together like cement. Entertainment was lingering round the petrol station, staring at vehicles.

Food was cabbages or maize and beans, sometimes with a small speck of meat thrown in.

I said to my brother: If this is life, then it is a meager portion, I swear it.

There was always work and more work. People were spending their bodies as if they would be given another when the first was used up. I myself was digging in the field, I was gathering wood, playing the role of responsible son. But looking down the road, I could see no place in the life, no opening for me.

As a small boy I liked to linger with the others in the marketplace. Sometimes a vehicle would stop at the Asian's for petrol. The wicked boys were begging for a spot of petrol on a cloth, to put to their noses and become intoxicated.

One day a vehicle stopped, full of Europeans with cameras and big hats and red faces. There was a woman in the rear; she looked at me and smiled. Then she opened that rear door a small crack and dropped a shilling into the dust. I covered it immediately with my foot.

When the others had gone off I lifted my foot and quickly retrieved the coin. It was not a shilling. It was an American coin, heavy and thick—a silver dollar from the United States of America.

I showed no one. The thing was mine and mine alone.

My one fear was to lose that coin. First I buried it. Then I feared the earth would move and it would be gone. So I tied it in a cloth and kept the cloth always in my pocket. Wherever I passed, the coin passed with me. At the end of a day I might sneak away up the path toward the mountain, to a spot above the village where there was a tremendous rock. The hills across the plain were sharp and black, with the sun just falling behind them. They looked like skyscrapers. I might take the cloth out and remove the coin and rub it for luck. The time was always short; my mother would be calling, Kimanja! Kimanja! Eventually the coin became shiny from rubbing; it was beginning to lose its features. So I left off rubbing it.

In school I was very bad. I was clever but lazy, with the reputation of a small scoundrel. I was not the kind of slave those teachers desired. *Ezekiel*, they said, *can you kindly explain why your brothers were prefects and scholars while you are an insolent, lazy boy?*

And so I was beaten. The headmaster was a small, cruel man named Mr. Chunga who spoke in whispers and was a champion of punishment. The others were always joking, *Hey, Kimanja, that guy's belt has passed more times against your backside than round his belly!*

There was a map of the world on the wall of this Chunga's office. When he would summon me, I was just staring past him at the map, at Europe and America. *Yes sir, yes sir*, I was responding; but in my mind I was saying, *Hey, one day I will be far away and you will still be here, a tiny pebble stuck in this miserable place!*

To receive punishment, one leaned over the edge of the desk with the trousers down. To distract my mind while being strapped, inwardly I was reciting facts, like the capitals of the states of America.

JACKson, Mississippi!

BOSton, Massachusetts!

DENver, Colorado!

Even when I cried I was smiling. It made that small tyrant quite furious. But I believed I had been chosen. Of all the other boys, I was the one with the coin in my pocket.

On the night when my father died, I sneaked away from the compound and went up the path, leaving the sounds of the women to melt away behind. I myself was not feeling sad. On the path I stopped to take the coin out and hold it up to the light of the moon. Yes, they had even been up there too—to the moon itself! There was no place they did not go.

From the top of the rock I looked out. Far along the plains some fields were being burned to encourage the new grasses. I held the coin between my thumb and fingers and rubbed it, never taking my eyes from that distant light floating and flickering in the air. I rubbed that coin and rubbed it some more, until it grew warm. Then I squeezed my fingers around it and let it burn quietly in the palm of my hand.

THE HOAX

IT BEGAN, INNOCENTLY enough I thought, with a joke.

In those days I taught high school English, and spent my summers at a grad school for teachers on an old estate up in the White Mountains in New Hampshire. My roommate that year was Elliot. Elliot taught at a famous boarding school in Connecticut, the kind of prestige place where half the students are kids of Fortune 500 CEOs. At thirty-one he was six years older than I but looked younger, thanks to a relentless regimen of exercise and diet, plus enough ointments and vitamins to keep a small drugstore afloat. Elliot was one of those invulnerable people: limited imagination, terrific party skills, gleaming good looks. Women offered themselves to him with monotonous frequency—this was 1970, after all, and two millennia of Judeo-Christian sexual repression appeared to be giving way to a new religion that stressed getting naked as its chief sacrament. Elliot's "guests" were sometimes loud, he himself was not shy; and the walls of our cottage dorm were flimsy. A consensus had developed among my dormmates (most of them married and missing their wives) that something should be done about the situation. Some of us had hatched a little trick.

Elliot had a tape of guitar ballads he liked to play during his romantic conquests. The plan was to secretly record one of these conquests, then record *that* tape over the original, so that the next time Elliot reached for the trusty ballads, he and his partner of the evening would have a little surprise. We ran a microphone from the window near Elliot's bed, along the porch to Pete Dorsey's room next door.

On a Friday night half a dozen of us huddled around the tape recorder in Pete Dorsey's room, waiting for Elliot. Eventually we heard my roommate come in—accompanied—and after a few minutes, sure enough, the ballads began. Through the wall came murmurs and rustlings. We flicked on the machine. Dorsey had rigged a second mike for a running commentary, and as the noise level in the next room rose, he began doing his imitation of Marlin Perkins on Mutual of Omaha's *Wild Kingdom*. "They're really going at it now!" he enthused. "It's a spectacular encounter of bloodthirsty predators!"

"Oh God!" Elliot groaned. "Oh Jeeeeeeesus!"

"A fight to the finish!" shouted Dorsey. "Claw to claw, tooth to tusk in nature's deadliest competition!" And so on.

Two days later I was at my desk when Elliot came in, waving the tape and shaking with laughter. Somehow he'd found out.

"Tooth to tusk," he was saying, over and over. Finally he got hold of himself. "You know, I'm a master at this kind of stuff. I *love* it." He smiled wickedly in the direction of Dorsey's room, then chuckled, looking again at the tape. "This thing could've caused me some real romantic problems," he mused.

I had my own romantic problems that summer, and they were far less racy than Elliot's. Things were bad with Monica, the woman I'd been living with for two years. We'd reached that stage where little habits the other person has offend you for no reason at all except the crucial one that it is *this* person who has them. Monica, for instance, had a way of putting on her makeup that involved suddenly smiling into the mirror, an exaggerated smile that showed all her teeth and gums. There must have been things I did that worked on her in the same deadly way, for we fought constantly. We were living on taunts and threats.

New Hampshire served as my summer getaway from a life that had become too familiar for comfort. After college, for lack of a better idea, I'd drifted back to Maryland and taken a teaching job two towns over from my hometown. My folks were glad I'd come back, particularly with a spiffy and ambitious girl who worked on Capitol Hill for a real live senator. But sometimes when they opened the door to welcome us on a Sunday visit I'd look at their smiling faces, and at Monica's, and feel a shiver of pure terror. I had the strange feeling that a gauzy, smothering substance was coming between me and the world, dulling my perception of things.

On the hall phone in the dorm I dutifully called Monica every other night. We argued, exchanging the kind of joke that is dead serious. Elliot regarded these calls with a mix of sympathy and scorn. "What are you doing to yourself?" he asked after one of them. I mumbled about love being complicated.

"Do yourself and her a favor," he broke in. "End this thing."

I told him I couldn't see taking advice on questions of love from someone whose romantic narratives always featured the refrain *So there we were, pumping away!* Still, at odd moments just after I turned out my reading lamp, or as I watched the light grace a door frame at sunset, I sometimes felt that I was less than happy.

Back in Maryland, meanwhile, Monica decided the best way out of our troubles was a flying leap into marriage. She proposed hopping a weekend flight up to discuss things. I hedged. Couldn't it wait until I got back? Truth was, I considered New Hampshire my personal retreat. This infuriated her. Thieves and murderers crossed safely into New England every day, she pointed out. "But if I get near the place, it's a crime!" She slammed the phone down.

The next day I found a phone message in my box at the campus P.O. I unfolded it wearily, wondering what new variation on our unhappiness Monica would now suggest. But the message wasn't from Monica. *Will be in NH this weekend,* it said. *Am coming to see you. Jill.*

Jill was a student of mine, or had been a year earlier—my best student. Her senior English journal had been one of the few pleasures of my first year of teaching; I would escape with it after a dreary ninth-grade class to a far carrel in the library and read for half an hour, filling the margins with comments in red ink.

Jill was beautiful, in a way that utterly escapes most adolescent males, engaged as they are in mindless pursuit of the Great American Breast. She was slender and boyish, with short black hair and thick eyebrows that dwindlingly approached each other above the bridge of her nose. Other girls would have plucked such eyebrows, but not Jill. She wore blue jeans and big roomy sweaters passed down from older brothers, and her beauty resided above all in her eyes, which were a changeable green and very wide—the pupils wide, I mean, as if permanently adjusted to admit as much world as possible.

Monica was jealous. When I showed her Jill's journal, she questioned my "approach"—all those comments in the margins. "I just think teachers shouldn't get mixed up in their students' personal lives," she'd said.

I wasn't mixed up in Jill's personal life; I'd made strict efforts to keep things in their places. But as her graduation had neared, and then passed, I'd let up on myself a bit. One night I went to a house where she and three of her friends were babysitting. When I arrived, they were sitting around drinking wine. Lightweights all, the girls got drunk easily, a silly drunkenness brimming with ecstasy. Jill sat Indian-style on the floor, rhapsodizing about the great writers she'd read in my class. "If Wordsworth were alive today, you know what I'd do, Mr. B— Oops!" She ducked her head, grinning, then called me by my first name. "I'd give him my virginity! I'd go straight to the doctor, get fitted for a diaphragm, walk right up to him, and say, 'Ravish me, Wordsworth, ravish me!' " She rolled back on the floor, laughing.

Earlier that summer, I'd gotten a depressed-sounding letter from Jill, who by now had finished her first year in college. She'd broken up with a guy she'd been seeing, and wasn't sure why. It worried her, she wrote—her "absurd" expectations. "After all, the next Wordsworth might not come along for centuries, and I can't wait that long!"

One night in New Hampshire, on an impulse, I'd taken this letter off my desk and showed it to Elliot. A smile crept across his face as he read.

"So what are you waiting for?" he said. "A formal invitation?"

I asked him what he meant.

He seemed indignant. "For Chrissakes, get on the phone and call this woman!" He put the letter back on my desk—glancing at himself, I noticed, as he passed the mirror. "She's not your student anymore, you know. She's a full-grown, voluptuous, fully legal—"

"Elliot!" His voice had slipped into a murmur.

"Okay, okay." He held up a hand. "What does she look like, by the way?"

I described her.

"Well, just imagine those big green eyes staring up into yours, Wordsworth. Imagine those lips trembling as you take off her sweater. Imagine—"

"You're sick," I cut him off.

Elliot laughed. "Hey, I'm the healthy one around here. Take a look at yourself sometime. This thing with Monica is aging you."

When I showed him the phone message from Jill, Elliot burst out in raucous congratulation. Clearly, he felt vindicated. "So she's not taking any chances," he gloated. "She's bringing it right to you."

Not at all, I said. Jill probably had friends in some summer program at Dartmouth and was visiting them. The thing was purely innocent.

"Not so innocent you'll be calling home about it though, huh?"

I tried to explain. Monica had a weak spot there. She wasn't rational about Jill. Why feed her anxieties?

"I'd say she's completely rational," Elliot smirked. "And by the way, I've got some good news for you." He was leaving for the weekend, he told me—driving to Burlington to meet a woman at a hotel. I'd have the room all to myself. He smiled lewdly. "Feel free to use my bed. It doesn't creak as much."

I protested; but Elliot insisted that until I was willing to call Monica and tell her I was having company, he couldn't take me seriously. So I let it drop.

Friday approached. A second message from Jill informed me she'd be arriving around eight. As I folded the pink slip and put it with the first in my desk drawer, a small voice inside me asked what I thought I was heading into. I ignored it, just as I'd ignored it when Jill had been in my class. Passion for a student, I'd told myself then, is not necessarily deadly to good teaching. We are like cars, getting ourselves to our destinations by means of raging explosions, the very power of which lies in their containment. The crucial thing about my friendship with Jill, indeed its very essence, was that it was *contained*. This was an idea whose delicacy people like my roommate could not be expected to grasp.

Friday afternoon I returned from the library to find Elliot's Mark Cross luggage posed in the doorway—three pieces.

"Traveling light?" I teased him. I was in a great mood.

"I've been looking all over for you." He seemed concerned. "Monica called. She's coming up. Today."

"She's *what*?"

"Three-ten plane from D.C. Gets into Burlington at five-thirty."

"Oh Jesus." I looked at my watch. "Jesus Christ."

"I tried to head her off, but she said she *has* to see you." Elliot patted my shoulder. "Want me to stop at the airport and tell her you died?"

I stood there shaking my head. It was a paralyzing thought, the two women headed inexorably toward me. It was horrible. It was almost too horrible to be true.

I looked up to see a grin tugging at my roommate's mouth.

"Elliot?" I said. "Is she *really* flying up here, Elliot?"

He backed toward the door, smiling.

All the way across the campus I chased him, bellowing his name and laughing hysterically. Finally I tackled him.

"I *told* you to watch out!" he said, as I pummeled him with harmless punches. "I *told* you I was a master!"

Two hours later Elliot left for Vermont, his blue MG spewing music and dust as he pulled away. I sat awhile on the porch, watching cars go by. Invariably they slowed as they broke from the woods to a sudden view of the campus with its birch trees and carriage houses, a kind of magic colony, the late-afternoon light washing the buildings in gold.

At seven I shaved and showered, dressed, and sat to wait for Jill. The cottage was quiet, empty save for a few people studying in their rooms. I thought of a fight Monica and I had had in a seafood restaurant the month before, the two of us shouting at each other amidst several dozen startled diners. Later we had made up, weeping and apologizing. This was a hard kind of love, exhausting and very loud. There were no silences in it anymore.

I put on a tape—smiling as I passed over Elliot's guitar ballads —and sat back with a beer, imagining the moment when Jill would walk through the door. She would be in jeans and a flannel shirt. She would toss her woven shoulder bag onto the bed, turn to me and say, simply, "Hey there!" Would I be nervous? I held out my hand and saw that it trembled.

Eight o'clock came. Eight-thirty. By now Elliot was in his suite at the hotel in Burlington. I tried to picture the woman who would drive up from somewhere to spend two nights in a hotel with Elliot. What would he say when she came through the door? *Hiya, babe?* Or *Hello, sexy lady?* I realized then I really didn't know much about Elliot. I'd thought I understood him, yet when it came down to it, I really just felt superior to him. What he wanted, what the women who came to him wanted: these were mysteries to me. At the same time—and this nagged me—I knew that somehow Elliot had figured out just what it was about Jill that moved me most. How many times had he repeated to me during the week, *Those eyes, Wordsworth, those eyes!?*

Something was not right. Nine o'clock, and Jill wasn't here. I tapped my fingers on the arm of the chair. Something was bothering me.

At my desk I pulled open the drawer and took out the two phone messages from Jill. For the first time it occurred to me that the handwriting didn't seem to match the scrawl of the old gent, Ben, who manned the campus switchboard. Something was wrong here.

The office was a forty-second dash from our cottage. I made for the wall of postal boxes. In mine was a folded pink slip.

Friday, 5:52 P.M., it said. *Monica was just the hoax within the hoax. . . .*

My fingers tingled, my neck felt numb. *Enjoy your weekend,* the note ended—*The Master.*

I stumbled off, out the door and onto the walk. Scenes of the last week rose before me: my rush back to the cottage with the first message; Elliot's loud camaraderie; his jovial teasing. All of it fake. An intricate, cunning prank. Jill wasn't coming. Hoax within hoax.

My disbelief burned away, leaving raw fury. Back in the room I punched the wall, and the whole cottage jingled. I looked at Elliot's stuff, his stereo and typewriter and guitar; if I didn't get out fast I knew I'd start smashing it. Back in the hall I dialed the number of the hotel in Burlington.

"Sorry," the desk clerk said. "There's no answer in Mr. Hayes's room."

In a twisted voice I heard myself saying I had a simple message for Mr. Hayes. "The message consists of two words," I snarled.

He took them down.

After hanging up, I went out onto the porch. Cool air played across my face, and I breathed deeply, trying to calm myself. But each time I thought about what Elliot had done, a wave of fresh anger crashed through me. One of the pieces of porch furniture, a green-painted Adirondack chair, floated into my line of sight. As if from a great distance I watched my hands grip its broad arms, lift it high over my head, and heave it down onto the lawn. With a howl I was after it. It was all right, I discovered, to want that chair to suffer, to want to hear its bones break; and so I threw it down again and again, until it lay there in pieces and I was satisfied it was dead.

Two decades have passed since that night.

If I could make this story turn out any way I wanted, I might choose a poetic-justice ending, allowing Elliot to become the respected headmaster of his ritzy school, then hurling him from grace at fifty into a scandal with a student. Or I might choose a good-springing-from-malice ending, with myself thanking God for Elliot Hayes each morning as I roll over, kiss my wife awake, and look into those big green eyes.

The truth, as usual, is less spectacular. I did not marry Jill. I never told her about the hoax, or how I waited, aflutter with anticipation, for her to walk into my life. When last I heard from her she was working in Seattle for an environmental group, had a couple of kids, and wrote at length about a hiking trip she and her husband had taken up Mt. Rainier.

As for Elliot, he went back to his famous school, and I never saw him again. Before we parted, he let me know how guilty he felt about what had happened. "I'm sorry," he said, glumly. "I had no idea you'd go nuts." I remember being disappointed by the lack of any diabolical intention on Elliot's part, any true malice that would correspond to the magnitude of what his hoax had uncovered in me.

That night, my rage finally broken, the chair in splinters at my feet, I'd wandered off into the darkness of the meadow behind our cottage. To my astonishment I was weeping, sharp sobs that jerked my whole body, as if some stranger residing inside me were lost in uncontrollable grief. Jill was not coming—far worse than that, she never had been. The whole thing had been a mirage; but the desire it had teased out of me was all too real.

It was a desolate moment. And yet I found I felt strangely alive, right down to the tips of my fingers. What was more, that gauzy feeling, that sense of living at one remove, seemed to have vanished. Several things were crystal clear. I knew I would leave Maryland, probably for good. Since I'd never really made an actual decision to be there in the first place, it would not be hard to go: I would simply stop coasting on childhood memories and do my good and irresponsible American duty to pick up and move on elsewhere. Monica would not follow me, and I wouldn't want her to.

After a while I was no longer crying. Toward the edge of the meadow I stopped, fifty feet from the woods, a dark mass of trees rustling and waving in the wind. I cocked my head and listened. My life was about to begin, and it seemed like a good idea to be paying attention when it happened.

FIREWORKS AT
NINE

ALL SUMMER KIM won't stop hassling him about the slide show. It began in April when he came back from Europe and showed her a print of Versailles. "Oh Jay, that's what I *missed*? All those fountains and statues and everything?" She'll catch him at the service bar, in the walk-in fridge, Oh Jay, pretty *please . . .* !

It's a singleness of purpose Jay both admires and finds maddening. "Listen Kim," he'll say to her. "I've got about six seconds to get these New Yorks out to E-9 and get back here for lobster for ten. Now don't you have anything constructive to do?"

At the ends of these evenings he's not tired. Kim is a big girl, but the weight of her feels good on his shoulder as they sit with Lyle and Bullet, counting out tips. Jay sips a Heineken and unlaces his shoes. "Hey Bullet," he says. "Tell me again why we wear boat shoes in a restaurant."

This isn't just any old steak house, Bullet reminds him; it's Barry's *Riverboat* Steak House. "See them nets? See them deck chairs? It's your basic nautical theme."

"Ah, right." Jay pulls Kim toward him. "And here's the goddess Nausicaa."

"I want a slide show," she says, turning down her lower lip.

"Come on, Kim, don't be such a—" *Baby,* Jay starts to say, but looks up to see Bullet and Lyle leering at him. He holds up his hands. "All right, all right. I know."

Jay is twenty-seven, Kim a senior in high school. It's not something Jay planned; it just happened that way. She came in last September to interview for a hostess job, and he found himself telling her, *If you were three years older I'd take you out.* The second time she came in he said, *If you were three months older I'd take you out.* The third time, he took her out. The Severins were not exactly thrilled when Kim showed up with him for a boyfriend. They want her to go to college and make something of herself, like her older sister Nora. As far as they can see, Jay wasted his own education, and they don't want her to catch the attitude.

The house Jay rents is a mere three blocks from the college he graduated from six years ago. Lately, this has come to seem like a standing rebuke, a reminder of decisions he has somehow failed to make. His roommates—Margot, Stuart, and the infamous McKenzie—are all younger than he, and all of them have plans. This year, before another fall swings around, Jay is determined to figure things out. Technically, he is co-manager of Barry's Riverboat Steak House; but the franchise is owned by a group of businessmen up in Boston, and his responsibilities are limited to hiring, ordering food, and depositing the money. It sometimes occurs to him that the only thing he really likes about life at the steak house is closing time. He and Kim will turn out the lights and stand in the doorway, the room lit only by the glow of the marina downriver or the blue light of the moon; and as he looks over tables set for the next night, the ridiculous thought strikes him that they are putting children to sleep.

Back from the restaurant, up in Jay's room, Kim sits on the bed while he stands frowning, trying to analyze his situation. He shakes his head, thinking about it. "What am I going to do, Kim?" he says. "I can't wait tables forever."

"Well, so?" Kim shrugs. "Then go and get a life."

"A wife?" He sits down and snakes an arm around her.

"A *life,* Jay. *L,* as in Listen when I say something."

"I thought you said *wife.* You know, *W,* as in Wild Woman." He smiles, remembering the Christmas dance at Kim's school. She wore a black miniskirt with a sequined top, dangling earrings, and outrageously high heels. Afraid he was going to feel like her father, he'd felt instead like an agent or manager. "Hey, that's what I'll do," he says now. "I'll be your manager."

"My manager? For what?"

"For anything you want," Jay says. There's a spot on her neck he's trying to get at, but she pushes him away.

"You wanna manage something?" she says. "How about managing to come over and give us a slide show. It'd be so nice, Jay! It'd be . . . informative."

Jay shakes his head. The slide show idea, he suspects, is Kim's way of punishing her parents for not letting her go with him on the trip; it's not a battle he wants to get involved in. He lifts

Kim's shirt and dives for her belly button, flicking his tongue out.

"Come on!" Kim says, again pushing him away. "You're like, slobbering all over me! I mean it, Jay!"

He stands. "Know what I love about you, Kim? You're so romantic. Makes me feel young again."

At the window he looks out at maple trees trembling bright green in the streetlight. In April, as the train to Tours zipped through the French countryside, he'd sat taking it all in, the orange-tiled roofs, the toylike cars, the bright blue overalls farmers wore. His first day in a foreign country and it felt like anything could happen, like life might take off on some wholly new course. If he *were* ever to give a slide show to Kim, he'd like to find a picture that conveyed to her exactly this feeling. But his fear is that it won't show up on any of the photos he took. He glanced through them once, looking for it; but it wasn't there, and he quickly put them aside.

It's surprising to Jay, the trouble he has figuring out what to do with his life. He's never relied on others to make his decisions for him; he's always thought of himself as independent.

At fifteen he had his own apartment. His mother had died of cancer two years earlier, his father had remarried, and along with the new wife came her son, a mean, oversized boy a year younger than Jay with the ridiculous name of Royal. Royal was a liar, a thief, and a pyromaniac who stole things from Jay's room and burned them in little ritualistic piles in the yard. He had screaming fits where he fell to the floor, kicking his legs out and knocking over tables and lamps. Soon he and Jay were at war, fighting ragged battles that didn't end until a year later when Jay's father, desperate, agreed to the solution Jay proposed. And so it was that in his last two and a half years of high school he lived by himself, downtown, in a two-room apartment above the Dunkin' Donuts a mile from home. His father paid the rent, $300 a month; he himself worked weekends for his spending money, first as a bagger at the Giant, then as a busboy at a family restaurant. He talked to his father daily, and on holidays he went home. But to Jay the house was alien ground now. It was messier, and it was louder, and Royal was in it; sometimes as Jay walked up the drive he'd hear a burst of yelling from inside, and have to force himself not to turn around. He considered the place a madhouse.

Lately the house on Cort Street has seemed like a madhouse. Stuart's off in Nicaragua, researching his dissertation, and in his absence Margot has been throwing one party after another. Jay worries about offending the scholars who live quietly on all sides, some of whom were his teachers and who, though they don't remember him by name, smile at him familiarly in the street. Margot also has a soft spot for refugees and wayward lost causes. Her current project is a sad-eyed girl from California named Serena. In the mornings Jay finds the girl dozing in front of the TV, her hair lying in a frizzy braid across her shoulder, or cleaning up out in the kitchen. One afternoon as he is heading out for work she catches him at the door with a glass of fresh-squeezed orange juice. "You're a nice guy," she says. "I can tell. You don't hurt people." Jay thinks of the people he has hurt. Serena goes on, telling about her boyfriend, a wandering poet named Rodney whose parents back East sent three men out to kidnap him from the trailer where the two of them were living. "They put him in a room with a horrible red painting on the wall, and they brainwashed him." She looks at Jay. "Red is war. Can you tell me a country that doesn't have red on its flag?"

Sweden, Jay thinks, but keeps it to himself.

And then there's the McKenzie situation. When Stuart kicked McKenzie out two months ago, Jay and Margot joked about missing him; but they both knew McKenzie was one of those people best appreciated in absentia. McKenzie, a windsurfer, tennis instructor, and jack-of-all-trades in the leisure world, had not run an orderly life. Women rushed in to scream at him late at night, sending other women diving under the sheets. His rent was chronically late; if an envelope had the little plastic window, he didn't open it. He came home from rugby matches dead drunk, climbed the huge pine tree in the backyard and sang old Supremes songs in a raspy falsetto. He used a briefcase of Stuart's —full of lecture notes—to prop up a Halloween jack-o'-lantern on the roof (so that kids could see it! he said later), then forgot about it all winter long, while Stuart madly searched. That had been the last straw. I WILL NOT CONTINUE TO SUBSIDIZE RENT, read the eviction notice Stuart tacked to the front door, FOR SOMEONE WHOSE CONGENITAL EFFRONTERY MAKES HIM IMPERVIOUS TO HARDSHIP. McKenzie was gone by the end of the month.

But now he's back, along with his best friend in the whole wide world, his German shepherd, Odin. The two of them pulled in in McKenzie's battered pickup at dusk one day, and don't show signs of leaving. All week McKenzie's been telling Jay about his adventures on the road: getting robbed in St. Louis, winning and losing two grand at roulette in Vegas, running a bungee-jumping concession outside a bar in Southern California. "It's wild out there," he says, as Jay imagines a trail of broken homes, coast to coast. McKenzie's current project is a homemade solar hot tub; he's convinced he can build them more cheaply than anyone else, and dreams of a line of McKenzie Tubs from Maine to Florida. Out in the yard he spray-paints aluminum sheets black, as Odin and Serena look on. The girl picks a dandelion and puts it behind her ear, and McKenzie half-turns, smiling over his shoulder. *Watch out,* Jay, spying from the kitchen, wants to tell her.

He wonders about people like McKenzie, or Stuart—people who just show up, saying here I am, this is what I want, and then take it, as if wanting and taking were the simplest, most natural things in the world. He recalls Stuart in the one class they shared in college, with his long hair and turtleneck sweaters and some sort of weird tin briefcase, hurrying up to the front of the room after the bell to hobnob with the professor as Jay headed out for the gym and track practice. Jay himself was the kind of conscientious student who got the work done, wrote the papers, took the notes, then never thought further about any of it. He still has the notebooks. When he looks through them now, he finds pages crammed with names and ideas that mean absolutely nothing to him. It's like some hobby he'd taken up with fanatical interest and then completely dropped. Except it's not a hobby, he knows; it was supposed to be life.

On his shelf he has a stack of catalogs for various graduate programs, and every six months or so he looks through them, checking out the courses and fellowships, figuring the costs. But who is he to say he wants to be a lawyer or a broker or a diplomat? There is a way of insisting on your own importance that is alien to him. At the restaurant he earns the confidence of his customers by speaking low and standing still, by strategically disappearing; if he succeeds, they won't remember him two days later. As manager he has other unspectacular chores. He counsels Allan, the college kid he hired for the summer, who gets flustered when the floor speeds up; he calms Keith, the broilerman, also known as Illinois, who is insane. Day after day, his life is spent averting small disasters, holding the fort. Meanwhile, Stuart and McKenzie and the others around him move onward and upward in the world, finding handholds in places where Jay, groping, encounters only smoothness. Even Royal, his stepbrother, far from becoming the derelict Jay always imagined he would, has turned into a respectable person, with a house and a wife and a steady job building houses in Virginia.

There's only one thing Jay knows he really wants, and that's Kim. He's not always sure just what it is he loves in her. There's the flash of woman's anger when she tells him about some injustice at school. There's the way she puts on her earrings, the sheer expertise of it, turning her head first to one side, then the other, as she stands before the mirror, talking the whole time. Or there's the mystery of her lone hobby, horses. Kim owns a dappled gray gelding, called Harlequin, which she keeps at a stable just outside town. She competes in equestrian tournaments, guiding the big horse through harrowing jumps over fences, bushes, and water-filled ditches. Jay has always been wary of horses, and the few times Kim has induced him to approach Harlequin, he has felt the horse register his wariness and return it with a restive, stamping nervousness of its own. With Kim in the saddle, however, it's a different story. Jay marvels at the way she leans low over Harlequin's massive neck, unawed by the creature's power, to take him gracefully over a jump. *It's no big deal,* she insists. *You just have to make him trust you, that's all.* But Jay is old enough to recognize that this is far from simple. He loves cherishing a gift in her that she herself is unaware of. It more than makes up for the jokes he has to take from everyone, all the robbing-the-cradle, violating-the-Mann-Act business. *Hey,* Jay's father said when Jay first told him about Kim. *Don't apologize, you're living every man's dream!* But that isn't it at all. All Jay knows is that when he holds Kim, when he slides down from her face to her neck, when he pulls out her shirt and buries his face inside, nothing else matters.

In the heat of late afternoon he sits on the bed, lacing up his boat shoes for work and thinking, for some reason, about his old apartment above the Dunkin' Donuts. He'd been famous for it at school, and wildly envied. But the truth was that he'd lived a quiet life there. Already as a little boy he'd been neat and self-contained, and after his mother died he'd become even more so. In his apartment he'd felt himself the master of every small thing. It was as if his mind held an outline of the rooms, with spaces traced for the objects of his life: here a trim rectangle for a perfectly made bed, here the stereo with the dust cover down, and so on. At the end of the day he'd put things where they belonged, and step by step the actuality of the apartment would swing around until it matched, precisely, the outline in his head. At ten o'clock or so, his apartment in shape, his homework done, he'd sit back in his chair, put on a record, and relax, staring out at the streetlight and sampling through the open window the sweet friey smell of the Dunkin' Donuts below. It was then, with everything cleared away and in order, that he would think of his mother. He'd remember how toward the end she'd drifted in and out of consciousness like a person half asleep, saying things that didn't quite make sense, then frowning when she realized it. The day before she died, she'd taken Jay's hand, and when he'd leaned close she'd whispered to him.

Be good, she'd told him. *Buckle up, and don't bother the driver.*

It's Kim's graduation night, and the event swirls with controversy. The Severins are taking her out to dinner before the ceremony—without Jay. At first he was not invited. Then he was invited, but Kim let her parents know his feelings had been hurt; then *their* feelings were hurt, and the whole thing fell apart. There's also the problem of what to get her for a present. When he asked what she wanted, she started hammering again on the slide show theme. *Look,* he finally said. *Think your parents need to be reminded how they almost let you spend your spring break sleeping with me in inns and castles all over Europe? Besides, your mother would fall asleep.* Mrs. Severin suffers from narcolepsy. She is known to nod off.

At eight o'clock Jay gets into his Fiat and drives to the high school, where he takes a seat in the last row of the cavernous gym. The Severins are here somewhere, with Kim's sister Nora, down from Boston. Nora is Jay's age, twenty-seven, and already a lawyer. All the Severins worship her. A framed copy of the newspaper article announcing her appointment to the firm she works for hangs in their TV room, enlarged to the size of a small poster.

At eight-fifteen the band strikes up a flimsy version of "Pomp and Circumstance," and the seniors file in, wearing purple robes. They cross the stage singly for their diplomas, some drawing cheers from their classmates, some titters; Jay feels surprised, and then vaguely guilty, that Kim gets no response whatsoever. She walks with her usual confident bounce, smiling toward where

her family must be sitting. Kim has a place at the state university
for the fall, but has told her parents she's probably not going. The
Severins fear she's throwing everything away for Jay. Whenever
Jay tells her she should go to school, she says, "But I'm too stupid
for college." Jay knows she's not stupid; she just hasn't yet figured out how to get out from under the shadow of the legendary
Nora and her accomplishments.

After the ceremony he's the first one out of the gym. Kim
wanted to meet him, but Jay, alert to the implication made by the
Severins that he has distanced her unhealthily from her peers,
insisted she spend the night celebrating with friends. He drives
through the parking lot, steering carefully among departing graduates. At home he watches TV for a while with Serena and
McKenzie, then goes to bed. His back has been bothering him,
so he arranges himself on his side with his knees drawn up. Lying
there, he hears sporadic shouts of kids on the avenue two streets
over, and horns wailing as cars take them to the beaches. Gradually the sounds bend and blur into each other. Half asleep, Jay
thinks of France. He sees the fields he cycled through, swaying
with wheat or corn, a hillside aflame with rapeseed plants—
staging, it seemed, for medieval villages where people actually
still lived, doing God knows what. Drifting into sleep, he
imagines taking Kim there and showing her everything.

At 3 A.M. she comes to him. At first he thinks it's a dream, the
hovering girl leaning down to kiss him. Then he smells the beer
on her breath.

"How was the party?" he says, pushing over to make room.

She laughs and tells about a bonfire at the beach, and some
show-offy boy who went to siphon gas from a car to get the fire
going, swallowed a mouthful, and puked.

"Well," Jay says, "at least you were entertained."

"No I wasn't. That's why I'm *here*." She rubs against him.

"Kim, have you been involved in the illegal consumption of alcoholic beverages?"

She giggles. "What are you—my father?"

"I sincerely hope not," he answers. "I sincerely hope you don't do that to your father."

"What?"

Mmmm, Jay says, *that.* And then she has shrugged herself out of her clothes and climbed on top of him, and he's holding on to her shoulders, to the place on her side where he can feel her ribs beneath his fingertips. Her breasts ride lightly on the backs of his hands. It's dark in the room, and all he can see of Kim's expression is her wide-open mouth, caught in its mute scream. Jay closes his eyes and softly groans her name.

Afterward she lies half on, half off him. Jay doesn't talk much during sex, but after it he chatters like a stand-up comic. Some of his best jokes, indeed just about the only times he's ever funny, come after making love—a side of him, he sometimes teases Kim, that far too few people ever get to see. Tonight, however, he doesn't feel like being funny. He tells her about things he saw in Europe: about a castle he visited where a man was training falcons in the garden; about riding out of the woods in France and seeing a flash of yellow sunflowers on the horizon. He wishes she could have been there, he says.

Out of nowhere she asks if he can imagine ever leaving her.

"Huh?" The question startles him.

"You know—just sorta, I don't know, blowing me off. Just taking off or something." Deciding to take a trip around the world, she says. Or getting a job in Chicago, or joining the navy, or winning the lottery and moving to Hawaii. Or meeting someone else.

"Hey." He pulls back, trying to see her face. "What's this action?"

She shrugs. "I dunno. I guess I was just wondering."

"Well, don't." He strokes her hair. "I'm not going anywhere," he says. "I'm not meeting anyone. I promise."

She nods, nuzzling into his neck as if digging a hole to sleep in; and sure enough, minutes later she's breathing deeply. But Jay lies awake. He thinks about his own high school graduation—an awkward dinner with his father, his stepmother, and Royal; and afterward, a few hours spent drinking rye-and-gingers at the local hangout, a parking lot outside a video arcade. If Kim had known him then, he reflects, she wouldn't have given him two seconds. And now she's worrying about him leaving her.

It's strange, though; when he thinks about it, he's not sure whether she said worrying or wondering. It nags at him. He wanted to reassure her, to let her know he'd always be there. But if she wasn't worrying, if she was just checking possibilities, imagining scenarios, then whom exactly was he trying to reassure?

Every Fourth of July, Barry's Riverboat Steak House is the place to be. At nine the town puts on a half hour of fireworks over the river, and Barry's customers have choice seats at the huge picture windows. For dessert they're served the Old Glory Special, blueberry pie topped with whipped cream and strawberries—a tradition rumored to have been started, once upon a time somewhere, by the original Barry himself.

It's the biggest night of the year, tables booked months in

advance. And it's on this night, of all nights, that the broilerman, Keith, decides to lose it. Keith, who wears a tattoo on his arm of a sirloin that looks exactly like the state of Illinois, is a Barry's veteran of twelve years' standing, but he's been acting strangely all summer—weird mood swings, outbursts of cackling laughter that drift over the floor and cause diners to look up puzzled from their steaks. He's been teetering on the brink of some abyss, and tonight Jay senses that he's finally fallen in. He's angry and loud, spewing bitter complaints: the steaks are cut wrong, the butter not seasoned, the mushrooms old. "Hey, what's Illinois got up his ass tonight?" Bullet mutters at the waiters' station.

Jay appraises the situation with concern. There are four hundred dinners to be served tonight, and Keith must cook every single one of them. Jay instructs the bartenders to go heavy on the alcohol. With strong booze, low lights, and the distraction of fireworks, just maybe they can get through the night. But it's dangerous. Already they're red-lining it; any stupid little thing can set it off. Out on the floor, he watches Kim busing a table. Butter from a lobster cup shines where she rubs it from the wood with a cloth; briefly Jay imagines her polishing things in some country home of theirs.

At eight-thirty, the stupid little thing happens. It involves Allan, the college kid Jay hired, and a loud drunk in his section who's misbehaving. Unbeknownst to Allan, the drunk is none other than Tommy Corkery, a former Barry's waiter with a habit of coming in and acting as if he owns the place. When Jay looks over, the kid is putting a hand on Corkery's shoulder and whispering something in his ear. Corkery stands up, a grimace of outrage on his face.

Jay and Bullet arrive together. *Come on Tommy,* they say, *give us a break here.* Corkery allows himself to be backpedaled into the bar. Then he stops. "Who is that sucker, anyway?"

"Name's Allan," Bullet says. "College boy."

"Well, I hope he has a degree in engineering, because I'm gonna take his fucking face apart."

"Okay, Tommy," Jay says, softly. "But you'll have to take mine apart first." Corkery gapes at him, then backs off, shaking his head.

The incident has removed Jay from action for a crucial five minutes; turning, he senses chaos in the room. A woman at A-1 beckons wildly for help. Her steak, she says. It's not even *cooked*! Jay retrieves it. Headed across the room with the plate, he fears for the moment when tables begin to communicate with each other. He imagines a general uprising. "Refry," he says to Keith at the broiler.

Illinois grabs the steak bare-handed and hurls it onto the grill. "Mother wants carbon, he's gonna get carbon!"

"Come on, Keith," Jay says, his voice quiet but firm. "Hang in there."

Illinois stares at him. "You know how long I've been hanging in here, J.M.?" he says. "Twelve fucking years. I figure that's a pretty sizable chunk of Colorado knows my name by now. In the bovine world, I mean. They must be having nightmares about me out in Colorado." Laughing, he leans across the counter. "Hey!" he yells out into the dining room. "Hey all you mothers out there!"

Reaching over, Jay pushes him back. "Listen up, Keith. It's a tough night, okay. But we gotta keep moving, buddy."

The broilerman glares wildly at him, and Jay realizes the man is crazy. "Keep moving? You wanna tell me about it, J.M.? Huh?" His hands pick at the knotted string of his apron. "I'll keep moving, all right!" He barges back into the kitchen and returns with his time card. "You always think you got all the fucking answers, don't you? Well, answer this one!" Thrown onto the grill, the time card bursts into flame. "I quit! I fucking resign! Effective pronto!"

The broiler door whiff-whaffs on its springs. The time card curls to nothing amid the flaming steaks.

Jay stands there, astonished that anyone should think he has all the answers. He has to fight back an urge to follow the broilerman and ask him what he meant. Or to simply grab Kim, walk out the door, hop into the Spider, crank the top down and drive off. They could head to Colorado, or California; or catch a plane to France and find that hillside with the mantle of golden flowers. Rent a cottage on the hill and sit there doing nothing in particular, playing cards, drinking red wine, taking care of Kim's horse, growing old together. They could learn French and get some kind of job, anything, in the village nearby. The thought rivets him—just walking out and leaving the broiler room empty, the Riverboat Steak House rudderless and adrift. He scouts the floor, but can't seem to find Kim anywhere.

A loud explosion, like a sonic boom, echoes over the river. *Ooooohhhh, aaaaahhhh,* says the crowd. The lights go down.

Jay faces the rack of hissing meat. Sighing, he unfolds his waiter's apron, hooks it around his neck, and heads for the broiler, where he picks up the tongs Illinois has flung on the floor and sets to work.

★   ★   ★

The slide projector whirrs and clicks. Jay presses the selector button and the carousel rotates another three degrees; Versailles is replaced by L'Arc de Triomphe.

"They call this place the Place de l'Étoile," he says, "because the avenues come out from it like the points of a star. It's crazy, trying to cross on foot."

"I'll bet it is," says Mr. Severin.

"Napoleon built the arch, Victor Hugo wrote about it, and the Nazis marched through it right down the Champs-Élysées." The sentence, Jay realizes as he says it, comes from a travel guide he had with him on the trip.

"Jay, you're a real wealth of information," says Mr. Severin, drawing on his pipe. "It sounds like quite an experience you had yourself there."

"Seriously," Kim says. "And that's what I had to miss, just because you guys—" Jay nudges her in the dark.

This slide show is a reconciliation on all sides. The Severins seem to have decided to officially recognize Jay. He, in return, has publicly affirmed the importance of Kim's going to college. No one knows what will happen next, but Jay senses the Severins feel they've done all they can. It's the first of August. In five days Stuart is coming home. McKenzie is gone, packing both his hot tub and Serena into his truck along with Odin, and heading for points unknown. Margot has carefully put the house back in order. Soon it will be September, and the town will fill once again with students. Labor Day, a big crowd at the steak house; and then the long slow falling off toward winter. On a Monday night in February they'll be lucky to serve forty dinners. Jay or Bullet can handle the whole floor alone.

"Hey," says Kim, tapping him on the arm. "Turn it to the next one. Press the thingy."

Jay presses the button, but nothing happens. "It won't go," he reports.

The living room wall reflects the awesome ramparts of Chenonceaux. A swan suns itself by the gatehouse. There is a moat. Jay recalls bats at twilight, darting sharply through the gloom.

A light buzzing commences at Jay's shoulder. Mrs. Severin is snoring. Kim reaches over and presses the button. Chenonceaux does not go away. "I mean, it's a nice castle and everything," she says, "but I don't want to spend the rest of my *life* there."

Mr. Severin stands up. "Sometimes it jams. Bugs the living daylights out of me." He moves by in a sweet waft of tobacco smoke, his hand patting Jay's shoulder as he passes. "Hold on, I'll get the lights," he says. "Wait just a second, will you Jay?"

"Sure," Jay says.

The moment seems wildly funny to him, so funny he thinks he's going to break out giggling. But the feeling passes, and he sits back in his chair, looking at the castle and the swan.

LIGHT

—It sure has, the younger man said, sitting down. Before knocking at the front door, he'd taken his sunglasses off, then changed his mind and kept them on. Now, in the dimness of the living room, he took them off again. —Too long.

The older man sat across from him in a rattan plantation chair. He was, according to calculations the younger man had made in the car on the way over, about fifty. He looked ten years older. —Cup of coffee? he said in his pitted, smoker's voice.

—Sure. Thanks.

The younger man watched him walk across the room, in corduroys and a plaid flannel shirt, sleeves buttoned at the wrist. The old touches were still there: rhinestone-studded boots, a string tie; the sly eccentricities they'd all admired. His hair had thinned and turned grizzled. He moved deliberately, touching his fingertips to the tops of furniture.

Alone, the younger man reacquainted himself with the room's exquisite objects. A chess table of glossy burled walnut. A Japanese dressing screen. The stained glass bay window, featuring a biblical scene he couldn't place; he wondered what church had been razed to set it free. Beneath it stood ferns and a row of stone cats, crouched in various poses. As he watched, an actual cat emerged from them and stood staring at him.

The older man returned carrying coffee on a silver tray. Sitting, he stirred sugar into his coffee and placed the spoon carefully on a napkin. Your mother tells me you're getting married next June, he said. —So who's the lucky girl?

—You'll like this. She's someone I met in a sculpture class I was taking at art school last summer.

—Fellow artist, or the model?

—Well, fellow would-be artist.

Reaching down, the younger man petted the cat, which had approached and begun coiling around his ankles. —Hey, remember the time you got that model to pose for your drawing class, and you locked the door and covered the window with cardboard so none of us could see in?

The older man laughed. —Do I remember? Halpern called me in and practically read me my Miranda rights. Apparently, some of our mothers were terrified about their *dear* innocent daughters confronting the dread secrets of the male anatomy. Hah! But listen to me, I'm getting cranky in my dotage.

The younger man finished his coffee and slid the cup onto the tray. —And what about Halpern? How's he these days?

—No contact. Can't say I'm too terribly sorry, either.

—And Mrs. Goddard? She still there?

—Louise Goddard will be in that school the day the saints come marching in! She's all right though. Did you know she actually took my painting class that last year? Came every single day too.

The younger man sat back. He could feel his nervousness sliding away. —Ah, Room 201, he said.

—That's right. Room 201.

—We loved it up there. It wasn't really like a class, you know? It wasn't really like . . . *school*.

—Funny, I seem to recall Halpern telling me that very same thing with deadening regularity.

—You know what I mean.

—Yes. I do know what you mean.

—You ever miss it? Ever wish you hadn't left?

The older man gestured vaguely. —Well, it was the Eighties. We all thought we were going to make a bundle, right? Even artists! But tell me. To what do I owe the pleasure of your visit?

The younger man shifted in his chair. —Oh, you know. Making the rounds. Filling people in on the wedding.

They sat there. The younger man looked around. Along the far wall, jade trees were arranged in a dense green row. The place, he remembered, had always had a lush, jungle feel to it. He started to speak, then stopped and cleared his throat.

—My mother also said you hadn't been feeling well.

The older man watched the cat slink to its favorite spot behind the ottoman. —That's gotta be the understatement of the century, he said with a wan smile.

★　★　★

Over a second round of coffee the younger man talked of his parents, now in their sixties. His mother passed whole mornings swapping gossip with a vast network of phone friends. His father had retired to the golf course.

—And what about you? the older man inquired. —How's business out there in the heartland?

Business, in fact, was good. An industrial photographer, the younger man spent his days taking pictures of products for large corporations. The job was challenging, he explained, and more than paid the bills. —But I mean, it's not exactly . . . well, it's not exactly art or anything.

—Art? The older man shrugged. —Hey, art is what you put into it. I've spent my life finding art in all sorts of places.

He waved his hand across the room, and the younger man followed the gesture, his gaze landing on a brilliantly painted effigy of a parrot. The house was packed with curious treasures. A dozen summers ago, just after high school, he'd spent a month housesitting here; and he remembered now the feeling, each time he had unlocked the front door, of stepping through some invisible wall into a different universe, one where beauty and imagination were the norm. Since then it had often pleased him to think about the house, lodged like a gem in this drab and run-down part of town. At one point in his life it had been the single most hopeful thing he'd known.

—It's not bad, is it? the older man said in a quiet voice. —See, people think taste is something you're born with. But they're dead wrong, you know. Taste is hard work. I suspect you've learned that by now.

The younger man leaned intently forward. —You helped me learn it, he said. —You, and maybe three others.

The older man paused to blow his nose into a handkerchief. —Well, you were exceptional. You saw how light worked. How things are lit from—

—From inside! the younger man finished.

—Exactly. From inside.

There was a silence. A smile came onto the younger man's face. —You know, he said, I have something to confess to you. It's a little awkward, but . . . Well, the truth is, I lost my virginity in this house.

—You did? With whom, pray tell?

Naming a former classmate, a girl he'd loved with a greedy desire, he nodded toward the bedroom. —My birthday. Night I turned eighteen.

—Well, what a fine present! the older man said, chuckling.

—I guess I was a little weirded out at the time. You know, my teacher's house and everything.

—Not at all. I'm glad I could be of some service in your, uh, moral education!

The two laughed, and the younger man shook his head, his face spreading in a sheepish grin. —I remember those hats you had on the wall. That collection. She and I, we actually took a few of them down and put them on. We sort of had a little private show.

The older man pursed his lips. A long moment passed. — Those hats were Edward's, he said.

Released at last from its cage, the name hovered in the air around them. They sat listening to it flutter and hum.

—Edward was always the kitschier of the two of us.

The younger man made a soft noise in his throat. —I'm so sorry. I'm just so, so . . . sorry.

—Well, thank you.

—Are you . . . ? Are you . . . ? He couldn't find a way to finish his sentence. —How do you feel?

—I feel pretty lousy, frankly. But you've got to play the hand you have, right?

The younger man attempted a smile. He could feel his careful grip slipping away. —If there's anything I can do, Roger. Anything at all. I mean it.

Outside in the street a truck rumbled by, rattling the house. A ray of sunlight caught the older man's face, and he closed his eyes and leaned into it.

—Well, there could be one thing, he said.

Its curtains drawn, the living room basked in a warm twilight. —Do you mind if I put on some music? the older man said.

—No, I don't mind, came the answer from behind the dressing screen.

He went to the stereo and pushed a button, and the dark, rising tones of Górecki's Third Symphony poured into the room. Sitting again in the big plantation chair, he rested his arms along the armrests and closed his eyes. When he opened them, the younger man was standing before him, by the bay window. The older man looked. —You can cover yourself if you're embarrassed, he said.

—I'm not embarrassed. I mean, I'm a little, but it's okay.

There was light to one side, spooling in through a gap in the curtains, and when the younger man shifted, it winked off his wrist. He had neglected to take off his watch.

—This could be an ad for Timex, he joked.

—Oh no it couldn't, the older man said. He laid his head back against the chair and closed his eyes. —*Shoulder the sky, my lad,* he recited softly. *Shoulder the sky, and drink your ale.*

At the door, the younger man found himself struggling for words, and the older man, for the moment a teacher again, helped. He asked how preparations for the wedding were going. —Where *is* the wedding, by the way?

—Louisiana. Outside Baton Rouge.

—Good Lord, a Southern belle!

They shook hands. The older man stood in the doorway, the younger a step below, and when their handshake opened into an embrace, the difference made it clumsy. Pulling back, the younger man tried not to sigh. He had to find a way to leave that would let him leave.

—Hey! He brightened. —Remember that tie you gave me?

The older man looked puzzled. —Which tie?

—For my graduation. The red, white, and blue one.

—No, I can't say that I do.

—Sure you do! You know, the Bicentennial tie! With the Liberty Bell and AMERICA all over the front—

—Uh-oh, the older man said. —Wasn't there something on the back of that tie?

—Yes! said the younger man. On the back of the necktie, the words IS A LITTLE CRACKED had appeared in bold block letters.

The older man rolled his eyes. —And that's what I gave a callow youth for his high school graduation? Now, what kind of educator does a thing like that?

—A damn good one, the younger man said. —I still love that tie.

The older man smiled. —Well then, wear it well, dear boy. In health and good humor.

He touched the younger man's shoulder; and with that he backed into the house, shutting the door behind him.

The younger man came down the steps, placing his foot with care on each one. He thought of his many friends, the old and the new; of his brother and sisters, scattered across the country and only half in touch; of the woman he was set to marry in ten months and the life that lay before them, waiting to be filled in with the children they would have, the places they would see, the work they would do. He felt himself a grateful messenger employed in vast purposes; an emissary to princes in an unseen land.

MAGENDO MEN

WHEN I TURNED twenty-four I was living in Africa
in a dusty mountainside village above a game park,
trying hard to be an English teacher. I'd graduated
from college two years before, in 1969, a bachelor
of arts less inclined to join America's Vietnam effort
than to go somewhere else and atone for it. Africa
had seemed the perfect place. It was virtuous and
needy; even better, it was exotic. But it hadn't taken
long for some of the exotic things in the village to
get on my nerves: like the screech of students following our headmaster in a 7 A.M. chorus of "Nothing but the Blood of Jeeeeesus," or the Masai herd
boy whose cows crossed my lawn, leaving huge
pods of olive-green shit. My letters home always
reported how big my world was, but in reality I'd

felt it steadily shrinking to the one square meter of my desk, where I sat every night in the hissing glow of a kerosene lamp, trying to mend my students' broken essays.

The night before my birthday found me drowning my sorrows at the New Life Day & Night Club, a dingy, windowless place where bartenders sold beer from inside a floor-to-ceiling metal cage. My drinking partner was Scott Mack, an American who did PR for the Safari Rally, an international road race set to pass through our town in two weeks. I was never quite sure what to make of Mack. He was the gung-ho type, always giving you the hard sell, always bantering good-buddy style about cars and women. In restaurants he'd call African waiters "Sam" or "Max" indiscriminately, then leave a huge tip. He talked about himself in the third person. "Just a boy from Illinois," he'd say, "looking to get a little less clean without getting himself killed." Which was funny, because Scott Mack was *exceedingly* clean, always toying with a Cross pen onto which he had grafted a tiny comb that could be flipped up, jackknife-style, to groom his black mustache. That was a dream of his, he'd confided to me—to go back to the States and patent some such gizmo, then make a quick million and "get the hell out."

Mack had visited often since appearing in the village months before, tossing T-shirts to kids from a Jeep bearing the logo of the cigarette company sponsoring the rally. He liked to pull up outside my classroom, leaning hard on the horn. One day he'd landed on the school field with his English girlfriend, Eve, in a helicopter piloted by a Brit he'd met that day in a bar, and had taken some kids—and me—for a ride. As Mack saw things, I was living a life of pointless hardship in the bush, and his job was to keep me cheered up.

Tonight my mood was especially glum. Leaving Africa in three weeks, I was wondering if I'd done my students any good at all. Mack wouldn't hear it. I was the Mr. Chips of the savanna, he said. The question with me wasn't whether I was any good; it was whether I was *too* good.

Too good? I asked.

"That's the problem with the whole Mr. Chips thing—it's too damn *moral*! You're teaching the three *R*'s, when what these kids really need—"

I knew what was coming. "The three *S*'s, right?" I said. "Smuggling, Stealing, and . . . Now what was that other one again?"

"Smoothing." Mack made a slow gesture with his hand.

The corruptness of Africa was Scott Mack's obsession. He talked about it a lot, and whenever he did, his leg jiggled. It was jiggling now. "You live on the *border* here!" he said. "Forget math! You gotta teach *magendo*!"

This was the word for black-market dealing. *Magendo* was everywhere in Africa, according to Mack. Firms funneling kickbacks to government ministers, MPs sitting on mountains of ivory: he talked about it with happy awe. I knew Mack had his own little bit of action, taking Safari Rally items he was supposed to be handing out and selling them instead, to traders in out-of-the-way towns happy to get their hands on T-shirts, lighters, and most of all on cigarettes. "See, that's the amazing thing about this country," he said now, excited as usual. "You write your own ticket, Delamere!"

I was never sure I liked being called after the notorious English settler, but what could I do? Besides, I knew Scott Mack meant it as a compliment. His girlfriend, Eve, was the daughter of a

wealthy coffee planter, Sir Richard, and Mack dreamed of marrying into the so-called White Highlands where she lived, a belt
of fertile land where the English settlers had granted themselves
thousand-year leases and built lavish farms.

We left the New Life at midnight and climbed in the Jeep for a
slow spin through town. Lanterns flickered inside the tea shacks,
rickety places where for the equivalent of a nickel you could buy
a greasy doughnut and a glass of sugary pink *chai*. I found myself
thinking about my best student, a bright sixteen-year-old named
Joseph Mungai, and how he'd made the day's journey to the
capital to get his driver's license, only to run up against an exam-
iner demanding a "special fee" of three hundred shillings. *I
quickly saw that I did not have the required skills to be a driver in this
country,* Mungai told me later. This was the other side of *magendo*.
Scott Mack might hear it as a magic word that opened doors, but
my students were from poor village families, and to them *magendo*
was a huge wall blocking them off from the better schools and
jobs, the better lives.

"I guess there are people who have more to be depressed
about than I do," I mused out loud.

We'd started up the road to school, and the mountain hung
above us, its snowy top blue in the moonlight. It was an awe-
inspiring sight. "Not too shoddy, huh?" Mack observed.

"Yeah," I said. "Too bad you can't get there from here."

The peak lay on the other side of a border closed by squabbles
between our country and its neighbor to the south. The beautiful
things in life, I reflected, were always unreachable; you could try
and try and never get your hands on them.

This seemed a profound idea, and I was about to elaborate it aloud when the Jeep jerked forward, engine roaring, stones clanging against the undercarriage.

"It's midnight, Delamere!" Scott Mack whooped. "It's your bloody birthday! You're the king!"

Up we went, rumbling past the school and the village's last huts and into the woods. Here the road disintegrated in a rutted trough, and the Jeep yawed like a boat in a storm. Ahead somewhere, I knew, lay the border post, manned by members of an elite army unit recognizable by their red berets and stony scowls, and by the wide berth people gave them in town.

"There's a checkpoint up there!" I yelled. "You can't get through!"

Mack hit the headlights, but drove on through the dark. A light flickered, and then the post appeared, a scant fifty yards in front of us. Belatedly it occurred to me that knowing someone well meant knowing what was beyond him, where his limits were. "Listen," I said, my voice rising. "These guys have *guns,* you know—"

I'd grabbed the door handle and was at the point of wrenching it open when Mack turned the wheel hard right, and the Jeep lurched off the road. Between two trees a crude passage opened up. Scott Mack said nothing, and as we humped along I wondered whether he had a secret life as a big-time smuggler, whether some shadowy *magendo* figure would now emerge from the trees hauling—what did I know?—a load of radios or elephant tusks. We veered off on a tiny spur, sloping to a clearing in the trees that peeped out over open hillside. Mack killed the engine and turned to me.

"You said something about getting there, right?" he said, chuckling.

I looked and saw that it was true. Before us lay a spectacular view of the mountain: from where we sat, the peak—framed perfectly by the circular opening in the trees—appeared almost within reach.

"Yup, Delamere," said Mack, "you're the king of the mountain!" Reaching under his seat, he pulled out a bottle whose squarish shape identified it as a quart of Jack Daniel's Tennessee whisky. He took a swig and sighed. "Just remember though—it's all relative."

I sat back. All night I'd been angling for this release, this sense of things floating away from me, of their not being my *fault*.

What did he mean, I asked. What was all relative?

Without answering, Scott Mack released the Jeep's emergency brake, and we rolled gently forward, out from the woods into open night. I looked up. Absent its frame of trees, the mountain seemed half as big and twice as far away; in seconds it had lost the better part of its grandeur.

Mack cranked the emergency brake and turned to me, grinning.

"*That's* what I mean!" he said.

As I'd said to Mack, others in the village had more to be depressed about than I did. One of them was Chandra Singh, the school's games master. A trim, turbaned Indian who spent three afternoons a week drilling our kids in netball and soccer, Singh had on his hands a family problem that had taken a turn from the difficult to the horrible. At the center of it was his niece, daughter of his brother, V. K. Singh, a wealthy merchant in the capital. It was bad enough that the girl, seventeen and still in school, had gotten herself pregnant; far worse, the boy involved was an African. Indians were clannish, their relations with Africans fraught with mistrust. In V.K.'s eyes his daughter was ruined; the "half-breed" would cover the family in shame.

All this I knew from rumor. People talked in the village, sunning themselves on stories that silted up from the river of gossip. But two days after my birthday, Chandra Singh came to see me in person. The situation, he said in his friendly nasal voice, had become "extremely complicated."

Had his niece's baby been born?

"Born, yes. Born and then . . . unborn again." He paused. "The girl. My niece. She . . . she got rid of it."

From a radio somewhere drifted the rumbling drums of the government news service. "They have put her under arrest, Jeff," Singh said. "She is in with prostitutes and common thieves. With women who have murdered their husbands with a machete."

I asked how it had happened—with the baby, I meant.

"It was night. The birth was three days before, and in those days her mother and sister were caring for her in a basement room. My brother, he was not allowing her upstairs." Singh's voice quavered. "In the yard is a servants quarters. There is an outhouse. The pit is very deep."

A servant had made the awful discovery and called the police. Now V. K. Singh had washed his hands of the situation, disowning his daughter. "So I find myself a solo player," Chandra said, "trying to find some way to grease the machine and liberate my niece from this living hell."

Lying in bed that night, I couldn't shake the feeling that in seeking me out, Singh had hoped for some dramatic intervention on my part. I might be only a low-paid teacher; but to him I was educated, and an American.

The thought gnawed at me. I recalled how, two years earlier, I'd descended upon my students like a tornado, urging them to "be creative," eager to free them from the dreary authoritarianism of my African colleagues. Then the year had ended and my Form Fours failed their English O-levels, every single one—and I'd realized with a jolt that none of them had ever imagined doing anything with their lives but hanging around town scrounging for work or, if they were girls, heading home to take care of siblings while waiting themselves to get pregnant. So this year I'd decided to focus all my hopes on two students: Joseph Mungai, and Clara Wanjiku, an earnest sixteen-year-old who spent her lunch breaks reading at the edge of the schoolyard and whom other kids called "the Professor." Night after night I'd prepped these two for O-levels in an empty classroom, pouring my energy into them at the expense of my other two hundred kids. I wasn't proud of this. It was the way people acted in burning buildings and sinking ships. It reminded me how drastically I'd adjusted my expectations downward; how helpless I was to help. Chandra Singh's appeal hit that same hot nerve.

The next morning I used the school's phone to call Scott Mack in the capital. When he wasn't out glad-handing for his tobacco company, Mack stayed at the Surrey House, a Tudor palace built at the turn of the century as a watering hole for European aristocrats. It was just before 7 A.M., and Mack sounded groggy.

"Rise and shi-ine!" I sang.

When he'd gotten himself awake, I related Chandra Singh's problem and asked what he thought the Indian could do to save his niece.

"You heard what he said," he answered with a loud yawn. "Grease the machine. Drink a little *chai* with the magistrate."

"Magendo 101, huh?" I said.

"You got it." Mack chuckled. "Hey, these Asians are rich, bwana. Go to the airport, they're smuggling dollars out in *suitcases*!"

I said I didn't think Chandra Singh was that kind of Asian.

"Well, maybe not." Mack knew Singh from the village's rally committee. "Look, you give the guy a tip from me. You tell him to sell the family cow and put it all on Altobelli. It's a sure bet."

Altobelli was an Italian driving in the Safari Rally, and according to Mack, all the smart money was riding with him—including his own. "It's make or break time, Delamere," he said. "Altobelli all the way."

We hung up then; and as we did I made an interesting discovery. One day over lunch at the Surrey House, Scott Mack had dumped a bunch of bills onto the table and played a little game with them, heaping the bright orange and blue notes into a kind of crazy salad, and laughing as he did. That had annoyed me; and I found now that if I concentrated on the image I could hold it in my mind and squeeze it like a sponge, eliciting a trickle of some mystery solvent that began sizzling away at the doubts I'd been having about my own mission in Africa. I thought about the Safari Rally T-shirts Scott Mack had unloaded in the village, turning half the town into a human cigarette ad. The more I thought about this, the worse he looked, and the better I felt; and I squeezed a little tighter.

Rally day broke sunny and cool. Shaving at my sink, I looked out the window to the mountain showing itself dazzling white, the savanna gray and patchy with fog. Often I'd watched as one of the zebra-striped tourist buses from the game park hotel chased gazelle and wildebeest across the plain. Fleeing, a herd of terrified animals would split into two or three smaller groups, and these into still smaller ones, until finally the bus would give up and turn away, looking bored. I splashed my face with cold water and took a last glance. It was hard to believe that in a week I'd be in New Jersey.

Someone knocked at the door. I opened to find my student Joseph Mungai, looking morose.

"Mwalimu," he said. "I am defeated." O-level results had come in, he told me, and Clara Wanjiku, the Professor, had bested him. Indeed, she had already left to join a fifth form at a school in the capital—he himself had just escorted her to the bus.

"I'm sorry, Joe," I said.

He shrugged. Perhaps, he suggested, he should marry Wanjiku now, and do it American style: the woman wears the pants. Mungai pulled at his baggy school shorts, turning them into a skirt. Then he suddenly stopped clowning. "Ah, *mwalimu,*" he said. "Me, I was born to be digging."

At eleven I walked to town for the race. A crowd thronged the market—rally officials and photographers, tourists from the park hotel, white faces everywhere. To the village these people represented the big world, the world not only of the capital but of Europe, too, and you could feel a panicky excitement afoot at the thought of finally being connected to it. I saw Chandra Singh putting up a poster of the local favorite, Ved Pranay Gooch, an Indian driver who lived in East Africa.

"Gooch will win this race!" Singh called. "He will win for Africa and the Indian people!" It was a brave face. Rumor had it that his niece, by now two weeks in jail, was to be charged within days. Whatever Chandra's attempts to grease the machine had been, they'd apparently failed.

For months, rally fever had been building in the village; and when a distant buzz floated up from the savanna just past noon, not even the soldiers from the border post could hide their elation. Necks craned in unison. Far below us, three tufts of dust crawled across the plain.

Wanakuja! someone shouted. They were coming!

First through was the red 77—Ved Pranay Gooch at the wheel, raising a gloved hand to the crowd. Next came Altobelli, the Italian, his yellow Fiat skidding around the curve, sending photographers diving. One after another the cars powered by, engines whining, wheels sending up a haze of dust that settled on the railings and in everyone's hair, giving the afternoon a spectral glow. The schoolchildren sang the national anthem. Little boys with long sticks steered miniature "cars" rigged up out of wire and tin cans. Women in costumes danced and sang. The mood rose, crested, and then, just when it seemed it would topple back, rose yet higher.

Most of the cars had come and gone when bad news came by radio from the final checkpoint: Pranay Gooch had gotten stuck in mud and been overtaken by Altobelli, now speeding toward the city and the victor's cup. Disappointment rippled through the crowd. By three the tourist buses had hauled their European guests off to the lodge; the photographers were packing their equipment. Soon the last straggling car passed. Nobody wanted to admit it, but the Safari Rally was over. People started trudging home.

I lingered. Passing the market, littered with the husks of vegetables sold that morning, I found myself imagining how the place would appear on somebody's TV in Europe—a fleeting view of a mountain, a crowd of black children hollering from a dusty patch of poverty. By the petrol station I watched a last team of photographers load a Jeep. The big world had descended for an afternoon, and now was packing its toys and leaving, taking everything of value with it, even the images inscribed on its films. I pictured Scott Mack, celebrating Altobelli's victory and the alchemy by which a little petty embezzlement had been redeemed in gold—his ticket, he hoped, into the White Highlands and its vestige of landed gentry. I pictured my own bags packed and waiting in my cabin, one of them containing the sign that had greeted me over my door two years earlier, YOU ARE HAIGLY WELCOME! In my mind flashed a chilling preview of myself back in the States, detailing "exotic" things I'd seen and done in my time abroad.

The vision took my breath away. It felt as if I were seeing myself for the first time. I winced to think of my former students hanging around town, jobless, hailing me with happy shouts from every store stoop. I winced to think of my parents, who had been full of fears about my coming to Africa, and to whom I'd seen fit to send a gruesome warning photo we were given here of the remains of a Corpsman who, wading carelessly into a river, had been ripped apart by crocodiles. Under that image I'd scrawled a line for my mother: *If you don't go to pieces, I'll try not to.* What could a person who would say something like that possibly be qualified for, I wondered now, beyond casually hurting people?

Behind me the photographers' Jeep revved its engine. I turned and ran toward it, sticking out my thumb.

★   ★   ★

It was night when we arrived, but you could see the capital had been cleaned up for foreign guests: the cripples and beggars gone, the garbage gone too. Near City Square we passed the stand where thousands must have cheered as Altobelli was handed the winner's cup. I rehearsed my pitch to Scott Mack. No plea of pity, just a cool business proposal: a loan, to be paid back—with interest. In the States I had some money in an account from my grandmother, plus what was coming from the Peace Corps. Not a fortune, but enough, I hoped, to get Chandra Singh and his niece off the hook.

I found Mack in the bar at the Surrey House. He introduced me to two English friends—"Hey, look who came in from the bush!"—then returned to some point he'd been making. "I'm telling you, the fix was in! I just can't figure the angle."

I asked what he was talking about.

What he was talking about was theft, he said; theft pure and simple. "I'm talking about *magendo,* bwana, big time! About disqualifying the winner and handing the race to some Asian who just happens to be a citizen of this wonderful democracy."

"To some Asian? You mean Gooch?"

"Yeah, Gooch." He offered a toast. "Here's to Gooch! Gooch the Pooch!"

When the others rose to head off to a party, Mack waved them along. He wasn't in a festive mood, he said. They left, and I asked him if he'd lost big on the race.

"Yeah," he said slowly. "I guess you could say that."

It was a gloomy moment, my whole scheme in ruins, and I could only hope that Singh *had* sold the family cow and bet on Gooch. But I doubted it.

Mack's plan for the remainder of the evening was to drink. At midnight I went with him to a nearby disco. The place was half full, the usual city mix of Africans and foreigners, and we took a table in a far corner. From under his jacket, Mack produced a fifth of vodka and broke the seal.

"So," he said, "I guess your man Singh's pleased, huh?"

I shrugged.

"Let me tell you something. These Asians, they have it pretty good." He took a slug of the vodka. "Your typical Asian, in Bombay he's a bloody untouchable, but here he makes it big. He should be *thankful,* Delamere!"

At that moment, as if conjured, an Indian in a tuxedo materialized, his hair slicked back in a glistening pompadour. "Good evening, gentlemen," he said. "I am Shekhar Chatterji, manager of this establishment."

Mack rolled his eyes. "See what I mean? What did I tell you?"

The manager was staring at the vodka and putting out a valiant attempt at a smile. "I'm sorry, but I am running an entertainment and refreshment club here," he said. "If I allow every patron to bring his own liquor, what is left for me?" He turned to Mack. "Sir, I promise you, you will get your bottle back as soon as you depart."

I was watching Scott Mack closely; for a second I thought I'd seen something menacing simmer up inside him. But whatever it was, it subsided. "Okay, bub." He shrugged, pushing the bottle across the table. "You win."

The Indian took the vodka with the discreetest of motions. He left, and we returned to discussing the rally. But all the while I could feel the heat flaming up again under Scott Mack. That menacing look came back on his face. "He's goddamn *right* I'll get my bottle back!" he muttered.

What happened next had a dreamlike quality. Mack stood and headed for the bar, and when I followed a moment later I saw him grappling with the bartender, the two men clenched like show wrestlers. A glass fell to the floor and shattered. From no-where, a bouncer and two blue-coated city policemen appeared. Peeling Mack away from the bar they dragged him, raging, across the room and out into the foyer at the top of the stairs.

I'd never seen anyone actually foam at the mouth before. But something seemed to have exploded inside Scott Mack. At the top of his voice he cursed the manager, the bouncer, and the policemen, who held his arms pinned behind him and seemed to be waiting for orders. Shekhar Chatterji stood in the door, fixing arriving guests with a pasty smile while trying to shoo us out. He shoved a fifty-shilling note into my hand. "Here is an entrance refund! Just take your friend away from here—for God's sake shut him up!"

"I won't shut up!" Mack howled. "I won't, goddammit!"

"Gentlemen." Chatterji motioned to the cops. "Please explain to this man—outside!—how lucky he is I do not press charges."

The four of us, tangled like some huge toy, started down the stairs. But Mack wasn't done. "Delamere!" he shouted in my ear. "Go back and get our bottle! Dammit, I don't want some greasy Gujurati drinking my vodka!"

Above us, Chatterji froze—I saw his back stiffen. He turned, his eyes blazing, and pointed a long finger. "I will *not* stand here and be insulted by this hooligan!" he shouted. "Officer, take him to the station, right away! I tell you, he will rue the day! He will rue it body and soul!"

★　★　★

It was a fifteen-minute walk to the police station. When I got there, Mack was being questioned by a lieutenant in a cramped cubicle whose walls were covered with snapshots of children and smears of cigarette ash. Mack's passport lay on the desk, while Mack himself sat with his head in his hands—his black hair mussed for once. Shekhar Chatterji stood glaring as the lieutenant, Okello, spoke to me. The situation was serious, he said, but not impossible. "Mr. Chatterji agrees that if Mr. Mack will apologize, the matter will be dropped."

"A sincere apology," Chatterji said.

"Yes." The lieutenant nodded. "It must be a sincere one."

I sat down. My friend Mr. Mack, I said, had had a long tough day—

"No no no!" Chatterji waved a finger. "He must speak for himself!"

"He's drunk," I said. "He's barely conscious."

At this Mack snapped up. Taking his wallet, he dumped its contents across the desk—credit cards, driver's license, everything. "Here I am," he said. "Mack, Scott, middle initial N, stands for nothing, Scott Nothing Mack." For an apology it wasn't a promising start. "I'm from Rockford, Illinois, my political affiliation is independent, religion Baptist, I studied at the Massachusetts Institute of Technology, I hold three patents registered with the United States, two checking accounts, Bank-Americard, MasterCharge, and this, gentlemen"—he held it up—"*this* is my American Express Card, good in places of *distinction* across the globe."

I booted him underneath the table, hard, and it seemed to shake him awake, for he made a mumbling, last-ditch attempt to save himself. "Look, I'm sorry about the whole ordeal with the bottle, okay? I'm sorry I didn't know that your . . . your customs over here . . ." He glanced up at the hovering Chatterji, and his face flushed red. "What I mean is, I'm sorry you don't do things over here the way we do in the *civilized* world—"

That was enough for the Indian. "Lieutenant," he shouted, "I will not have this man spreading manure all over me! I want him charged—no tricks!" He slammed his hand on the table; then checked his watch, adjusted his cummerbund, and strode out the door.

When he left, the room seemed eerily quiet. With a what-else-can-I-do? shrug, Okello motioned to an officer who stood Mack up and led him, limp and unresisting, across the room to the lockup. A jailer with a ratty grin opened from within; he held out a bag and ordered Mack to empty his pockets. I could hear the voices of women—prostitutes, I guessed—hooting in delight as the jailer pushed Mack inside. The door clanked shut.

Back at his desk, Okello lit a cigarette and inhaled gratefully, as if the interrogation had interrupted an evening of smoking pleasure.

"Your friend is a fool," he said, sighting along the side of his cigarette. "You see, the Asian in Africa is a rich man, and a peaceful one. You can take his money and he will not resist. Step on his pride, however, and he becomes quite dangerous to you." He closed his eyes and rubbed them. "Your friend should very seriously follow a course in foreign relations."

"Well"—I nodded toward the lockup—"I guess he's getting one now."

"Indeed." The lieutenant chuckled. "Indeed he is."

He offered me a cigarette. Taking it, I sat back and smoked while he worked his way through a stack of papers. We talked on and off. He asked whether I'd visited a certain town in the western part of the country.

"That town is near my home," he said. "Near where I was a tiny boy with legs like sticks." He smiled. "In that place we had rivers where the fishes would actually jump from the stream onto the bank for you."

His father had worked as a gardener at a French mission, he told me. "In that church there was a statue of the Virgin. A pasteboard statue, due to lack of materials." He put down his pen. "One night some wicked boys spread mud on this statue. For some time my father was assigned to guard it. I could go there very very late and see him just sitting at the foot of that Blessed Virgin, with his machete across his knee." Okello looked at me. "Of course, now it is all gone. The mission, Père Leroux, everything. I believe that statue melted in a terrible rain some years ago. Myself, I have got a wife near that place now. Also six kiddies."

When he finally stood up, I was surprised to find Okello was smaller than I—a shortish man, really. "Do you suppose your friend has finished his course by now?" he said.

I shrugged. The clock showed three-thirty.

"In any case, I think I could see my way through to releasing him. As a personal favor to you."

"You could?"

He gestured. "I have got too much paperwork already," he said. "I wouldn't mind to spare some more."

We stood facing each other over the cluttered desk. "Listen," I said. "You're doing something for me. I'd like to do something for you."

He made an almost imperceptible bow.

By the time Scott Mack and I emerged on the street it was 4 A.M., the city dead still. We stood under a weak and buzzing streetlight. Mack took his pen-comb gadget from his breast pocket, dabbed at his mustache with it, and put it away. He was sorry, he said, about the whole mess. "I lost my head, I know it. Dumb as sin. Mind like a sieve."

I looked past him toward the city skyline.

"Gotta tell ya though, Delamere, I didn't think you were gonna come through for me there. Whoo-hoo, was I dead wrong! I mean, there I am, wondering what act of God is gonna get me out of this hellhole, and meanwhile, Magendo Man here is busy serving our Lieutenant Sam tea and cakes!" He slapped me on the back. Time to hit the Surrey, he said, and scare up a Tequila Sunrise for breakfast. Digging in his pocket, he pulled out his billfold. "So what's one boy from Illinois worth around here, anyway? A hundred? Two?"

I pictured the scene back at the Surrey House, all the furious preparations for the day's pleasures: drivers gassing up vans, cooks in the kitchen squeezing fresh orange juice with exactly the kind of little gizmo Scott Mack might wish he had invented. A tingling warmth flooded my cheeks and forehead. I knew what I was going to say before I said it; what I didn't realize was how good it would feel—one of those defining moments, one for the permanent collection.

"Fuck you, Mack," I said. "Okay? Just. Fuck. You."

Then I walked away, leaving him standing there, his mouth as wide open as his wallet.

I never saw him again. Days later a plane whisked me off to another world, closing a time in my life that has turned out to be so different from what went before or after that my memories of it have remained fixed, like the room of a child who has died.

With one exception.

Eight years after leaving Africa, I got a surprise phone call from Clara Wanjiku. My former student was in New York City, of all places, going to NYU and working part-time for her country's delegation to the U.N. I drove in and had lunch with her: a handsome young woman who laughed easily and carried her accomplishments with a stately grace. It was somehow wonderful to sit in an East Side restaurant, trading stories of the village on the mountain. About Joseph Mungai, Wanjiku told me he'd completed an agricultural program and returned to work on projects around town—and to marry Chandra Singh's niece. The girl, it turned out, had been released from jail just days after I'd left the country—the case against her dropped—and had come to live with her uncle.

This much I knew already, from various letters I'd gotten in the first year after my return. But I wasn't prepared for what Clara Wanjiku said next. She was recalling the day after the O-level test results came in, when Joseph Mungai had brought her to the bus in the marketplace.

"He was so disappointed," she told me, pushing her coffee cup aside. "You know, *mwalimu,* I was in love with that boy. If he had wanted me to marry him, I would have stopped everything on the spot."

She glanced out at pedestrians on Second Avenue. "In fact, on the way to the bus we had decided that Mungai would come with me to the city. But he had no money, nor did I. He asked the driver for a free ride, he begged him, but it was useless. The man just sat there racing the motor."

I imagined Joseph Mungai turning on the charm, cajoling the driver, smooth-talking him, offering the world—all to no avail.

"At that moment, *mwalimu,* I had practically decided to throw everything aside and get off the bus and stay. But then a funny thing happened. An old woman sitting in the back said she knew someone who had received a lot of money. She said someone had brought several thousand shillings from town that same morning for Mr. Singh, and so we decided—"

"Wait a sec," I interrupted. "For Chandra Singh? That morning?"

"Yes, that morning. In a package. With a messenger."

"On that very morning? *Before* the Safari Rally? Are you sure?"

Wanjiku shrugged. I motioned for her to go on.

"Well, Joseph jumped off the bus to run after Mr. Singh, just to borrow enough for the trip. But as soon as he was gone, that driver pulled away. He just left, just like that. And so I left too." Clara Wanjiku shook her head. "You know, that money was used to free Chandra Singh's relative—and then she came to town and married Joseph. Now she is there and I am here." Wanjiku fingered an earring, and I recalled that eight years earlier she'd been the only girl in school to obey our headmaster's silly injunction against jewelry. I called for the check.

Outside on the sidewalk we shook hands. It was funny, we agreed, the way fate tossed people around like toys. "One last thing," I said. "That money—the money for Singh—do you happen to know where it came from?"

She looked at me. "In fact, *mwalimu,* I always suspected it was you."

That night I wrote to Joseph Mungai, and four months later I received a blotchily typed letter. Mungai greeted me on behalf of his father-in-law, Chandra Singh; thanked me for having always pushed him forward in his studies; and told me that yes, Mr. Scott Mack had indeed most generously sent Chandra Singh a sum of money before the road race eight years ago. In fact, he himself had been wanting to get in touch with Mr. Scott Mack for a long time. He hoped that when I saw him I would greet him on behalf of his wife, his father-in-law, and his five-year-old son, Scott Mungai. He signed the letter "Your Faithful Former Student, 'Joe'."

I tried writing to Scott Mack. But I had no address; the Rockford, Illinois directory gave no such listing; and MIT, which I remembered him boasting about that night, had no record of him among its graduates.

At one point I picked up the phone, thinking to call him directly, but of course I had no idea what number to dial. Standing there, I felt a funny little jog in things, as when a familiar room flashes for a second back into the strangeness of the first time; and as I put the receiver in its cradle I could only hope that wherever Mack was, he had somehow made his little gizmo, his quick million, and gotten the hell out.

THE
WEDNESDAY
NIGHT
CLUB

THEY WERE SIX, charter members all, and they'd come by plane, train, and car from distant corners of the land to meet at their alma mater. Cromby did advertising in Manhattan; Hodge had run a waterbed outfit in California and was currently bankrupt; Freeman practiced law in Chicago. Lowery sold muni bonds, Mikulski was an oral surgeon, and Green, the group's intellectual, taught English at a women's college in Virginia. The scene of their reunion was a private dining chamber at the Squire's Nest, that venerable New England inn just off campus; the occasion, Lowery's impending wedding—the last of the Wednesday Night Club to fall.

"Here's to Larry!" Mikulski, the Chairman and Ultimate Leader, lifted a glass of champagne and peered slyly into the bubbles. "May his mastery of *bondage* stand him in good stead on his honeymoon!"

"And to the Wednesday Night Club," added Freeman, rising to his not-so-full height of 5′ 4″. "May its decadence forever flourish!"

Hear, hear! the others clinked in.

Sixteen years before, as rowdy college sophomores, they'd convened every Wednesday in the windowless basement of their dorm, a pleasingly squalid room containing a pool table and a sofa whose foam guts bulged through several gaping wounds. There, guzzling Budweiser in front of an ancient Philco that Lowery had cadged from his dying grandmother, they'd spent their evenings trading friendly insults and plotting their next escapade, from fire extinguisher raids through the campus's steam tunnels to the annual safari in Cromby's Jeep across the quad, chased by a bellowing security officer named Felker.

"Those were the days, huh guys?" said Cromby now. "A little pool, a few brewskis, a little Heeeeere's Johnny . . ."

"A coupla tokes on the evil weed . . ." Hodge grinned. The club's Secretary of Agriculture, he had supplied extralegal smokables.

Mikulski rumbled his insinuating laugh. "Hey, you turkeys remember when you leashed me to that tree?" The school in their day had been a men's college, necessitating regular forays to the women's college two towns over, where one memorable Wednesday Mikulski had been tied, buck naked, to a maple at the center of campus, a sign around his neck reading SOCIETY FOR THE PROTECTION OF TINY ANIMALS, with an arrow pointing downward.

"Amazing," said Freeman, shaking his head.

"Yup, those were the days, all right," Lowery pitched in.

There followed a murmuring silence, during which the members of the Wednesday Night Club sat pondering the past and covertly studying each other. Time had been active, altering features and doling out new mannerisms. Cromby, once kidded about his movie-star looks, ran a hand oh-so-carefully through thinning hair; Mikulski stroked his belly fondly like a pet. Green swished his tongue in his closed mouth, lending himself an air of sober reflection. Lowery had added an unconscious wink to his homey Midwestern smile. How strange it was, the six of them here at the Squire, in ties and jackets, enjoying the overpriced champagne and stuffy ambience, glancing out the very same window they'd once walked by countless times on their way to the bars in town.

"Sixteen years," ventured Green. "It changes you."

For a moment it seemed the remark might tumble them headlong into introspection. Mikulski frowned. All weekend he'd been hearing Green professing strange new sympathies, showing dead places where he'd used to show bounce. With a mighty scowl the Chairman splatted a palm on the table.

"What's this philosophical crap?" he cried. "Come on! What we need is to party till we bleed! A team of nymphos to sit on our faces and *squeeze*!"

Cromby, ever the gentleman, tipped an avuncular look toward the waitress, busy clearing dessert plates. The Wednesday Night Club waited politely until she was gone, then exploded in snorts and hiccups of glee. In short order the talk turned to wild parties they remembered, to the heroic performances of a notorious Amazon from the women's school, and thence to the exotic delights of Bangkok, a city whose charms, it turned out, not only

Mikulski but also Hodge and Freeman had had occasion to sample during travels in the Far East. The Chairman smiled, glancing at his watch. At eleven o'clock, in a special attraction he himself had arranged, a stripper dressed as a college security guard was due to walk through the door, handcuff Lowery to his chair, and do nasty things to him.

"Hey you guys!" he saluted them all, raising his glass yet again. "This is the life, ain't it?"

The group had kicked things off the day before with a late-afternoon stroll around the college. Caught in mid-September splendor, the campus called forth agreeable shivers of memory. The six could muster little sense of connection, however, to its current denizens, highly evolved creatures capering about in strangely hacked haircuts, nose rings, black pants, and designer T-shirts protesting various global outrages. They found it a stark contrast to the woodsy comfort of their own era, with its trusty blue jeans and down vests; the whole school seemed caught in a weird ideology of fashion and hurt feelings. The Wednesday Nighters stood perplexed before a bulletin board proclaiming lesbian defense groups, Third World councils, a gender studies symposium on something called "Cross-Dressing and the Construction of Eros in the Elizabethan Drama." "Doesn't anyone around here study anything like history anymore?" asked Lowery, who, truth be told, had spent more time as an undergraduate analyzing his pitching motion in the mirror than hitting the books in the library.

For the lowdown they turned to Green, their academic. "Everything's more . . . politicized nowadays," the English professor said, shrugging. "There's a kind of . . . self-consciousness."

Freeman shook his head. "Hey, I'd be self-conscious too, if I went around all day with a ring in my nose!"

"They at least doing some decent drugs?" asked Hodge, only to be hooted down by the rest, who reminded him that if he hadn't smoked away so many brain cells over the years he'd be in the White House by now.

The biggest change from their era, of course, was the presence of females on campus. A rumor of youthful beauty seemed to float about the school like the scent of fresh bread, and the group trailed it helplessly. In the snack bar at the new student center they speculated on the smorgasbord of libido that was campus life in the nineties.

"Jesus, think about the dorms!" Mikulski drew his bushy eyebrows lewdly together. " 'Hi, I'm your neighbor, wanna screw?' "

"Whaddya mean, neighbor?" said Lowery. "Roommate!"

"Do they room together?"

"Hell, they *shower* together!"

"No!" "You're kidding me!" "Say it ain't so!"

This time Green, whose school was a women's college, could offer no definitive word; and so in the glorious light of six o'clock they marched, puffed up like conquering heroes, to Wiggins Hall, their old dorm.

In the basement they found that renovation had obliterated their former lair in an antiseptic dazzle of carpet and fluorescent light. A circular TV den bestrode the middle of the room, the set playing to empty leather couches. Like a dowser hunting the ghost of water, Hodge wandered to the corner where their own vile sofa had stood, amid a chaos of old beer bottles and grease-stained pizza boxes.

"Man oh man," he said, remembering. "Did this place reek, or what?"

"It reeked all right," cried Freeman. "Of Mikulski!"

But their chairman was already on the stairs. "Shower time, gentlemen!" he called back. "Soap me up, Susie!"

Two flights up, they bunched before the very bathroom where they themselves had once brushed and combed and shaved. Sure enough, inside someone was showering. They listened to the hiss and patter of water.

"Well?" said Mikulski. "Are we men or are we wusses?"

"Tell you what, guys." Green took a step backward. "I'm gonna wait outside. This is getting a little racy for me."

The professor bowed out with a smile and a wave. As the remaining five stood vacillating, a door down the hall opened and a girl stepped out, carrying a bowl of popcorn.

"Um, excuse me," inquired Freeman, "but can you tell me where the men's room is?"

The girl tipped her head. "Right there."

"Ah, I see, I see." The barrel-chested little lawyer nodded like a puppet. "And, uh, is that also the, ah, the . . . um . . . ah . . ."

"See, we used to go here, back in the old days," Mikulski stepped in, "and I guess we're, well, kinda curious how you feel sharing bathrooms—you know, with guys."

Cromby turned away, sighing, and Hodge grinned as the girl looked the Chairman up and down with the faintest shimmer of a smile.

"That depends," she said slowly, "on the guy."

Without waiting for a reply she walked on, slaloming through them with her bowl of popcorn; further down the hall she knocked on a door which opened and swallowed her in a burst of hearty male greeting.

Mikulski's mouth hung open.

"That does it," he said. "I'm coming back here. Special student. I don't care what the hell I study."

The five clomped their way down the stairs at the end of the hall.

"You're a married guy, Mack," reminded Cromby. "You've got kids. You're a respected member of the community."

"You're a *dentist,* man!" Hodge clapped the Chairman on the shoulder. "It's your karma!"

Outside, Green was waiting on the dorm steps, gazing thoughtfully across the quad. "So," he said, "did you find the fountain of youth?"

Mikulski glared at him. "You used to be good for a laugh, Greenie. What the hell happened?"

The English teacher removed his glasses and polished them with his handkerchief, a tactic from his years in the classroom. "Well, I guess the question is what kind of laugh one wants to be good for, right?"

He put his glasses back on and looked probingly around. Nodding, mumbling, the group shoved off toward town and the inn.

In their marital arrangements the Wednesday Nighters spanned the spectrum from stoic misery to desperate bliss. Bliss was the lot of Lowery, at thirty-five marrying a twenty-two-year-old he'd met on a Caribbean weekend and hastily proposed to. Misery, on the other hand, had been Cromby's; the Gorgeous One had made the mistake of marrying someone even more handsome than himself, a would-be movie star who relentlessly cheated on him, bringing torment he'd needed the better part of a decade to extract himself from. Hodge was luckier. The Californian was well matched with his wife, an HMO manager years older than he who loved nothing more than to come home from the office and relax with her husband and a joint in bed, and who furthermore was happily supporting him through the interminable legal acrimony into which his relationship with his former business partner had crumbled. In Chicago, meanwhile, Freeman had married a successful sculptor whom he slavishly venerated, receiving obscure pleasure, after a day spent wrangling with corporate contracts, from being ordered around the house like a butler and lectured to over dinner on modern art, which he knew nothing about.

Of the club's two fathers, Green presented the happier prospect. The professor was snugly lodged in a brick house with two daughters, a wife who baked bread and kept him up on the *New York Review of Books,* and a view across rolling Virginia farms to his women's college, where the occasional advances of his students—all so far resisted—were erasing a long-standing anxiety about his looks. Mikulski's situation was trickier. Five years earlier the Chairman had surprised the rest by marrying not the sheeny bimbo they'd predicted, but an intelligent and vaguely boyish PE instructor at a local junior college. In short order the couple produced two children, inducing in Mikulski a trapped feeling he regularly bemoaned to drinking pals, implying he'd been somehow duped into matrimony by his wily wife. In fact, the intriguing question was why his wife had married him. Though he didn't know it, she'd been on the rebound from an affair with, of all people, another woman, and was eager both to nail down an ambiguous sexual identity and to have children—

purposes to which Mikulski, whom she'd met in a weekly volleyball game, was conveniently suited.

But all that was far from the private room at the Squire where the six now sat, swilling champagne and anticipating the arrival, due any minute now, of the stripper.

The stripper had caused unexpected dissension in the ranks. Mikulski, telephoning around, had been disappointed to find Hodge indifferent and Green opposed. The Chairman studied Green now, deep in conversation with Lowery. What could Larry Lowery possibly be saying that was so profound? Nothing, he decided; it was just Green and his new, oh-so-serious self. It irked Mikulski, the professor's solemn nodding and frowning, the earnest stutter he was sure hadn't been there fifteen years before. He also didn't remember Green being so young and trim looking.

"Hey Greenie," he called down the table. "What's the situation at your school these days? They kick your ass outta there if they catch you diddling one of your students?"

"Yeah," said Freeman. "You got one of those guideline deals —you know, those step-by-step things where the guy has to ask, 'Want me to take off your shirt now? Want me to take off my underwear now?' "

"Do you desire me to lick your earlobe at this particular moment in time?" queried Hodge, as usual adding his own special twist.

Tittering, the five amused themselves with variations on the guideline theme while Green sat brooding. Lowery shook his head. "What about these cases where some guy asks a chick out a coupla times, takes her out, then wakes up to find his mug shot all over campus saying he's a rapist! How about that?"

"Harsh," said Cromby, wincing. "Tough world for dating."

Green interrupted. "Well, it *is* a tough world. Always has been."

At the head of the table Mikulski sat envisioning a professor's life, that endless succession of squash matches, vacations and free lunch. "Now what the hell does *that* mean, 'it's a tough world'?" he bristled.

Green turned to face him. "I mean the world women live in, Bill." Cheeks afire, he summarized the injustices women from time immemorial had suffered. For centuries the law had been wielded as a tool to keep them down. Now it was being levered the other way, and men didn't like it. "I don't like it myself," he said stoically. "But I accept it. How can I not?"

The others stared at their fingernails, all but Mikulski. "Yeah, you accept it all right, Greenie," he snorted. "Like the time you sleazed that scrawny little girl at Smith and then blew her off the next morning when you got a good look at her, for instance?"

Sensing conflict, Cromby weighed in with a gracious smile. "It all used to be so much simpler, didn't it? Guy likes girl, calls her up, they go out, fall in love. . . . Nowadays you both have to bring your lawyer along." He turned to Freeman. "No offense, Mickey."

"Hey." The lawyer waved a hand. "We'll take it where we get it."

The others chuckled; but Green couldn't let go. It pained him to think about the girl at Smith. He recalled a pale rabbity face, a string of strained phone calls, his own hot relief when she'd finally gotten the hint and stopped calling. "Look," he said now, boffing his fist on the table. "What's wrong with guidelines anyway? I mean, the Bill of Rights—there's a set of guidelines for you!"

But Mikulski had the upper hand. "Greenie," he cried with open glee. "Wake up, buddy! *Guidelines* for sex? That's like . . ." He scoured his brain for a figure of speech. "Like trying to put a straitjacket on a jellyfish!"

Quickly Green was ready with a counter-analogy; but the image of the straitjacketed jellyfish proved too much for the other Wednesday Nighters, and the air in the small room grew shaggy with mirth. Green looked over at Mikulski, basking in the laughter. He imagined stepping on the oral surgeon's face, grinding his heel into the soft white jowls. "It's an interesting metaphor, Bill," he remarked, "because if you ask me—"

A loud knock at the door quashed the argument.

"All right Larry, I know you're in there!" a voice, female, intoned from the hall. "You gonna be good, or do I have to come take care of you?"

The men blinked and fell silent. *Me?* Lowery's mouth formed the word.

"Now, who do you think that could be?" asked Freeman, smirking.

"Sounds sorta like Felker, back from the dead," mused Hodge, referring to the harried security guard of yore.

"If so," Mikulski gloated as the door swung open, "then heaven's been pretty goddamn kind!"

The stripper was a pro. In short order she had Lowery reduced to boxer shorts and handcuffed to his chair, and stood before him in her police outfit, one hand on an out-thrust hip, the other waggling a finger in his face. "I hear you've been a *baaaad* boy,

Larry,'' she scolded. Scarlet splotched Lowery's neck and chest. Try as he might, he couldn't chase a humiliating tremor from the smile plastered on his face.

"Oh, he's been *extremely* naughty," chirped Freeman by the window, where he'd hurried to close the curtains—Cromby standing guard at the door, in case the waitress got any ideas.

"You guys," mumbled Lowery. "You guys."

The stripper reached back and pushed a button on a cassette box she'd deposited on the table behind her, and music flooded the room. Gyrating to its silky beat, she began teasing open the buttons of her blue shirt. With a foxy wink she tossed off her outer garments and, shortly thereafter, her exceedingly flimsy inner ones as well.

"Jesus," Mikulski gasped. "That's absolutely the most beautiful sight I've seen in ages."

"Thank you!" said the stripper spryly, her gaze locked in on Lowery. Bending, swaying, she passed closer and closer, swinging herself hypnotically before the shackled and trembling bond salesman. Lowery's eyes goggled out of his head.

"Hey Larr," croaked Freeman. "What's that crawling around in your shorts there, guy?"

"Whaddya want me to do?" In fact, to Lowery's relief, embarrassment so far was winning out over lust for control of his all-too-public anatomy.

And so it went, the woman cavorting about the room, the Wednesday Nighters looking on in various attitudes of rapture. Only Green refused to join in. He sat rigid in his chair, grimacing disapproval. To a man, the other Wednesday Nighters deemed this lofty bearing contrary to the spirit of their reunion. It was a dash of cold water; a weed that needed weeding.

"Come on Greenie, loosen up!" commanded Freeman, to no avail.

At the end of her routine the stripper treated each of them to a democratic stop-and-shimmy. Approaching Green, she plunged her hands in her hair and, elbows up, struck a bunnyish centerfold pose.

"What's the matter?" she cooed. "Don't you like me?"

"No no no," Green murmured. "It's not that. It's just . . . just . . ."

"Hey Greenie," kidded Freeman. "You insulted her feminine charms!"

"That's right," agreed the stripper. She began an intricate pelvic swivel, purling side to side and then fore to aft as well.

"Jeez," sighed Cromby from his spot by the door. "I insulted my ex-wife plenty, and she never did *that*!"

Green's face wore a stricken look as the stripper, flexing backward, lowered herself limbolike and began approaching him knees first.

"Hey Greenie!" said Lowery. "If you can't get into this, buddy, you're already dead!"

"He's not *allowed* to get into it!" Mikulski jeered. "It's not in his Faculty Handbook! It's not in his Code!" They taunted him as the stripper limboed closer, their chant echoing in the tiny room: *Gree-nie! Gree-nie! Gree-nie! Gree-nie!*

In fact, behind his mask of composure the professor teetered on the edge of a perilous abandonment. Lust pooled in all corners of his being. Sweat dappled his upper lip, and his body vaguely shook as the stripper, with a deft tug at his lapel, lifted him from his chair. Spellbound, Green watched her perfect form massaging the space between them with a luxurious undulation.

It was unbearable. He thought of his wife, he thought of his little daughters, of his office at the college with its piles of books—he clutched at these images like a drowning man at a spar of wood.

Without breaking rhythm, the stripper reached up, grasped his necktie by the knot and shook it loose a little; and with this simplest of gestures, Green felt the dike inside him crumbling away, unleashing wave after wave of dark desire. Again a vision of his wife and daughters crept to the edge of his mind, but this time he booted it away like a mangy begging cur. Hips and elbows swinging, he shimmied to the music, face to face with the smiling stripper. The Wednesday Nighters hooted and howled.

"Now *there's* the Greenie I know!" rasped Mikulski.

"Greenie, you animal!" Freeman was beside himself. "Look at him—he's a TOTAL ANIMAL!"

Green hardly heard them. With an audible sigh he ceased clenching, he ceased clutching; after years of holding himself carefully back, the professor tasted the savage bliss of letting go.

A little later, with the stripper paid and gone, the members of the Wednesday Night Club sat indulging a mellow retrospective of their receding but still vivid youth. They were glad, they decided, to have been college students during the seventies, an interval of fun between the religious zeal of the sixties, the yuppie striving of the eighties, and the political correctness of today; they felt nostalgia for their decade with its innocent pleasures.

All agreed the stripper had been an excellent culmination to the weekend. "Where'd you get her, Mack?" asked Freeman. "Friend of the wife?"

"Yeah, *right*!" Shaking his head, Mikulski reached for the nearest champagne glass. He pictured his wife doing dishes in the kitchen, and pondered the maw of family life, gaping to swallow him again on the morrow.

"Hey Greenie." Cromby raised a teasing eyebrow. "I think our performer liked you a little, huh guy?"

"Yeah, Greenie, you stud!" teased Freeman.

But Green had fallen into something like a state of mourning. He looked around at the other men slumped in their chairs, swirling remnants of lukewarm champagne in smeared glasses.

"I need some fresh air," he announced, rising and striding across the room.

Outside the night was cool and soothing. Green removed his necktie, loosened earlier by the stripper, and unbuttoned his top shirt button. Up on the hill, the tower clock of the college chapel rang 1 A.M. The professor glanced back toward the Squire's Nest and the room where his comrades sat. Any time now Lowery would trot out his famous bullfrog imitation, a freakish anatomical trick whereby he bugged his eyes and blew his neck in-out, in-out, like a bellows. *The world begins in tragedy,* Green ruminated, *and ends in farce.* Who had said that? Nietzsche? Nabokov? He wasn't sure. Literature always seemed to desert him just when he needed it most.

He looked up from these musings to see the stripper, leaning against a car not a dozen feet away. In the dim light Green studied her: arms alluringly crossed, hand floating up to bring a sip of cigarette to her exquisite face. The professor's heart leapt. Crazy though it might be, he'd had the feeling earlier, as the woman had stood before him, her gaze smoldering into his, that she'd pierced some fragile membrane in his soul, and he in hers, both of them penetrating to regions of tender sympathy. Here was his chance to let her know he was different from the rest; that he hadn't lusted after her in the brute way of a Mikulski or a Freeman. Taking a deep breath, he propelled himself out onto the sidewalk.

The stripper seemed lost in thought as Green, approaching, aimed what he hoped was a warm but respectful grin in her direction. He trawled by, unnoticed, and hove to at a No Parking sign a little further along to recoup his forces for a second pass. As he stood puzzling over what to say, the woman reached for another cigarette. Groping in his pocket for his lighter, Green launched himself at a half-trot back along the walk.

"Need a light?" he said, brandishing the gadget.

Her glance, though friendly, was devoid of recognition. Green waited while she blew a plume of smoke into the night air. Again her eyes sifted blankly over his.

"I, uh, I really enjoyed the, uh, show," he managed, nodding back toward the inn. "Do you . . . Have you been doing this a long time?"

"Too long," the stripper said, flicking ash. "Much too long."

Once more Green waited, but nothing followed. With chagrin he felt himself sinking into the blurry anonymity of customers who had paid; of men in ties. He opened his mouth to protest, but succeeded only in emitting a slight strangled noise. Face flaming, he pocketed his lighter and lunged off into the night.

For her part, the stripper had barely registered the encounter. She had other things on her mind. A hairdresser in a grimy mill town a half hour to the south, she'd started doing shows years before on a dare, and it had become a lucrative little hobby. She had a three-year-old daughter, and while stripping didn't strike her as the most motherly thing to be doing, the money was good and the work easy. Her boyfriend, Fred, handled the business and advertising; all she had to do was undress.

At the moment she was wondering exactly where Fred was. Tonight she'd taken one look at the inn—BMWs out front, a lobby with a fireplace—and knew there wouldn't be any trouble. No one would touch her, and the money would be better if Fred wasn't lurking by the door. He'd been only too glad to oblige her—heading into town, he'd said, for a pizza. Now she wondered just what that pizza had become. She'd promised her babysitter she'd be back by 12:30, and here it was 1 A.M. already and no Fred. She decided to set the end of her cigarette as a deadline, not just for tonight but for forever; and powering her way down the smoke she smiled a wicked little smile to think of Fred out there enjoying himself, unaware of the death sentence hanging over his head.

Green, meanwhile, had stumbled blindly off, cutting across the lawn between the inn and a pair of darkened, stately homes. The professor's lungs were working in choppy little bursts, and he forced himself to take a few deep breaths and relax.

He emerged on an unfamiliar street along the edge of campus. Through maples overhead, streetlights spilled gently swaying shadows. A group of students passed on the sidewalk, twittering like birds, and shortly afterward another. No one noticed him. A third troop clamored by, and Green, drifting aimlessly along, began to imagine he was invisible. It was as if through some horror-movie metamorphosis his blood and matter were draining away, preparing him to join a spectral procession of dead and departed graduates returned to haunt the campus forever.

The vision left him strangely thrilled. Everything, he reflected, everything is temporary: youth, love and family, even literature itself would pass. The professor's eyes brimmed. He felt himself winging upward, as if toward some transcendent Archimedean point from which life and its predicaments could finally be grasped, the shape seen whole. Eyes closed, he stood dead still, listening for whatever message the invisible choirs might be lofting back from eternity. But all he heard were the inconspicuous sounds of night in the exurbs: a bus somewhere steaming to a stop; the breeze playing in the treetops; an obscure crepitation, as of distant gunfire. Remoter still, he picked up a mysterious and familiar noise, one he'd noticed before in his life, shadowing the edge of his consciousness like a kind of aural déjà vu. He listened harder, and then there it was; it sounded distinctly like laughter.

THE REPRIEVE

THE DAY SEEMED to Krieger like any other day—
that was precisely the problem. Finishing practice at
five, he had jogged as usual from the boathouse to
the gym. *Hey Jake, what's shaking?* he'd said to the
equipment man. "Another day, another dollar," the
old man answered, pushing clean sweats across the
counter. "Just don't tear the whole town down tonight, okay, Coach?!" Only ten minutes later, under the shower, the spray pleasantly needling his
back, did Krieger understand. He laughed out loud,
and the three or four students in the shower room
glanced at him quizzically.

"It's my birthday," he explained. "Forgot all
about it."

For nine years Krieger had been coaching crew at

the university. Though young for the job at twenty-four, he'd been an NCAA pairs champion, and they'd hired him. He liked the life. He liked standing on the porch with his German shepherd, Rocket, watching the sun rise over the river, or running country roads on an autumn afternoon. He'd never considered himself lonely. But now, walking home across the campus, past students tossing Frisbees and loafing in happy aimless herds, he wondered what it meant when the only person in the world who knew it was your birthday was a seventy-year-old equipment man who read it off an ID card. Was there something wrong in that? he wondered, something he should be worried about? Approaching his house, he suffered an unsettling vision of himself as others saw him: a man who lived alone with his dog; who entertained rarely; who plied the river at all ungodly hours. *There goes Krieger,* people thought, *that fanatic.*

When he opened the door, Rocket hurtled out, furiously wagging; but Krieger went straight inside. He had a call to make, one he'd been putting off.

He'd met her three weeks before, at a party thrown by one of his former rowers in a city halfway across the state. It was a loud party, foggy with cigarette smoke, the crowd ten years younger than Krieger. He took refuge on the balcony, and was surprised when she came out to join him—he'd noticed her inside, a short woman with jet black hair and a sly, laughing look. "I'm Maria," she said, offering her hand. "Massage therapist, failed grad student, and at the moment slightly intoxicated." Krieger himself was tall and boxy, with thick reddish hair, and believed, from his experience, that opposites attract. "Krieger," he said. "Carl Krieger." He took her hand. "Crew coach. And all too sober."

They had talked, the city lights stretched out below them.

Suddenly she'd grabbed his arm and wheeled him around. "Carl," she said. "I need your help on a question of character." Through the window she pointed to a slouching giant deep in conversation with a stringy blond girl. The giant—Krieger put him at 6′4″, 250 lbs—was Maria's roommate and former boyfriend, Jack. Jack was a grad student in philosophy: a genius, she said, but impossible to live with. He never made plans; he refused to lock the apartment; he drowned out his cigarettes in Coke bottles and let the dishes pile up until she did them. As they watched, he made a vehement point to the blond girl, raking his hands back through his long hair and grimacing as if the heat of his ideas was scorching his brain. Krieger knew the type. "Some people are actually a lot less complicated than they think," he said, choosing his words with care. Maria had laughed then—*You know, Carl,* she'd said, *you're right!*—and before going in she'd handed him her number, written in a looping script on the back of a bank deposit slip.

It took him an hour, but after searching the whole house he finally found the slip—crumpled up in the wastepaper basket in his office. He sat by the phone for a moment, considering what to say. Then he dialed.

To his relief, she answered, and not the boyfriend.

"Hello Maria," he said. "This is Krieger." A long, sinking silence followed; he resisted a powerful urge to hang up. "We met at a party a couple of weeks ago," he stumbled on. "I . . . I guess maybe you—"

"Oh," she broke in, *"Carl."* She laughed, then lowered her voice a level. "God, Carl," she said. "What *took* you so long?"

★   ★   ★

For three months they traveled back and forth, seeing each other. It was a long haul for dinner and a movie; Krieger would leave midmorning and return, dead tired, at 3 A.M. Soon they began to spend whole weekends together. For Krieger these times were full of surprises. Maria knew things, like the names of flowers or the directors of foreign films, and he listened closely when she talked. In a fish restaurant at the shore she got him to try oysters. *I've never been big on this stuff,* he said as she speared the pale mass with a fork and held it out to him, quivering and dripping. She shook with laughter. "God, Carl," she said, "I wish you could see yourself!"

He found her mysterious. In bed she had a way of staring at him, wide-eyed and mute; then, suddenly giggling, she'd climb over on top, her long hair hanging down and enveloping his face like a dark tent.

The summer passed, and with September came the annual onslaught of students and the start of another year. Krieger was pleased by his life's new shape. On Sunday evenings when he and Maria parted, he felt aloneness had once again been warded off, and real life with its workaday tasks could safely resume.

The one shadow in all of it was Jack. Ex-boyfriends, Krieger's instincts told him, should quietly disappear. But Jack was still very much in the picture. Maria, in fact, still lived with him. Jack refused to give up his apartment, she reported, simply because the two of them weren't sleeping together anymore. They had decided to "be reasonable" and continue to share the place while she looked for something she could afford.

The world was full of people, Krieger knew, who operated perfectly well by rules he himself couldn't begin to fathom. Still, the situation seemed unnatural. With no car of her own, Maria used Jack's, a rust-riddled VW Beetle plastered with bumper stickers for Greenpeace and festooned inside with animal statues and Mardi Gras beads. Krieger hated seeing it parked in his driveway. Visiting her at her apartment was worse. He hadn't the foggiest idea how to act when Jack greeted him at the door, a look of absent politeness on his face. The big man spent whole days reading in the kitchen, sitting with a huge foot up on the table, smoking one cigarette after another and stubbing them out in a blue plastic ashtray pocked with melted brown spots. Krieger thought of the beating his lungs and bronchials were taking. Nights, Jack slept on a foldout couch in the living room, crossing right past their bed to get to the bathroom.

"Doesn't he hate my guts?" Krieger asked Maria.

"He says he's evolved out of jealousy," she informed him. "He says I need a father figure, and you're it."

"Give me a break," Krieger said.

As soon as she found something decent, she assured him, she'd move. But he began to wonder how hard she was looking. It irked him to see her things and Jack's stashed together in the bathroom—their two toothbrushes leaning on one another like old pals in the pink plastic cup.

Things came to a head in the fall. One Saturday night he and Maria were asleep when Jack, coming home dead drunk at 3 A.M., stumbled into their room, tripped over the corner of the bed, and toppled headlong on the floor. A minute later, Krieger heard him throwing up in the bathroom.

"This is not healthy," he told Maria the next morning.

"What isn't?" She was sitting in bed, eating a croissant.

Krieger waved his hands. "This guy lends you his car to visit your new boyfriend, you share the same apartment, you share the same *shower*—"

"So?"

"So?!" He opened the door to reveal Jack asleep on the couch, mouth gaping. "I mean, look at this. It's a mess! It's crazy!"

"You're pacing, Carl."

It was true; he was. He sat down next to her and tried to get hold of his thoughts. "This whole thing's making me nervous as hell."

She took his hand. "I'm sorry," she said. "But this is how things are right now. I mean, my life is down here, and you're up there."

From the front room he could hear Jack snoring. He closed his eyes and rubbed the bridge of his nose. "Look, we've gotta do something about this," he said. "I'm not sleeping nights."

On the first of October, she moved in.

At the outset there were adjustments to be made. Over the years he'd become the type of person, he saw, whose eye went right to that long black hair in the bathtub, that spot of dirt squashed into the carpet. Living by himself he'd had a rule, no shoes in the house. But you couldn't go around making rules for another person—that was the whole point. Then there was the sleep problem. Maria liked to bury herself in a mountain of quilts, beneath which she generated a volcano-like warmth; during the night it seeped out until Krieger, engulfed, woke sweating and kicking at the covers. For her part, she was horrified to learn that he actually rose at 5:30 A.M. four times a week, for an hour of single sculling on the river. The transition from sleep was too abrupt, she said, and was sure to wreak havoc with his body's natural rhythms.

The other issue was Rocket: she was allergic to him. Reluctantly Krieger fixed up a place in the basement. "Sorry guy," he said as he took the dog down. He rubbed the big ears. "Maybe you should've tried that new aftershave after all."

These problems negotiated, things moved swiftly. It seemed to Krieger that Maria made more friends in her first six weeks in town than he had in his first six years. Her massage business thrived. Arriving home he would hear the soft music and wonder whom he'd find stretched out on the living room floor. One day it was Ellen Petarski, the women's lacrosse coach. She laughed, looking up at him. "You live here too, Krieger?" she said.

"No, *she* lives here too," he answered, smiling.

His social life, latched to hers, took a sharp upward swing. As autumn moved into winter they fell in with a roving party of assistant professors and grad students, people his age or slightly younger, that touched down once a week for dinner at someone's house. Always the main course was something unpronounceable and fiendishly spiced, served with detailed accounts of the host's travels in far corners of the world. Krieger enjoyed the group without ever feeling quite at home in it. Often during dinner he found himself inwardly hung up on some vexing, basic fact, like whether Spain or Portugal had colonized Brazil, while the conversation careened onward around him, allusions and jokes spinning off at high speed. It was unnerving. *How do they know all this stuff?* he asked Maria one night in February as they drove home at 1 A.M. through a wet snow.

It's just talk, she reassured him. *They skim a book, they get the names down, the ideas.* He made a noncommittal noise, and she smiled. *Most people aren't like you, Carl. If you had to read all those books, you'd really* read *them.*

A half hour later they lay in bed, her head resting on his chest. Something, he wasn't sure what, was still nagging at him.

"Hey," he said. "Why did you come out to the balcony that night, anyway? At the party, I mean."

"It was the way you looked," she answered after a moment.

"Oh yeah?"

"Yeah. I mean, not just that you were good-looking or something. More like you were . . . solid-looking. Like you had a real life."

He thought about it. "So then you come up here and find I have these bad qualities."

"Mmmm?" He had dragged her back from the brink of sleep. "Bad what?"

"Bad qualities. I'm too intense. I don't notice things like you do." He paused. "Antisocial qualities."

"Mmmm . . ."

Krieger wanted to talk, but her voice was growing creamy; within seconds her breathing lengthened and she was asleep.

For a long while he lay awake. Outside, the snow had changed to rain—he could hear the drops splatting on the roof. Having grown up in New England, where snow was snow, it annoyed him to live now in the kind of border climate where everything was mixed, and the best February could muster was a gray sopping slush. His head vaguely ached. The strong red wines that were the group's drink of choice had a way of disguising their effects, so that often he had no idea how drunk he really was until hours afterward when he'd wake in the middle of the night, temples throbbing, tongue swollen and dry. More than once he'd been forced to forgo his morning sprints on the river. This bothered him.

His arm, pinioned by Maria's head, had fallen asleep. He flexed his fingers, gasping as tingles raced along the nerves. Listening to the rain outside, he felt a surge of restlessness, as if the time was overdue when some important decision had to be made. But he had no idea at all what that decision was supposed to be.

The next weekend he took her up to New Hampshire—a trip he'd been promising for months. They drove by the house where he'd grown up, and where his father had run a hardware store; then past the famous private school where his folks, saving every penny, had sent him as a day student. Maria whistled, looking at the immaculate brick buildings and the serpentine walks crowded with kids in fancy overcoats and down jackets.

"You little *preppy,* Carl!" she laughed.

"Who?" said Krieger, who had always felt like an outsider at the school, a townie. "Me?"

At the nursing home they stood by his father's bed while the old man lay there sticking out his lower lip at them. Krieger recounted how, after his mother had died, his father had started selectively pretending not to hear people. After a while he really had stopped hearing them.

"Glad to meet you, Mr. Krieger!" Maria said, leaning in front of him.

When she went off to find a bathroom, Krieger put his hand on his father's shoulder. "Hey Dad," he said, "can we talk?"

The old man paid no attention, and Krieger felt another layer of hopelessness being papered over the memory of his real, living father. "Come on, Dad," he said. "I came up here to tell you something!" He passed his hand back and forth until his father's eyes locked on to the motion. "Dad, you remember our confirmed old bachelor conversation, right? How you were afraid I'd never find the right girl and so on? Remember that?"

A bead of saliva welled in a corner of the old man's mouth, then broke and flowed down the deep crease in his chin. His eyes followed the white uniform of a passing nurse with a look of sorrow.

"Oh Christ," Krieger muttered. He wiped his father's face, then squashed the Kleenex into a ball and threw it aside.

Turning, he saw Maria approaching, gazing at him fixedly.

Back in the car she put her arm around him. But he said nothing, and she took it away.

"What was going on in there, anyway?" she asked.

Krieger shook his head. He started the car, and they drove out through the town, its streets hulked high with plowed snow. He remembered how as a child, waking from the recurring dream of a shapeless, nameless dread, he'd wander into his parents' room and stand trembling at the foot of their bed. *What's wrong, honey?* his mother would say, and he'd stand there, unable to describe the thing, until his father would roll over and order him back to his room.

"What *is* it, Carl?" Maria said.

"I don't know," he answered, staring straight ahead. "I really don't." He accelerated onto the highway. Everything was fine, he told himself, everything was going according to plan; and yet he couldn't shake a sense of some ragged trouble lying in wait for them around the next curve.

★   ★   ★

One evening in March, it happened. They were in the kitchen eating spaghetti, the TV in the living room making the background babble Maria claimed essential to her peace of mind, when Krieger looked up from his plate to see her face going pale in big white splotches.

"You okay?" he said, alarmed.

She pushed her chair back. "I just heard something."

He put down his fork and followed her into the living room. On TV the local news was giving details of a plane crash in the Bahamas. *Once again,* said the anchorman, *two state men are believed to have been on the doomed aircraft. . . .* He gave one name, and the second name was Jack's.

"Oh Jesus," Maria said. "Oh Jesus no."

She went to the phone and dialed. Krieger, still wearing his napkin tucked as a bib into his shirt, sat down beside her on the couch. Someone answered on the other end of the phone—he could hear the tiny voice.

"Lorraine," Maria said. "It's me."

He watched her hair up close. Each ray of light that hit it seemed to break apart and scatter itself in specks of color. *Oh God,* he heard her saying. *Please tell me this isn't true.*

Strange things began to happen in the next days. Waking at 3 A.M., he found her sitting by the window. She was agonizing over Jack's funeral, she said, over whether she ought to go. Seeing her upset, he wondered aloud whether the funeral might upset her more. Her words leaped in the darkness. "Is that what you think a funeral's for—to make you *feel* good?"

She'd never spoken like that to him before. "Okay," he said. "Then maybe you should go."

She didn't, and the funeral wasn't mentioned again. But things stayed tense. Krieger chalked it up to mourning—and yet at times he was sure he felt something personal in it. Her eyes, landing on him, frowned. In bed she turned away, presenting the smooth white shell of her back. *Hey,* he wanted to say, *I didn't kill the guy.*

Coming home from crew practice one day a week after Jack's death, he found her sitting on the living room floor, weeping.

"Why was he on that plane in the first place?" she wailed. "He never went on any tropical vacation before."

Krieger knelt. "Listen to me. I know you feel guilty about how things went last year with Jack, but that doesn't mean—"

"Oh *please,* Carl. Don't analyze me." Tears poured out of her. "Jack never analyzed me," she whispered.

"No?" His face flamed. "Like that father figure crap, for instance?"

Hate gleamed in her eyes.

After that, they both avoided Jack's name. But Krieger could feel the dead man's presence between them, growing larger and more heroic each day. It was as if all Jack's bad qualities had died along with him, leaving only his boldness, sensitivity, and legendary brilliance. Krieger could sense the life he was offering Maria being checked against her old life with Jack. It appeared she'd been keeping certain judgments to herself. The house was too neat. They went to bed too early. Their social life sucked.

"What do you mean?" said Krieger, incredulous. He had the feeling they lived at the center of a furious social whirlwind.

"I guess I just expect too much," she said, turning away.

On a Friday night he took her to a movie. It was an action film, and as the shootings and batterings piled up he could feel her squirming. *This is horrible!* she whispered. Finally she grabbed her jacket and left.

Out on the sidewalk he found her standing in the bright light under the marquee. There was a heavy silence during which she refused to meet his gaze. "Let me guess," he said finally. "Jack wouldn't have taken you to that, right?"

She shrugged. "You said it, not me."

"Listen, Maria." He glanced around; they were alone. "Do you know that whenever we go out, there are *three* of us—you, me, and Jack? I mean, I can practically *hear* the guy."

"That's your problem," she said. "I can't help what you hear."

Krieger's anger flared. "This is ridiculous," he said. "I don't want a threesome here, okay?"

"Well, you had one before, so welcome back!" She turned and started hustling away into the dark. He pictured her naked on the bed in her old apartment, and Jack sitting in the next room.

"Oh great!" he shouted after her. "That's just *terrific*!"

That night she slept at Ellen Petarski's, and the next day, when she came back, Krieger apologized. She accepted, then reached into her pocket, pulled out a pack of cigarettes, and shook one out.

"Old habit," she said. Krieger turned away, shaking his head. It troubled him to think how much he didn't know about her.

Other things troubled him too. His crews were having a dismal season. His best varsity rower quit, and even as he dealt the boy a stinging rebuke, Krieger was inwardly blaming himself. It was a question of intensity. Over the months his own rowing had dwindled to once a week, and he could feel himself growing slack, losing his legs in the sprints. As if to compensate, he drove his rowers harder, keeping them overtime on the river; they looked at him from the boats with blunt and sullen stares.

Coming home from these lackluster practices, he continued to find the living room occupied by Maria and her massage clients. The fruity odor of the massage oils followed him upstairs, spreading throughout the second floor. Krieger found it hard to believe that someone so disturbed by the mild scent of a dog had no problem whatsoever with the heavy smell of those oils. One afternoon he went to take Rocket for a walk, and coming up out of the basement the dog wriggled past him into the house. For five minutes he spread his scent around before Krieger collared him. When Maria came back from her aerobics class, she noticed nothing. The next day he let the dog upstairs for a full hour, barely managing to herd him back down into the basement as Maria came up the front walk. This time she frowned and walked around the house, twitching her nose.

"Did that Rocket get up here?" she asked.

"Not that I'm aware of," he said.

He was surprised how easy it was to lie to her. It made him feel guilty; and as a gesture of peace he took her out to their favorite Italian place, where they drank a big bottle of Chianti and managed to get through the evening without even a veiled reference to Jack. At one point Krieger held his hand out on the table, and she put hers alongside, offering a wan smile when he stroked her palm. He took it as a small but welcome sign of progress.

In May the miserable crew season ended, and suddenly he had time on his hands. Each summer it was his habit to choose a few big reading projects; this year he was starting with Trevelyan's

History of England. It was a calm Friday evening as he settled in his leather chair in the living room. Maria sat sprawled on the couch, reading a magazine. Seven weeks had passed since Jack's death, and Krieger had the feeling things were finally returning to normal. He was relieved to have the disarray of the spring behind him. Hefting the massive book, he paged through the chapters, getting a sense of the task ahead. What he liked about history was the orderly way eras and movements yielded to each other, creating a visible bridge from distant times and places to the here and now.

Maria sighed loudly. She was flipping through the magazine, licking her index finger and slapping it against the pages.

"Are you going to be reading all night?" she asked.

Krieger shrugged. "Not all night," he said.

He watched out of the corner of his eye as she tossed the magazine aside and went to the window. Dormitory lights sparkled in the distance—a city rising abruptly out of farmland. The breeze carried in a waft of rap music. Classes were over, and the campus was one huge party.

"I wouldn't mind dancing," she said. "I never go dancing anymore."

"There's probably not a heckuva lot of actual dancing going on over there." Krieger told her about the year students had bought a couple of junk cars, wheeled them onto campus, and staged a sledgehammer party. At the end of it they'd doused the cars with gas and torched them.

But she wasn't listening. "I used to dance a lot," she said. "All the time, in fact." She was sitting on the windowsill, her head pressing against the screen.

"It's so terrible, Carl," she whispered. "So terrible."

Weariness overwhelmed him; he'd thought they were past this by now. For a long moment he gazed at her back. He tried to return to his book, but couldn't concentrate; the sentences swarmed on the page.

The next afternoon, heading across campus toward the boathouse, Krieger found his mind wrenched from Trevelyan's handling of the clans of Wales. A familiar figure was sitting at the outdoor café—a huge figure reading and smoking a cigarette, one foot up on the low terrace wall.

He drifted over as if in a trance.

"Hello there," Jack said. "Figured I might run into one of you."

"What . . . what are you doing here?" Krieger managed.

"Using the library. Is that allowed?"

"No. I mean, I . . ." There was only one way to say it. "I thought you were dead."

"Hey, I can't do everything for you, pal." The big man squinted up at him, and his look softened. "Don't you read the newspaper?"

He hadn't been on the plane that went down, he explained; it had all been a big mix-up. He'd had a ticket, true, but a fender bender in Miami had kept him from the airport, and then later the airline had mistakenly announced—

He stopped. "Wait a sec. Didn't Maria . . . ? Does Maria still . . . ?"

Krieger looked at his watch. "Look, can you still be here in fifteen minutes?" Jack nodded. "Okay," Krieger said. "Just don't budge."

Jogging home seemed to take no time at all—one second he was leaving the student center, the next he was in his driveway.

He found Maria in the backyard, digging in her new garden with a trowel.

"Guess who I just saw," he told her. "Jack. I just saw Jack."

Her hand stopped. Then it started again.

"Did you hear what I said?"

She stared at him and slowly shook her head.

"Maria. Jack is sitting over at the student center right now, reading a book. *Your* Jack. I just talked to him."

When she kept on digging, Krieger grabbed her arm, jerked her up, and pulled her toward the car.

"What the . . . ?" she sputtered. "What are you doing?"

"Come on," he said, opening the door and pushing her in.

"I don't know what the *hell* you're up to, Carl," she hissed as he got in beside her. "But it better be damn good."

They rode over in taut silence and parked by the student center. Rounding the corner of the building, they stood where Krieger had stood.

"Oh God." Maria ducked back. "Oh God oh God oh God."

Krieger explained what Jack had told him. He took her hands and massaged them while she calmed down. "Go ahead now," he said.

He waited a few minutes, then followed. She was sitting on Jack's lap, her head buried in his shoulder. Krieger went over and put the car keys on the table.

"I'll be at home," he said.

Back at the house he paced restlessly. Picturing Maria on Jack's lap, the big man repeating *It's all right, it's all right,* he felt the way he used to at a regatta, moments before the start—arms and legs twitching, ready to go.

After a while he heard his car in the drive. When she came through the door her face was red and swollen, as if her allergies were acting up.

"So," Krieger said. "He lives."

She rubbed her eyes. "Let's talk, Carl."

"Who—the two of us or the three of us?"

"You're pissed at me," she said. "I know you're pissed at me."

He went to the window and glanced out. "So where is he?"

"He left. He went home." Krieger could feel her eyes on his back. "Hey. Carl. Look at me."

He turned around.

"It's *you* I want, Carl. Not Jack. That was just some morbid thing I was doing. You were wonderful about it, and I was such a shit."

Krieger said nothing. A smile came weakly onto her face, fell off, then crept partway back again. "Look," she said. "I'm going out in the garden. When you feel like talking, come on out. We can start putting this thing back together."

She touched him on the shoulder as she went. He listened to the screen door smack and her feet tread the back stairs.

In the living room he wandered around, straightening pictures and slipcovers. His rowing trophies on the mantel had collected a film of dust, and he wiped it away with a paper towel. The two throw rugs had been moved from their usual places, revealing pale rectangles where for years they had protected the wood from wear and sun. With his foot he slid them back.

Crossing the room, he went out to the screened-in porch and the pile of newspapers. During crew season he liked to keep the papers stacked and in order; at the end of a busy week he usually got around to looking through them. But this year there'd been problems. All too often, sections from one day's paper had ended up mixed in with another's, or had simply vanished. He started through the pile, looking for the days after Jack's reported death. For fifteen minutes he spread the papers out on the floor. Then he found it. Man Gets Reprieve, said the headline. Reports of Death "Greatly Exaggerated," Quips Grad Student.

The page had been folded to make sturdy backing for a crossword puzzle, which had then been shoved, half-completed, into the classifieds.

Krieger brought the paper into the kitchen. With scissors he cut the article out, cutting carefully along each edge, and left it on the table. It annoyed him to think how much grief could have been avoided if his system had only been followed. A little, simple thing, but it would have made a huge difference.

At the kitchen table he tried to get a handle on himself. He felt angry and mean, and didn't much like it. He found his mind wandering back to New Hampshire, to a turtle pond in the woods behind his parents' house. As a boy he had believed that if you could only succeed in separating a turtle cleanly from its shell, a little green man would jump out, happy to be free. A half dozen times up in the woods he had tried to do this, with horrifying results.

Standing, he crossed to the sink and washed the newsprint off his hands, the soap sudsing up a gray lather the color of ash. Through the back window he watched her. She was kneeling, working away with a trowel and a tiny spade. The hole in his yard was getting bigger and bigger. Soon there would be plants, their roots forking and curling deep into the earth.

Krieger went to the basement door. He opened it and looked down into the darkness. There was a friendly jingle of dog tags.

"C'mere Rocket!" he called. "C'mon boy!" He stood aside and smiled as the dog came bounding wide-eyed up the stairs and into the house.

BIG AS LIFE

BY THE TIME they enter the mall it's already well past four, and the whole ride over his son has been so hyper, tapping and jiggling and banging his fists on his legs, *Think he's still there, Dad, huh, think we'll still see him?* that he considers it lucky the boy hasn't peed his pants. Alec races off, heading for the east hall, and he follows along at a measured pace, crossing to the far side to pass the store; the last thing he wants is Jaspers spotting him and coming out to harass him about inventory or some damn thing. Watching his son disappear in the crowd of shoppers, he shakes his head, thinking again about the whole mess. How does he always get himself into squeezes like this? he wonders for the umpteenth time.

All he'd wanted was not to disappoint the boy. It was an afternoon three years ago, they'd been watching a Celtics game, and the sportscaster had mentioned Bird's college days at ISU. His son had piped up, *Hey Dad, that's where you went, right?* and before he knew it, out it had slipped—*Yup, good old Terre Haute, me and the Bird Man*—and Alec had run with it. *You mean you know Larry Bird?! I can't believe you actually know LARRY BIRD!!* He couldn't seem to keep the thing from steamrolling. Watching the Dream Team later in the summer, he and Alec together, they'd see Bird blow a jumper and he'd say, "Jeez, Larry's back's sure hurting today," and the two of them would shake their heads, commiserating with the great player in the twilight of his career. The story grew. He told his son about playing with Bird in a pickup game one day in the gym. One time became half a dozen times. He and Bird became buddies. Bird suggested he go out for the ISU team, and only an old injury kept him from doing so. Only a bum ankle kept him from being Larry Bird's teammate. Alec's eyes went wide.

His wife had been eavesdropping. "Did you really know Larry Bird?" she asked him as they sat in bed. It was one of the nights she was talking to him.

"Well, I don't know exactly if he'd remember me person-ally—"

"I didn't think so." She went back to her book.

"Hey, look, the kid's ten years old. I'm just giving him a card to play, okay?"

But the card was *fake,* she reminded him. What would happen when Alec found that out?

How? he asked. How was Alec supposed to find that out?

Between them hovered the invisible list of her disappointments, from the lack of a second child, to his half-dozen jobs in twice as many years, to the broken promise of moving back East to her beloved New England.

"I did," she said, shrugging.

When the news came that a local charity was sponsoring a wheelchair hoop tournament, and Guess Who was coming to town, his first thought had been to come clean. *Look, Tiger,* he'd say. *About this whole Larry Bird thing . . .* But he pictured his son's face crumpling, and knew he couldn't do it. So he looked for some other way out. First he wrote to Bird himself, c/o the Celtics; no answer. Then he tried calling Bird's restaurant out in Terre Haute. His idea was to get hold of a couple of gift certificates and smuggle them into Bird's hands at the signing session, maybe sending Alec back to the car for something. Bird had a heart, he'd play along. But the gift certificates didn't come. He called the restaurant again, talked to the manager, and waited. Nothing. He was stumped.

His last hope was that he could somehow make the problem just go away. But when his wife found out what he was up to, just a half hour ago out in the kitchen, she was furious. Alec had come bursting into the room, phone in hand. "Daaaad! It was at *two* o'clock, not *four*!" Jamal and Lee had already been there and back. They'd already gotten autographs!

"Jeez, Tiger," he said. "I coulda sworn the paper said four." He looked skeptically at his watch. "I don't know if we can—"

His wife grabbed his arm and pulled him aside. "Now, you listen. You get that boy over there and you get him in, or I swear—!" She left it hanging, and hammered him with a killer of a look. He's used to her eyes telling him he's being selfish or crude, but this was different. This was the way you'd look at a war criminal.

It isn't fair, he thinks now as he makes his way down the mall. There are things his wife just doesn't understand, never will. She doesn't realize being a hero to your kid isn't so cheap when your own father screwed up so bad that when he dropped dead one day, you couldn't even cry. He himself never means to gild the lily so wildly with Alec—but then he sees the awe in his son's eyes and he just can't ease off. He can't explain it entirely, but he knows it has something to do with that sudden feeling of being twelve himself again, huddled with his sister and brother in the tiny back room of the trailer, feeling sick to his stomach as they listen to their father stumble around in the kitchen, raving at their mother, breaking things. His wife can't understand this. She comes from a family where everything worked; one that had money, that could afford to tell the truth.

He reaches the east hall. At first glance it looks how it always looks. There's the waterfall and tropical display, the African guy Sheikh Whatsisname selling handbags, the candy shop with nineteen kinds of popcorn where he and Jaspers take their coffee breaks.

And there, at a table over in the corner, is Larry Bird.

It's a remnant of a crowd, no more than a dozen kids and fathers. He spots Alec, hanging shyly at the back edge. As he does, Bird stands, towering over the small group. A guy in a blazer at his elbow is pointing at his watch and saying something. Bird nods and shrugs at the rest of the kids.

Alec charges over, panic written across his small round face. "Dad, he's *leaving!*"

Next to them the waterfall loudly splashes away. "Well," he says, "I guess the guy's pretty busy, you know? Probably has to see the mayor and about a million other people."

"But can't you, can't you go get him or something, I mean go tell him we're here or something . . . ?"

"Well, what did he just say?"

His son's answer comes in tight snorts of desperation. "He said —the other man said—they're running late—there's no *time!*"

Across the hall, Bird and his entourage peel themselves away from the last clinging kids. In seconds they'll be out the door and gone.

He can't let it happen. He tries, but he can't pull it off. *All right, dammit,* he mutters, grabbing Alec's hand. *We'll head 'em off at the pass!* Taking aim for the door, he starts across the room.

It plays out as in a dream. As they converge on the group, he knows he needs a good opening line, but has no idea whatsoever what it's going to be until the very second the words pop out of him: "Hey Bird Man! Been down to the Romp lately?" A bar in Terre Haute, popular with ISU students, a place he'd all but forgotten about until right now.

Bird turns and stares, his face funny with its beaky nose; and then they're standing in front of him—under him is more like it —the Celtics star frowning with a look that all too clearly says, *Am I supposed to know you?* It makes him want to apologize. "Look, uh, Larry," he manages. "My boy here, Alec . . ."

He wants to say more, but Bird is way ahead of him, already reaching out for the Celtics roster in Alec's hand, wiggling his fingers in an impatient, *Come-on-let's-have-it* gesture.

Seconds later it's over.

★　★　★

Outside, his son standing quietly beside him, he squints into the white light of late afternoon and watches Larry Bird duck into the passenger seat of a blue minivan and be driven off.

Nothing could have been more obvious, he knows, than that look on Bird's face, the two seconds it took him to size the situation up and decide that the person standing in front of him was not anyone he knew, but just another anonymous fan. No handshake necessary. No joyous reunion of old buddies. Just a few mumbled words and then gone.

It's exactly the nightmare he's been trying all along to avoid. And yet as he considers what to say to Alec about it, how to begin to peel the lie back to the core of something true, he's surprised to feel a weight being lifted, a big one, as if some chunk of granite he's been lugging around inside him has left with Larry Bird in the van. He's almost glad the boy has seen through his charade. There are things he'd like to explain, things he has never told anyone, not even his wife, not even back in the early days when they were still telling each other things. He pictures himself driving his son through the cornfields of Indiana, through the town and past the grain elevator and out toward the hated trailer park, if somehow it has survived all those years of his violently wishing it away.

"Look, Tiger—" "Hey, Dad—"

They speak at the same moment, and he yields to the boy.

"Dad, is he like you remembered him, like he was back then?"

"Who?"

"The Bird Man!"

Incredibly, his son is staring wide-eyed up at him, eager and breathless as before, still hungry for the story. "I mean, is he, like, you know, the same guy and everything?"

It takes him a long time to answer. He frowns, and shifts his weight from one foot to the other. "The same guy?" he muses, looking out over the vast parking lot. Only now does he realize they're not parked here at all, they're way down at the other end, thousands of cars away. "The same guy? Hmmm . . . Well, that's hard to say. I guess I'd say old Larry seemed a little . . . a little smaller somehow."

It's not the answer Alec expected. "Whaddya mean, smaller?"

Heat wobbles off the tops of the cars, and his knees go suddenly rubbery on him. He's remembering, very exactly, the feeling he had when his father died, twenty-one years ago. It was a feeling of relief. The bad things his old man had done were complete—not a single one more would be added—and now he could get on with the work of erasing them and inventing some good ones to take their place.

A fierce love for his own son flares up in him, and he turns and squares the boy around by the shoulders, squatting to talk face-to-face.

"Listen, Tiger," he says. "Everything's always smaller, okay? Nothing's ever as big as you remember—nothing! Not Niagara Falls, not the Empire State Building, not even Larry Bird. You can quote me on that, okay?"

"O-kay!" says Alec, chiming out the syllables in his singsongy boy's voice. He stands and ruffles his son's hair, and together they step off the curb, out into the sea of gleaming cars.

WHAT THEY EAT
IN WHANGOOM

As LONG AS I can remember, I've thought of Harperton as a nothing-happening place. I grew up over in New London—a town on the shore, between Boston and New York; a spot people visited, or at least had to pass through to get where they *were* visiting. New London had colleges and a newspaper, it had doctors and stockbrokers sporting around in BMWs. What did Harperton have? Dead mills, Polish-American clubs, and a drive-in where the waitress brought Mom-and-Dadburgers on a tray to your car window. The town existed in a place outside time; it was still actually doing things other towns had already revived as nostalgia kicks.

In sixth grade we came up for Pop Warner football. The Harperton players wore crew cuts and that chipped and snarling look of white man's poverty. Harperton was a whole city that looked like that. Trash clogged the river-bank. Battered cars lined streets of dingy frame houses, some trimmed in black. (Nobody in New London ever trimmed a house in black.) The teenagers hanging around the doughnut shop were going out of their gourds with boredom. After the game we drove off. "Deadbeat dump," we muttered.

That's where I decided to start a career and a family.

When I finished law school, my parents assumed I'd find some hotshot situation in a city somewhere. My father owns a travel agency in New London, my mother's a school psychologist; the two had had hopes. To them, my city of destiny could have been New York or Chicago, or maybe San Francisco. But Harperton? *Our* Harperton? Where there wasn't a single decent restaurant, and the main cultural attraction was some nut who filled his yard with statues of the Blessed Virgin in upended bathtubs? It was a jolt for them. Jolt Number Two was my marrying Jess when I was twenty-seven and she fresh out of high school: an innocent, my mother commented; a babe in the woods. Before long Chucky and Ben came along, and my folks got used to the situation. But nowadays I suspect they think I'm paying the price for stepping back from the plate fifteen years ago—now that Jess has left, and everything's fallen apart.

I caught my wife in the act.

That's the headline version. Caught in the act, in flagrante delicto on the living room floor. Buck naked and banging away.

It was last June, a Sunday. I'd taken Chucky and Ben for an afternoon with my folks—Jess had begged off with a headache. In New London I realized I'd forgotten two bags of cement my father needed; and before he could talk me out of it, I unloaded the boys and turned the pickup around to Harperton.

I'm tempted to say I had a premonition. Maybe, maybe not. Anyway, I walked into the living room and there they were, down on the Navajo rug. Jess's eyes were closed, her mouth open. He was tanned above and fish-belly white below. His hair lay in a ponytail on his back, jiggling. Witnesses to disasters—it's one way you know they're being truthful—often seize on some trivial detail. I watched that ponytail jiggle; then I heard my own voice laugh. Jess opened her eyes.

"Oh shit!" she said; and Ponytail stopped jiggling.

A break in your marriage is like any sudden injury: you sit, stunned, and you wait. Is this an apple falling on my head or the sky itself? Ponytail, Jess told me when I inquired that evening whom she'd been screwing in our living room, was a professor at UConn. An archaeologist.

That kid? I said.

She rolled her eyes. "He's thirty-three. He's three years older than *I* am."

"He's got a ponytail, for Christ's sake! You're telling me he's a professor and he's got a ponytail?"

She held her hands in front of her face like a cage and groaned into them. "You *see*? You *see* how narrow-minded you are?"

She'd said this as if it was a point she'd made a hundred times. We were in the kitchen, the boys out back playing. All right, I decided, let's stir things up a little here. "An archaeologist?" I said. "It's this Indian crap, isn't it?" I put my hand to my mouth and went *HOW-wow-wow-wow!,* hopping around on one foot like Chief Jay Strongbow.

Jess tore off the apron she'd been wearing. "You know what that is, Gary? That's cultural genocide, that's what that is!"

I remembered having once felt responsible for every big word she had in her vocabulary. Suddenly I got scared. "Jess," I said, and stopped hopping around. "You're about as Indian as I am. This is just some . . . some *idea*."

She tossed her apron aside and walked out the door and into the yard.

That was a year ago.

I believe in trying to see the humor in things—it's usually there whether you want to see it or not. Ponytail was, in fact, the Indians' archaeologist: the tribe's bone man, you could even say. He turned out to be a removable part; but the tribe hasn't. Call Jess's answering machine these days and you'll hear Jess saying: "Fast Water, Golden Bear, and I are out right now. . . ." As I told my father, I have a special distinction among cheated-on husbands: I'm probably the only one in North America whose wife *defected*.

A decade ago the tribe wasn't much to boast about, just a few dozen people living in trailers in the woods east of town. Then in the eighties, things started happening. First they got official recognition from Washington. (Reagan was good for Indians, he cut deals.) They opened a bingo hall that turned a tidy little profit. Some investors lined up, and before anyone knew what was happening, across the river on Route 7 stood a spanking-new casino, open for business.

The casino is amazing—a 24-hour-a-day, 365-day-a-year geyser of tax-free gold. For the tribe that means $50 million a month in gaming revenues. For the rest of us it's real estate gone haywire and bumper-to-bumper traffic on what used to be an empty country road. It's *Time* magazine and *60 Minutes* turning the lights on and making us feel we never really existed before. And it's wild rumors about what the tribe has up its sleeve. They want to link Harperton to the casino by monorail. They want to buy the Deering Mansion, one of Harperton's few attractions, as a personal guest house for Frank Sinatra. And on and on.

In this kind of atmosphere a community can get unhinged. Recently a teacher from Chucky's middle school came to my office. His son had broken an elbow rollerblading, and he wanted to know whether there were "grounds for action" against the skate company. He had a game plan: Ask a million, settle for a hundred thou. When I told him he had no case, he smiled and left. Through the window I watched him get in his car and drive off. Here he was, this real Knights of Columbus, Harperton-born-and-bred type, cruising around town chasing some pot of gold. He scared me.

My wife's pot of gold comes thanks to a woman named Annie Banks, who died way back in 1910. This Annie Banks belonged to a tiny tribe that's cousin to the casino tribe. Last year the two groups banged out a profit-sharing deal that, when it goes through, could make every member of the Annie Banks tribe very comfortable.

Jess claims Annie Banks was her great-great-grandmother. Thus she herself is—abracadabra!—a Native American!

Her evidence? A name in a Bible, a memory of her grandfather's "Indian stories." Plus two brothers ready to swear up, down, and sideways that their father's dramatic last words before he died were that they were Indians and he'd been ashamed to tell them all his life. It's pretty hilarious to hear Jess's brother

Roy, who in my view has about as much spirituality as your average tree stump, discuss his Indian soul. "It's like, hunting and walking in the woods," he says. "You know—being one with nature or whatever."

I don't mean Jess fabricated the whole Indian thing overnight. In fact, she and I used to joke about it: Chucky would act up, and we'd look at each other and say, *Must be that Hackett Injun blood!* But before the casino came along it was way, way in the background. I ask Jess: Even if the Annie Banks connection *is* real, what about the $^{15}/_{16}$ths of her that aren't Indian? And what about "Fast Water" and "Golden Bear"? They've got twice that much Italian in them, four times that much Irish—on both sides! So why not answer the phone with "Seamus, Patrick, and I are out right now . . . ?"

"We're not going to have an argument, Gary," she says. "That's what you want, but I'm not going to give it to you."

After I caught her in the living room last summer, Jess stopped seeing Ponytail, then went back, then stopped again. For two months I was coming home from work every day not knowing whether I still had a wife. At night we were hashing it out. Jess felt smothered by me, she said. She'd been too young when we married. She needed to try some things. She needed a life of her own. "*This* is your own!" I'd say, pointing around the house. "*This* is. *This* is." But in October she packed a few bags and moved to an apartment, a monthly rental near the river. She needed this for now, she said.

The boys have coped pretty well with the situation. Ben is Ben: a dreamy bundle of five-year-old who trails along entertaining himself with singsongy chatter about Mr. Happy Turtle. Chucky's tougher; he's eleven and he likes to dig. When the two come back from Jess's apartment, he'll stand around the kitchen, frowning, then suddenly hit me with something Jess told him, something like *Mom says this whole town really belongs to the Indians!* or *Mom says you didn't let her go to college!* If I don't take the bait, he sulks; but if I show any real anger, he's liable to burst out wailing. It's a tricky balance.

As for me, I've tried hobbies to fill the new gaps in my life. I started reading again; I took up brewing root beer. Still, after Jess left there were dead times, especially when the boys were at her place—long hours when I'd sit and wonder what she was doing. I'd try to picture her out there, going from place to place in a new life with people I didn't know. One Saturday night when she had the boys, I called and found she'd gone to a party. I finagled the name and number from her babysitter, did some checking in the phone book, and at about 10 P.M. I drove out to a ramshackle place in the woods off Route 7. There I found Jess and a dozen others—in a huge teepee out in the yard. This was December, about 40 degrees out, and there it was, this huge canvas thing with poles sticking every which way out of the top.

I don't know what I expected, probably headdresses and peace pipes; but when I ducked in, what I found was a group of people in their twenties sitting around a space heater, listening to music. A joint was going around the circle. Needless to say, Jess was surprised to see me. "This is Gary," she said, and the group shifted to make room. I couldn't tell whether they even knew who I was.

As it turned out, despite the teepee, only a couple of people there were actual members of the tribe. The rest were groupies and wannabes. They were nice, you couldn't help liking them; but they were just kids. Jess was sitting across from me, and I kept trying to catch her eye. She felt me fishing and evaded at first; then changed her mind and bit. What I saw on her face surprised me. She wasn't angry at my snooping around. There was no meanness there, no desire to hurt me. But I didn't see any grief, either, or guilt. What I saw in her eyes was more like nervousness. It was the look of someone who badly wanted something and was holding her breath until she got it. A look so innocent and selfish it almost knocked me over.

When I met Jess a dozen years ago, she was just eighteen: kid number six out of six in her family; her father unemployed, her mother an alcoholic. Up to then she'd been living a pretty standard Harperton life—driving around in cars drinking rum-and-Cokes, messing up in school—and she was looking for someone to show her a better one. That someone was me.

I'm not saying Jess didn't love me; I'm saying we tend to love what we can use. She claims I kept her from college, but the truth is I *was* college. At the start she hung on my every word. Sometimes I'd hear her on the phone with a girlfriend, repeating an idea I'd expressed a few days before. I liked hearing how she had run it through herself and given it her own twist. She wasn't parroting, she was learning; and she did it fast and well.

Now it's the tribe's turn, and they've launched Jess on a nice little career. She's studying communications, she's working as a spokesperson for the Tribal Council. A couple of times I've turned on the news and seen her. Jess is a knockout on TV. She's got high cheekbones, and sky-blue eyes with tiny purplish rims to them that give her gaze a weird intensity; on the tube it's mesmerizing. It's just the local news, but Jess doesn't seem local; she seems national. She seems like a star.

Chucky and Ben love it. *Look!* they squeal, gathering around

the set. *There's Mom!* We stand there watching. And then I picture some little thing, like the look Jess would get on her face
while hanging laundry in the basement of our first apartment.
Jess is not a great natural mother or housewife, more like a great
adaptation of one, and I loved the bite-your-lip concentration as
she lined up each piece of clothing and slid it between the rails of
the drying rack. And now there she is on the tube, drop-dead
gorgeous as ever, talking away about the need for the red man to
control his images. I click off the TV, and the boys yell at me
until I turn it back on.

When your wife screws around, you're expected to do some
heavy hitting back. But revenge wasn't what I had in mind when
I called Rick Giorgio, a private investigator friend of mine, and
told him I had some work for him. This was four months ago, in
March. Jess and I had been sharing the boys in a "friendly arrangement" with no legal basis; but I told Giorgio that if the
time ever came, I knew she'd fight for custody, and I wanted to
be ready.

I hear you, Giorgio said. You're laying a foundation. You
wanna lay stone, you gotta dig dirt.

I'd had him do some digging for clients over the years. Standard divorce dirt—who slept with whom when, who drank and
drove, who smashed what in a fit of rage. In my own case I
wasn't sure what he'd come back with. Maybe Jess had been
leaving the boys alone in her apartment to go gallivanting about
town. Maybe she was sleeping her way up the Tribal Council. I
wasn't exactly looking forward to finding out.

Giorgio phoned a couple of times to report some nickel-and-
dime stuff. Two weeks went by, then he called from some bar.

The thing was taking on a whole new angle, he said. "Actually it's getting kinda wacky." He sketched it in for me.

Three weeks later we met downtown at the Bottom Line. Giorgio dresses like someone's idea of a detective, in a rumpled suit and loose tie. He was drinking bourbon in great gulps, ahh-hing at the glass with comical gusto. I sat down, and he tossed an envelope on the table.

"This'll change the little lady's tune," he said.

As it turned out, I wasn't the only one skeptical about my wife's claim to being an Indian. Someone in the tribe had tipped Giorgio to a rumor. The tip had led him out to Wisconsin, on the trail of an old woman whose mother had been a cousin of Jess's Annie Banks. Six months before, this old woman's grand-son had done some research in an attempt to lay claim to a piece of the casino action. Unfortunately for him, his family tie wasn't direct enough for the tribe's $1/16$th rule. In the course of check-ing, however, he'd learned that one family—the Hacketts, of Harperton, CT—had successfully asserted membership through Annie Banks. This was intriguing to him, because, according to his grandmother, who'd known her personally, Annie Banks had never married and never had children.

Eventually, Jess's brother Roy got a surprise phone call from the grandson (this is one part of the story I like imagining), asking if the Hacketts would be interested in "making an offer" for this "extremely important material" he had gathered. The material consisted of a letter—notarized—written by the grand-mother, who since then had died: a letter, complete with family tree, saying that Annie Banks had died childless, and thus that the "Ann Banks Hackett" in my wife's family Bible could not possi-bly be the Annie Banks listed on the tribal rolls of 1910.

What Giorgio had in his envelope was this letter. The smoking gun, he said.

As I sat there, the thought of my wife's destiny reduced to a bureaucratic oversight made me laugh, then laugh harder, that flapping, giddy kind of laughter that loosens you from your moorings. Something went the wrong way and I choked a little.

Whoa, buddy! said Giorgio, handing me his bourbon. Down the hatch!

His bill was $3,100, and I wrote out a check. Giorgio took it and gestured toward the envelope on the table. So what was I gonna do? Spill the beans or no?

I told him I guessed that was the $64,000 question.

"At least," he said, and slipped my check into his jacket pocket. We shook hands and I left.

Giorgio had called the Annie Banks letter a smoking gun, but in the days that followed it seemed to me more like a loaded one. I put the letter in the safe in my office, but then I brought it home. I liked having it within reach, where I could take it out and read the opening lines: *To Whom It May Concern—I am an 88-year-old woman of sound mind and body.* . . . If I hadn't wanted revenge before, that was because I hadn't had a weapon; now that I was armed, I didn't feel so Christian about things. I imagined Jess on her knees, begging for the letter. In the living room I rolled it up, aimed it at her picture and said "Bang!" Once I even managed to place it briefly in her possession without her knowing. She was coming to take the boys to the library, and I put the letter in an envelope with my name on it, sealed it and stuck it inside one of Chucky's books. The thought of Jess driving her own doom around town gave me an almost pornographic pleasure. And when she handed the envelope back to me

—unopened—at the end of the day, I felt as if I'd given her her shot at a pardon, and she'd refused it. Now the blade could fall. I could destroy her. Torpedo the fantasy boat she'd hopped and watch it go under. *If* I chose to.

But I didn't choose to. As the weeks went by I put the letter away and managed not to obsess about it. Spring came, Jess was still in her apartment. I concentrated on work and on the boys. I painted the back deck. I brewed root beer.

I've always loved root beer. As a kid in New London I'd order a large one at Michael's Dairy and watch, fascinated, as the soda jerk pumped the syrup, then nozzled in the seltzer and mixed it with a long spoon. In recent years the drink's been making a comeback, but for a while in the seventies and eighties it looked like it might disappear. The main ingredients of root beer are sassafras, anise, and molasses. To make it you can either hunt all this stuff down on your own, or do what I did and buy it ready to go, in little foil packets, from the Barrel Brew Taste Factory: ten batches worth, brewed in easy-clean barrel-shaped jars—fifty gallons in all—for $49.95, including the jars. The process involves a lot of boiling, sifting, filtering; then letting the brew sit. I decided to keep it in the basement. I liked thinking about the root beer down there, slowly bubbling away. It sounds macabre, but on nights when Chucky and Ben were at Jess's, it was almost as if some other living being was in the house.

June 20 was my birthday, a Sunday, and my parents came over for an afternoon picnic on the patio. My father gave me a bottle of Jameson's Irish whisky, my mother brought a whole meal— lasagna, coleslaw, all my old favorites. During dessert, I was watching Ben make an unholy mess of his key lime pie when it occurred to me: my folks hadn't mentioned Jess's name, not once, the whole time.

When the boys took the plates to the kitchen, I leaned across the table.

"I *can* talk about her, you know. She didn't die. We're just separated."

My mother gave me her calm, therapist's smile. "We know that, Gary. We thought if you wanted to talk about it, you'd talk about it."

"We didn't want to spoil your birthday," my father said. "It wasn't a conspiracy."

"No?" I raised an eyebrow. But I could see he was telling the truth. It had been eight months since Jess left; they'd decided to move on.

That hit me hard. I'd been acting as if Jess and I had hit a snag in our life together and put things on hold, as if we'd called time-out to figure it all out. But the truth was that the game was going on; *I* was the only one standing still.

After my parents went home, and the boys had gone outside to play, I sat down in the living room with the Jameson's and a tumbler. The whisky did its work, and around six o'clock I found myself reaching for the phone. Muddled thoughts were running around my brain.

Jess wasn't home. Her answering machine came on, and I listened to the spiel about Fast Water and Golden Bear. I decided I'd heard that a few hundred times too many. "You know what, Jess?" I said after the beep. "I'm feeling kinda left out without one of those nifty Indian names! Whaddya think—how about . . . Laughing Cuckold? Or He-Who-Sleeps-Alone-on-His-Fortieth-Birthday? Or maybe—"

A clashing sound, and Jess broke in on the line. "What are you, drunk or something? What do you think you're doing?"

It hadn't occurred to me that she'd been listening; I'd thought I was alone. I didn't know what I was doing, I mumbled. I was just calling.

"Well, if that's your idea of 'just calling' . . ."

"Jess," I broke in. But I had no idea what was supposed to come next. My hand on the phone was filmy with sweat. "I've been trying to get the boys interested in root beer," I said finally.

"Gary, are you all right?"

I closed my eyes and rubbed them. I was sorry about the Indian jokes, I told her, really sorry.

"Yeah, well. Let's just forget about it, okay?" She expelled a short, determined breath. "Listen. Maybe it's not the best time right now, but sometime soon we have to sit down and talk about the next step."

"The next step? What do you mean—what next step?"

"You're not in any shape to talk about this right now. We'll talk soon, okay?"

She hung up.

I listened to the dial tone until it went into its warning mode, then turned back to the Jameson's. As I did, a tremor passed through my entire body, and I thought I would be sick. I put the tumbler down and stood.

Out back I told the boys I had an errand to do, then climbed into the pickup. Just drive somewhere, was the idea. I let the wheel do its own steering—down Main Street to the north end of town, back along the river. The sky was sharp, more September than June, with that hard blue light that frames objects clearly, as if the weather has decided to tell the truth about things. To me it seemed the shabby core of Harperton was being laid out plain, the town caught in its long-term project of crumbling, brick by brick, back into the earth.

I took a left on Bridge, crossing the river, my mind turning dizzy loops the whole time. I was thinking about how Jess's career as an Indian had gotten started, in a Native American history class in New London, and how I'd given her the fateful push to do it. She met Ponytail there, he introduced her to people in the tribe, and the fun began. Soon Ponytail was jiggling away on our living room floor. Picturing his rope of hair and fishbelly-white ass made me feel sick all over again. I pulled off the road, rolled up the windows, and made some loud noises.

I've always seen myself as a coper, as someone who takes the situation and deals. There in my truck, as I sat pistol-whipping myself with images of my wife and this hippie archaeologist on our living room floor, I decided I had to act. Maybe there was a way through, I thought. This whole thing had happened in the first place because Jess had gotten this crazy idea of herself as an Indian. That idea had been a mistake. Cancel that mistake, and all bets were off.

From a gas station I called Jess's apartment. "We have to meet," I said when she answered. "There's something you should know about."

"What?"

"Something important." I was having trouble catching my breath. "New information."

"Look, I wanted to tell you—I'm going to be reasonable about the boys, I promise. And I don't want a thing for myself. Not a single penny—"

It wasn't that simple, I broke in. The *reason* she didn't want anything, I explained, was that she thought she could afford not to. "And that may be contingent upon things you can't control, Jessica."

"Gary, don't go lawyer on me. Just tell me what you're talking about."

Not over the phone, I said. We had to meet. Today. Right away.

I could hear her mentally reshuffling the deck. "All right," she said in an icy voice. "I'll meet you *in* a half hour, *for* a half hour."

I knew where it had to be. Up till now I had avoided the place, but suddenly I felt I had to see it.

"Meet me at the casino," I said. "Front entrance, twenty minutes." And before she could change her mind, I hung up.

This summer I decided to revive an old family tradition of Midnight Walks. My mother did it when I was a kid, waking me for a stroll in the night, and now I wanted to pass it on to my sons. For weeks I built the idea up until they were so jazzed they could hardly sleep. Finally last night I went into their room and woke them. *Midnight sharp, guys,* I crooned. *Time for a walk on the wild side.* I helped Ben pull a flannel shirt on over his pajamas, and out we went, through the yard and onto Meeting Street, heading for Old Town. Old Town is what's left of the original Harperton, a couple dozen colonial saltboxes and a church. The three of us walked through the narrow streets, Ben still wrapped in sleep, Chucky jabbering away, wired as usual. *It's so dark, Dad!* he chattered. *What if we meet a murderer or something?*

"There aren't any murderers here," I said. "Just lions and tigers and bears, oh my!"

"But what if one jumped out and wanted to *kill* us? What if he had a gun and blew us away?"

"Nobody has a gun around here, Chuckster," I said with a sigh. "It's not one you have to worry about, okay?"

He gave me a grudging nod.

At the top of Pequot Road we reached the statue of Captain Harper, standing tall on its granite pedestal. It's a nifty jungle gym, one of the boys' favorite places, and I sat on the stone step at the base while they clambered on up. Originally, in the 1800s, the statue was meant to glorify Harper, but nowadays the figure of a swashbuckling soldier unsheathing his sword just seems brutally accurate. So does the inscription: "On this spot in 1682, Captain Isaiah Harper and his men overthrew the Indians and made the settlement safe." Recently there's been a controversy about the appropriateness of the statue—the tribes on one side, a handful of old Yankees on the other. A commission was formed to find an "alternative home" for it; but when they cast around for takers, they didn't find a single one. Nobody wants Harper anymore. Wait long enough, history evens out all the hurts.

"Hey Dad." Chucky broke into my thoughts. "Are you a millionaire?"

"Good God! I'm barely a thousandaire."

"Thousandaire, that's *weak*! I'm gonna be a millionaire! I'm gonna be a billionaire!"

Ben chimed in: "I'm gonna be a ten hundred thousand million billionaire!" The boys giggled, and I listened to their voices rise and fall.

To the east, the lights of the casino were spreading an orange glow in the sky. I pictured the vast parking lot as I'd seen it when I'd pulled in, ten minutes after telling Jess to meet me there. All around, America was pouring in to gamble—young, old, rich, poor, black, white, you name it; the buses rolling in like troop transports. As I sat waiting, the panic in my body subsided, bit by bit; and with it I felt my plan fade away into a shimmering mirage. I was still drunk, but not drunk enough to kid myself: If Jess was ever going to come back, it wasn't going to be through some scheme with a letter or any other kind of trick I might come up with; it was going to have to just happen. I spotted her then, standing by the front entrance among the valets. I pulled to the curb and watched her walk the twenty feet or so to my window. *Look, I lied before,* I said when she got there. *There isn't any new information. I was just being drunk.* She shook her head and said nothing, looking off over the top of my truck to something I couldn't see. She would be all right, I saw then; whatever way things went, she would be all right.

"Hey Dad!" Above me, Ben started in on his favorite game, Guess What They Eat. "Dad, guess what they eat in Hopsaroppsa!"

"I dunno, chum, what do they eat?"

"They eat . . . black rocks, with eggs on top! And guess what they eat in Boolermooler!"

"Hmmm . . . Poached turtle toes?"

"No!" He chortled. "They eat big big big garages! And sunglasses!"

Chucky groaned; he considers Guess What They Eat a huge waste of time. Below us in Old Town the church clock chimed 1 A.M. I stood. "All right, you two tough guys. Hop on down. Let's go get some shut-eye."

They slid down from the statue, and we started back on Pequot Road, Ben bopping along with his funny skipping walk. "Dad, now guess what they eat in Whangoom!"

I patted his head. "In Whangoom? Hmmm . . . Let me think about it."

A dog bayed inside someone's house; we were approaching the bottom of the hill. Ben tugged at my sleeve, his voice growing whiny. "You have to *guess*! You have to guess what they eat in Whangoom!"

Chucky made a noise of disgust. "Dad, there *is* no Whangoom! It's just some stupid made-up place."

I asked how he knew.

"I know! Ben just makes up these places. It's so stupid!"

At the corner we turned onto Meeting. "Now hold on," I said. "Not only do I believe in Whangoom, but this time I also happen to know what they eat there." I paused for effect. "They eat . . . root beer!"

My sons joined in a spasm of groaning. *Yuck,* they gargled, *blech, uchh!* "And by the way, Dad," added Chucky. "You don't *eat* root beer, you know."

"Ah, but in Whangoom you do," I said.

We crossed to our side of the street, away from the streetlights, and I took the boys' hands and spoke in a low voice. In Whangoom, I told them, everything was different. Food was different. The language was different. Even sports were different. Furthermore, the population there consisted largely of ghosts. At night, if you listened very carefully, you could hear them in the wind, whispering Whangoomian secrets. I cocked an ear.

"Are we there?" Ben said. "Are we in Whangoom?" He was holding tight to my hand. On the other side, Chucky kept quiet for once.

Along the sidewalk, we stepped over places buckled up by the roots of Norway maples that line our street. I squeezed my sons' hands tight. "I think we're just . . . approaching . . . the border," I said.

We neared the house. As we did, an image of Jess came to me: I saw her as I'd seen her the night I asked her to marry me. We were sitting in my car outside her parents' place, engine idling, and she'd just given me a look that said loud and clear exactly how much she was prepared to need me. It had melted me, that look. I had never felt so *useful* before.

My sons and I reached the edge of our yard and stood for a moment. I hadn't left any lights on, and at this creepy hour it was possible to imagine our house, hulked high and dark against the sky, as the capital of an alien, possibly forbidding world.

"Okay," I whispered. "Now—we may have to slip by a sentry or two. Are we up to that, men?"

They nodded. I looked to the left, to the right; then the three of us crept forward, quiet as burglars, step by step into the yard.

THE WAY
THINGS ALWAYS
HAPPEN

OF THE FEW TRICKS he'd mastered in his forty-one
years, like wiggling his ears or singing "Santa Claus
Is Coming to Town" backwards, Reardon was most
proud of the secret of carrying on a conversation
with someone while thinking about something altogether different. It was a mental trick he used at
the office, talking with one client while inwardly
rehearsing a meeting with a more important one; or
on the train, fending off a talky fellow commuter.
Sometimes, guiltily, he used it at home. He was
using it now, in fact—a summer evening at dinner,
his thirteen-year-old, Paul, telling about a man he'd
seen standing on a box in Washington Square, naked
but for a loincloth and a sign reading MUSEUM OF
LIVING ART; his eight-year-old, Julie, giggling

slyly ("*Naked*? Could you see his grinder?"); his wife, Carolyn, shaking her head; and Reardon himself, thinking annoyed thoughts about the $200,000 a jury had awarded that morning to plaintiffs suing his client, a neurosurgeon named Armbruster. The plaintiffs' daughter had had the bum luck to slip in the hospital shower; their lawyer, a handsome, Kennedyesque figure of about thirty with a tiny diamond earring, had argued negligence on the part of the surgeon for not *expressly forbidding*—

"Frank? What do you think?"

Reardon blinked into his wife's doubtful gaze. His son had been saying something about a Haitian he'd met in the park. Or was it a Hawaiian? "What was that guy's name again, Paulie?" he asked.

The name was Boniface. Boniface was from Port au Prince, his son informed him, and he was for democracy and everything. "But these really repressive guys, they like, beat him up and smashed his store and shot his brother."

Reardon's grasp of Caribbean realities was less than sure. "Politics in underdeveloped countries," he observed. "Now, there's a dicey business for you."

"Yeah, well, that's why he needed help."

"Help?" Reardon set down his fork and turned to his son. Giving money away had become one of the boy's favorite hobbies of late—a streak of helpless generosity he seemed to have taken over whole from his mother, famous for her inability to Just Say No to the herds of cheap con men, political wannabes, and religious cranks who made their living grazing off the gullible and the polite. Under cross-examination Paul admitted having given the Haitian money—twenty dollars toward a bus ticket for a cousin in Miami. It wasn't a big deal, he insisted. *Au con-*

traire, Reardon argued, and took a moment to demonstrate that twenty dollars from Paul was the equivalent of himself handing out six or seven grand.

The boy's answer was a pouting frown. "But you're *rich*!" he said. "And besides, he's paying me back."

Reardon smiled at his wife. "Honey, how do you think old Boniface'll use that twenty? Little peep show in Times Square? Couple rocks of crack?"

"Well, maybe he was telling the truth, Frank," Carolyn offered.

"Yeah," laughed Reardon. "And maybe the pope's my uncle."

"God, Dad, you're so . . ." His son, groping for the word.

"Cynical," said Carolyn, with a glance at Reardon.

After dinner, as they cleaned up together in the kitchen, she asked what he would have done at Paul's age. "At his age," Reardon began, "I didn't have twenty cents, let alone . . ." From out of nowhere, he remembered a bum in Prospect Park, an old man whom he and Jimmy Connally had teased, sticking a quarter to a string with bubble gum and dragging it back and forth in front of his bench. He told his wife the story.

She wasn't listening. "You're hard on him, you know," she said.

"Who, Paulie? Oh, come on, honey."

"He takes it hard."

Reardon thought about how tougher boys bullied Paul at school, battles from which his son straggled home tear-stained and furious. *Why do they pick on him when he doesn't do anything?* Carolyn had asked. *Exactly,* he had tried to explain. *He doesn't do anything. He has the look.* His wife's eyes had narrowed. *What look? What are you talking about?*

Tossing the dish towel aside, Reardon exited the kitchen and went down the hall to the TV room, where his kids were watching *Wheel of Fortune,* sitting cross-legged on the floor and gaping mesmerized at the screen. "So," he said to Paul. "When's your man allegedly paying you back?"

"It's not allegedly, Dad. He *is* paying me back! Friday."

Reardon made sure Carolyn wasn't lurking. "Wanna put your money where your heart is?" he said. "Ten bucks says you never see that twenty."

When they shook on it, he was surprised at his son's grip, at how far the fingers went around his own hand—another reminder, he decided to tell his wife, that the boy was growing older, and the universal indulgence granted children to be foolish, to take things back, would itself soon be withdrawn, piece by piece, until nothing stood between Paul Reardon and the world except his own wits. When Carolyn thought this over she would absently nibble her lower lip, an earnest little habit of hers Reardon found perpetually endearing. He smiled, picturing it. Too many men he knew had developed over the years a perverse contempt for their wives—first sheltering them, then blaming them for being sheltered. It was an inconsistency he prided himself on not committing.

On Friday, as usual, he took the 7:22 Metro-North from Westport into Grand Central, emerging on Park Avenue to walk to his office at Sheed Wellman. The morning was hazy, and air conditioners on all sides gurgled and whirred, struggling for a head start on the day. Reardon barely noticed them. Having walked these fourteen blocks every weekday for twelve years, he'd come to think of them as a kind of extended foyer to the Hitchcock Building, and nothing short of a screaming ambulance could pierce the cozy cocoon of his thoughts.

Reardon made his living defending doctors. As a boy watching Ben Casey, later as a biology major at Fordham, he'd wanted to be a doctor himself. His science grades had been too soft, and he'd stayed on at Fordham for law school instead; but his old dream had remained with him, exerting an invisible pull on his decisions and landing him, after a dismal stint as a public defender, in medical liability at Sheed Wellman. He liked physicians, identifying with their overworked, misunderstood air, and took pride in the small victories he won on their behalf. Secretly he regarded his work as almost a kind of medicine itself: emergency triage on a legal system bleeding through the pores.

The very idea of responsibility, Reardon believed, was heaving its last gasp in America. On the TV talk shows, freaks and losers spilled out their sad stories to audiences wallowing in sticky sympathy. Instead of obesity there was sugar addiction; instead of squandering your paycheck on the horses, gambling addiction; there even existed, he had discovered, a support group for the grandchildren of alcoholics. If anything bad happened to you, if you were lazy, if you simply hated your life, there was always someone to blame, and usually to sue. Everyone was a victim. Liberals had installed the great gripe as a national birthright—with lawyers, to Reardon's chagrin, as their chief architects. For his part, he was happy to lend his own talents to the other side. Each time he got an award reduced or a case dismissed, he felt the satisfaction of seeing America nudged a tiny step back from the precipice.

At one-thirty the air over Manhattan visibly shimmered. Twenty stories up, Reardon stood at the window of his office and watched people below moving punily in the cruel light. Random reflections streaked like quasars off car windows and mirrors. It sometimes occurred to him that the city was on the verge of some spontaneous calamity, a magnificent combustion after which, through the great gash blown in its side, cool clean night would come roaring in. Pushing the thought aside, he called Ernie Cross, his broker and squash partner, and begged off from their afternoon match. At two he tied up a few loose ends, wished his secretary a good weekend, and left the office.

Out on the sidewalk he stood deciding which way to go. As a boy in Brooklyn he'd reveled in an afternoon in the city; now he was surprised to find it had become a mysterious, even a daunting challenge, as if he had suddenly been put ashore in Lisbon or Shanghai. People swarmed, babbling cacophonously, on their unimaginable errands. A bus hulked by, trailing noxious fumes. An old woman in a filthy raincoat sat on the curb, eating cottage cheese with a plastic spoon and smacking her lips.

He pictured Paul in his room in Connecticut, sitting at his computer, drawing complex designs with the mouse, inputting melodies which the machine printed out in musical notation. It sometimes troubled Reardon to see his son growing up without the city running in his veins; he worried that the life he and Carolyn had fashioned in the suburbs, with its peace and comfort, might not be the best incubator of character for a boy. Lately Paul had shown a troubling tendency to sulk—like the night before, when he'd barged into Reardon's discussion of the Armbruster case with a *Hey Dad, what is redistributing income, anyway?*

"It's taking from Peter to support Paul," Reardon had answered with a smile. "Or taking from Paul to support Harry the Haitian." The boy mumbled something into his shirt, and Reardon urged him to speak up.

"I said at least that's better than taking boat people and putting them in concentration camps!" he blurted.

Those were *holding* camps, Reardon had pointed out—a crucial distinction. But his son waved it off. "Why do we have to put them in *any* camp? This is supposed to be a free country, isn't it? I mean, *we're* here. What gives *us* the right?"

Reardon had found himself wondering just when the boy with the toothy, jack-o'-lantern grin had been spirited away and replaced by the hunched, resentful figure peering at him from across the table. *I blame YOU!* that look clearly said—as if Reardon were beating up on him, and only the gross injustice of the world prevented some hero from materializing to protect him from further wounding.

Giving the change in his pocket a jingling shake, he pushed his way against the wall of heat across Forty-sixth Street to Fifth Avenue, where he boarded an M4 headed downtown. The air-conditioning on the bus was not functioning, and a film of misery lay over the dozen passengers. Reardon found that whistling "Moon River" made him feel somehow cooler. He felt grateful when a pair of teenaged girls got on at Thirty-fourth Street, laughing and joking, and sat across from him. He checked his watch. Three o'clock, his son had said, Washington Square. Under the arch.

It wasn't spying, Reardon told himself. His son was going to learn something about how the world really worked, and he wanted to be there to help focus the lesson. He rehearsed how it would go. Doing good, he'd tell Paul, wasn't always a question of having the biggest heart. Take a surgeon, for instance: in order to save people, he had to be clinical and cold, he even had to hurt—a ruthless kindness.

The highest truths, he would explain, were paradoxes.

The bus lumbered on. Reardon smiled over at the girls, who giggled, exchanging secret looks. He adjusted his tie and went on whistling, a little louder.

The scene at the park was hectic, a motley mob of roller skaters, folksingers, and bums. In the middle of it Reardon spotted Paul, sitting on the pavement reading a comic book, his back up against the concrete base of the arch. With a newspaper he installed himself on a bench in the shade, near where a German oompah-pah quartet stood belching out quaint melodies.

Three o'clock came and went, and no Haitian. At three-thirty Paul stood up and looked in several directions, squinting in the hot light. Reardon studied him from behind his newspaper—a neat boy in jeans and sneakers, unmarked by tattoos or jewelry or bizarre haircut. He recalled the years he would bring Paul in to Shea for a Mets game, the pleasure he'd taken in leading him across the vast parking lot, a tiny trooper toting his oversize mitt and talking a mile a minute. After fifth grade, sports had abruptly given way to music and video games, and Reardon had stopped getting tickets.

At four his son walked out from under the arch, retreating ten paces to a bench. A garbage can stood at one end, and as he slumped down, he tossed his comic book into it. The gesture of surrender tugged at Reardon's heart. He looked around at the accordion player in his lederhosen, the black-clad college girl sulkily reading poetry, all the bit players in the miniature tragedy his son was experiencing. He pictured himself sitting down on the bench and slipping his arm around the boy's narrow shoulders.

So caught up was Reardon in this vision that he lost track of things, and was startled to look over and find the bench empty. Scanning, his eye located Paul, huddled with a small, balding black man in a floral print shirt. Paul was just pocketing his wallet, nodding and smiling as the little man talked rapid-fire at him. A minute later they shook hands and parted in opposite directions, the Haitian disappearing back into the park, Reardon's son striding swiftly beneath the arch and off up Fifth Avenue.

Reardon stood. The heat was suddenly very hot, requiring him to take out a handkerchief and mop his brow. Crossing to where the two had stood, he lingered there for a few moments. Then, tossing his newspaper into the trash can—it landed on top of his son's comic book—he left.

At dinner that night he waited for his son to claim victory. But the boy held back, and finally Reardon, antsy, decided to get it over with. "So," he said. "What about your Haitian friend and our little wager?"

"Little wager?" Carolyn squinted at him from her end of the table.

"What's a wager?" chirped Julie.

"A wager," answered Carolyn, "is when your father acts like a big baby."

Reardon held up his hands. "Let's see how it comes out,

okay?'' He produced his wallet. ''Go ahead,'' he said to his son. ''Make your mother's day.''

Oddly, Paul's face displayed no triumph. ''Well,'' Reardon pressed, ''did you meet him or did you meet him?''

''I met him.''

''And? Did you get your twenty?''

''Um, not . . . not exactly.''

''Aha.'' He returned the wallet to his pocket. ''Well, well, well.''

With a sigh, the boy turned to his mother—whenever this happened, language magically began pouring out of him—and launched into a breathless account of how the Haitian's cousin had had to rush off to Washington to testify before a refugee commission. The trip was urgent. So urgent, in fact, he'd had to buy a plane ticket.

''Oh Jesus.'' Reardon slapped his forehead. ''He soaked you again!''

The boy groaned, as if the very limits of a reasonable patience were being tested. ''Mom,'' he said. ''Can you please tell him to stop being so cynical?''

Ten minutes of patient effort were needed to drag out the sorry truth. His son had indeed forked over ten more dollars. This time the Haitian had promised to pay him back in two days —indeed, had even promised to come out to Westport to do it.

''You didn't give him our address, did you?'' breathed Carolyn.

''No, I *didn't*.'' Paul rolled his eyes. ''We're meeting at the station. He's visiting some friends out here. In Fairfield or somewhere.''

Reardon leaned forward, clasping his hands together. It was

time to introduce some reality into the proceedings. "Paul," he said. "Now, what do you think the chances are that a Haitian who spends his days panhandling in Washington Square has friends out here?"

For the first time all evening, his son looked him square in the eye. "Just because he's black, or he's not rich, or he doesn't play *tennis* or something, does that mean he doesn't have friends?"

"No. It just means he doesn't have friends out *here*." Calmly Reardon laid out the logic of the situation. "Look, estimate the probability, that's all I'm asking, Paulie. Would you say it's highly likely? Possible but not probable? Or would you say it's—"

"Dad. I *believed* him, okay?"

The boy was near tears. Reardon glanced over and saw Carolyn fixing him with a raylike glare.

"All right, all right," he said. He stood and, reaching over, swept his daughter up out of her chair. "Come on Jules, let's you and me leave these two bleeding hearts and mosey on out to the corral."

But his son wouldn't let it go. "Hey Dad, he's gonna pay me back, you know." The whining voice trailed him across the room. "I mean, I'll bet you *again* if you want! Double or nothing!"

Reardon turned in the doorway, grinning.

Around midnight he sat in bed, propped up with pillows and Frederick Forsyth. Reardon liked spending time at home, relaxing. Never a workaholic, he had once envied those sleek Wall Street lawyers who put in seventy-hour weeks, pulled salaries in the high six figures, and flashed about town in limos, while he was busy taking his wife and kids for weekends to the beach. But somewhere along the line the dangers of workaholism had surfaced in the public awareness—its stresses, its moral emptiness—and Reardon had been relieved to discover he was the type of person you were supposed to be, after all.

The night was dead quiet, save for the occasional swish of a passing car. Carolyn lay next to him, facing the wall. His wife had never learned the art of the poker face, and so to hide some thought had to resort to blunter strategies, like turning her back. Reardon found this amusing.

"Hey, you over there," he said. "What's up?"

She rolled over. It was Paul, she sighed. She was worried about the meeting Sunday. What if this Haitian had a gun or a knife?

Reardon assured her there wasn't going to *be* any meeting. No one was going to take the train all the way out to Connecticut just to squeeze ten bucks out of a thirteen-year-old kid. It would be bad business.

"You think so?"

"I know so. What's going to happen is, Paul's going to go and sit on his butt at the station for an hour, then come back. Okay?"

She nodded, her face still creased with worry. Reardon experienced a small swoon of anguish at the thought of her having someday to live on, after his death, without him. He rested the book on his chest. "Look, how about if I go down Sunday and make sure he's all right, okay?" He leaned over and kissed her forehead. "Oh, and by the way. Thanks a bunch for the whole 'cynical' thing. I can see I'll never hear the end of that."

He went back to his book, and was immediately absorbed in it, so that when, somewhat later, he heard her quietly say, "Well, you *are* sometimes," it took him a moment to realize what she was talking about. When he did, he put the book down and stared at her.

"You are, Frank," she said. "I'm sorry."

"So that's the thanks I get for pledging to protect our kid from the dreaded Haitian knife-murderer." He shook his head. "Jeez, it's tough to score a point around here sometimes."

"Don't worry," she said. "I'm not keeping score."

Reardon grunted and returned again to his novel. But her unfairness stung him. He pictured her alarm when Paul had disclosed that the Haitian was coming.

"You know," he said, "you can't have it both ways. You can't be terrified of this guy *and* call me cynical too."

"Why can't I?"

"Because it's contradictory. Look, either you believe the Haitian and think I'm cynical, *or* you fear the Haitian and think I'm right."

Her answer was a great show of rustling sheets. "Good night, Frank," she said.

He hated how women did that—treating the discussion like a taxicab they could order to the curb whenever they felt like getting out. Annoyance crested and toppled over inside him. "I don't see how we're going to get anywhere if we can't agree on the basic principle of noncontradiction," he said.

She spoke without turning. "I was scared, that's all. For Paul."

"I see. With you it's concern, with me it's cynicism."

"Well, Frank, different people are different." She burrowed down into the mattress, yawning greedily. "I'm going to sleep now. Good night."

Instantly her breathing deepened. But Reardon lay wide awake, churning out dire scenarios. So different people were different. Would she want different laws for those different people? Different schools? How about different movie theaters and buses? And who would decide?

"It's totalitarianism," he said. He reached over and poked a finger in her back. "Hey. It's apartheid, your little system. It's homelands."

She rolled over and looked at him through filmy eyes. "I was asleep. I was dreaming about those silly little drawings you used to do. Remember those?"

In college he'd drawn caricatures and cartoons. He didn't see what relevance they had to the present moment.

"Those were so funny. I laughed and laughed. God, you were funny then."

Reardon said nothing. There was a wistful tone to these remarks he found not entirely satisfying. He glanced over and saw that degree by degree she was waking up, the dreamy look seeping away.

"You know," she said, "I wish you could have seen your face. Tonight, I mean. With Paulie."

"Well, I was annoyed. I still am. Aren't you?"

"No, I mean before that. When you found out he didn't get his money back. It was like . . . like it made your day, Frank. Like you enjoyed it."

They lay there. From out in the hall he could hear the jolting whimpers of their black Lab, Jordie, caught in a dream.

"That's ridiculous," he said, and reached for the light.

Sunday morning found him on the clay courts of the Woody Creek Country Club, laboring to serve just one ace past the sleek seventy-year-old who was his father-in-law. W. Cummings

Randall—Reardon, in his mind, always put a "III" after the name—had captained the tennis team at Yale in the Forties. Silver-haired, humorless, and graceful, Carolyn's father was a man whose bearing suggested both monumental accomplishment and, at the same time, an easy freedom from having to have accomplished any actual thing, other than being born, in order to claim such a bearing. Walter Randall exuded "culture," but had little use for music, art, or books, and kept such intrusions upon his serenity to the absolute minimum necessary to placate Carolyn's mother, Prilly. In truth, Reardon had no idea what his father-in-law, retired after forty years of bond trading, did with his spare time, other than play tennis. He was a ferocious competitor, and conducted his "friendly" games with Reardon like rear-guard battles in the old war to prove that Carolyn had made a terrible mistake.

Today had begun typically, Reardon losing the first set 6–2, suffering through rallies in which his father-in-law stood lodged like a pivot in the center of the court, gleefully swinging him from side to side. In the middle of the second set, however, a wondrous thing happened. About to serve, Reardon was stopped by Walter's raised racquet. He watched as the older man, stooping, proceeded to peel a leaf from the clay and carry it over to the fence. The ludicrous care with which his father-in-law deposited the leaf through the mesh fence onto the lawn, as if it were a precious jewel, had a magical effect on Reardon's mood—he found himself struggling to restrain laughter—and after that he was unstoppable. He aimed for the corners, catching his father-in-law deep in the backhand. He crunched overheads and lofted killer lobs that elicited from Walter a curt, "Yup, that's too good!" The second set was won in a tense tiebreaker, the third in a rout. When it was over, he pumped his fists like Jimmy Connors and trotted to the net.

"Well, Frank," said his father-in-law, approaching slowly. "That's some little leap into the court you take on that serve of yours. I remember getting called for a foot-fault once against Harvard. Tricky little line judge . . ." But nothing could conceal the man's bitter disappointment.

On the way home Reardon, jubilant, put the top down and cruised the turnpike with the air roaring one ovation after another. It was well past noon when he got back to town. Checking his watch, he realized that in the excitement of victory he'd forgotten all about his son and the Haitian. Quickly he turned the car in the direction of the train station. But when he got there, the platform was empty. He drove off.

Three blocks from home he saw his son, riding his neon yellow mountain bike. Reardon gave a toot as he went by, then pulled into the drive and waited, leaning against the car.

Paul rode up slowly, wrenching his handlebars from side to side, scooping sharp turns out of the road.

"Hey, champ," Reardon called out. "At that rate you'll never get here."

The boy pedaled over, looking conspicuously glum.

"You went down to meet your Haitian friend, right?"

"Uh-huh," his son said, looking away.

An image of him alone on the platform drifted through Reardon's mind. "Look, Paul," he said, as gently as he could. "I know it hurts. But it's the way things always happen. You gotta take your hits and learn." He reached out and rumpled his son's already rumpled hair.

To his surprise, the boy ducked out from beneath his hand, flashing him an evil look.

"Dad, you're just, like, *assuming* he didn't show up. That's pretty bogus, you know, just assuming."

Reardon straightened. "Okay," he said in a measured tone. "So tell me. Did he show up?"

He watched his son struggle with it, saw the precise moment when he decided to lie.

"Yeah," he said. "He showed up."

"I see." Reardon nodded. "And he paid you back too, I assume."

"Yup."

"I see."

They stood there: the boy glaring, chin thrust out; Reardon with arms folded, waiting. "Well, glad to hear things worked out," he told his son. The boy frowned tightly. In a matter-of-fact voice, Reardon asked if the Haitian had paid back the whole thirty dollars.

"That's what he owed me, isn't it?"

"Absolutely." Reardon stroked his chin. "So . . . Then I guess you wouldn't mind giving me a look in your wallet to see those thirty dollars."

His son's face told it all: the impulse to cover the first lie with a second; then the furtive glance down toward the pocket of his blue jeans—his front pocket, where Reardon had taught him to keep his wallet as a precaution against pickpockets, and where, unmistakably outlined in the faded denim, it now was.

"Gotcha, huh?"

The boy had dug his toe into the grass and was working away

at a piece of sod. He mumbled something; Reardon made out "no right" and "private property."

"What's that? Speak up if you've got something to say, for Pete's sake!"

The clot of grass sprang loose from the lawn, revealing the black earth beneath. "Are you saying I'm lying or something?" the boy said in a thin, wailing tone.

Reardon motioned with his hand. "I'm saying let's have a look at that wallet, mister!"

"Why? You think you can just—"

"Give . . . me . . . the goddamn . . . *wallet*!"

With a convulsive motion his son tore the wallet from his pocket and flung it at Reardon. It thunked against his chest and fell to the ground.

"He was a *refugee*!" the boy cried in a choked voice. "They were going to *kill* him!" Grabbing his bike, he tore across the lawn and crashed over the curb. Reardon watched him pump off down the street.

As he did, the front door opened, and Jordie barreled out into the yard, followed by Carolyn. The dog lunged up to him in a frenzy of wagging. His wife's attitude was less friendly.

"I saw that," she said. "Don't think I didn't."

Reardon explained how he'd caught the boy in a flat-out lie. "If there's one thing I can't stand, Carolyn, it's a liar. You know that."

She stared at him as if at an alien from an incomprehensible world.

"What?" he asked. "Why are you looking at me like that?"

"This whole thing makes you *happy,* doesn't it, Frank! He gets his heart broken and you get a charge out of it."

"Now hold on a sec—"

"But then I guess you have your little double-or-nothing to think about, right?" She looked away, biting her lip.

A dozen angry rejoinders clamored in his mind. But as he was about to select one, he spied a single tear rolling down her face.

"Hey, honey," he said, instantly softening. "Come on. You know I'm not going to make him pay." He was just trying to toughen the kid up, he explained. It was a man-to-man thing. He reached out to stroke her face.

She twisted free. "You really don't get it, do you, Frank? He's going to pay you that money if it kills him."

Her mouth banged out a harsh laugh. She shook her head, then turned and went back to the house.

Reardon stood for a while in the yard, the dog sitting patiently alongside. He found himself remembering a bully who had tormented him in Prospect Park thirty years earlier. Night after night he'd come home complaining about it, until one night his father called him over, gave him a long look from head to toe— then abruptly hauled off and hammered him on the arm, hard. *He hurt you that bad?* he demanded. Reardon, tears welling, had shaken his head. *Good! Then you don't have anything to be scared of, right?*

Bending, he picked his son's wallet out of the grass. As predicted, it was empty of money, save for a single dollar bill, limp with age. He took it out and folded it, then folded it again and a third time, and stood there absently turning the dingy green square over and over in his fingers.

His wife was right, he knew. In his mind he saw the boy slaving away—mowing the lawn, mowing other people's lawns, washing windows, collecting bottles and cans. And when the debt was finally paid off, it would be another thing the boy had accomplished, had *done*.

He examined the rest of the wallet's contents. A stamp, a cash register receipt with a phone number written on the back. A baby picture of Julie; two ticket stubs; a playing card—the jack of hearts—folded in half. With these odds and ends his son was practicing the magic trick of identity. It wasn't much to go on, but it wasn't nothing, either; it was far from nothing. Reardon wondered whose number the boy was getting up the courage to call. He pictured him carrying the phone around the corner into the hall, taking a deep breath, counting to five, then picking up the receiver. That, at any rate, was how he himself would have done it at that age. His son would be smoother, perhaps; not so nervous. Maybe not nervous at all. He couldn't be sure.

With a sigh he closed the wallet and slipped it into his pocket. Inside him a voice was madly chanting, *Reardon, you idiot, you fool!* He took a long look around at his property, half hoping the house itself might offer a rebuttal, or perhaps the wrought-iron lawn furniture he'd bought, or the mulberry trees he'd had planted. But these serene objects kept their silence; nothing spoke on his behalf.

Jordie, meanwhile, sat nearby, staring up at him abjectly.

"What are *you* looking at?" Reardon said. "Go on, get outta here!"

He watched the dog skulk across the yard. Then he got in his car and drove slowly up the drive.

A SOLDIER
LOYAL
AND TRUE

THE STORE-IT FACILITY sits in an acre of roadside
just off the Merritt Parkway, an hour north of the
city. A dozen years ago she passed here daily, but it's
one of those anonymous stretches of car washes and
liquor stores that could be anywhere. FORTRESS
AMERICA, the warehouse calls its row of red, white,
and blue aluminum sheds.

He must have liked the name.

For more than a year she's been putting this off.
A project in her pottery studio, the libretto she was
writing for her friend Roger's opera; something always came up. From Chicago, her brother began in
his friendly way to threaten her. He'd done his part,
he told her—the will, the whole legal-practical side
of it—and wanted her to do hers. *One of these days,*

Cass, I'm just gonna pick up the phone and send some guys in there. Leave it to her brother to make moving men sound like hired killers.

The shed, #23, is full, a reminder of how little her father took with him when he left Connecticut for his strange and solitary new life out West. The condo in Montana had come furnished, right down to the glum landscapes on the walls. He had his computer and fax machine, his Nordic Trainer; a box of income tax returns; a few family pictures. That was it. She picks up a leather travel bag, studying the gilt-edged initials—PHC, Pierce Hemmings Chandler, Jr.—before tossing it down on the far side of an invisible line dividing the room into hemispheres of Yes and No.

Why her? she asks herself. Why should she be the one?

Of the three of them she was certifiably the least close to him. Her mother, after all, had been his college sweetheart, and her brother, Trip, still lived according to his master plan. She was the rebel, the odd tick in his smooth-running family; the girl who never fit his picture of what a girl should be. She didn't like the boys he wanted her to, didn't take up tennis or cheerleading, didn't worship Trip the way the rest of the world allegedly did. Summer afternoons she spent in the dimness of the living room, practicing the piano, until he'd lean in shaking his head and tell her to get the hell outside in the *sun!* for God's sake.

Why can't you get along with your father? went her mother's eternal refrain. But he was all boarded up to her. With Trip he did things, tennis, fishing, tossing a ball in the yard. The two had a language of their own; they were always *patting* each other. With her, however, after she'd turned thirteen or so, he'd stopped rumpling her hair and teasing, and begun *addressing* her.

More and more she seemed to annoy him. Even when she tried to please him, she annoyed him. She might remark that if she were running the world, people would go off to work dancing, nobody'd ever be bored—and he'd turn on her, angry. At thirty she still feels a shiver of dread at the years spent trying to scrabble up onto the icy rock of him, propelled by the merciless fact of being his daughter. She pictures what she'd normally be doing with her Saturday, jogging in the park or working in her study with her cat, Juan, slinking around underfoot, the stereo sending something trivial by Puccini skittering through the apartment. That's the life she's made for herself, piece by piece, and thinking about it steadies her.

She finds the chairs beneath a blanket: two black-enameled hardwood armchairs with the seal of his college silk-screened in gold on the backrests. Her father had kept their house stocked with an endless array of college coffee cups and calendars, college towels and ashtrays and coasters. She studies the chairs. Pompous and uncomfortable, to her they embody his beloved alma mater exactly as she remembers it, all too well, from her brief stay there. In her junior year of high school, after centuries of admitting only men, his college had abruptly seen the light and changed its mind. At school and at home it was made clear to her that if a place like that took you, you went. So she did, for one miserable year.

It was like living on another planet. Football players stampeded her hall at 3 A.M., pounding on doors. Sister schools delivered busloads of women to frat parties where the brothers drank themselves sick. One day in the cafeteria, a boy called Hooter drank twenty glasses of milk on a bet and then, as a happy crowd looked on, threw up. Her father's precious glee club, meanwhile, consisted of fifty boys in bow ties and tails who began each concert by dashing down the aisle like berserk butlers, leaping onto the stage, and bursting into the college song, a chant of tribute to the school's founder. *Ohhhhh, Lord William Gloster was a soldier of the king, and he came from across the sea. / To the Frenchmen and the Indians he didn't do a thing, in the wilds of this wild country* . . . Everywhere she turned, someone drunk seemed to be inciting someone drunker to sing that ridiculous song. Unable to see herself in any of it, she spent whole afternoons staring out her window at the Vermont woods and a stretch of railroad track on which, every night at around 2 A.M., a train clacked softly by, heading north and filling her with an inordinate desire to see Montreal. She ached with loneliness; save for a few kindred castaways in the Music department, nothing whatsoever at her father's famous college made her feel wanted.

It's not nursery school, Cassie, he told her at Christmas—*it's an education!* But gradually the feeling that something was wrong with her gave way to a breathtaking suspicion that no, it was *them* something was wrong with; it was *him*. At home again during spring break, reading on the porch one Sunday afternoon, she heard him in the house, humming the Lord William song. *And for his Royal Majesty he fought with all his might, for he was a soldier loyal and true! / And he conquered all the enemies that came within his sight, and he looked around for more when he was through* . . . How bizarre it seemed to her, the very notion of loving your school. If Lord William hadn't done anything to the Frenchmen and the Indians, she asked herself, then who were all those enemies he was so busy conquering?

Going into her father's office, she told him the rumor she'd heard, that the actual, historical Lord William had circulated blankets infested with smallpox among local Native Americans. She didn't see why people should celebrate someone who'd done that, she said.

Oh, come off it, Cassie, he replied—then blinked and went back to the bill he'd been paying.

In his blunt silence she found herself contemplating her recent discovery of opera, an astonishing world where people sang out in joy or sorrow at the slightest provocation—glancing up at the moon or sealing a letter or looking around for a lost door key. She saw now what would happen with her: very soon she would leave her father's famous college, move to Boston or New York and find a small apartment full of plants and light, and start being the person she wanted to be.

She was nineteen years old.

In her motel room she sits listening to *Don Giovanni* and eating a pizza. The restaurant they used to go to, owned by a clan of Greeks named Panakos, is no more; on Main Street she found a place called the Pizza Works, gleaming and overpriced like the rest of the town, run by a team of twenty-year-olds. She saw nobody she knew. Driving back past the sprawling houses and lawns, she was struck by how foreign it had all become. The very bulk of the homes, their furious striving for permanence, gave the village the air of an opulent graveyard and underlined to her the slipperiness of all attachments. She thought of her parents and how, after she and her brother left home, they'd begun to float free—first from their neighbors, then from each other. Visiting, she'd been shocked by how they'd reduced their talk to a short-hand of necessities: *You send Welch that check yet? The window-well guy coming tomorrow?* When the split came, it was with an eerie lack of rancor on both sides: "a structural recognition," her father put it in a letter, "of ways that have been going separate for some time now."

Turning down the music, she takes up some odds and ends from Fortress America: maps with family trips outlined in Magic Marker, papers from the various companies her father worked for. She takes up a *Lord William* magazine, his alumni quarterly, and pages through obituaries from his era. *"Fred was a veteran of the Naval Air Corps, where as a blimp pilot he took out several German U-boats. . . ." "After graduation Bob joined the family steel business and served for thirty-six years. . . ." "Three themes ran through Scooter's life: his love for Ruth, wife of four decades; his commitment to our fair college; and his lifelong devotion to golf."* She can hardly imagine a world more alien than this one, with its strange loyalties to games and corporations, and its ceaseless pose of stoicism. *"In his last year Spence was fighting his body on several fronts, but kept mum even to his closest associates."* These are her father's pals, these men of the 1950s. "Successful" men, who proudly freed themselves from art and religion, from tenderness itself, consigning the whole load of it like so much laundry to the women in their lives —only to find themselves struck dumb when, at fifty, they peered down from the top of the hill to where mortality crouched waiting in the shadows. *"I remember Arnie as a terrific athlete and a heckuva guy —a tireless long-distance man who never threw in the towel. . . ."*

She thinks of her father's place out in Montana and of her lone visit in the four years he lived there. She'd hoped the crisis of his life would change him, but instead found him continuing exactly as before, only now without the distraction of friends or family—a hermit consultant sitting in his mountaintop condo, issuing edicts by phone and fax. He'd seemed surprised that she found his situation anything less than excellent. *I like it here,* he said. *It's warm, it's clean. It suits my needs.* All garbage in the condo, he told her with enthusiasm, was sorted for glass, paper, and plastic. He took her to the window to watch as garbagemen wheeled the containers onto a platform behind their truck, then pressed a button and stepped back as the trash was lifted and dumped. "See that?" he said at her shoulder. "There's your future right there!" If she had any money lying around, he advised, she could do worse with it than waste disposal.

The last time she saw him was one year later, at her brother's in Chicago. His health seemed fine, no hint of the heart attack that would kill him in six months. He'd been skiing, and his skin glowed as if someone had been polishing him—stiff and shiny, he reminded her of an andiron. He was friendly in his distant way; but when, claiming too much work, he announced after three days he was leaving, she felt the old anger rising at his stumpish, unquestioning assumption of importance. Who was waiting for him out in Montana anyway, she wanted to ask, other than his fax machine?

When the taxi came to get him they embraced, and she saw he was looking at her closely.

"Why, you're getting gray!" he said.

It was true—for a year or so, coarse white hairs had been sprouting from a single spot on the top of her head. She tipped a dubious look at his own silver hair.

"Yes, well, I guess I see what you mean," he said. Outside, the taxi honked again. "But you can color them, you know. Women are allowed to."

Seconds later he was gone.

She shakes her head, thinking about his last words to her—
women are allowed to!—and goes to close the magazine. As she
does, something leaps out at her:

GEORGE L. HUTCHINS, '47

The College has received word of the death of
George Hutchins. A member of the Debating Society, George also acted as manager of the swim team.
After graduation he served in the U.S. Army, then
took an MBA from the Wharton School before going to work in 1953 for DuPont in Wilmington,
Delaware.

Pierce Chandler has written:

"I was shocked to learn of the death of Georgie
Hutchins on May 6. Georgie, also known as 'The
Mole,' a name he pretended to loathe, was a quiet
person who called or wrote me occasionally from
his home outside Philadelphia—usually with a wild
invitation to join him on an Alumni Cruise to Zanzibar or some such place. He worked his entire career at DuPont, rising steadily but not spectacularly,
as befitted his dependable nature, and took early
retirement at sixty last summer.

"Georgie and I were roommates for two of our
four years—no real plan, it just happened that way.
A few years later at Wharton I looked up and there
we were again, in the same program. By then Georgie had succeeded in getting the world to address
him with a respectful 'George,' but as someone who
knew him from earlier days, I was granted an ex-
emption.

"George was a quiet but true friend with a subtle
sense of humor who loved the College and sup-

ported it loyally and generously through the Alumni Fund. Never married, he was especially devoted to his sister's children. George, Georgie, The Mole, a lifelong distant friend. I shall miss him.''

Her father's words fascinate her—there's some muted note in them she can't place—and she mulls the piece over as she undresses for bed. *George, Georgie, the Mole. I shall miss him.* She considers calling her brother; but it's ten-thirty in Chicago, and besides, to ask him what? Whether he remembers their father talking about someone named Georgie the Mole? It sounds like a line from some gangster film.

But she can't get it out of her mind.

At the tiny desk by the window she opens her notebook.

The Mole, she writes. *A lifelong distant friend.*

As befitted his dependable nature.

Just looked up and there we were again. No plan, it just happened that way. George, Georgie, the Mole.

For her writing she favors oversized sketch books, not only because they leave space to draw and doodle, but because of how the thick paper pushes back a little against her pen, as if the page itself is meeting her thoughts with thoughts of its own. *He just looked up,* she writes, *and there he was again. Standing in the dorm hallway smiling. The Mole!*

What the hell are you doing here, Mole! You little son of a gun!

They shook hands. —By the way, it's George now.

George?

Sure, you know. Can't be a mole your whole life, right?

Okay, well, I'll do my best—Mole!

She waits for something else to happen; but nothing does.

After a few minutes she puts the pen down, turns off the lamp, and goes to bed.

Lying in the dark, she tries to picture her father the way George Hutchins might have seen him in the dormitory hallway in Philadelphia. She chases the notion through dim alleys and strange curved rooms; and finally, just as sleep is washing warmly over her, she catches a glimpse of him: a tall man, handsome, handshake swung in a wide arc to clap, *whap!* against yours—Pete Chandler! She sees him standing there in the hall grinning, and hears a sound she recognizes from years ago, when she was a child: the sound of him laughing.

At Fortress America the next day she scours his past for a trace of George Hutchins. She finds fraternity newsletters, a college letterman's sweater. Was her father on the swim team? She has no idea. It recalls the frustration she often felt as a girl, trying to pin down just what it was he actually did in his job. He worked for the telephone company, she knew, but he didn't make phones. He made decisions. He made decisions about people who made decisions about people who made phones. At dinner her mother would ask how work had been, but nobody expected him to say much. It was as if the family ran on an unspoken agreement to keep that part of him hidden.

I looked up and he was standing there in the hallway, the son of a gun. I shall miss him.

A man like that could grieve, she thinks, and no one would know.

Back at the motel she calls her brother. She asks him whether he thinks their father was depressed out in Montana.

"Depressed? Whaddya mean, depressed?"

She has forgotten how easily annoyed he is. "I mean," she says, carefully, "don't you ever wonder what he was running away from out there?"

"He wasn't running away. He wasn't depressed. He was active."

"Well, but—"

"He was skiing every day. He was *working*." Her brother makes a sound resembling part of a laugh. "Christ, Cassie, the guy was earning more than I do." Changing the subject, he starts telling her about something he and his wife, Jeannie, are having done to the living room.

"Hey Trip," she breaks in. "Did Dad ever mention someone named Georgie Hutchins to you?"

Briefly she tells him about the obituary in the *Lord William* magazine—the sense she has of George Hutchins's devotion to their father, the fact that Hutchins never married, the stranger fact that their father never mentioned him, even though they lived together for two years. Hutchins's death, she adds, happened six months before Pierce Jr. left for Montana. She has the feeling he was mourning out there, she tells her brother.

Silence. Then: "So what are you trying to say? Are you trying to say Dad was *gay* or something? Is that what you're saying?"

"No, I . . . I don't know." She thinks about it. "I guess that wouldn't be very likely, would it?"

"Likely? It would be crazy, that's what it would be."

But everything's crazy when you think about it, she tells him. "I mean, going out there to live alone on top of a mountain is crazy, isn't it?"

He ignores her. Give him evidence, he says. An obit in a

magazine is less than nothing. "You're just reading all this into it, Cass!"

"Yes," she says. "I know I am."

"Well, all right then." She can see her brother shifting his shoulders and stretching his chin out, settling himself down. "Now. My advice to you is you make some decisions about that storage junk and then get the hell out of there. Okay?" Friendliness seeps back into his voice; he's on solid ground again, where he likes to be, giving orders.

When they hang up, she tries watching TV, but can't follow the action and turns it off. At the desk she opens her notebook and takes up her pen, waving it absently over the page like a wand, as if to coax George Hutchins from the air itself. Finally she begins to write.

He was always in the background, they called him the Mole. Now, why did they do that? Thin shoulders, thin smile, very quick at math . . . He'd tell a joke and because he wasn't supposed to be funny nobody laughed until ten seconds later. Then they'd realize it and say, Not bad, Mole, not bad!

She's reminded of Verdi's Rigoletto, the suffering jester, now exhilarated, now sunk in gloom, terrified his deformity will be mocked at court. *They didn't know it,* she writes, *but he was also the Mole because he had a secret. It was a time and place where that kind of secret stayed secret. The Mole, living underground.*

There was someone. He was smooth and popular and handsome; a tall athletic Someone who knew what he wanted and never had to shout to get it. The Mole felt warmed by his presence, as on a beach in summer.

The Someone didn't suspect, and the Mole wanted it that way. Just being together was his goal. In chapel for morning prayer. Drinking beer at the football game. A late-night cram session in the library. He wanted

*to let him know without letting him know. Without spoiling anything.
That was the absolute rule.*

She stops, unsure where to take it. Does Hutchins tell his
truth, or endure in aching quiet? She thinks of the rapturous
''Un' aura amorosa'' of Mozart's Ferrando; of Wagner, his heroes
like gods, commanding blind devotion, his Isolde dying her perfect *Liebestod*. She writes:

*A Friday night frat dance. The Mole sipped beer and watched Some-
one doing the fox-trot with his date, admiring how he led her through the
moves. They came off the floor by where he stood.*

*''Hey, Mole-man!'' To the date he was introduced as the roomie from
last year. ''Sonofagun put up with one of history's worst snorers!''*

The date's face reddened and she smiled.

*''Georgie.'' A firm hand on his shoulder. ''Feel free to dip into the
brothers' brew over at the punch table. But watch out, it'll knock yer—''*

The phone jangles her back. It's her brother, calling to inform
her that he's angry. He's been sitting there for half an hour
thinking it over, and he can't believe she has the gall to insult
their father like that.

"I'm not trying to insult anyone," she says.

"Yeah, well, that's the problem with you, Cass. You never *try*
to insult anyone."

"What do you mean?"

"I mean this whole ridiculous smear campaign of yours.
Think about it! Dad slaves away so you can have your alternative
lifestyle, or whatever it is, and not worry who's gonna pay your
goddamn nursing home someday. Meanwhile you act like he's
America's last robber baron, then no sooner is he in the grave
than you start spreading the story that he was some kind of closet
queer! Now, you don't call that insulting anyone?"

She would answer, but he's barreling onward. "Dad *gay*? I mean, give me a break, will you, Cass? *You're* the one who started the whole homophobic business, remember? Whatever happened to that? And remember our little evening with that composer friend of yours? Would you like to know what Dad had to say about *him* afterward?"

"No," she says, "I wouldn't."

"I guess not. But let me tell you something, it wasn't too friendly."

Past arguments with her brother have driven her to tears, but this time she finds herself riding his anger with an easy calm. "You have it all wrong, Trip," she says. "You may be right, but you have it all wrong."

A snorting sound, like a bull in a ring, and he reels it all back at her again, the outrage of it, his loyalty, her treachery, blah blah blah.

"I'm leaving now, Trip," she says.

Hanging up on him, she returns to the desk, where George Hutchins and her father stand waiting in the crowded fraternity living room.

He sits by the phone in his house in Philadelphia, trying to get his nerve up. September outside, green and lazy. On the table the brochure and its bright pictures of palm trees in sunlight, a woman balancing a basket on her head. He watches his finger tremble as it dials.

"Hullo?" On the third ring.

"Pete? George here—George Hutchins."

"Georgie! Hey, what a surprise! Where are you calling from?"

From home, he says, looking out the window at two kids throwing a Frisbee in the street. "I was just sitting around waiting for my niece and nephew to stop by later for a cookout, and I thought, what the heck, why not give old Pete Chandler a call."

"Well, terrific. I'm glad you did."

To ease his nervousness, he talks about his sister's kids. The girl sixteen and beautiful. The boy eighteen and starting at Penn next week. How time flies. "You realize that exactly forty years ago today, you and I were carrying our trunks into Simms Hall, Room 208? Freshman year."

A low whistle. "Jeez, don't get me looking back over my shoulder, Georgie." *His own kids, he says, are suddenly grown up on him—Pierce III doing a clerkship in Chicago, Cassandra a would-be bohemian in Boston. Liz is doing her usual, gardening and cooking up a storm. And what about the Mole? Still the confirmed old bachelor?*

"Well, you know me. Just trying to spare womanhood some grief!"

They chat about old professors, football games and classmates who incredibly have died. Finally he picks up the brochure and clears his throat. "Listen, uh, Pete. I have in front of me the latest travel prospect from the alumni office. Now, I haven't been on one myself, but I hear they do them very nicely. A professor comes along and lectures on art or history. It's not just a tourist thing, it's more . . ." *He searches for the word.* "More inclusive. Anyway, this year it's Zanzibar. Three weeks. Boat and bus and plane and just about everything else you could imagine."

"Oh yeah? Sounds like fun, sounds like fun." *Last cruise I took was thirty-five years ago, with the U.S. Navy!"*

In the street one of the kids runs, hand outstretched, toward the hovering Frisbee. "Well," *he says into the phone, trying to sound nonchalant,* "so what would you think about taking one this winter?"

"One what?"

"A cruise—you know, this alumni thing."

"What, you and me, Georgie?"

And Liz too, he hurries to say. And anyone else they can dragoon into it. His kids could even come if they wanted to.

"Jeez, Georgie, I don't know. Zanzibar, huh?" A tiny chuckle. "Where the heck is Zanzibar, anyway . . . ?"

After they say their good-byes, the Mole folds the brochure back into its envelope. Five o'clock, time to get ready for his niece and nephew. Outside, the kids with the Frisbee are gone.

He thinks about how much he likes young people—being with them, listening to them talk, watching how they react to things without having to decide what to feel or show. It's not so much their youth itself he envies as its timing, their great good luck in being young in an age when everything is so open. Looking back, he feels regret at his own life, with its large burden of secrecy; but in all honesty he can't imagine having done it any other way. He tries to see himself living as many today do, openly, and it takes his breath away.

In another year he will be sixty.

He recalls the night he almost let it slip, at the fraternity after the dance. How dangerously drunk he'd gotten, drinking with the brothers in their dank basement. First beer, then punch, then more beer, layering it on until he felt the wall inside breaking down. He was standing next to him, shoulder to shoulder. The date had disappeared somewhere, they stood in a circle singing. Ohhhhh, Lord William Gloster was a soldier of the king. . . .

In the drunken sentiment and loud lunges of affection his own intentions sat camouflaged. A group of five, singing arm in arm in the basement. Swaying back and forth, shouting out the lyrics. They made rude jokes. They pledged eternal devotion to the college and each other.

And then he simply turned and threw his other arm around him.

Willed the whole world away and buried his face in his neck and held on tight.

—Whoa, Mole, wait a sec, hold on there fella! Hey you guys, make room, we gotta get the Mole here some fresh air!

Fortunately, he was about to be sick.

Outside then, on his hands and knees, retching into the bushes. Trying in between to apologize, for everything.

—Take it easy now, Mole-man. Go ahead, let it all out! There ya go.

A hand under his armpit, helping him up. A handkerchief. —Jesus Christ, Mole! I toldja it'd knock yer socks off, didn't I?

Sorry, Pete, he said, wiping his face. Sorry sorry sorry.

A laugh, a clap on the shoulder. —Ah, Mole, if you could only see yourself, you little son of a gun!

Four decades later in his living room he remembers that laugh and how listening to it he knew in a burst of joy and misery this was a person he would sacrifice everything for, if only life would give him half a chance to do it. He thinks about the voice on the other end of the phone. The laughing is gone now. The swearing is gone too, Christ this and goddamn that and you little son of a gun. All gone. He takes the brochure out of its envelope for a last look at Zanzibar. Are there really places on God's good earth, he wonders, that begin with Z?

On Sunday morning, her VW and the U-Haul packed full, she takes the long way out of town, past the house. The drive through the village and into the woods has the easy fit of old jeans. Turning onto Lantern Lane she passes the farm where a couple named Wimser lived, holdouts from a lost rural past. She remembers pacing their field with her brother, collecting stones, as Wimser or his wife tossed feed to chickens in a coop. The coop is gone now, the farmhouse renovated; a sleek black Volvo sits in the drive.

Their own house comes upon her suddenly, looming behind the blind curve where her mother always feared a terrible accident. The town, she notices, has installed a mirror. She parks beneath the bulky outcropping of rock on the south edge of the property.

Climbing up to her old place, a benchlike cleft in the rock about ten feet off the ground—her office, she used to call it—she takes a slow look around. The yard appears more ragged than fifteen years ago, when twice a week a trio of rough-talking brothers from the town came out to keep it in shape. She wonders whether her father was embarrassed about being the kind of man who never did anything around the house himself, who always hired people.

Her perch faces the room at the house's back corner. Through the sliding glass doors she can see that the current owners are using it as a playroom—toys lie scattered across the floor—but back then it was his office. Saturday mornings when she got up he'd be there already, drinking coffee and paying bills; he must have liked the morning sun through the glass doors, though he never said so. At night he sat in a leather armchair in the corner, reading and chewing on his pipe stem. The Encyclopedia Britannica was there, and as a grade schooler she would go in to use it for a report on Argentina or electricity. He'd ask a question or two and she'd answer, then sit there reading the big page and trying to outquiet him.

It's in this room that he would have written the obituary for George Hutchins. She imagines him sitting there, wondering what to say. She hears him sighing, sees him crossing out lines, starting over, tossing the pencil aside; sitting with his head in his hands—afflicted, for the first time in a career of churning out memos, by writer's block. Her mother would pass in the hall, perhaps with a cup of coffee, perhaps leaning in to ask him, Was everything okay? And he'd fling a hand up to wave her off, but without turning around, because too many years of not sharing such things had passed for him to shock her with the fact that he was crying, actual tears dropping down on his half-written page as the awkward thought thudded through his mind, *He loved me! That little son of a gun* loved *me, dammit!*

For the first time all weekend she feels a flash of her father's living presence: the warm, rich odor of him, a mixture of pipe tobacco, liquor, and something stale like old slippers. It strikes her as the essence of fatherness itself, and she stands dead still, trying to get a bead on it. But as quickly as it came to her, it slips away, she can't find it anywhere; and after a last look around she climbs down off the rock and goes to her car.

GOING THE
DISTANCE

"DORIS, WHY ARE we doing this?"

Culpepper stands at the window, watching the moving van rumble off down Beinecke Street. It's not a local outfit; his son, Robbie, arranged it from New England. Culpepper hopes the van's tires are in better shape than they look.

"Did you say something, dear?" His wife's voice hovers behind him. Culpepper turns; in the emptiness of the front room she looks overdressed and silly. "Is there something you're not telling me, Owen? You didn't have another spell, did you?"

He shakes his head. "Ah, there's nothing wrong with me, Doris."

"Well, at least we've got a beautiful day." She reaches up and kisses him. "You couldn't ask for anything more."

When it comes time to leave, the odds and ends she thought too fragile for the movers turn out to be almost more than they can fit in the Dodge. In the backseat Culpepper shifts things around, trying to create some visibility.

"I don't know why we're bringing all this stuff anyway," he says. "It's a small house, you know. Heckuva lot smaller than this one."

His wife gets in the car, sighing, and closes the door. "I guess we'll miss this old place, won't we, Owen?"

Culpepper starts the engine. "Forty-four years," he mutters. He backs the Dodge into Beinecke Street, and they pull away in silence.

The decision to move, it seems to Culpepper, sneaked up on him, building like a wave, then breaking on him when he wasn't looking. First Robbie opened his orthopedic practice in Massachusetts, he and Elise buying a big house and later, when Cindy and Judd came along, trading for a still bigger one. Culpepper and Doris began visiting north, once a year, twice. One day his son phoned. *Dad, there's a nifty little place around the corner that's up for sale. . . .*

Now, taking the northbound out of Philadelphia, Culpepper points out that New England really isn't so far. They could have kept visiting.

"These drives are hard on you," Doris says. "You get tired and start swerving."

"I don't swerve. It's these young punks who swerve."

"And who was grumbling last Christmas about never crossing that George Washington Bridge again in his life?"

He waves his hand. "You're the one who's afraid the damn thing's going to fall down. Not me."

"Now don't be cranky, Owen. You're going to live near your son and daughter-in-law and your grandchildren who love you."

He isn't being cranky, he thinks. It just annoys him that he can't pinpoint a moment when he, Owen Culpepper, made the decision to leave the only home they've known for forty-four years. "I just wish I could get the thing straight in my mind," he says as the Dodge struggles up a long hill.

He feels his wife's hand on his arm. "Robbie knows what he's doing," she says. "Didn't you always say he had a good head on his shoulders?"

"Did I?" He frowns, and presses on the accelerator.

There isn't a lot of closeness between Culpepper and his son; there never has been. Part of it was lack of time—he worked hard, six days a week, often at two jobs. But then there was the boy himself. From the start he was different from Culpepper: born smooth, it seemed, where Culpepper was rough. He was dark like his mother, and had Doris's father's long face. She fussed endlessly over him. One day when he was twelve, she dressed him in his Sunday suit and took him across town for a singing audition at a prep school with a famous boys' choir. The two of them came back flushed with victory—the boy had been given a partial scholarship. Culpepper, whose own schooling had stopped in the seventh grade when his father died, gladly paid the rest. But he always felt uneasy at the big ivy-covered school where boys in ties and navy jackets strolled the lawns. In meetings with teachers it was Robbie who was at ease, Culpepper scratchy and speechless. Robbie sang solos in the glee club, and

Culpepper would sit in the audience listening with pride and a kind of astonishment. The boy loved the limelight; he himself would have run and hid.

Somehow they were always just missing, the two of them. There was the time Robbie came to him and asked to be shown about engines. Pleased, Culpepper chose a Saturday afternoon. With the Nash parked in the drive and his tools spread out on a cloth, he waited at the appointed hour. After twenty minutes, a car driven by one of Robbie's pals pulled to the curb, and Robbie got out, running toward him and calling, "Sorry I'm late!"

The lesson was a failure. The boy had no patience. Again and again he interrupted Culpepper with questions; he wanted to learn everything all at once and get back to his Saturday fun. "Slow down," Culpepper said. "You'll never fix anything in a hurry like that." Twice he caught the boy looking at his watch. The third time, he stood and wiped his hands on a rag. "Son," he said, lowering the hood. "I'm not doing this for my benefit. You go enjoy your Saturday with your friends."

Traffic picks up as they approach New York. In his mind Culpepper sees how carefully his son rolled up his shirtsleeves, one fold at a time, under the hood of the Nash. He sees the boy's hands fluttering over the engine. Smooth white hands with perfect nails—the hands of a man who would someday work with his mind.

His wife speaks in a dreamy voice. "Robbie was always a good, good boy," she says. "What I'll never understand is how he could have left the church. It's my one great sorrow."

"Some people are quitters, Doris," Culpepper says.

"What do you mean?"

"I mean they start things and don't finish, that's what I mean."

"But surely you don't— You're swerving again, Owen!"

The George Washington Bridge looms before them, teeming with cars. Culpepper grips the wheel harder. At the crown of the bridge, with the metropolis sunk in smog off to their right, they slow to a crawl.

"This goddamn George Washington Bridge," he mutters. "I'll be goddamned if I'll ever—" Then, remembering, he cuts himself off.

They arrive in the town just after three and drive down Main Street. College students sit at outdoor cafés; fancy shops display rugs and baskets from exotic lands. Nothing useful is being sold anywhere. There's a square with a bandstand and big frame houses on all sides, porches green with hanging plants. On one corner sits a little stone church.

"It's like a picture, isn't it?" says Doris.

They pass his son's house, Culpepper recalling the day five years ago when he stood with Doris on the wide lawn, looking up at the diamond-paned windows and walls of ivy. It was the kind of place which as a boy he had always imagined the great, invisible factory owners living in. Half a mile further on, he turns the Dodge onto their new street. "Go *slowly,* Owen," says Doris, pulling on her gloves and staring over the dashboard, excited like a girl. And then there it is, a single-story brick place behind hedges in a trim yard. As they pull in, the front door flies open and their grandson Judd comes running out, waving, followed by Robbie and Elise.

The moving van in the drive looks bigger than the house

itself, Culpepper notes. It's even smaller than he remembers; a bungalow really, hardly a house at all.

"Toot the horn, dear," Doris says, and he toots.

When the movers leave, the five stand in the front room, among boxes and furniture. Elise has found a scratch in the dining room table.

"I knew better than to trust that outfit," Culpepper says. "Should have gone with someone local."

"That scratch has been there for years," says Doris, "and Owen knows it."

He glares at her.

"Dad," says Elise, "tell us about your party at the Academy."

For the past six years Culpepper has worked part-time as a handyman at Robbie's old prep school, waxing floors, fixing leaks—the kind of work the doctors told him he could safely do. "It was your typical going-away affair," he says. "Three cheers and a box of cigars."

"Was Hanley there?" asks his son. Hanley is his old choirmaster, older even than Culpepper.

"Hanley was there."

"That Mr. Hanley loves you, Robbie," says Doris. Turning to Elise, she recites a list of Hanley's praises of the boy, which she seems to have memorized, word for word, over the years.

Culpepper watches his son smiling. He remembers him at fifteen, when he got his growth and suddenly towered over everyone. He was handsome; girls fell for him right and left. To Culpepper the boy seemed to be living in a movie, where only good things happened. He was always changing his mind and never having to pay for it. He'd work an after-school job for two months, then suddenly quit and throw his earnings away on a leather jacket. He'd quit the baseball team, then three weeks later change his mind, and the coach would take him back. *I worry about that boy,* Culpepper told Doris. *He's smart, but does he have any sense?*

He takes a turn around the tiny front room, stopping to inspect the small fireplace. Doris, he knows, has always wanted one. She'd hoped for one when they built the house on Beinecke Street, but the mason wanted too much for it, and Culpepper, though handy, did not trust himself to do the job. Culpepper has been many things over the years—has worked in the shipyards in Philly, driven a cab, tried his hand at carpentry; was, for twenty-three years, a milkman—and somewhere along the way he decided never to do something unless he could do it right.

"This fireplace," he calls over to his son. "It's real?"

"One hundred percent," says Robbie, coming over. "The real McCoy."

Culpepper kneels, peering up the flue. "Pretty shallow," he says.

Robbie grins. "We'll have Santa do some slimming before he comes."

"My question is whether it'll draw right."

"It'll draw right, Dad. It'll draw."

Standing, Culpepper faces his son. "I guess you're wondering why we didn't have a fireplace down at 749," he says.

"No," says Robbie, carefully. "In fact, I wasn't."

Culpepper grunts, then moves on. "What's this?" He points to something big under a sheet. His son and daughter-in-law trade glances.

"Go ahead Rob, show him," Elise says.

With a magician's flourish, his son whips the cover off, and Culpepper finds himself looking at a burgundy-colored easy chair. "It's a Vibra-Lounger, Dad. Designed by an orthopedist I met at a conference out in Chicago. Press the button and it starts doing some pretty soothing things to your lumbar paraspinous muscles."

"It goes tickle tickle tickle, Pap!" cries Judd.

"It's sinfully comfy," says Elise.

"And real leather," says Doris. "My stars!"

Everyone looks at him. He wishes his wife would take her hand away from her mouth. "Well, it's some chair all right," he manages finally. "But do we have room for it? Remember, this isn't the size house we're used to."

"We'll *make* room, Dad," Robbie says. "Jeez. Don't you even want to try it out?"

"Later," says Culpepper. "Let's get this stuff unpacked first." He takes off his sweater, rolls up his sleeves, and moves to the boxes in the dining room.

"Now don't strain yourself, dear," Doris warns. She turns to Robbie. "He had another spell last week. He's fine if you can just get him to take his medicine." She has developed a habit of speaking about him, Culpepper realizes, as if he's not standing right there. It annoys him.

As the afternoon wears on, he finds himself getting more annoyed. He can feel the others trying to slow him down, keep him off to the side. It makes him itch to strike back. When Robbie explains where an air conditioner might go, he interrupts: "Didn't need one down home. Don't see why we will up here."

A moment's silence; then conversation resumes as if nothing has been said. Again he butts in: "If the builders had had their heads screwed on right, they'd have given you some cross-ventilation in here and you wouldn't *need* air-conditioning. You could let Mother Nature cool you off."

"Now that's the kind of thing I never think of!" says Elise.

Culpepper shrugs. "You would if you were building your own place. Build your own place and you know what you're getting." He glances at his son. "Now, I know Rob here doesn't agree with me. See, he never really liked 749—" The boy's head jerks up, but Culpepper continues, raising a hand. "No, he never liked the place. It embarrassed him in front of his pals—"

"Owen!" Doris cuts him off. "What in the world are you talking about?"

"Oh, I don't know." He turns away, swatting the air. "Look, why don't I just do us all a favor and stay out of everyone's hair here."

No one argues.

Out in the kitchen, Culpepper sets himself to working on the oak table, one leg of which is loose. *Bear up now, Owen,* he mutters. But he finds it hard to concentrate. It's as if leaving 749 has opened a floodgate inside him; things he never realized annoyed him, things decades ago, are floating to the surface. An evening in a fancy restaurant one summer at the Jersey Shore, for example. The boy had opened the menu and gone, as usual, right to the most expensive item. *You got a real taste for steak there, kid,* he hears his own voice saying. *I hope when you grow up you find a wallet for it too.* And the boy looking up, wounded, to his mother, and Doris's voice, gently pleading, *He's been such a good boy, Owen, maybe we can spoil him just this once. . . .*

In his own childhood there had been no question of spoiling anyone. That and a lot of other things had vanished in a snap the day he and his brother Billy found their father lying crooked and cold at the bottom of the stairs. He remembers standing at the door as they took the body away, his mother sobbing hysterically behind him, and knowing that his real life had just begun. Who would pay the meat man when he came? How little coal could they get by on over the winter? He was thirteen and the oldest of five children. That night he reached into his drawer and took out his corncob pipe—the pipe he used for smoking tobacco with Arnie Foxx down by the creek—and threw it away. It angers him now, sixty years later, this solemn sacrifice. So much has been demanded of him.

Their voices bring him back. In the front room Doris is raising the subject of her one great sorrow. *Are you by any chance going to church these days, Rob?* he hears her hopeful voice asking.

"Religiously, Mom. Religiously." The boy is always joking.

Doris laughs. "Oh, go on with you!" Then, to Elise: "He used to sing in the choir at St. Mark's, you know. Sang like an angel."

"Now he sings in the shower," his daughter-in-law says.

"That's right—hymns every Sunday, from the Waterproof Hymnal," jokes Robbie. "Just for you, Mom."

Culpepper barges into the room. Their faces turn to him, alarmed. "Everyone's too damn good for church these days," he says. "It's a crying shame, if you ask me."

Again the silence. Robbie stands hefting a box of dishes, and Culpepper catches him glancing at his wife. A slow frown moves across the boy's brow. "Hey Dad," he says. "Why don't you find

Judd and take him outside. He'd like that, and maybe you could relax a little."

His son's practiced, professional look reminds him, maddeningly, of the awe he has felt all his life in the presence of doctors.

"I don't *want* to relax!" He punches out the words. "How can I relax with you throwing all my furniture around the house like it's some kind of goddamn garage sale?"

The doctor smile vanishes. Putting the box down, Robbie takes Culpepper by the arm and turns him aside. "Would you mind telling me what the hell is wrong with you today?" he says.

Culpepper shakes his arm loose. "Nothing's wrong with me! Look, I could've handled this whole show from the start, but you keep getting in my way. I'm trying not to complain but it's getting pretty goddamn tough!"

Suddenly he's aware of his own voice shouting, and of the others gathered around, staring. He closes his eyes and rubs the bridge of his nose. A long sigh escapes from him like steam. "Okay," he says. "All right."

Opening his eyes, Culpepper sees Judd, hanging back beyond the adults, studying him with a troubled and curious look. "Come on, kid," he says. "Lemme take you out in the yard and show you a move or two." Striding across the room, he takes his grandson by the hand and heads for the back door, leaving the three of them whispering in his wake.

The yard is a plain box edged by bushes, with patchy grass and a single maple in the center. Culpepper guesses it will take him two years to bring it up to what they've left behind down home. He turns to his grandson. "Where's your sister today?" he asks.

"She's at *Girl* Scouts. Probably making pot holders or some stupid thing."

"Girls have their business and men have theirs, Judd."

"I know, I know. Hey, Pap—" The boy pulls him toward the maple. "Think we could build a tree fort up here?"

"Don't see why not." Solemnly Culpepper scratches his chin. "Of course, we'd need an eager builder, someone who could scamper up and down. Younger man, I'd say."

The boy's hand shoots up. "That's me—I can do it!"

"I'm sure you can, Judd." He musses the boy's red hair. "You know, you've got your old grandpappy's hair. Just hope you hang on to it a little longer."

"Did you really have hair, Pap?" The boy shows disbelief.

"Well, I guess I did—red hair too." He tries to picture this; it seems like a lie. "I was a tough little runt. Didn't let the bigger fellas push me around. Probably like you."

"Dad says you were a boxer and you knocked guys out."

Culpepper smiles. In his twenties he was, indeed, a boxer—first in the army, then as a semipro in Philadelphia. His friends down at Studemayer's Gym called him Red Pepper, which pleased him. As a boy he had always dreamed of being called "Mike" or even "Irish Mike"; he had hated his parents for giving him such a dull and serious name as Owen.

"I was a bantamweight," he says to the boy. "Tough little rooster."

"And were you the champ?"

"Not exactly. I was one of the . . . contenders, I guess you could say." The truth was he'd been a mediocre fighter. The good fighters knew how to work themselves into a rage, and this he was never able to do. At twenty-five he stopped fighting altogether; Doris thought it beneath his dignity.

Judd puts up his dukes. "Show me how you used to fight, Pap! Come on!" And even though it's been almost half a century, before Culpepper knows what's happening, there he is, fists up, giving the boy a lesson in the basics: showing him how to angle his body, how to feint and duck; positioning the skinny arm to flick a jab. It's all still there, after all these years. "You gotta keep up your guard, see?" he tells the boy. "Like Jimmy Studemayer used to say—'Make 'em pay to get in, Red! Make 'em pay double and they won't come back!' "

The boy is serious and steady; he wants to be taught. Culpepper throws a few quarter-speed punches, easy to deflect, then crowds him toward the tree. "Now you're backed in the corner, kid—you've gotta get out, out of the corner—" With a neat swivel Judd ducks out from underneath, popping up behind Culpepper, laughing.

"Good move, good move!" He squeezes his grandson's shoulder. "You're like me, kid. You've got grit. You've got those freckles. You've even got a dumb name like me. What're you gonna do with names like Judd and Owen, huh?" Culpepper feels light on his feet, lighter than he has in years. He executes a feint and shuffle step, and the boy's eyes go wide. "Okay. Now, this round we'll work on counterpunching. That's when the other guy gets too confident, see, and you stick him a good hard one—"

The screen door bangs. He looks over to see Rob standing on the back porch, staring at him.

"Refreshment time, boys!" Elise calls from the kitchen window.

"We'll be right in, dear," Culpepper says. "Just one more round."

"Judd," says Rob. "Pap's had a long drive today. You let him relax a little, okay?"

The boy starts to move, but Culpepper grabs his arm and holds him. On the porch Robbie shakes his head. "Dad," he says. "Listen, why don't we—"

"No, *you* listen." Culpepper grits his teeth and grinds the words out. "We're in the middle of something here! We're busy! Can't you see that?"

His son stalks back into the house.

The boy never was one for boxing, Culpepper reflects. It was Culpepper's chief pleasure, but his son had never cared for it. Once and once only he took him, over Doris's objections, into Philadelphia to the fights. The main bout on the card was a brawl between two clumsy heavyweights. In the late rounds one fighter opened a gash on the other's eyebrow, and blood began leaking all over the ring as the two men staggered around in a blubbery embrace. *Those were a couple of bums we saw in there,* he said to the boy afterward. *Don't you get the idea your old dad was a bum.* The boy was silent. When they got back to 749 his mother embraced him as if he had been lost in the desert for weeks.

Shaking the memory off, Culpepper turns back to his grandson. "Now, where were we?"

"Counterpunching," says Judd. "A good hard quick one."

"Right. Okay." But Culpepper can't get back on track. He imagines the three of them huddled in the kitchen. *He gets cranky in the afternoon until you give him his sherry,* Doris would say. Anger prickles his neck.

"All right kid," he says to Judd. "Forget about counterpunching. It's round fifteen now. You're down on points, you need the knockout. Let's have your best stuff!"

Smiling, Judd steps in with a flurry of sloppy jabs Culpepper blocks with his forearms. In his ear he hears the scornful voice of Jimmy Studemayer, whipping him up. "You're holding back, Red!" he shouts, startling the boy. "Joe Louis held back against that German fella and what'd it get him? Come on! You scared of me? Huh? Sissy boy?"

The boy takes a deep breath, collects himself, and charges in, arms windmilling. Sidestepping, Culpepper swats the back of the red head, just hard enough to send him sprawling—just enough, he hopes, to get him a little riled. On the ground the boy blinks, looking up. Culpepper dances on the balls of his feet.

"Okay," he says, "so you get a cheap shot! Happens all the time! What're you gonna do—quit? Gonna wilt like a little pansy?" The boy shakes his head—no smiling now—and stands. Culpepper sees he's getting to him. "Your great fighter is never a quitter!" he goes on. "He might not give you the prettiest show, but you know he's gonna go the distance. What about you, Red? Gonna quit and cry to your mother?"

The boy flushes behind his freckles. He avoids Culpepper's gaze, staring into his midsection with a grim intensity. Waiting, Culpepper feels a tickling thrill in his arms and chest. The boy bores straight in, and this time manages to slip a right under his guard and land a glancing blow to Culpepper's ribs. He grunts, and the boy backs off, unsure again.

"Better!" Culpepper barks. "But where's the follow-up?"

From his crouch he taunts him. ''Your contender, he's the one who finishes what he starts, and isn't afraid to get his hands dirty doing it! That's what I always tried to tell your father, and he never had the faintest idea what the hell I was talking about! And you wanna know why?'' He shouts it out. ''Because he's a quitter, your father! Always was, always will be! A spoiled, whining, gutless little quitter—''

''No!''

With a sharp snort of rage, the boy lowers his head and comes at him, steaming in like a locomotive. Culpepper tries to cover up, but the next thing he knows, he's on the ground, his wind knocked out of him; the boy standing above, hands clenched, eyes wide with fear.

''I'm . . . okay,'' he manages. ''No knockdown. Just . . . a slip.''

Sobbing, the boy turns and runs into the house.

For a long moment Culpepper rests on one knee, waiting for his wind to come back. His own gasping strikes him as ludicrous; he sounds like a donkey. Not a very impressive return to the ring, he reflects.

There was another time when he'd made a boy cry, in a different backyard. It was his son's first year of medical school and he was struggling—taking the train into the city and coming home night after night whining and complaining. The professors were unfair, he whined, the tests were unfair. For the first time in his life, the boy knew hard work, and he didn't like it. One evening Culpepper took him out into the yard. They stood listening to a train go by on the tracks two streets over.

You're having a tough time of it, aren't you, Culpepper said. *The world's treating you pretty bad.*

You don't know the half of it, Dad. They make us do the stupidest, most trivial stuff—

Listen, son, he cut him off. *You're twenty-two years old. If you can't take the heat, get out of the kitchen.*

Tears glittered in the boy's eyes. Without a word he went back to the house. Culpepper stayed outside, thinking, as dusk came on.

Now the lone maple in his new backyard waves limply in the breeze, mocking him. He brushes off his trousers, checks his teeth—at least his plate hasn't fallen out—and heads for the house.

Inside the three of them gape at him.

"What did you do to that boy?" Elise asks in a whisper.

He laughs. "Dear, that boy gave me a head butt that would've made Jake LaMotta proud."

Robbie stands with his arms crossed, glaring at him. "Dad, what the *hell* do you think you're doing?"

Ignoring this, Culpepper raises a hand and walks through the kitchen. "Where's Judd?" he asks.

"He's in the back bedroom." Elise offers a tiny smile. "He likes to be alone when he's upset."

Culpepper walks down the empty hallway to the last room. He leans his head against the door.

"You're one tough little flyweight scrapper, kid," he says. "Fighting way out of your weight class and still you get the K.O." Silence. "Listen. Don't ever pay any attention to what the other fella says in the ring. He'll do anything to get your goat. Oldest sucker play in the world."

He imagines he can hear the boy holding his breath inside the room, and lowers his voice. "One last thing. In real life, the fella who's gonna go the distance is the one who fights with his head. You remember that." He taps a knuckle on the door, once, and goes back down the hall.

In the front room he finds a glass of sherry waiting for him on a box next to the lounge chair. He sits, groaning a little, feeling soreness on his ribs where the boy's blow stung him.

The sherry eases him, and he lets his mind drift back again to that evening in the yard in Philadelphia, twenty years ago. After his son had turned and marched back into the house, Culpepper stood in the twilight and smoked a cigarette. Sunset was painting pink across the western sky, the city spreading its hazy glow in the east. From a cell in the police station a block over he heard the voice of a local drunk, Collins, singing *Oh, my darlin', oh, my darlin', oh, my darrrrlin', Clementine* . . . One light shone in the kitchen of his house, where Doris was doing the dishes, and another upstairs, where his son by now was once again huddled over his medical textbooks. Culpepper tossed his cigarette butt down and ground it into the grass with his foot. The boy, he thought, would soon quit; would slide back and join his old grade-school pals putting in their forty hours at the paper mills and chemical companies, breaking their backs and struggling to get the mortgage payments in—would do, in short, what Culpepper himself had done. He lit another Lucky Strike and stood in the yard with his arms loosely crossed, enjoying the soft night air and the sounds of his neighborhood.

But Robbie had not quit. Somewhere along the way—Culpepper still isn't sure just where—that whining boy had disappeared, and a man stood in his place. He can hear him now, his deep bass voice telling some story out in the kitchen, the two women murmuring laughter. Reaching down, Culpepper's fingers find the button on the side of the lounger. A low hum begins from somewhere deep inside; it vibrates through his body, through his arm and the hand that holds the sherry glass.

"You ass, Owen," he says aloud, and watches tiny ripples race across the surface of his drink.

THE COBBLER'S KID

CARUSO SITS AT the window, waiting for Germany to appear through purple mist below. The jet softly bounces; he watches its engines suckling the wing. *How's this for a wild-goose chase, Katie May?* he thinks, feeling again in his jacket pocket for the snapshot. Next to him his neighbor, a woman from Buffalo, has been running a cheery monologue. "Wait'll you see those crazy Germans," she's telling him. "They bring their yappy little dogs right into the restaurants!" On and on she talks, as if doing them both a favor.

There's something about a widower, isn't there, he wants to say. *You can spot us a mile away.*

Caruso's wife died two years ago, halfway through a beautiful autumn in which the birds lingered late, as if they might change their minds and stay. Three weeks before, he'd left the marina in his son Tony's hands and devoted himself full-time to her—carrying her around the house, sitting her by the window as he raked leaves in the yard. Every afternoon they played gin. Then one day she stopped being able to do that. "Vince." She smiled as he tried to help. "You can't play both hands, you know." He leaned close. "You take care of yourself, Vince," she breathed.

A week later she was gone.

Life attempted to go on. He rose as usual at dawn, driving to the marina with a cup of coffee on the dash. Dockbuilding with Tony, working the crane as the pile driver struck its booming blows, he'd stare out over the water and think absolutely nothing. *Dad,* Tony would say, *you're spacing out on me!*—and a door would jerk open and the world come tumbling in again. Alone in the kitchen he'd speak to her, always expecting her voice to answer from the next room. It never did.

His children worried. Julie sent boxes of grapefruit from Florida. Tony's wife, Serena, dragged him to a travel agency downtown and stood him in front of posters. *How about a trip down the Nile, Vince?* she said. *Check out those pyramids and camels.* Or how about Germany? Hadn't he always said he wanted to go back to that village someday—*you know, where you met that kid, Little Whatsisname?*

Fritzie, he said. *Little Fritzie.*

Caruso met Little Fritzie after the war, in a village beneath a castle near the Rhine. His days were spent walking guard on a PW cage full of German soldiers, his nights quartered in a crumbling hotel. One afternoon, passing a bombed-out cobbler's shop, he spied a barefoot boy sweeping through a mess of lasts and templates, singing in a thin falsetto. The melody drew Caruso in. The boy turned and eyed him warily, and he took a D-bar and held it out. Snatching the candy, the boy ran out of the shop, into the house behind. *A cobbler's kid,* Caruso thought, *just like me.*

In the next weeks he came to see Little Fritzie often. He took him to open-air movies at night, took him rabbit hunting with a clip-fed Mauser he'd lifted from the body of a German infantry-man. With hand signs, shy pats on the shoulder, and the few words each knew in the other's language, the two became friends. The boy took to following him around everywhere, run-ning errands for him, keeping him company. *Hey, Caruso!* other soldiers would call out. *Where's your little slave?*

Before leaving, he'd promised to give the boy the Mauser. When the orders came, however, they'd had to move quickly, and in the confusion of departure he forgot. Later, back in the States, he'd show the gun to someone and think about the boy. For a while the idea of going back for a visit remained strong, but as the years passed, work and family had occupied him, and his memory of the six weeks in the village fell away in bits and pieces until little was left beyond the boy's crooked grin and the sour taste of his own unkept promise. Somewhere along the way, with two kids of his own romping through the house, he boxed the Mauser and stashed it in the attic.

Now he takes the snapshot out again and studies himself, a high-waisted figure in an army uniform, and the scrawny, grin-ning boy with shorts held up by suspenders of string.

"There's a bag of bones for you," says his neighbor, peering over.

The plane tips, revealing a vast quilt of greens and browns.

Caruso sits back, closing his eyes. As they nestle into a descent he pictures the gun, traveling cool and black in his suitcase in the cargo hold below.

And suddenly there he is—climbing out of a rented car on a street called the Burgstrasse, looking up at the ruined castle. The tiny dorf has grown, new neighborhoods rolling up onto hillsides where he remembers only trees. Fritzie's street is one of these: trim stucco homes, neat gardens, flower boxes stuffed with geraniums. FRIEDRICH UND ANNA SCHULTHEISS, reads the brass plate on the door. Caruso stands there, holding his breath. *Turn around,* he thinks, *go back where you belong.* But he has pressed the bell. A tall, silver-haired man appears before him. Caruso holds up the snapshot.

"Fince?" Fritzie peers at the photo, eyes wide. "*Mein Gott*—Fince!"

Hugged, Caruso finds his face crushed into the taller man's shoulder, and for a wild moment he wonders whether the whole thing is a charade cooked up somehow by his son and daughter-in-law. Shaking the feeling away, he follows the silver-haired man into the house.

Over lunch he's introduced to Fritzie's wife, Anna, and daughters—Birgit, a ten-year-old, giggling and flashing a familiar grin; and Steffi, dressed in black and a lopsided haircut, sitting half-turned from the table in what Caruso recognizes as a universal posture of teenage rebellion. He and Fritzie trade stories. He learns how after the war Fritzie studied machine design, then went to work for a paper factory nearby, rising to become a manager. A good position, Fritzie says; a position with responsibility.

The older girl rolls her eyes.

Caruso sums up his own life as if from a recipe. *My wife passed away, year before last . . .* he hears himself saying. *The marina, that's been a nifty operation. Guess I've spent half my life on the water.*

Fritzie raises a glass of wine. "Fince, America is good to the Germans. You give us Marshall Plan. Then we have . . ." He turns to his wife.

"Miracle," Anna Schultheiss says. "Economic miracle."

"*Jawohl!*" says Fritzie. "Economic miracle!"

The older girl snorts, and with a ducking motion leans toward Caruso.

"At the *Fabrik* where my father is working," she says, "they make a paper bag for dogs. You go to the park. You follow your dog and when it makes shit, you use this bag my father makes."

She sits back smiling.

After lunch Fritzie takes Caruso in his gray Mercedes up to the castle. From the parking lot they take a path along a ledge. Fritzie steps with care, as if moving recklessly might send them toppling over the handrail. They look out over the valley and its villages, dense clusters of orange-tiled roofs laid among the greens of forests and fields. A hang glider hovers in the middle distance. Suspended in his cocoon, the pilot dangles like a larva soon to be transformed into something beautiful.

"A very gross danger," says Fritzie, shaking his head.

Caruso nods. But it thrills him, that sense of the bottom dropping out, of suddenly finding yourself moving in three dimensions instead of the usual two. His foot loosens a pebble that scuttles off the ledge toward the treetops below, and he feels Fritzie's hand on his elbow.

"*Vorsicht,* Fince." Be careful. "Come . . . we go to the castle."

But Caruso doesn't move. "You know, Fritzie, I never was much of a tourist," he says. "Me and the wife, we stayed pretty close to home."

"Liberty Statue, Niagara Falls!" Fritzie ticks America off on his fingers.

"Look," Caruso says. "About why I came over on this whole escapade in the first place. See, my wife, Kathleen . . . When she . . . when she passed away . . ." He wants to explain how it was, not hearing her voice anymore; but he can't get a handle on it. He imagines what Fritzie would normally be doing with his Sunday: dozing in his easy chair, watching soccer or whatever it was you watched over here. "Hey. Remember when we hunted rabbits with that Mauser?" To illustrate, he makes a hippity-hop motion, holding his hands like floppy ears. "You know, bunnies. Cottontails."

Fritzie looks doubtful. "Cotton . . . tells?"

Laughing, Caruso claps the German on the shoulder. "Jeez, look at me. Seventy-two years old and I'm over here doing the Easter Bunny!"

It's time, he decides, to do what he came to do; and so when they arrive back at the house, he digs in his suitcase for the Mauser. "Bugged the heck outta me I made off with this," he says, unwrapping the towel he packed it in. Fritzie takes the gift with a smile. "We shoot, Private Fince Caruso!" he says, pointing the Mauser. Anna scolds him, and Fritzie, nodding sheepishly, puts the gun in a cabinet drawer in the living room. Then he zips down into the basement. When he returns, he's carrying an old, torn baseball. Waving it wildly, he calls out in what

Caruso takes to be German; only the third time around—*zis ze raid huid inza kettbud zeet!*—does Caruso hear, with a stab of recognition, the long-forgotten voice of Red Barber, *Hiya folks, this is the redhead in the catbird seat . . . !*

The strangeness of it all doesn't hit him until later, as he unpacks in his room upstairs. The gun has been given, the promise kept; what now?

He takes off his shoes and, immediately tired, lies back on the bed. There's a snug thickening of his vision; and then Kathleen Monaghan is before him, a girl of seventeen in a pale green dress, walking up Lincoln Avenue with those springy strides—like a farmer, he kidded her. He sees his mother, in black from head to toe like a tremendous beetle, limping toward Taglione's Fruit Stand; and the girl in the green dress stopping to greet her.

A hovering presence nudges him awake. Fritzie's older daughter is standing by the door. Caruso sits up slowly.

"Excuse me. My parents say I must apologize. For spoiling the meal."

"It's okay. No harm done. You didn't spoil *my* meal."

The girl's hair falls down in front of one eye, and she pushes it away with a finger. "My father allows nothing. He is a dictator."

"Go easy on him," Caruso hears himself saying. "He's just a boy."

The girl laughs. She wanders to the window that looks out over a small balcony into the backyard. "Do you know this was my *Oma's* room? The mother of my father. She was here ten years and then she died."

"Ah," says Caruso. "I see."

"She was crazy for Hitler. Her man too."

"Fritzie's father? The shoemaker?"

The girl just shrugs. Caruso looks at her. How old are you? he asks.

Seventeen, she tells him.

"You should smile more. Pretty face like yours, it's made to be smiling."

Her answer is a broad frown. She looks around, her eyes landing on his open bag and the pairs of black socks he's been wearing since his wife's death—a small badge of mourning. "My boyfriend, he says black is the only honest color to wear in Germany. It is my favorite color." And what about him, she asks—has he got a favorite color?

In his mind Caruso sees the Germany he knew—splintered trees, a church spire against a smoky sky—and recalls a drunken air corps bombardier somewhere in a bar, boasting about what he and his crew had been doing to the Germans.

"Green," he says.

"Ja." Fritzie's daughter solemnly nods. "That's good too."

All weekend he's taken around in the Mercedes: to the paper plant, to the old shoe store, now a supermarket; and farther, to the Rhine, gray-green and slow in the hazy sun. Caruso isn't used to doing so much smiling. *Schön, sehr schön,* he says, over and over. *Spoken like a true German!* Fritzie tells him. To Caruso it sounds as if he's saying *chairman.*

The boy who swept up the ruins of his father's shop, Caruso sees, has become a careful, orderly man. In his work room, tools hang on pegs set to fit outlines traced on the wall, each with its name underneath—as if you might wake up one morning and forget what a vise grip is called. Before dinner Fritzie measures his blood pressure, pumping up the cuff and frowning as the numbers mount and settle. Caruso watches with a scratchy, distracted sensation.

On Monday the week rolls around. Fritzie goes off to work, Anna shops, the girls ride their bikes to school; and Caruso, though never much of a hiker, takes walks. He follows the footpaths, crossing streets of new houses overlooking vineyards where wine trees dangle from wires like snakes. At night he returns, weary and aching, to tell them what he has seen: the view from the castle, or the sheep he stopped to watch an elderly *Bauer* and his wife shear. Fritzie raises a glass and toasts him. "Fince," he says, "you become a *Wanderer!*" They're pleased to think he's out there enjoying himself, and he lets them; it's easier that way.

But the girl, Steffi, is not so easily fooled. Tuesday night he's sitting on his bed, rubbing Ben-Gay into his sore feet, when she barges in.

"This walking walking walking," she says, shaking her head.

He looks at the door. "You know, I was always taught to knock."

She flops down on the floor. "I myself don't like walking. I prefer to ride a motorcycle."

Steffi's boyfriend, Gunther, has a big Kawasaki. Caruso has seen him—a spiffy young man with a trim mustache and leather jacket, leaning against his motorcycle, waiting for Steffi. Fritzie is berserk on the subject of Gunther, but Caruso likes the stylish way the young man steps aside and gestures toward his bike, with a slight bow, as Steffi comes up the street. He thinks about Tony, and the long, losing battle he fought against a succession of Harleys his son kept showing up with. "Well," he says to the girl, "just don't go do something silly and hurt yourself."

"And you—why do you hurt yourself?" She is looking at his veined and knobby feet.

"Hey, just seeing the sights," he says. "Just out and around."

"My boyfriend says every person searches for something. The honest man admits it, the liar hides it, the fool doesn't know it."

"A regular philosopher, your boyfriend." She frowns, and Caruso feels a spike of regret. "Look, don't pay attention to me. I'm old and cranky."

He meant it as a throwaway, but the girl picks it up. "How is it to be old?" she inquires. "Do you have pain?"

"You get used to it." You get used to a lot of things, he tells her.

"Like what?"

"Oh, like not having all your teeth. Like resting every third stair." He looks at the girl, sitting on the floor, feet pressed together in some kind of yoga position. A wasteful way to design bodies, he thinks: having them peak so early, then linger so long.

"Tell me." She looks up at him. "Tell me what you remark— what you notice—about Germans."

Caruso thinks it over. "Well, first of all, they dress real nice. It kinda throws you off." He keeps passing working men like himself, he tells her, dressed up in fancy sweaters and cotton dress shirts.

"Hah! In America, only the rich have good clothes."

"No, not that." He pictures his grease-ridden overalls at home. "Well, I guess I always was a slob. Used to drive my wife crazy."

The girl's sigh brings him back from far away. Personally, she announces, she would like to go someplace where there are no clothes whatsoever—an island somewhere in the sun. "People," she says. "They have such fear of natural things." Caruso nods, and she sees he is tired. "Okay, Mr. Wanderer," she says, standing. *"Schlaf' gut."*

He escorts her to the door and closes it after her. The air, he notices, carries a ghost of her fragrance. Caruso shakes his head. If she ever saw *his* body, she'd change her mind about that island. But that's the mercy of being young, he thinks: you have no idea what's in store.

Slowly, bit by little bit, things are coming back to him. In the center of town he closes his eyes and hears the *ka-swooosh!* a PFC from Kentucky—Carter? Carson?—made as he fell over backward into the fountain one night, dead drunk. In the woods, a swish of breeze plays among the treetops, and suddenly his hands are moist and he's trembling, waiting for the shriek of screaming meemies and the hollow *plunk!* of mortar.

At night, back in his room in Fritzie's house, he takes these stray pieces and tries without success to meld them into a single meaning. At the window he closes the *Rolladen,* a jointed shutter the Germans use like a blindfold to keep out the outside world, and in the total darkness lies awake, memory galloping him back to the war and the boy sweeping through rubble in the cobbler's shop—and then beyond, to Lincoln Avenue and his own father's shop, with its piles of scrap leather and tins of shoe polish. Huge flakes of ash float from the chimney out over the street; eggplants glint in his mother's shopping net as she returns from Taglione's. He hears the clop and clang of Larsen the milkman and his horse in the street at dawn. At St. Mary's a circular stained-glass window shone, on sunny days, blood-ruby and deep violet, a gem-like brilliance he would stare up into as Father Passero intoned the mass. He always tried to concentrate on the Latin words, but inevitably his attention returned to the circle of gems and the way its pieces seemed now scattered, now joined; now flat, now deep—the colors alive and breathing in the Sunday morning light. He knelt with his parents and brothers, the unpadded wood of the kneeler pressing his kneecaps. In the choir sat his future wife, that willowy Irish girl with the crippled brother. A cloud moved behind the window, darkening the gems; when it passed, they glowed with new fury, brighter and brighter, until he had to look away—a tiny boy, a collection of puny hopes and huge sins.

Katie May? Katie May? he whispers in the dark.

At thirteen he knew he loved her. There was a day when it happened. The end of an afternoon, just before dinner, and he was down in the shop with his friend Tommy Antonelli, fooling around by the shelf of special shoes his father made for clubfeet and hammertoes. His father himself had gone upstairs to wash up. "Hey Vinnie," Tommy said, grabbing a black shoe with a six-inch elevated sole. "Betcha can't walk in this."

Taking the shoe, he pulled it on and hobbled across the room, hunching his back and making his best Lon Chaney face. "I am the hideous Quasimodo," he groaned, "a freak in my pitiful towerrr—!!"

The bell jingled; he turned to the front door and there she was, standing beneath his father's statue of St. Crispin.

"I'm Kathleen Monaghan," she said with a look of pity and blame, "and I'm here for my brother Michael's shoes."

He remembers lying awake that night, wondering what hell would be like. It seemed he had offended an angel.

★   ★   ★

Fritzie and the girl argue, fights full of snorting silences and killer glares. At dinner Fritzie's trying to tell Caruso about a scam by which the notorious Gunther managed to collect unemployment while riding across Africa on his motorcycle, and Steffi plays games with the translation. "He says he is jealous of Gunther, because Gunther has freedom," she tells Caruso. "People like Gunther, they are the true heroes of life." Suspicious, Fritzie stalks across the room and returns with a big yellow dictionary. "No hero!" he says, scrabbling through the pages. He stabs the air with a finger. "Parasite!" he shouts. "Refuser! Do-nothing lazybones!"

The girl, meanwhile, has picked up a milk carton. Look at this, she says. Look at the paper napkins, at the paper tablecloth, at everything.

"Garbage!" she says to Caruso. "Everywhere garbage! Their whole generation, they pollute and pollute! My father, he drives on the autobahn like the typical German man, he thinks his Mercedes is a rocket."

"Not true, not true!" Fritzie shakes his head.

The girl keeps her gaze fixed on Caruso. There was a TV game show in the sixties, she informs him. The host held his hand over each contestant's head, and when he got to your favorite, you voted by turning on appliances in the house. The results were registered by a phone link to the power company, which measured the energy drain.

"I tell you," she says. "My father was using the wash machine and vacuum machine and *everything*!" Standing, she turns and stomps off through the living room, out the sliding doors into the yard.

Fritzie's face wears the panicky and exhausted look of a man whose life is being ruined by one nagging problem.

"She makes him crazy," says Anna. "The poor man."

"Hey," says Caruso. "They're kids. They live in another world."

In the silence, a motorcycle passes in the street.

"They are sneaking!" Fritzie bangs the table. "Come Fince, we go!"

He rises, and Caruso follows. Into the yard they go, hustling up the orchard, past the hutch where Fritzie's younger daughter keeps a rabbit. Caruso lets himself fall back. He's too old to be charging up hillsides.

The path crosses a dirt road and dips into woods. Following it, Caruso is assailed by a queer feeling of having been here before— a tingling that starts in the tips of his fingers and works up his arms. Below he sees a glint of sunlight on water.

This is it, he thinks. *This is the place.*

Fritzie is standing by the edge of a pond. There's a skater's hut and the ashes of old campfires.

"So they're not here," Caruso says, approaching.

"No, *verdammt!*" With a roundhouse kick Fritzie boots a twig into the water. Turning back to the path, he takes a few steps, then waits.

Caruso waves him on. "You go ahead, Fritzie. I'm gonna rest a bit."

Alone, he lowers himself to a sitting position near the edge of the pond. The tingling feeling is still with him. He looks at the water; by a switching of visual gears he finds he can focus now on the surface picture of trees and cloud, now on the deeper one of rocks and mossy sticks on the mud floor below. He tries to focus both at once, but it's impossible. He picks up a pebble and tosses it in—

And remembers. *Of course!* he thinks. *The fish! The fish, Katie May!*

"Mr. Caruso?"

Startled, he turns to see the girl, Steffi, sitting down next to him.

"Well, hello there," he says.

He can see she's been crying. "It's all shit," she sniffles, hugging her knees. "Everything shit shit shit."

Since nothing better occurs to him, he decides to tell her what he has just remembered. "You know, I took your dad fishing here once. Fishing GI style. Know what that is?"

She shakes her head.

"Well, all you need's a hand grenade. You pull the pin, you toss it, and—*poof!!*" He sees in his mind the white spout of water. "It's the concussion. Kills the fish. They float up easy as you please."

"That is cruel," she says in a faint voice. "And unfair."

"Unfair?" Caruso turns the word over in his mind. He tries to think what he can tell her about the last time he was in Germany —about seeing bodies flung like rags, villages reduced to kindling; about dreaming day after day of a tidy green lawn and a white house with Kathleen Monaghan locked safely inside it. He holds up a hand in a wandering gesture.

The girl rocks on her haunches. "You leave this weekend," she says. "Well, I leave too. With Gunther. We leave on his bike. To Greece." He doesn't argue, and she seems disappointed. "It is a question of freedom. Perhaps when I come back my father sees I am to be handled as an adult."

"Or perhaps," says Caruso, "he throws you out of the house."

"It's the same to me. He can do what he wants, like always."

Caruso ponders. "Look," he says. "I know you kids don't realize it, but the reason we folks give you grief sometimes is because we love you. Like my wife used to say—"

But Fritzie's daughter cuts him off. "*Love?* That is not love! Did you make your wife free or did you bundle her in a chain?"

He frowns. "I gave her a house. A place to be safe and sound in. A place to count on."

"And that is love?"

He shrugs. "I thought it was."

The girl stares with a jagged intensity that makes him look down. They fall silent. After a while she unfolds herself and moves off.

Caruso sits, listening to his own heart's distant flutter, as dusk gathers in the trees around the pond. A stilt-legged bug tracks across the water, stepping uncertainly, as if each time it might go through.

He never believed he deserved her: that was the problem. She had come back from college to teach school at St. Mary's. Walking by, he'd see her policing the children at recess, Miss Monaghan on the playground; but looking from her to the church's stone spire he felt accused and guilty, and hurried off before she saw him. He was twenty-four, had tried half a dozen jobs in as many years, and still lived with his mother. It was time to enlist. Maybe the war would change things.

A foolish idea, he soon saw. There was nothing heroic about soldiering. You ate, you slept—both badly. You killed and tried to avoid being killed. You learned how easy it was to knock down a house, or to pay no more attention to a German corpse than to a puddle in the street. His buddies talked as if these experiences would return them to civilian life armed with a powerful magic. For him it was the opposite; the very things that were supposed to be making him bold were actually unnerving him. He'd been writing to Kathleen Monaghan, and she'd answered his letters, dutifully at first, then—to his astonishment—tenderly. *Pop her the question, for Christ's sake!* his buddy Gustafson taunted him as he hunched with pen and paper in their foxhole. *Make your reservations before someone else takes the table!* But it was impossible. More and more he found it hard to believe that the world containing Kathleen Monaghan was the same one that contained him and the life he was living. He began to despair.

Then he met the boy. *There's a kid here,* he wrote to her. *There's something about him, the way he sings. . . .* He wrote about the candy bars he brought him, the bananas and tinned meats, the cigarettes to sell or trade. The boy was his prince and lucky charm; he'd give him some small gift, stroke his golden head like a rabbit's foot and wait for the crooked grin. That grin was his reward. Each time he made Fritzie smile like that, it seemed to him that a door to his own future nudged open another inch. *Kate, there's something about his voice, it's like hearing an angel. . . .*

It all comes back to him now. How the two of them stood by the edge of the pond as he reached for a grenade on his belt. How the water churned and spouted, and the boy's eyes went wide as the mud cleared and one by one fish appeared, belly-up and silvery in the sun. How Little Fritzie rushed into the pond, up to his knees, to his waist, splashing in a frenzy of gratitude and wonder, smile wide as a mile; and how he himself stood on the bank, thinking about what he'd write to Kate Monaghan, picturing her in her green dress and trying out under his breath words he hadn't dared think about before: *I love you, I want to marry you.*

He sits perfectly still, tears pouring down his face. He imagines floating up out of himself to join her in the cozy dimness beyond those birch trees. *This is it,* he thinks. *I'm here. I'm ready.*

Caruso waits. Night thickens, smothering the birch trees. The trill of a bird drills a hole in his solitude. His left leg has fallen asleep, sending a prickly wave rolling upward through him. He groans aloud; he is still there.

The next day, Friday, he doesn't walk. He's tired, he tells them; he's already seen the whole town. Plans are being made for his departure: a *Weinfest* in the village on Saturday night, a Sunday drive to Frankfurt to see him off. He feels the girl's eyes boring into him and looks away.

In the afternoon he sits on his balcony over the yard, postcard and pen in hand. The postcard shows a kaleidoscope of castles and sparkling lakes. He turns it over. *Dear Kids,* he writes.

In the orchard Anna and Birgit are picking apples, the rabbit hunching nearby in its pen. Caruso remembers the bunny he and his wife bought their daughter Julie for her tenth birthday—a quivering fat thing she named Rex. Rex lived happily in his coop for a couple of years; then he mysteriously began to dig holes. Caruso would go out and fill in the day's effort, and the next day the rabbit would start in again. His daughter begged him, please let Rex dig, oh please: it was his *fun,* she said. He gave in. The hole got deeper, a foot deep, two. Then one morning he went out and found the rabbit curled up inside it, dead and cold.

His pen hovers over the gleaming blankness of the postcard. He puts it down and closes his eyes.

That night he lies fully dressed on his bed. He has left open the *Rolladen,* and moonlight fills the room with a numb blue radiance that reveals the shapes of things but not their colors. Quietly as he can, he puts his shoes on and goes down the stairs into the living room, crossing to the cabinet, where he opens the top drawer. Flat and black, the gun looks more like an absence than a presence, and he's surprised to feel its hardness as his fingers go around it. Taking the clip along, he slips out the sliding back doors into the night.

Through the orchard and into the woods, Caruso breathes easy. Something his body has been holding onto these many months, some insistent vigilance over its own borders, has loosened: it's as if his pores are wide open, and he is being filled with the silvery light and the thin must of apples dissolving on the ground. At the pond he finds his spot and sits. The water shows a round reflected moon, like the pendulum of a stilled clock.

From his pocket he takes the clip and eases it into the Mauser. He looks at the moon and its reflection and back again. No telling which is which; one is as real as the other. It seems it has taken him years, his whole life, to realize this. He sees St. Crispin above the door in his father's shop, his father's broad back disappearing beneath it, the window at St. Mary's, breathing in and out, in and out—

A noise. Caruso lowers the gun. Off to his right, striding briskly down the path, is the girl. At the edge of the pond she stops, mere feet away from where he sits in the darkness.

He watches as she lifts one knee, then the other; hears the *thop* of a sandal on the ground, the thin razz of a zipper. Sliding into the pond, the girl strokes toward the center, tugging a vee of ripples across the surface.

At the middle she dives, her legs going up and then down like a sinking ship. Caruso feels a flash of panic; he's about to jerk himself to his feet when she surfaces with a gentle *plip!* and swims toward shore. Soon she's standing naked in the moonlight. He sees the curve of her hips and waist, the dark circles of her breasts. It used to excite him, the way a woman's nipple furrows and hardens in the cold. He has forgotten this. The girl pulls on her jeans, balancing like a dancer. From down in the village floats a bell chiming two o'clock. She picks up her shirt and shrugs herself back into it; then, sandals in hand, disappears back up the path.

It's astonishing to Caruso—the ease of her nakedness, the beauty she's been carrying around with her beneath her black clothes. He wishes he could tell her. He wishes she knew he has seen only one woman naked like that in his whole long life.

When the bell chimes three, he raises himself up, his joints cracking comfortably. With a sweep of his arm he tosses the Mauser out into the darkness, and hears the *plosh!* as it hits the water. Heading back up the path, he pictures the pistol at the bottom of the pond, a single bubble escaping from its nose.

Saturday evening. The *Weinfest* is a maze of food stalls and wine bars in the center of town, outside the old hotel. Wives and daughters, pressed into service as waitresses, serve huge plates of wurst. Cigarette smoke fogs the air, a band plays marches and waltzes. People at the long tables link their arms and sway back and forth, singing.

Caruso sits with Fritzie and Anna, sharing wine out of a single tall glass. Birgit is at a friend's house, Steffi at home. He pictures her riding away on the back of her Gunther's motorcycle, holding on tight; unpacking her tent on an island somewhere.

On the platform, the band members set aside their instruments as a man, the mayor perhaps, reads from a proclamation. At the edge of the stage stands a teenaged girl in a colorful dirndl like the ones on the posters in the travel agency where Caruso bought his ticket. Anna points at her. "The Wine Queen," she says.

Old men line up to aim trembling kisses at the Wine Queen's cheek. The band starts up again, couples rise to dance. Caruso takes a long drink and leans across the table.

"Boy," he says. "This sure is special."

He wants to find something to weigh against the hurt they're going to feel when they get home and find the girl gone. But Fritzie's gaze is fastened somewhere behind him. Caruso turns.

"Say!" he blurts out. "Look who's here!"

"Hello," Steffi says.

She approaches and stands by the table. Caruso feels an idiotic grin spread across his face. "Hey," he hears himself say. "Think maybe I could have the honor?"

And then he's out in the middle of the square, waltzing across the cobblestones with the girl. He tries to move in some relation to the music, but he's no dancer, and when after a few steps he feels her taking the lead, he doesn't fight it; he lets her steer them around and concentrates simply on not planting one of his heavy feet on hers.

"Well," he says, "you're pretty darn good at this."

"As a child I was in the *Tanzschule,*" she tells him. "We learned waltz, tango, rumba, cha cha cha. . . ."

"A regular Ginger Rogers," he says.

"In Germany you learn a lot of things you never need."

Silently they revolve. In his arms she feels stiff, and he wonders if she's mad at him or whether it's just the way you're supposed to waltz. He glances over to see Anna and Fritzie smiling.

The song merges into another, slower one, and he feels her expertly adjusting their step.

"So you're still here," he says to her. "That's good."

He wishes he could explain it, this lightening sensation he's had all day, the feeling of finally having slept and wakened refreshed in every atom of his body. Where yesterday there was only a blank, today he can see himself puttering in the garden back home, driving piles on the barge, firing up the Webber for a cookout with Tony and Serena. He sees how they'll congratulate themselves: *See, Dad, didn't we tell ya everyone needs a little relaxation sometime, a little change of scenery . . . ?* He glances over at the band. The tuba player, a young man, has a curious way of tooting into the mouthpiece, his lips set in a smile, as if he is telling the horn some wicked secret.

"Listen, Steffi." He fumbles for words. "Last night I, um . . ."

"You know, Mr. Caruso," she says. "Germans are not like Americans. We are not Puritans like you."

"No?"

"No. For instance, we swim without clothes."

"Without clothes."

"Yes. It's called Free Body Culture."

"Aha," he says. "I see." She leans back, but he pulls her close again, so she can't see his embarrassment and pleasure. "By the way. Nobody but the bill collector calls me Mister. You call me Vince, okay?"

"Okay. Vince."

He feels in her a slight shifting toward him. His cheek is very close to hers, close enough to feel warmth surging across the tiny space between them. *Vince.* The music spins, a voice vibrates in his ear, the voice he has been waiting for: *Vince. You take care of yourself, Vince.*

The dance is over. For a second he holds on, his eyes squeezed shut. "Thank you," he says into the dim fragrance of her neck. "Thank you."

RAND RICHARDS COOPER grew up in Connecticut, graduated from Amherst College in 1981, and recently returned to the U.S. after four years in Germany. He has worked as a teacher, newspaper columnist, and basketball coach; his writing has appeared in *Harper's, The Atlantic, GQ, The New York Times Book Review,* and other magazines. Mr. Cooper is the author of a previous book of stories, *The Last to Go.*